MW00487615

To Bob who picked up the shattered pieces
of my life.

And to Brian who figured out how to put
them back
together.

This book is dedicated to my family.

In Cahoots

A Novel

**By
Jilda Unruh
&
Bob Horton**

CHAPTER #1
WEDNESDAY

"Why do you want to be a teacher?" That question from his first job interview in Miami, came flooding back to Carlo Ferrini as he cradled the bloody body of his nemesis in his arms.

Moments earlier, Dr. Hank Maine, the second most powerful man in the Miami School System, had been talking to Carlo about an item on the agenda of the school board's monthly meeting, that was about to start. The next thing Carlo knew... Hank, "the Nazi," was dead in his arms, the victim of a vicious stabbing. The knife still jutted from the Nazi's chest. The "Nazi" was a name Carlo had coined for Deputy Superintendent Dr. Hank Maine almost from the moment he met him.

Carlo remembered staring across the desk at his potential employer, the first time they met. Dr. Maine was a man, who by all standards was Adolf Hitler's CLONE! He wore a well-coiffed toupee that mimicked Hitler's trademark, shoe polish black hair. He also sported a misplaced eyebrow mustache, just like Hitler's. He even acted like a man who actually believed he was "the Fuehrer." He ruled imperial, and through fear. He barked orders, talked down to most employees, treated women with disdain, and was the first to extract revenge on any employee who crossed him.

Moments before Hank Maine's blood began to gush all over Carlo Ferrini, the two men had stepped off the elevator into the lobby of the school board headquarters building. It was a sea of humanity jam packed mostly with the hordes of parents and teachers who'd come to photograph, videotape or generally fawn over the kids and students who usually performed music, drama or gymnastics at the beginning of the board meeting.

Because the meetings were televised via public TV and radio, school principals worked overtime for the opportunity to showcase their students. It was a bit of recognition for the professional educator, who labored long hours for menial pay, to teach the next generation something that might make them contributing members of society one day.

Maine and Ferrini exited the elevator and turned left toward the auditorium doors... where inside, the audience had just concluded the Pledge of Allegiance and was ten seconds into a moment of silence... when the Nazi let out a bloodcurdling scream, and dropped like a rag doll to the floor. Carlo, who'd turned to speak with the president of the teachers union, whipped his head around and gasped in horror! In the center of the Nazi's chest, rose the very big handle of a huge knife. Carlo was transfixed by the size of it.

Sure, Carlo saw the Nazi's mouth open, as if in a perpetual scream. Blood was everywhere. Screaming people were everywhere, but Carlo, in shock, saw and heard none of it. His knees began to buckle and he dropped to the body of the Nazi. Carlo's rehearsed answer to the question 'why do you want to be a teacher,' flooded his thoughts as he lifted the Nazi's head in his lap. "It's in my bones. It's my calling to help people," Carlo silently recalled.

Suddenly, Carlo's silence within himself was shattered! He now heard the screams and shouts that signaled the panicked chaos that had erupted in the lobby. Carlo lifted the Nazi's head up to his mouth. From all appearances, he was trying to give comfort to the deputy superintendent. As the bloody man's ear was all but next to Carlo's lips, Carlo whispered, "May you rot in hell, Hank."

Then Carlo took his free hand and closed the Nazi's eyes . . . having heard the "death gasp" as his words ferried Dr. Hank Maine out of this world.

In one of the school board auditorium's press galleries, Investigative TV Reporter Jez Underwood sat alone. For several years, the woman who'd made her reputation busting the balls of the school board and administrators, in the hardcore, corruption, capital of the world, known as Miami, had been boycotting the regular pressroom, the one that had soundproof glass, along with tea, water and cookie service.

She'd objected to the fact that the teacher's union used the pressroom as a meeting room. When her investigations into the union's finances heated up, union representatives would personally attack her whenever she showed up simply to do her job which was covering the school board meeting. So she'd found a new place to work.

Now Jez hung out in the makeshift press gallery at the back of the school board auditorium . . . the one that had no soundproof glass, and no hospitality service.

On this particular day, she sat quietly, listening to her voice mail messages, while the school board and the audience recognized a moment of silence, which Jez knew, was really a code word for prayer. So much for the purported separation of church and state, Jez thought, as she forwarded past messages from her Mom, "Hi honey! Nothing pressing;" her hair stylist, "your appointment is Saturday at 11am . . . "and a missive from her news director that tomorrow night's story was too long! "You don't work for Dateline," he'd concluded. "No duh," Jez said to herself. If I did, I would receive constructive feedback from a manager more concerned about content than time constraints!

She'd just begun to mentally edit Thursday night's script when she heard the scream. It was a life ending, unbearable pain kind of scream. It was also a man's scream. Immediately, she knew it was close by. Jez jumped out of her chair, opened the door to the adjoining TV control room that was broadcasting the school board meeting on public television, and all but jumped down the three steps that led to the lobby door. When she pulled it open, it was as if she'd opened the door to Armageddon. People were running and screaming... hands were waving, police officers had their guns drawn and were shouting at people to get down... people who were clearly frozen in their tracks in shock. Shouts of "call 9-1-1!" and "who did this?" bounced off her brain as she tried to process the grisly scene in front of her. There lay the Deputy Superintendent, a huge knife jutting from his chest. Holding the Nazi's dead body, was Carlo Ferrini... one of Jez's best, and most super, secret sources!

Jez knew Carlo as a man of impeccable ethics and profes-
sionalism. She also knew he had a "loathing" streak for the
Nazi going back years. So why was Carlo holding the Nazi's
lifeless body? What was he whispering into the Nazi's ear?

Jez ran over to Carlo, dropped to her knees and begged him
to answer just one question, "Who did this Carlo?"

CHAPTER #2

"We want you live at 5:00, 5:30, 6:00 and 11:00. Capiche?"

Jez's news director, Boris Danken, had this annoying habit of lapsing into Italian whenever he got excited. Not that he was Italian, or knew more than a handful of Italian words and phrases probably picked up by watching the "Sopranos," she thought! She suspected he did it to make himself appear "continental." You see, whenever Boris Danken took time off from making his employees in the newsroom miserable, he always traveled to Europe. "Io capsico!" Jez responded, in Italian, with a small dose of disdain in her voice. It wasn't like she didn't know she'd be the lead in every newscast. After all, the second most powerful asshole in the school district had just been murdered in the lobby of the school board's headquarters! Fortunately for Jez, he'd died in the arms of one of her sources. Unfortunately, Carlo hadn't seen who'd stabbed the Nazi and neither had anyone else, at least anybody who'd admit to Jez that they'd seen the doer. And since the dead man was universally reviled by just about everyone in the system, Jez knew the list of suspects would resemble the Miami phone book!

Jez clicked her Nextel. "Boss, you do understand that my reports will have to be by phone, don't you? I did tell the assignment desk that the police have locked down the building. No one is being allowed in or out they say. This place is a crime scene. Capiche?"

Jez really wished she could see Danken's face! The idea that his lead story would be a "phoner" and not a live shot from the only reporter who was there when the dead man took his last breath… would drive the newsroom, slave master, insane!

A lead story in the world of TV news that wasn't "Live," was "Verboten!" That's German for "forbidden." Jez privately smirked. See, I can be continental too you jerk, she thought. Then her smirk turned to a full throttle smile. She loved it when her boss couldn't control things… especially her!

CHAPTER #3

The police had taken Carlo up to the superintendent's office. Based upon eyewitness accounts, he was not considered a chief suspect, however, forensics protocol had to be followed, and he was not allowed to use the restroom to wash the blood of Hank Maine, off his body.

While waiting for the crime scene technicians, Carlo was lost in thought, as the blood of the Nazi dried on his arms, hands and clothes. "So, why do you want to be a teacher?" Maine had asked him that question during his first job interview in Miami. Carlo remembered wondering what answer he could give to that question that hadn't already been given a million times, since the first public school was established in Boston in 1635.

He'd rehearsed his answer a dozen times since moving to Miami from Naples, New York, bottom of Canandaigua Lake, the little finger of New York State's Finger Lakes. He'd left the small; patrician Yankee mindset behind, for the lure of a city with the promise to be big one day, even if it's current status in 1965 was as a racist, segregated, backwater, swampland caught between the Old South and South America. Those were the reasons why Miami wasn't exactly a candidate for America's most livable city. But Carlo didn't care. He was in Miami, where the average temperature was 74+ degrees.

It was a place where homes looked like taffy, painted all shades of pastels (peach, baby blue and butter)... where the ocean and bay waters were shades of royal blue, that nuzzled against hues of green, creating, on sunny, cloudless days, a color that lit up like neon aqua. Miami swayed to a Latin rhythm, just like its palm trees swayed in the tropical breezes. It's what lured the northerners out of their cold, red brick and stone homes, where snow shovels, not convertibles, dominated. It's what awed the land locked visitors, who'd never seen an ocean. This delicious blend of sun and sand, water and colors is also why Carlo had wanted the Miami job so badly.

Carlo had started to repeat his practiced answer to the hated question... the answer that talked about wanting to change the world and help young people. It was in his head like a bubble thought! It was not what came out of Carlo's mouth."Sir, it's in my bones. I want a fresh new start and adventure. I want to be so excited about each new day that my skin tingles every morning when I wake up, because I am filled with the anticipation of what I'll encounter and experience that day. If my life can change each day, then I damn well know I can change young people's lives in the same positive way. "The Nazi hired him on the spot.

In his reflections, Carlo remembered his 15 years in the classroom. They were very happy years, because of the children he'd helped to grow and succeed in school. Then one day, he was offered an administrative position at the school system's headquarters. It was then that Carlo's own education began. He would soon learn the politics of public education. The lessons would turn his stomach, and ultimately shock the unsuspecting citizens of Miami, when the school system's "dirty little secrets" began to be exposed. Carlo suspected the unraveling scandals were behind the murder of the Nazi. The only question Carlo had, was which of the power hungry, desperate, hypocritical, back stabbers had finally decided to mount a frontal assault on the treacherous Dr. Hank Maine?

"Mr. Ferrini? Mr. Ferrini?" The sound of Miami Schools Police Detective Rogelio González's voice, snapped Carlo out of his stupor. "I need to ask you some questions sir," the detective said. "Of course. I uh . . ." Carlo looked down at the bloody mess on his arms.

"I'm really sorry sir that I can't allow you to clean up just yet, but we've called in the Miami Police Department to handle the investigation and you'll have to wait for them to get here."

Detective Gonzalez was part of the school districts own police force, and would be an integral part of the investigation, but would not act as the lead detective. Still, he had the authority to begin questioning potential witnesses, and that most certainly included the man who was found holding the dead Hank Maine.

"Sir, I need you to tell me everything you can remember, starting with the reason you were with Dr. Maine in the lobby." Detective Gonzalez waited.

"Hank had called for me for advice," Carlo began. "He insisted I meet with him at his office before the school board meeting."

Carlo Ferrini recounted for the detective, how Maine was imploring him for help with a particularly controversial and public issue. Maine had allowed his ego to get the best of him and turn an otherwise internal situation, into a media frenzy. Carlo explained that Dr. Maine was in a rage about the single maverick board member, Dr Amelia Salas, who had failed to fall under his spell. She was proposing an audit of the district's compliance with the law that made all district records available to the public.

"To hell with that ditz's demand that we comply with public record's laws," the Nazi barked at Carlo. "Who does she think she is? First Amendment Amelia?"

Because Maine was the keeper of the public records, he'd refused to comply with her request. Hell! He didn't comply with anyone's request for public records, including the media's. He knew full well that most news outlets were too cheap to sue the district for violating the state statute that required him to produce all district documents, per Florida's Sunshine Law. So he'd figured he'd just ignore Salas' requests too.

Amelia Salas wanted to find out how the FEMA money was being spent on the school system's hurricane repairs. Maine had managed to get her tossed out of a financial committee meeting a few days earlier, when her incessant questioning had rattled the other committee members. Now she'd decided to take her conniption fit over his refusal, public. The Nazi was worried her proposal would stir up a shit storm and possibly motivate the media to band together and do the unthinkable… sue the school system.

"He'd summoned me to help him strategize about how to shut Salas up!"

"Why would he call you of all people," Det. Gonzalez asked.

"Good question, Detective." Carlo replied. "I only wish my answer was as good."

Carlo began telling the Detective how he had once been the right hand man for the current superintendent of schools, and in that capacity, once held more power than Maine. He also was incredibly adept at handling the local media hound dogs.

The Nazi had tremendous admiration and respect for Carlo, whom he knew was honest and capable. But Maine also knew Carlo was an obstacle to Maine's long-range plan to gain full control of the school board and school system for his own personal gain.

"One major point of contention was seeing those Ivy-League university diplomas hanging on the wall above my office credenza," Carlo informed Gonzalez. "It disturbed him to the point of actually abstaining from entering my office!" Carlo threw his head back in laughter, amused at the absurdity of Maine's jealousy.

"Why?" asked Gonzalez.

"Because Maine's own credentials were not only non-Ivy League, they were not even legitimate. They were mail order diplomas!" Carlo was chuckling so hard, his bald-head looked like the bouncing ball that used to move over the words of a song as it showed up on the screen during a performance of the Lawrence Welk Show.

"Adding insult to injury," Carlo continued, "was the fact that Jez Underwood had uncovered Maine's college transcripts. She'd broadcast a story about how his grades were so bad, he'd been put on academic probation three times while in junior college, and he'd flunked "Education 101!" For God's sake, thought Carlo, how does anyone but a moron do that? Carlo remembered Jez's comments during one of their secret meetings after that story aired.

"Only in Miami can a dimwit with a C- grade point average, and diploma mill degrees end up one heartbeat away from being the top educator," she'd said. Carlo remembered laughing, even though he knew he should cry. Public education, once a bastion of caring and committed teachers and principals had turned into a billion dollar business held hostage by corruption and cronyism. "Student" was a word rarely heard at school board meetings. "Teachers" were mocked for not wanting "out" of the classroom, and most principals found every excuse in their arsenal to be away from their campus. Carlo knew why... and so did most school board employees.

The job of school principal had become, for the most part, a patronage position for every girlfriend, sister, mother, father, brother, wife, husband, cousin, neighbor, boyfriend and mistress of board members and powerful school system administrators. And let's not forget campaign workers and contributors who had a girlfriend, sister, mother, father, brother, wife, husband, cousin, neighbor, boyfriend or mistress! Qualifications were exaggerated, competence was compromised and leadership was a liability. School system administrators didn't want innovative thinkers running schools; they wanted, or rather needed, puppets. Who better than a grateful incompetent, Carlo thought. Those principals had to stay away from their campuses out of fear that someone might discover that they really didn't know what they were doing! Carlo remembered some principals who had to make, every two weeks on payday, cash payments to board members, who had literally sold them administrative positions.

Maine's jealousy over Carlo's legitimate educational credentials and his closeness to the superintendent eventually led Maine to orchestrate Carlo's ouster from the halls of educational power. But because Carlo was a team player, he'd come when Maine called.

"That's right," Ferrini informed the detective. "I came to help the man who was responsible for exiling me to the school system's equivalent of Siberia."

"I don't get it," Detective Gonzalez said, as he cocked his head. "So the two of you were rivals?"

"If by rival you're implying Hank Maine was my equal, he was not." Carlo stiffened at the detective's implication. "Hank Maine was an arrogant, duplicitous, phony, son of a bitch, detective. Hardly, a man I'd be in a rivalry with."

Suddenly, the door opened and just about every important person in the school system and the City of Miami, walked in.

CHAPTER #4

The school district's Chief of Police entered first, followed by Miami's Police Chief, the Mayor, the president of the school board and the superintendent.

"Carlo!" Suddenly, Superintendent Rod Vascoe had Carlo locked in a bear hug. The gesture appeared to convey concern. It was anything but! "Keep your mouth shut. You've been warned," he whispered into Carlo's ear while patting him on the back. "Don't fuck with us!" R.V., as he was often referred to, released his grip around Carlo.

"I understand the police need to interview you. Please Carlo, take all the time you need," Rod Vascoe declared. "You know my office is yours." R.V. smiled.

Anyone else would have thought it a warm and sympathetic smile. Carlo knew differently, because he knew R.V. For five years, Carlo had been R.V.'s right hand man. He'd written his speeches, prepared him for presentations, responded to his school board follow-ups (questions raised during meetings by board members requiring staff responses), and basically was totally devoted to the deceitful asshole. He'd helped the humble Cuban rise to the district's highest position. It was no easy task! For starters, R.V. was a superintendent without a doctorate degree... not even a phony one like Maine! And then there were the dumb things R.V. did, that were so typical of the way powerful administrators scammed the unsuspecting taxpayers.

R.V. had gotten his mother a job at a vocational school. On paper, she was supposed to teach typing. But "mama" didn't know how to type! So she sat in the school's cafeteria all day, earning her paycheck by gossiping.

If that wasn't bad enough, R.V. had also gotten his niece a "do-nothing job" at the same school. Technically, she did do things; it's just that teaching wasn't one of those things. She'd been placed there because she was the principal's mistress! The two of them used a room on the school's fourth floor that used be a mock hotel room, when the school had a

Hotel Hospitality Course. The whole sordid affair was a poorly kept secret at the school.

It chilled Carlo to the bone to see his boss be so stupid. All Carlo could do was try to make sure that as few people as possible, knew that R.V. was... "Un echón," an empty suit, as the Cubans says. That is, until R.V. fell under the spell of the Nazi.

Carlo burned with anger every time he thought of what the Nazi had done to him personally and how he'd allowed R.V.'s incompetence to become public by not protecting the superintendent, as Carlo once had.

The group briefly gathered around the superintendent's conference table. At this point, Carlo looked around and saw what had been in one of Jez Underwood's reports... furniture that would have made the Queen of England smile!

He gazed at the sumptuous Knoll mahogany-top, Saarinen Tulip table that stretched like an airport runway from one end of the superintendent's massive office suite to the other. They sat in large swiveling Tulip chairs, upholstered in the finest black Italian leather. In the center of the Florence Knoll credenza, was an ornate Christofle silver tea and coffee set. Windows swagged in lustrous silk, oriental themed fabric, revealed a stunning view of a glimmering Biscayne Bay, while on the opposite wall... six, not one, but six, 50" flat screen plasma TV monitors were mounted... one for each of the English and Spanish language TV stations.

The superintendent's desk was the same "surfboard-shaped" oval Saarinen table in the smaller version with the matching top, but with four Knoll Brno chairs in polished stainless steel and black leather.

Carlo thought this was a far cry from the days when he worked for R.V. and they had hand-me-down furniture. No wonder schools were deprived, he thought to himself. The district's taxpayer money was on display in the superintendent's office. When Carlo was there, R.V.'s saying was, "we're here to give, not to take." That concept had surely slipped from his philosophy in recent years.

The superintendent's suite was the size of a top-floor condo in one of Miami's luxury high-rise buildings that were spreading across the former swampland like Kudzu. Five secretary desks also from Knoll, were strategically placed in the outer office. High-tech was an understatement in this case. Carlo wondered which high-end design firm had whipped up such lavishness. Was it done "pro bono" in exchange for a lucrative school construction contract? Carlo knew that's how things worked in the school system. He also knew that the Nazi was behind this luxurious, up-scale office appearance. He most likely had brokered the exchange, for a cut of the action.

Hank Maine was big on image and Carlo was pretty sure Maine's reason for such a sumptuous office for a public school leader, was based on Maine's belief that R.V. should portray the success of a CEO or "captain of industry." Knowing he was second in command, he actually thought that he could muster the board votes, by favors or by blackmail, to succeed R.V. When that time came, the Nazi would want an office, befitting his title. So Carlo was pretty sure, Maine had used R.V. to fade the heat for the cost of a swank office; an office that Maine firmly believed, would one day be his.

Detective González had never been in the superintendent's office before. But he was pretty sure most humble public educators' offices didn't look like this palace!

At the imposing conference table, he listened as School Police Chief Luis Pérez explained to the others why he'd called in the City of Miami Police Department to handle the murder investigation. Sure his officers were pretty good handling thefts, assaults and even computer crimes, but a homicide investigation was out of the school police's league.

Perez was aware that he'd inherited a group of officers that were mostly rejects from other reputable law enforcement agencies or well-connected former security guards. He'd even discovered that some on his staff, who wore a badge, had criminal records! His job was to weed out the bottom feeders, and build a department that taxpayers could be proud of. But until he'd gotten rid of the losers, he wasn't going to risk a major homicide investigation being botched by the collection of nitwits he now commanded. Of course, he didn't say any of this out loud. He merely informed the powers that be, that it was best to let seasoned homicide detectives take the lead. No one argued with his decision.

As the top officials got up to leave, Superintendent Vascoe glared at Carlo, who remained seated. Carlo was about to continue his talk with Detective Gonzalez. The very idea sent shivers down Vascoe's spine. He knew, nothing good could come from Carlo Ferrini, chatting with cops!

CHAPTER #5

"I'm investigative reporter Jez Underwood. Tonight, 11 News has shocking details about what police discovered on the body of the murdered deputy superintendent of schools in Miami. I'll have our exclusive report... next!" Jez finished her headline tease... covered the microphone with her free hand and said to her photographer, "That should get their attention!"

11 News needed viewers' attention. The once vaunted station was in a race for its life... meaning ratings and advertising dollars. Jez's school district scoops had proven to repeatedly keep viewers awake and tuned in over the last few years, especially for the all-important late news.

The school system's scandals had become a running soap opera in Miami. Viewers couldn't seem to get enough! Even Spanish language radio commentators paid attention when Jez broke another school scoop. In Miami, where Hispanics were the majority, being quoted on Spanish language radio was the ultimate compliment for a white, blonde chick of WASPY heritage from Kansas.

Jez had come to Miami 13 years ago, after a brief stint working in Topeka and then Minneapolis. Although she'd once been a competitive downhill skier, she'd wearied of winter weather, and had jumped at the chance to work in a warm climate. Her preference would have been San Diego, but beggars can't be choosers in the TV business. You go where the job offers are.

Over the years, she'd gone from a rookie night reporter, to Weekend Anchor, to Chief Investigative Reporter. She'd never married, but had dated one man for nearly nine years. He'd tried to get her to commit, but Jez was married to her job and wasn't interested in settling down, since children were not at the top of her list of things "to do."

Jez's kids, were her stories. Her passion for rooting out corruption was close to becoming an obsession. As she got older, and she went from a size 2 to a 14, nothing seemed to matter as long as she was kicking ass and taking names.

Since her breakup with the mortgage broker, few men could handle the weird hours she kept, the dedication to her job, and her inability to put them first in her life. They inevitably drifted away, almost without her noticing. Jez was astute about a lot of things, but her love life wasn't one of those things.

"One minute," the producer yelled into her earpiece.

Jez recoiled! "Damn it Sophie! That's my eardrum you just shattered! Unless you can produce 'sotto voce,' I'm unplugging you!"

"Sorry Jez. I'm just so excited! This is such a killer story! You are the bomb!" Sophie whispered.

"A nuclear bomb tonight girlfriend," Jez replied as she opened her compact to powder her nose and check her hair one last time.

It'd been a day of blood, guts and police interrogations and nobody's make-up looked TV ready after 14-hours... especially in Miami's heat. Newspaper people had it so easy, Jez thought, as she closed her compact. All they have to do is... well, nothing. She figured half of them worked from home in their PJ's, with a laptop and phone as the only tools of their trade. TV people, on the other hand, carted around oversized briefcases that looked more like luggage, filled with blow dryers, make-up bags, curling irons... no scratch that.... straightening irons, this was Miami, where humidity was mother nature's curling iron. Then there were the big styling brushes, hairspray, gel and mousse. And that was just the stuff the male TV reporters carried around!

"Ten seconds to the special open," Sophie informed Jez in her best sotto voce.

It was another of her boss's Italian phrases he dropped on Jez whenever she was screaming at him about his lack of vision, news judgment and overall capitulation to the cash, crazed, corporate heathens, now running most TV stations around the country. Under pressure from those Wall Street stock analysts "BIG J" journalism was swiftly being replaced by "BIMBO" journalism, and to Jez, it seemed as though Miami was the test market for the dumbing down of news.

One last, good, deep breath, Jez reminded herself. It was an old acting trick she'd learned as a theater major at the University of Texas. Her parents had encouraged her to go there, in hopes she'd find a wealthy oil heir, and land herself an MRS. degree.

Instead, she'd found herself a handsome actor, who encouraged her to pursue her dreams of going on the Broadway stage. Jez had ultimately, come to her senses, when she found out her handsome, actor, boyfriend had been sleeping with one of her sorority sisters! She dumped the "hunk of love" and traded in her dreams of the big stage for the small screen of TV. Now she was the "feared Investigative reporter" in the best news market in the U.S.

She used to tell her friends and family… most of whom still lived in America, which was anywhere, north of Ft. Lauderdale… that every big story had a Miami connection. Some of the Watergate burglars lived in Miami. The U.S. government snatches Panamanian President Manuel Noriega and brings him to . . . Miami! A drunken Saudi Princess gets arrested after becoming unruly on a flight into… Miami! The only Category 5 hurricane to hit the United States in nearly 100 years makes landfall . . . in Miami! And when gold medal gymnast Nadia Comaneci defected from Romania, did she head to Houston, New York City or even Chicago where they actually have a Romanian enclave? No! She defected to Miami! Well, really it was Hollywood, Florida, which is just 20 minutes north of Miami. Same thing, Jez knew. Hell, even the 2000 Presidential race hung in the balance because of pregnant or hanging chads in Miami! Jez loved this asylum called the "MAGIC CITY." How many times had she muttered to herself…"Toto, I don't think we're in Kansas anymore!"

"Tonight…. an 11 news exclusive," boomed the voice of the most popular news anchorman in South Florida, Dean

Sands. What a perfect name, Jez thought, for a guy who lived in a community with miles of beaches!

Sands continued reading, as video of Dr. Hank Maine rolled across TV screens in South Florida.

"Will women's lingerie help police link a suspect to the murder of Miami's Deputy Superintendent of Schools? That's what is puzzling authorities tonight, less than 12 hours after Dr. Hank Maine was stabbed to death in the lobby of the school board auditorium. Joining us live from just outside the scene of today's murder, with exclusive details, is Investigative Reporter Jez Underwood. Jez, I understand you've got the scoop on "Hanky's Panky!" He's got to stop writing these inane lead-ins, Jez fumed, realizing he'd tinkered with the script she'd phoned in earlier. Damn anchors. They just can't leave well-enough alone, she thought... trying to stifle a chuckle that was working its way up her throat.

Jez began. "Dean, the horror of a bold, daytime stabbing in the public school headquarters, is matched only by the stunning discovery that was made when Dr. Hank Maine's body was taken to the county's morgue for an autopsy." Jez paused for affect. "According to sources familiar with the investigation... deputy superintendent of schools, Hank Maine, died wearing a pair of ladies underwear! Specifically, last year's bestselling Victoria Secret's "Angel" line. I'm told it was an ice blue pair of bra and thong panties."

CHAPTER #6

Carlo sat on his couch laughing like a hyena. Jez had just
"made his day," as Dirty Harry would say. Revealing that the
Nazi had died with his blue lace undies on was nothing less
than a home run, Carlo thought.

He was sitting in his living room on the 49th floor of one of
Miami Beach's most prestigious condos. Like so many in the
school district, Carlo had heard rumors of Maine's secret life
as a "cross dresser." But Carlo had never known it to be anything but a rumor. He remembered Jez asking him about it.
Wow! Now he realized all those rumors might have been
true. Her sources were accurate. He was stunned!

Carlo figured he'd call Jez in about an hour. By then she'd
have cleared her live shot and driven home. Such delicious
details about Maine's Victoria Secret's secret deserved a follow up and Carlo was ready to dish!

Jez and Carlo both knew Maine had risen to power through
blackmail. Now he was dead, and his "male" was in question.
It was 11:15 pm, and after the day Carlo had had, he decided
he'd earned a Martini... Bombay Sapphire up... shaken with
a twist. "Ferrini. Carlo Ferrini," he muttered to no one in particular, as he poured the gin and vermouth, imitating James
Bond. Waiting for the martini to chill, he lifted his prize show
dog Samba and began stroking the top of her head . . . just
like "Dr. No" did with his white Abyssinian cat in Carlo's favorite bond film, "TO RUSSIA WITH LOVE." Carlo had felt
like Dr. No all day.

"No! I didn't see who stabbed him. No! I didn't do it. No, I'm
not lying or hiding anything." The "no's" were piling up.The
truth: Carlo didn't see who stabbed the Nazi . . . but he knew
the list of suspects was long. He wondered which of Maine's
misdeeds had gotten him killed. He could easily name at
least 100 people who would want to "off" the Nazi. That's
what he'd told the cops. "Short list the people who loved him,
liked him, or tolerated him and work backwards from there
Detective González." He also warned González that this
might take up the better part of the cops 10 years until retirement. González had laughed. But Carlo knew the Detec-

tive wouldn't be laughing when he figured out how many enemies Hank Maine had cultivated... and he began to uncover the secrets a school system some might kill to protect.

Already, some of those secrets were getting out. Jez Underwood had tangled with Hank Maine last year, when she discovered that he'd been bugging administrative offices at the downtown headquarters building, including those of school board members. She'd reported that he'd even installed hidden cameras in the restrooms! Despite the public outrage, the Nazi kept his job and the power that came with it.

Hank Maine controlled the security staff assigned to the administrative offices. And like Hitler, Maine even had his own Herr Himmler. The guy was a humorless security guard at the headquarters building who had a swastika tattooed on the left side of his neck. If ever there was a white supremacist on the school system's payroll, Webb Streck was it! He was also Dr. Maine's personal enforcer and errand runner. That was just one of the reasons nearly everyone in the district hated Hank Maine. Parents hated him, secretaries hated him, teachers, principals, and custodians hated him. And the news media really loathed him! He had the audacity to act as if they didn't exist. But few news managers cared. It was the school board after all! School boards were not thought of as "sexy news." Their meetings were usually boring and the public didn't really care. That was the thinking when Jez began unearthing school scandals, such as the one about a maintenance supervisor who was caught giving a blowjob to another man in a public park. Jez had found out that he'd been driving his district vehicle and was on the clock when he was arrested. But his boss had altered his time sheet, indicating the guy was out sick. He was never fired.

Carlo remembered the story she broke about the secretary making $100,000+, who only had a high school diploma, and the one about the high school athletic director who was recruiting high school graduates from the Bahamas to play for his championship football team. Was the athletic director fired? No! But the coach suspected of blowing the whistle on him was.

Jez had discovered that an assistant principal at an adult education school, who held a doctoral degree, had been assigned to monitor the staff parking lot from 3 to 11 pm, by the principal. It was punishment for going public about the fact that he used a school custodian as his chauffer.

And Jez had gotten her hidden cameras inside a kindergarten class in an inner city "F" school, with 50 kids and only one teacher. Jez then confronted the principal with an enrollment sheet he'd doctored, showing only 21 children were in that class. The principal was only reprimanded.

But it was the shocking story about the hidden cameras in the school board's headquarters that prompted Hank Maine to launch a vendetta against Jez and her station.

Jez was not allowed on any floor, except the first floor of the school board headquarters. If Jez was in the building, a guard shadowed her everywhere . . . bathrooms included. They would camp outside the ladies room, not allowing anyone in... until Jez was out. It ranked among the silliest, most stupid, yet revealing tales of just how insulated and paranoid the culture of one of the nation's largest school systems had become. One had to wonder... what else were the district's powerful and influential hiding?

With that one story of the Nazi's own personal "KGB" tactics; Jez had earned a special place in the "black heart" of the second most powerful administrator. The minute she'd aired the story, all hell broke loose! That investigation had unleashed madness, Jez would later tell Ferrini. Her phones wouldn't stop ringing. E-mails poured in and the frenzy of trying to absorb everything she was being told, mostly by strangers, not yet tested sources, was taking its toll. Jez wondered what prompted these people to move from apathy to active whistleblower.

She soon learned that it was because of the blatant and flagrant abuse of school board rules, cronyism, nepotism, and the anger that arose from the jealousy of human nature, by people who'd been slighted by the gravy train.

Jealous people bear watching, Carlo's grandmother always told him. Now, those who'd been passed over for a promotion because of a lack of connections to management, or who'd refused to compromise their principles, saw a chance to get even.

One hundred hour weeks suddenly were the norm. How else could Jez possibly sift through all the tips, hints and positively riveting tales of what was going on under the noses of the unsuspecting taxpayers, without whose dollars, such decadent corruption would not have been possible? It was the same for Jez's producer, Adele Morris. The two of them basically had to stop working during the November sweeps period in order to keep up with the volume of e-mails and phone calls... and in some instances the regular mail. The information, source name and phone number were entered into the station's computer. As the weeks passed and the information continued to pour in... Jez decided to catalogue the information as chapters. By chapter 13, she knew this document required a name. "The Bible," she said. "That's what we'll call it... the Bible of the school system." The name wasn't intended to be blasphemous, just descriptive. It was after all, the most comprehensive compilation of sources' names, phone numbers, addresses, stories, tips, and hints that any reporter had probably ever managed to assemble, involving the school board.

"The Bible?" Adele asked, somewhat aghast.

"Yes!" Jez replied excited about the idea.

Adele, a devout Catholic, didn't respond. Instead she crossed herself and nodded. Because Jez didn't trust computers, she backed up the Bible in a number of files... and then printed copies, one of which was kept in her bank safe deposit drawer, and the other she kept in her briefcase. If her enemies had had any idea of the damning information she was collecting and walking around with... Jez knew she wouldn't live long.

She'd been warned repeatedly to watch her back. No one had directly threatened her life... but more than a few people, including Carlo, were concerned enough about her safety to talk to her about it.

Carlo had insisted she get a device from Germany that lit up if her phone line was tapped and instantly cut the call. She did. Emeril, her photographer demanded she use different routes to and from work and home. She did. And the station refused to allow any package she received, to be delivered to her, until the mailroom guy had taken it outside to the far end of the parking lot and unwrapped it. Poor Juan, she thought. Her heartless employers had turned the Mexican immigrant into a bomb-sniffing dog, without the training a bomb-sniffing dog would most certainly receive!

Jez wasn't naive. In fact, she was very aware she was playing with fire. It came with the territory when you were an investigative reporter, especially when one focused on public corruption, as Jez did. She was always on guard. Mostly she kept her eye out for people who might be following her. Jez drove a candy apple red convertible... turbo charged. So Jez knew she could leave most "tails" in her dust. She also knew that a cherry red convertible, driving at ridiculous speeds attracted the attention of cops in any uniform. So, if followed, Jez's back up plan was to drive like a bat out of hell, and hope to be pulled over. She had to laugh! Who in their right mind would want that? Jezebel . . . that's who!

That's the name bestowed upon her by her father, a Bette Davis fan! As a young child, she'd wished her mother had won the name game. Mom's pick was Pamela. It was a nice name that people could spell, and didn't laugh at when informed that "yes," it was her real name!" Later as an adult, during a family dinner when she'd moaned about her name being so infamous, Jez's father had laughed and told her, "If the shoe fits Jez, wear it." Even Jez saw the humor in that. It seems she'd grown into her name in more ways than one.

Carlo decided it was time to call Jez. He was ready to throw a few new clues in her direction. Screw R.V.'s warning. Times had changed. The district was under assault... and Carlo knew where the bodies were buried. It was time for one of his secret meetings with the "diva of personal destruction... Jez Underwood."

CHAPTER #7
THURSDAY

At the Miami cop shop; most of the city's best detectives weren't waiting for the forensics from the medical examiner. They were busy comparing interview notes from all those in the lobby when the Nazi was bludgeoned to death. The chiefs of police for both the city and the school district had made it clear that the murder of Dep. Supt. Hank Maine was the top priority.

"How could no one have seen someone jab a dagger into the guy's guts?" Det. González asked the seven detectives gathered around the conference table in homicide's wing of the department. "The place was filled with at least 100 people."

"105, sir," one of the detectives corrected.

"Yeah, yeah, 105. That's five more reasons I don't understand why everyone in the lobby was deaf, dumb and blind," barked González. "Has CSU come up with anything Davis?"

"No. They're still there processing the scene," Detective Hal Davis informed his school police counterpart.

"I want to know the minute they have anything. Got it?" González asked Davis.

"Yes Rogelio, I've got it. But with all due respect, this is our investigation now. Your support is appreciated, but don't ever talk to me like that again!" Davis replied.

*****

Lee and Lilly Molina weren't detectives, but the death of Hank Maine had them as anxious as the guys at the cop shop. Not because the forensics was slow in coming, but because of what each privately knew about the Nazi. Lee and Lilly were a power couple. They liked to think of themselves as the Bob and Elizabeth Dole of the Miami School System.

Lee had risen to power by using his school to raise and hide funds that various top administrators tapped into. Molina's' school slush fund was used to pay for personal parties, including baby and wedding showers, meetings, campaign fundraisers and any personal necessities. If a board member needed business cards for his or her real job, Lee Molina had his school's print shop whip up a few hundred business cards. If a board member or administrator's wife's car needed repairs or maintenance, Lee had it brought into his auto repair shop at the school. It was then taken to a service station he co-owned with the automotive repair instructor at his school. The car would be fixed for free. Favors were Lee's method of career advancement.

Lily on the other hand, had a more traditional approach to the subject. Simply put... she put out! Lily was presently an associate superintendent. It was a position she'd gotten through hard work on her knees and back. Lily was the "not so secret" lover of one school board member, and the sexual satisfier of a top administrator. The latter was Dep. Supt. Hank Maine.

He'd loved her blowjobs so much he'd thrust her out of the classroom and into the board's administrative headquarters. But he'd dumped her like a hot potato when Dr. Moses Josiah Moorehead became her lover and mentor. Even the Nazi knew better than to hang onto a woman that Big Mo had eyes for.

Dr. Moses Josiah Moorehead was not just another school board member. He was widely known as the "Stealth Superintendent." Moorehead had the power, even if he didn't have the title. But it was not having the title that often drove him mad with jealousy.

Dr. Moses Josiah Moorehead grew up in rural Mississippi, one of 12 children born to sharecropper parents. He was a depression-era baby, whose young soul was nurtured in the "old South," which was steeped in racism. It was a time in which black men weren't respected and generally referred to as "boy..." often before a mob of white crackers, or rednecks, lynched them from a tree.

On his first job application, he'd chaffed when he was forced to check his race as "Negro." Decades later, when Negroes were now referred to as blacks, Moorehead wanted nothing more than for the black man to be more powerful than the white man.

He'd gone into education, not because he loved children, in fact, he didn't like them one bit. What Moses Josiah Moorehead liked was, women, booze, drugs, money and power. He pursued a career path he knew would put him in an environment surrounded with women and provide him with a decent salary that could support his other vices... including, he hoped, the power he yearned for. He was determined to escape the fields and a lifetime of picking cotton.

Ultimately, Moses Josiah Moorehead went from being a classroom teacher, to school principal, to an administrator on the fast track. He earned a doctorate degree. It was a legitimate doctorate, not one of those fraudulent degrees, so many of his colleagues favored. He was a smart man who was determined to be somebody by hook or by crook. He'd done just that. But his rise had not been without periodic falls.

There was the time Big Mo had used a few of his closest associates, also top school administrators, to raise money for his school board campaign. They got caught twisting teacher's arms for contributions as part of raffle ticket scam. His henchmen forced teachers, custodians and other low rung school employees, to take a book of 20, $20 tickets to sell for Moorehead's campaign war chest. Too afraid to say no to the omnipotent Dr. Moorehead and his gang of thugs, most of these poorly paid, and overworked school employees, simply reached into their jar of grocery money, to meet the monetary obligations Big Mo surreptitiously demanded of them.

Then there was the time that Mo and a principal opened a bakery at one of the high schools. Top administrators, or anyone who could keep their mouth shut, could go there to get cakes and cookies for anything from weddings to Sunday brunches. The students did it all for free. But Mo and his partner, charged a nominal fee and kept every penny. When the authorities moved in, Mo eluded an indictment, but his pal, got caught... not only for using public facilities for a private business, but authorities soon learned that the gold plated faucets in his Miami Beach home... had been bought and paid for by the taxpayers!

Enter Jez Underwood. Although she could expose other failings and mismanagement, which continued unabated since Big Mo had temporarily been silenced by authorities in the 80's, she was never going to dampen his enthusiasm for what was his primary goal... black domination of the school system.

As hard as he'd tried to put loyalty ahead of competence, as many investigations as he'd dodged, and as often as he'd had to slink out of the spotlight, waiting for the right time for the Phoenix to rise again... Moses Josiah Moorehead had hit a dead end in his quest for dominance... at least the kind that gave him public recognition for dominance. The chance to hold the title as the "Wizard of the welfare state" he'd worked so diligently to create inside the school system, was getting farther and farther from his grasp.

You see, no matter how he had twisted and cajoled the system so that blacks truly had a chance at power, Miami's geographic location had turned it into a city dominated by Cuban exiles. It now seemed that Moorehead had to battle on two fronts, one the ancient enemy, the white man, and the second, the newest arrivals. In theory, Moorehead's power and knowledge should have ensured that anyone within breathing distance of the man would reap the benefits of those attributes. So why then, weren't the schools in his predominantly inner city district the best? In fact, far from being the best, they were notoriously the worst.

The truth: Dr. Moorehead had successfully grabbed the top rung of the ladder for himself, but in so doing, had selfishly and shamelessly, left his people at the bottom. Why?

It would be the one question about the enigma of this intelligent individual, that Jez would never be able to answer.

CHAPTER #8

Lily Molina, knew her relationship with Moorehead was fleeting. It's one of the reasons she cozied up to Lee Molina. People who knew Lee and Lily were convinced that they were made for each other. Both were diabolically ambitious, mean, hateful, and devoid of morals, ethics or common decency. When the two decided to marry, (his fifth, her fourth) they were so full of themselves and the power they'd accrued in the school system... they actually had the nerve to use taxpayer money to pay for their wedding reception. Jez had recently uncovered their bar bills, and party rental fees, including wine glasses, champagne glasses, ashtrays, cutlery, tables, tablecloths, booze, food... you name it. Jez even located one of the four school employees they recruited to act as servers at the reception. The person told Jez how the four had been given compensatory "comp" time for working the wedding party. That allowed Jez to reveal how taxpayers had funded four employee's days off... because they worked a wedding reception, illegally billed to those same taxpayers. The marriage of Lee and Lily Molina only clicked when "mutual destruction" was assured. He'd accuse her of prostituting herself with every Tom, Dick and Hank Maine. She'd accuse him of fucking anything that moved in a skirt.

Lily wasn't half wrong. In fact, Lee Molina was the system's leading defendant! If there had been an award for the most lawsuits filed against one man for sexual harassment in the Miami Public School System, Lee Molina would have won the title! Lee was a "horn dog." That was Jez's Kansas expression for a man who couldn't keep his pecker in his pants. Carlo had died laughing when she'd first used the phrase.

The idea that women employees of the district were nothing but sex slaves... was a recurring theme Jez kept uncovering.

There was the middle school principal who'd chased his pregnant secretary around the conference table... waving a wad of hundred dollar bills at her, demanding to have sex!

Then there was the principal who had a teacher on a special beeper. Whenever he wanted sex, he'd beep her and she had 20 minutes to hook up with him. The fact that she was married didn't bother the sicko one bit. He took demonic pleasure in making it hard for her to explain to her husband where she was going and why. One time, he had her meet him at his church where he was an elder. That title gave him access to a key to the church.

He'd opened the door to the sanctuary... took her hand and led her toward the altar. As they stood under the stained glass depiction of a crucified Jesus on the cross... the pervert pushed his pathetic secretary onto the altar and mounted her.

Lucky for the lady, nothing was happening. His penis was small. It wasn't getting larger. It wasn't doing anything. Period. He ordered her to blow him. She did. But nothing happened. So he stood, took a piece of paper from his coat pocket, wrote the words, "You are a lousy lay." Then he stuck a gun in his mouth and pulled the trigger.

When these stories broke, Jez used to say... "I can't make this stuff up!" Who could? These were educators after all, not pimps and prostitutes!

But Jez had learned, that no matter how demeaning, inappropriate or vile the behavior, getting subordinates to open up about what they were being subjected to was damn hard! Their fear of retribution was real, and real frightening. Never was that more apparent than when Jez tried to gain the trust and confidence of a caller known only as Carlita. Carlita called Jez, like about 300 others had, following Jez's report on the hidden cameras in the school board administrative offices. But Carlita refused to give Jez even a hint of her identity or how to reach her. Instead, Jez had to wait for Carlita to call each time. It tested Jez's ability to relate to the frightened human race, her ability to massage a source, and it made her painfully aware of the powerful people she was pissing off. Jez wanted to wrap her arms around her sources and tell them that everything would be ok. But she knew she couldn't do that. Hell, even she didn't know if everything would be ok. It was a fact she adamantly kept from her darling parents and siblings.

They knew what she did for a living, and she knew it worried them. Jez needed to keep their worrying to a minimum. Mostly because she wasn't sure her parents weren't above having her removed from Miami... just like parents did when their kids became Moonies or Hari Krishnas. Jez knew she was part of a cult. But it was called TV news! Her cult worshipped ratings and big stories. It was a cult that had no use for people with morals or ethics. In point of fact, the TV News business was only one notch above a mafia hit man, lobbyist, politician or personal injury attorney... at least in the public's eye

Carlo was also part of a cult... called the public school system. It worshipped money and power. It was a fact that disgusted Carlo, who thought educating children should have been the primary concern of anyone who worked in public schools. Sadly, he'd learned quite the opposite.

Too many people in the district just wrote the kids off. Carlo remembered one of his former teachers who'd recently spent time in what was considered one of the toughest schools in town, telling him how she was told by her principal, "These kids can't be taught anything, so don't bother trying. Just take attendance and keep order."

Seeing what the district had become, and desperately wanting to let the public know, is the reason Carlo had agreed to meet with Jez when she called the first time. Jez was straight up with him."I know you used to be Vascoe's right-hand man, "mano derecha," and I know he didn't treat you right. I figure you know where lots of the bodies are buried and I'm wondering if you'd care to share any of that information with me," she told him. It was true! Carlo did know where the bodies were buried and he was pissed off. That's what Jez loved about him the minute they met. He was passionate about education, had nearly 30 years with the school system, knew all of the major players, and he was scorned! Jez believed a scorned lover, wife, husband, business partner or chief of staff... made the best sources. Why? Because they were usually pissed-off and looking for revenge. Jez provided them an avenue to do just that.

She'd heard how Superintendent Vascoe had dumped Carlo in favor of the Nazi. She'd heard that Carlo was sick with Cancer, probably because of all the stress the Nazi had caused him, Jez thought. And so, that's why she called Carlo. It was a whim, but ultimately proved to be a very fruitful meeting. For two hours, Carlo had spilled his guts to Jez and her photographer, Emeril. The meeting at a trendy SoBe Lincoln Road restaurant had led to a great friendship along the way. It also meant Jez had someone who could provide her with documentation, tips, leads, phone numbers, payroll records . . . you name it. Carlo didn't blow the whistle to Jez; he helped her interpret data, financials, and personnel codes. He could navigate the system easier than driving a car. If Carlo didn't know something, he knew people who did, and he could get stuff for Jez like no other source she had. Now they were meeting again . . . less than 24 hours after Dr. Hank Maine's death.

CHAPTER #9

Because Dade County was the size of the state of Rhode Island, there was no shortage of places to hook up where it was a pretty good bet you wouldn't be seen. If anyone at the school district had found out that Carlo was meeting with Jez... his job and retirement would have been in jeopardy.

Investigating the school district required a lot of "cloak and dagger" stuff for Jez and her sources. Jez had become real good at finding restaurants that were "here today, gone tomorrow... " Meaning, by the time word got out about its menu, the owners had gone out of business. These kinds of places meant a sparse crowd and a 90% guarantee of privacy. Sometimes, the food was even surprisingly good!

One of Jez's current spots was in a "transitional neighborhood," as she called it. Basically, it was a bad neighborhood in the process of being revitalized. The Lamplight Restaurant was located on a poorly traveled side street in Miami's design district. It didn't look like much from the outside, but once you entered the unassuming art deco arch that stood as an invitation to anyone strolling down the sidewalk, you discovered the hidden patio with its overgrown palms and gigantic hanging ferns. It was a wonderful place to eat during the winter, when the average temperature in Miami was 76-degrees and no humidity. Inside, there was a dark oak bar and grand piano. The inside portion of the restaurant was a mix between Miami chic and a Washington D.C. power lunch spot. The menu touted everything from salads and hamburgers to mango salsa covered Sea Bass.

But what the Lamplight had, that Jez just loved, were two corner booths with heavy tapestry draperies that could be pulled for privacy. Jez always arrived a few minutes before it opened for business... greased the hostesses palm so she'd be discreet, and would tell her to escort anyone asking for the "Dee Dee party," to her table. Today, Carlo would be that someone.

"Hi," he said pulling back the drape.

"How are you holding up?" Jez inquired, concerned about
the toll yesterday's events had taken on him.

"A little shaky," Carlo confessed as he sat down. He waited
for the hostess to pull the drape closed before he continued.
"I'm ambivalent! No one deserved death more than the Nazi!
He actually changed the entire course of my career. Now, in
retrospect, I am better off emotionally because of it, but certainly not financially."

Carlo's reaction didn't really surprise Jez. She wondered how
many school employees were toasting the first day without
the Nazi in their lives. Probably thousands, including the district's "Parent of the Year." Maine had actually given her the
"finger" in the middle of a televised board meeting! It was
caught on tape, and Jez broke the story the next night...
complete with the middle finger highlighted! All the better to
get a look at what Dr. Hank Maine thought of dedicated parents, who suffered through long board meetings that went
past midnight, just so their children's education might be im-
proved.

"Are you sure you didn't see who stabbed him," Jez asked
again. "You were right there, Carlo!"

"Jez, I swear I didn't. Vito Sindoni had just grabbed my arm
and told me he needed to speak to me. I'd turned away from
Maine to talk with Vito. I didn't see who did it."

Vito Sindoni was president of the teacher's union. He was a
portly man, who was the epitome of a "union boss." White-
haired, and as short and he was wide, Jez had often thought
he looked like the "Penguin" crime character from the Batman cartoons. Sindoni was so powerful, it was rumored that
most board members didn't cast a vote on anything without
consulting him. His backroom deals and his temper were no-
torious. Jez had encountered both!

She'd exposed how he'd gotten the board to award a health
insurance contract to one company. A company that had then
turned around and hired Sindoni's lobbyist pal, Sid Messing,
for millions of dollars in consulting fees. She'd then linked
Messing to the Sindoni Family Trust Fund. It was a clever

way for Sindoni to collect the kickback on the deal, since he'd made sure all other health insurance companies were shut out of the massive request for proposal... or RFP.

"What did that tyrant Sindoni want?" Jez asked.

"I never got a chance to find out. Maine screamed before Vito could tell me." Carlo opened up his menu. "But I do know something about the murder weapon if you're interested."

"Carlo! You are such a tease! What? Tell me." Jez was leaning across the table with anticipation.

"Semper Fi." Carlo went silent.

"Yeah, yeah the Marine's motto," Jez responded. Her hands were in a rolling motion... indicating that Carlo should keep talking."That's what I saw on the handle of the knife."

"Are you saying, you think a Marine killed him?" Jez paused. "Why would a Marine kill him? What could be the significance of a Marine's knife being used to gut the Nazi? Maine wasn't a Marine was he?"

"No little girl, he wasn't a Marine, but he collected everything military. He became a teacher to avoid the Vietnam War with a deferment." Carlo looked at her somewhat surprised. He figured she knew all this. "You've been in his office. Don't you remember his collection?"

"Carlo, Maine barely let me in the building, so no, I was never in his office. The few interviews I did with him before he cut me off, were conducted in the lobby.""Oh, well then let me tell you my dear, Hank Maine was a military paraphernalia freak!"

At that moment, the waitress pulled the drape back and asked if they'd like to order. Both ordered the grilled ham and cheese Panini with a Diet Coke. The waitress closed the drape again. Jez was getting impatient. "O.K., so the Nazi had a thing for military stuff! He also apparently had a thing for lacy underwear! What is it you're trying to tell me?" she demanded.

"Jez, that knife was part of Maine's collection. It hung on the wall in his office!" Carlo was almost breathless as he related this huge lead to Jez.

"Oh My God!" she exclaimed. "He was killed with his own knife... meaning whoever did it... had been in his office, seen it, and had access to the office." Jez's mind was racing. She and Carlo both knew, that clue strongly favored a district employee as the "doer. "Do the police know this Carlo?"

"I didn't tell them, " he replied. Then a slow grin began to spread across his face. A similar one was dawning on Jez's lips. Just then, the waitress pulled back the drape to serve them their drinks. "Cancel our order, Sally but, put your tip on my tab," Jez instructed the waitress.

Then she turned to Carlo. "I'd say I have tonight's exclusive lead story, wouldn't you?" Carlo nodded. Then the two of them all but ran out of the restaurant.

CHAPTER #10

It was Jez's close relationship with the district's security staff that helped her get into the Nazi's office. After leaving the restaurant, Carlo had headed home. Jez had called Emeril and instructed him to meet her at the school system's head-quarters. "Hi Charlie." Jez greeted her most devoted fan and favorite security guard. "Girl, this place is still spinning like a top over Maine's death. You must know how many people are walking around today with smiles on their faces."

Charlie Hopkins was openly gay, and thought Jez Under-wood walked on air. Ever since she'd started exposing the school system's dirty laundry, Charlie had watched in awe at the increased paranoia pulsating through the headquarters. He knew most all the top people would sooner pee in their pants than get a phone call from Jez. He loved watching them squirm.

"Charlie, I need a huge, huge favor," Jez informed him.

"Sure, sugar," he responded. "Anything for you Jez. What is it?"

"I need to get my camera inside the Nazi's office, pronto! There's your own batch of cookies in it for you." Not only was Jez an investigative reporter… but she made a mean cookie. Usually her baking creations were holiday gifts… sugar cook-ies shaped like Santa Claus, Easter Eggs, Halloween witch-es or autumn leaves. She covered the designs generously with sugary icing in every color of the rainbow and then dec-orated them with sparkles, sprinkles, M&M's… you name it. Her creations were more addictive than crack… and in gen-eral, men went wilder over them than women. She suspected the gals didn't like to admit eating sweets. But, the cookies had been her calling card for sources in all parts of the school system. While some female reporters might sleep with men to get information… Jez just baked for them.

"Holy Moly girl! Are you for real?" Charlie was clearly ner-vous at her request."Listen Charlie, you and I both know that with the Nazi dead, the rules about my access to this building died with him. I even suspect his hidden cameras have been disconnected. So all you have to do is hand me a badge to visit the 9th floor, give another one to Emeril and let us worry about getting caught. I'll tell them I snatched it while you argued with Emeril about crossing the police tape. I mean you were just doing your job making him go around to the other entrance, and he's old and lazy and didn't want to." Jez held her breath as Charlie contemplated the worthiness of her story. "I bet I can even make some porno cookies that will impress your friends, Charlie. I have food coloring they call "nude." Know what I mean?" Jez winked at Charlie.

"Oh to hell with this place. Go get 'em girlfriend." Charlie then handed her two 9th floor visitor passes.

"Your sweet tooth will be handsomely rewarded, my dear," Jez told Charlie as she grabbed the passes and pushed the up button on the elevator.

Inside Maine's office, Jez not only got to see the missing slot where the "Semper Fi" knife had once hung... but she had a few good moments to go through the Nazi's papers on his desk. "What are ju doink?" Emeril asked with his eyebrows raised.

"Making the best use of time while your slow ass shoots some videotape, poor refugee!" Poor refugee was a phrase Emeril used to describe himself whenever he tried to gain Jezs' sympathy about something. As in... I'm just a poor Cuban refugee. His repertoire on the topic was limited. But, now, the refugee's eyebrows were raised in a disapproving stare. Emeril wasn't the best photographer at the station. But he was the best if you needed someone who could sit still for hours on a surveillance, read the tea leaves of a stake out, and then catch the subject on videotape. His investigative instincts were the reason Jez didn't want to work with anyone else. It's also why she put up with his broken English... half of which she never understood.

But his raised eyebrows spoke volumes. Emeril was from the old school of broadcasting... back when they had morals and ethics, just like educators. Jez wasn't that far off the mark from Emeril's old standards, but occasionally she knew she pushed him. Sifting through the paperwork on the Nazi's desk was one of those moments. "God will get ju blondie," Emeril announced.

"Then light a candle and say a prayer for me at church on Sunday." Jez responded sarcastically. "This is one story they aren't going to kill, Emeril."

"How can they blondie, the guy's already dead." Emeril's words rang in Jez's ear. He was so right, she thought.

******

It had only been a year since her station had started concocting all sorts of excuses why her stories about Vito Sindoni, the teacher's union president, weren't making air. Among the reasons... "You don't really have evidence," or "there could be a perfectly logical explanation for that." Her favorite, however, was, "the audience is bored with this story." Somehow, a weekly publication had picked up on 11 News's lack of Underwood vs. Sindoni reporting and started asking questions.

One day after the weekly hit the newsstand, Jez found herself in the General Managers office, where happy wasn't exactly the "word" of the day! "I can't believe you said 'no fucking comment.'" The man screaming at the top of his lungs was Tab Tanner, the station's general manager.

"I didn't say no fucking comment," Jez insisted. "I said no comment. There was no fucking in my response."

"Don't get smart with me Jez." Tanner almost sounded serious. "When you're asked if this station has killed a story, you say No! Hell No! You defend this organization to the death! Got it?" Tanner was seething over an article in a local weekly newspaper that indicated the station had backed off Jez's stories about Vito Sindoni and his misuse of teachers' union dues, all because he'd filed an FCC license challenge against the station.

Some reporters would have considered such a lawsuit, a badge of honor. Not Jez. She wanted to vomit when she heard what Sindoni was up to. Tanner had assured her that it was just part of the business and that she was just doing her job. But she saw that look in his eyes... the one that said he was frightened half to death. A General Manager, who lost a license challenge, would never work in the business again. Jez was well aware of the realities of this broadcast challenge, and the cost to the company.

Kitty Haas was dead... and not one employee working for her TV stations, believed her heirs, had the stomach their mother had, to stand up to people who might cost them some legal fees. In fact, the last time a person tried to eviscerate her Florida Broadcast licenses... the man was stopped dead in his tracks. His name was President Richard Nixon.

"Tanner, all I was doing was . . . " Jez stopped in mid-sentence. Tanner had grabbed his crystal handled letter opener and was holding it up high above his head as if he was going to plunge it into Jez at any minute. He was threatening her with it.

"I don't give a fuck what you think you were doing. What I'm telling you is that you defend this station, no matter what!"

By now, Tanner was waving the letter opener wildly, as if he had pirates to slay or had channeled Freddy the Slasher. "Are you going to stab me with that thing or open envelopes?" Jez asked.

Although she was perspiring like a stuck pig, she understood the importance of not letting Tanner know she was fucking scared out of her mind! "Shut up!" Tanner replied. . . as his blood vessels appeared to burst from throbbing. "I'm your God damn boss."

"All the more reason you should put that thing down Tanner. A boss who threatens his employee with a dangerous weapon, won't be a boss very much longer." Jez stopped talking and held her breath.

Jez had known Tab Tanner for over 20 years. She knew he was just having a "moment." Tanner had a secret that few people knew. That secret was that Tanner's bark was worse than his bite! Jez had known it for a long time. Now it was time to call him on it.

"Isn't it enough that you have the entire station convinced you're the devil? Do you have to act like him too?" Jez was defiant. She knew he ate wimps for lunch, and she wasn't about to be one.

"Go to hell," screamed Tanner, as he put the letter opener down. "I've worked hard to cultivate that image among my employees, so don't go screwing it up by telling people the truth!" Jez and Tanner erupted into laughter! She knew he needed a hug . . . and he knew she needed one too. Neither got one. And both knew why.

CHAPTER #11

It was all starting to become a bit much. A hated man had been murdered with his own huge dagger he'd kept in his office as part of a military memorabilia collection. No one saw the doer and the victim died in the arms of a man who he'd screwed professionally. Pathetically, the cops had not one suspect. "Priceless!" Jez muttered to herself, as she contemplated the realities of the situation.

The cops were scurrying to interview most of the system's top administrators. They'd already finished their interviews with all the people in the lobby at the time of Maine's death. Now they were branching out . . . reportedly to the very people who might have had motive to kill the Nazi. Detective González was sitting in Superintendent Vascoe's office. This time, he was interviewing the Superintendent. "Did you like your Deputy, Mr. Superintendent?" González asked.

Dodging his true feelings and playing the party line, R.V. responded, "Well of course, Detective. I'm the one who promoted him to the very powerful position he held. Hank was a cleaver man, with incredible ambition. I liked that in him."

"Did his ambition ever get him in trouble, sir . . . or you?" The Detective was probing.

"His ambition served me well, Detective González. What are you driving at, if I may ask"? R.V. was now suddenly suspicious of González's questions. Detective González pushed on.

"Did you and Dr. Maine socialize outside of work, sir?"

"We often attended the same affairs such as the Superintendent's Ball, or the Barbara Bush Family Literacy Foundation's cruise ship luncheon. We'd always show up at the Annual Teacher-Of-The Year Luncheon, Principal-Of-The-Year Luncheon or dinner, etc. Those and many similar school system events fell under Hank's administrative role. Beyond that, no, we weren't drinking buddies in a skybox at a Dolphins game, if that's what you're asking. Hank and I had a strictly professional/social relationship. I really didn't know much

about him, other than the fact he was married to Donna."
Superintendent Vascoe gulped. It did not go undetected by
González. As R. V. went on to explain, Donna was Hank
Maine's wife. Years ago, she'd been his student! But somehow, teaching her American history had turned into an illicit
love affair between the Nazi and the young Donna Carson. It
was scandalous then, and would have been more so now.

But scandal never seemed to bother Hank Maine. He
seemed to wear it like gum on an old shoe. There was the
time he orchestrated the purchase of land for an elementary
school that was contaminated with paint toxins, just to make
one of the board members happy and to appease a powerful
lobbyist.

Then there was the rundown apartment building the system
owned, but never used. So the Nazi decided to set up a sort
of brothel for top administrators! The property was less than
a block from the main headquarters... so all the big guys
could set up their trysts and not even have to really leave the
office to get a piece of action. Jez and Emeril had run surveillance on the HOTSPOT, as it was called, and the reports
were expected to end Maine's career. But R.V had refused
to dump his deputy... and so the Nazi's myth and madness
grew like a cancer. After wrapping up his questioning of superintendent Vascoe, Detective González headed off to interview Maine's office staff.

There was Betty, his personal secretary, Kristal, Manty, and
Pauline. And these were just the office slaves. Maine also
had hundreds of people in various departments from mid-
level administrators to low-level administrators, who reported
to him. González was weary just thinking about all the work
he had in front of him. "Do you have any idea who killed Dr.
Maine?" The question to González came from Betty Pardue.
But González noticed her question had more curiosity, than
concern in her voice. "Not just yet Mrs. Pardue. Do you have
any ideas on the subject?" he asked.

Betty Pardue was a "lifer" at the district, and she was well
loved. Nobody could understand how she'd ended up working for the Nazi, and nobody could understand how she'd
survived doing so. Hank Maine wasn't just known as the

Nazi because of his identical Hitler looks . . . he was also a tyrant and any person who survived his office "work camp," was a marvel. Betty was just that person. "Detective," Pardue began, "I can't think of anyone who didn't want him dead and that includes me. Dr. Maine was a pompous jackass! Please excuse my language, but there's no other way to describe him. He was always granting himself special privileges. For example, while other employees had to go to the district's dining room or out of the building for lunch, Maine's food was prepared by the dining facility manager and delivered to his office free of charge. His title as the Deputy Superintendent of the Miami School System meant that he controlled and supervised many of the system's critical departments. So yes, lots of people hated him. People inside the district hated him. People outside the district hated him. I had absolutely no respect for him."

"Then why did you work for him Betty," González inquired.

"Because, he paid more than any other administrator." She paused for effect. "Want to know why? Well, he had to . . . otherwise, no one would have worked for him. No one that is, but Pauline."

"Why Pauline Finch?" González asked.

"The truth?" Betty suddenly seemed very ill at ease.

"The truth," González responded. Betty bit her lip and looked down at her hands wringing themselves from the anxiety she was feeling. Betty had survived the mad, mad world of Miami's school administration by keeping her mouth shut and burying whatever she saw or heard that she shouldn't. Now she was being asked to spill her guts! Slowly, she turned her wedding band around her finger, over and over again. It was a nervous habit. Detective González noticed the seemingly innocent movement and realized that he had a "live one" on the line.

González was into sport fishing... and equated everything to hooking the "big one." Her actions told him she was faltering and may break. He didn't need to know about fish to figure that out... it was Psychology for Cops 101. Finally, Betty raised her eyes toward González, and then slowly lifted her head to look him straight in the eyes. "They were lovers! Everyone knew it . . . including the news media." Betty felt the burden of decades of secrets suddenly lift from her shoulders as she spoke. "That Jez Underwood revealed how Pauline had gotten two $20,000 raises in one year . . . all because Maine pushed it through the board he owned and operated." Betty stared at the ceiling.

"Did you ever see, first hand, any proof of this alleged relationship Mrs. Pardue?" González held his breath. At first, Betty Pardue was silent, as if contemplating her response. In fact, she was contemplating how her response might get her fired. But with the burden of keeping secrets already lifted Betty responded with unabashed candor. "Does seeing them do it doggy style on his conference table count as proof?"

CHAPTER #12

Detective Rogelio González was a standard issue Cuban male. He was obsessed with everything macho. He thought being a cop was macho. He thought wearing a gun was macho, and driving a patrol car with multi-colored lights was macho. The bulging arm muscles that jutted from his uniform were the result of his macho obsession with weightlifting. Now days, he didn't have as many chances to show them off, since detectives wore suits. Fortunately, Miami's tropical heat gave him a chance to shed his suit jacket, more often than not.

González had gone from working a patrol car for the Miami Police Department on the tough streets of Little Havana, to homicide detective, almost in the blink of an eye. He'd never spent any time working domestic violence or sexual assault cases, before leaving for a more peaceful job with the School Police, or so he'd hoped.

So listening to Betty Pardue's revelations both shocked and titillated the detective. González had to ask Betty for details because his job required it. But he locked on her every word because he personally enjoyed hearing all the salacious sexual details. He thought that was macho too. "What date did this sexual act occur? What time? Was anyone else present? How is it that you witnessed this act? Did you confront them? Did you tell anyone? Was this the first and last time you witnessed said act? Or were there other times?" Betty flinched at each question. But she realized the answers were necessary, in order for truth to be served.

"October 2000. It was about 7:45p.m. No one else was present that I saw. I was working late, unbeknownst to Dr. Maine, who'd been in meetings all day. He must have thought they were alone... because the door wasn't closed all the way. I most certainly did not confront them Detective! What do you think? I'm crazy? And I most certainly didn't tell anyone. I needed my job. No one in this school system knows whom to trust. If I were to tell anyone, I risked the Nazi finding out. He had just about everyone in his pocket. And yes, this was the first time I'd witnessed "said act." But it wasn't the last time. Those two apparently felt invincible!

Maine thought he owned the school system... and Pauline thought so too. She has no morals. The entire secretarial pool knew she would do whatever was necessary and with whomever, in order to advance her career. Lucky for her, Maine liked having a buxom, leggy blonde by his side. I think it made him feel masculine or hot or something."

Gonzalez had another question. "To your knowledge, did anyone else know about their sexual relationship, Mrs. Pardue?"

"Sure! Are you kidding me?" Betty exclaimed as if incredulous the rumors hadn't made it over to school police headquarters. "It was the buzz of the entire building, once people started seeing the kind of money Finch was taking home. She was a secretary with only a high school diploma, and she made more than most principals and a few deputy superintendents! Before I got my little peep at Adolf and Eva... word on the street was that the previous superintendent had caught them together on the couch in the Nazi's office. Rumor has it he used it to blackmail Dr. Maine. You see, Miss Finch was sort of the "pass around pack" among the leadership troika. A certain board member provided job protection in exchange for sex. He also got her to spy on Maine by using her feminine charms on the Nazi, as well as the previous superintendent! It's how he gathered his intelligence on the top dogs... or should I say pigs! This place used to make me race home to take a shower. I felt so filthy at some of the stuff I saw and heard. It was like working in a brothel instead of an institution of learning!" Betty was venting... and it felt good.

"No shit," thought González, as he tried to fathom that these were the people in charge of the education of his three children... and 363,000 other young minds.

CHAPTER #13

"Tonight, an 11 News exclusive." Dean Sands was at the anchor desk. "Investigative Reporter Jez Underwood has identified the weapon used to stab the Miami school system's number two man, to death. Jez joins us live from outside the school district's headquarters, where Dr. Hank Maine was slain last night. Jez?"
The camera was now on Jez, full screen.

"Dean, 11 News can confirm that Dr. Hank Maine was cut down by a Marine's knife that was part of his military collection kept in his office. We have exclusive video of where the knife once hung, before it was used to kill the school system's number two man. Let's roll the videotape."

As Jez was announcing information the cops had not authorized for release, the police were working overtime on Maine's slaying. They'd learned that there were no fingerprints found on the murder weapon. The killer obviously wore gloves.

The police had hoped for at least a partial print, since all district employees had to undergo a fingerprint/criminal background check before being hired.

Of course, as Jez had discovered months earlier, if an employee had a powerful mentor in the district, even the most horrific of criminal charges wouldn't stop a "favorite" from getting hired... no matter how bad their criminal background. She'd discovered that the godson of Dr. Moses Josiah Moorehead had gotten a job at the district, even though he'd fled Birmingham, Alabama... having been convicted of sexual assault on a child, child abuse, and had signed away his parental rights. It seems the child he'd abused, was his own. Then when he got hired in Miami, he'd racked up a slew of battery and assault charges, some of which were sexual, but they were always ignored by the district, because of who he was related. School board members were, of course, the exception to the fingerprint rule because they were elected officials. Besides, all of them had been eliminated as suspects, since they'd been in their seats on the dais when the Nazi was slain.

Jez and several other members of the Miami media used to joke about what a collection of buffoons the public always managed to elect to the school board.

There was, of course, Dr. Moses Josiah Moorehead, the "Stealth Superintendent with his greased back, banana flip, "That Girl" hairdo. He usually wore nice suits, but he and Dr. Jesse Joe Crandall appeared to have some sort of competition to see who could own the most gaudy gold watch and rings!

Crandall was a former state representative and minister, who blamed the white man for every black person who was in jail, under investigation, or not filthy rich. He'd lecture from the dais as if it was his church pulpit, always trying to sound like Martin Luther King Jr., but managing to sound more like Louis Farrakhan! He had a penchant for the same thick, chiseled gold jewelry as Dr. Moorehead, but that's where the similarities in attire ended.

Jesse Joe always showed up looking like he just stepped off the cover of "PIMP AND WHORE" magazine… that is if there was such a publication. Because of his girth, reporters suspected his clothes were custom-made by the Easter Bunny! He'd show up in an entire outfit of lavender, orange, yellow, gold lame and bright blue. He had a red one that made him look like Santa Claus in June, unless, of course he wore it in December, when it might have made sense. Often times his shirt and tie also matched the color of his suit. But without fail, his shoes were always dyed to match.

Patty Sable was a former teacher, with long flowing brown hair, flicked with blonde highlights. She was a pretty woman, that is, until she opened her mouth! Once the lips started flapping you had to wonder if she was the dumbest blonde since Barbie, or the meanest soul since Beelzebub!

She was always saying the most vicious things to, and about, Amelia Salas. Maybe it was just petty jealousy.

Salas was a petite, wisp of a woman, who was independently wealthy because of a successful career as a sales executive for Ferragamo Shoes International. She could be an airhead one minute, and a tiger fighting for the taxpayer the next. That's what so endeared her to the public, whether they lived in her district or not. Nothing got past her. Unlike Hammond Garfield.

Half the time, the retired accountant dozed on the dais. Talk about overstaying one's welcome! Garfield had been on the board for 40 years! He was crotchety, unpleasant and totally disengaged from the board's business.

Dr. Cecil Raymond, an ophthalmologist, was the complete opposite. The silver-haired fox, as the media called him, stuck his nose and hands into everything. He made sure his family members got board contracts or were on the board's payroll. He personally selected every principal and adminis-trator in his district. Raymond was smooth enough to keep his constituents fooled for nearly 20 years. If they'd only known that Raymond never saw a conflict of interest he couldn't ignore.

But the real clowns in the circus were Bitzy Champlain, a nearly 80-year old, elderly airhead, who started every sen-tence with "Well, when I was a young girl in school..." a di-rect reference to 1910.

Then there was Mario Castro, a local Cuban radio personali-ty, who required English subtitles on the public TV station when he spoke at the school board meetings, because his English was so bad! It drove Jez insane that she lived in an American city, where English had to be translated for English speakers! But his ownership of private schools left him vul-nerable to attack and charges of conflict of interest, especial-ly when the governor pushed vouchers for private schools through the legislature as a way to give students in failing public schools a chance at a supposedly "quality education." There was just one problem! While Mario Castro didn't charge the new transfers from public school for the first three months... he went into bill collection mode on the fourth month... and literally bankrupted many immigrant and low income families he was supposed to be helping.

Lastly, there was the President of the school board, Jewel Haynes... aka "the Queen." President Haynes was an attractive blonde, wealthy, and well-dressed, but a demanding diva in her 60's, who spent so much time thanking everyone at school board meetings, that those meetings often droned into the wee hours of the next day. Many in the pressroom, who had to stay until she banged the gavel, closing the meeting, were convinced, Haynes' slow, deliberate, overt attention to "thank you" came from a bottle of medicine.

The press members laid bets at 1:00 or 2:00a.m. about what it could be. Valium? Xanax? Lithium? Or something stronger? Either way, there wasn't a member of the press who didn't think the Prez wasn't "on something."

CHAPTER #14

"Dinorah! I need some water, now!" The command for H_2O came from "the Queen."

It was late Thursday night, and Jewel Haynes was still at her school board office trying to finish work that had been put on hold because of Hank Maine's death the day before. Dinorah appeared at Ms. Haynes's office door, holding a Grand Baroque silver platter with a 3 oz. bottle of water and a small Waterford crystal tumbler, filled with ice. "It's about time," screeched Jewel.

"Yes ma'am. Sorry ma'am." Dinorah sat the silver tray on President Haynes' desk then walked away, stepping slowly backwards, as if she was in the presence of royalty. In Jewel Haynes' mind, Dinorah was in the presence of royalty. Her Serene Highness, the President of the Miami School Board. Dinorah quickly realized why she was Ms. Haynes' 50th assistant in four years. The woman was a monster for whom nobody wanted to work! Dinorah was already counting her days.

Meanwhile, Jez was counting a few things too... mostly the number of hours she'd been on a stake out at the school board building. It was less than 36 hours since Hank Maine had been killed, and it wasn't stopping top administrators from burning the midnight oil. Unfortunately, Jez and Emeril had to burn it with them. It was nearly midnight on Thursday. It was Carlo who had suggested weeks before Maine's death, that Jez check out what R.V. and his two "other right-hand men," were up to. One was Deputy Superintendent of Human Resources, Joe Nunez. The other was Deputy Superintendent of Maintenance and Facilities, Nestor Padron.

And so she'd booked overtime for Emeril to do just that, long before the two would spend sleepless hours covering Maine's homicide. It's why she was sitting on the hard cement floor of a parking garage, located right across the street from the headquarters. They were there because the spot gave them a clear view of the superintendent's corner office. Carlo's tip to Jez was that R. V. and Maine, Nunez, and Padron, were in cahoots, spending late nights, moving money from one account to another. He'd claimed that some were supposedly "off shore" accounts.

Jez was no accountant, but she knew that public officials weren't supposed to move money into offshore bank accounts!

So she and Emeril had set up shop across from R.V.'s office, after her 11:00pm live shot announcing the identity of the murder weapon, in hopes of getting "the goods."

They'd started this stakeout long before the Maine murder. They were back, this particular night, to see what kind of activity would continue, if any, now that cops were crawling the halls of the headquarters trying to solve a death. Jez and Emeril had already shot some good video of the superintendent and his trusty sidekick Nuñez "cooking the books." With Emeril's telephoto lens, he could easily zoom in on the computer screens and document every money transfer R.V. was making with his trusted "aide de camps."

Emeril and Jez were certain this was the same stuff R.V. was up to with the Nazi before his death, but that couldn't be proven now! At least not with the videotape camera they were using to capture "corruption." Jez was certainly interested in who'd whacked Dr. Hank Maine, but her job now, was to let the cops do theirs. Now was a critical juncture in really going after the corruption in the district. Unfortunately, her boss was more concerned with the "nuts and bolts" of the murder of Hank Maine. But Jez knew how incredibly shortsighted that attitude was. A bigger story lay just beneath the surface of a basic homicide... and that was what she was after... even if her gnat-brained boss didn't realize it.

She was growing weary of serving two masters: one being Boris Danken... her adult attention hyperactivity deficit disorder boss. The other being herself, and her reputation as the best investigative reporter in South Florida.

"Transfer $10 million out of Title One. Move it operations. We only need to cover the deficit for a few days," R.V. ordered. Nuñez clicked the appropriate keys on the computer. "We'll replace it in five days before accountants get a whiff." Nunez didn't look all that convinced. In fact, he looked pale.

"The Title One Grant funds will be transferred before you can blink!" R.V. might have sounded like a man trying to calm his cohorts in crime, but it was really himself he was trying to reassure. Doing this kind of money shuffling might have been fun at one point, but doing it in the shadow of a police murder investigation gave R.V. the flop sweats!

Title 1 of the Elementary and Secondary Education Act of 1965, was enacted by Congress to ensure that all children have a fair, equal, and significant opportunity to obtain a high-quality education and reach, at a minimum, proficiency on academic achievement standards and state assessments. Because the funding comes from Federal income taxes... the regulations are very strict and specific on how the money can be spent. Using it to cover an operating deficit, is not one of those specifics! "Et lukes like the saam $10 million za ass-hole move lust wick." Jez marveled that she actually under-stood what Emeril had said in his broken Cuban/English. In her head she translated . . . " it looks like the same $10 mil-lion the asshole moved last week." Emeril had fled Cuba 40 years ago, so Jez had a hard time understanding why he still talked like the "caricature" on Saturday Night Live . . . the one who always said . . . "Baseball has been belly, belly, goot to me."

"How do you think these people sleep at night, knowing what they've done with dollars meant to educate children?" Jez asked Emeril.

"I don't know blondie," he responded.

"Monopoly money Emeril. That's what Ms. Salas called it. Remember? You shot the interview. Play money, she said. Imagine, Emeril, so much money that it has stopped being real to these people."

"Take a look at dis Jez!" Emeril sounded excited.

Jez instantly turned around to face the school board building. She was now on her knees instead of her ass.

"What's going on?" she asked.

"Dat dirt bag Moorehead jus showed up," Emeril whispered.

Jez was totally surprised. In all their other surveillances, they'd never seen him be a part of any of this money shuffle.

"He never works this late," she whispered back. "What's he doing?" Jez had forgotten her binoculars, so she had to rely on Emeril and his telephoto lense to keep her informed.

"I tink he just ordered Nunez and Padron out of the office. Either way, day're leafing."

"Weird," Jez commented. "What now?"

"He and Vascoe are talking. Now Vascoe is sitting at the computer..."

"Yeah! And?" Jez's gut told her something big was happening.

"Moorehead just told him to transfer $1 billion dollars to a Cayman bank, gringa!" Emeril was about to bust with knowledge.

"What?" Jez nearly got whiplash, she turned to face Emeril so fast.

"One billion blondie! This old Cuban reads lips!"

CHAPTER #15
FRIDAY

Carlo sat in his office staring at the newspaper on his desk. The headline read: SCHOOL DISTRICT MURDER MYSTERY.

It was his first day back to work since he'd found himself at the center of the Maine murder mystery... and now Carlo was trying to put it out of his thoughts and get his mind wrapped around the staff meeting that was five minutes away. It wasn't a special meeting prompted by the Nazi's death... just his normal, routine, every Friday at 10am meeting with his top staffers. It was what principals were supposed to do... meet, discuss lesson plans, get updates on students and keep the focus on teaching and learning.

Carlo had started his career as a classroom teacher, proved himself to be a leader, and went on to become a "teacher-on special-assignment." The latter position was one that took a teacher from the classroom to function in some devised administrative capacity for teacher compensation. It had long been the norm, but was not condoned by the teacher's union. They were considered neither fish nor fowl. Many high-ranking district administrators had a TOSA flunky to carry the load and cover their ass (CYA as it was commonly referred to). This enabled the administrator to have plenty of free time, lunches, social events, trysts, and still keep up with the position's responsibilities, through "smoke and mirrors." Carlo had functioned in that capacity for 14 of his 31 years in education, since he was first hired by Dr. Maine. Just a few years previously, the same Dr. Maine had seen to it that Carlo was booted out of the school system headquarters and his role of covering the posterior of the superintendent.

With Carlo out of the line of fire, Hank had complete control of Rod Vascoe. He had managed to convince the superintendent that he could do no wrong. R.V. eventually began to believe his own hype, as presented by Hank Maine. That would ultimately lead to his downfall, especially with the media.

Behind R.V.'s back, Hank maneuvered the politics and finances of board agenda items, members, and top ranking administrators, more commonly known as the "palace guard." The name for this type of "blackmail" and getting the goods on one another, was known as "MAD..." "Mutually Assured Destruction." Hank Maine was a master. Eventually, just about everyone in the district was beholding to the Nazi.

Carlo remembered how Maine had worked a deal with a lobbyist for millions, in which the lobbyist convinced a clueless board member to place the purchase of an Indian burial ground on the agenda for purchase to be the future site of a school. The board approved the item, and when it hit the news, the board member was skewered by the media, and especially by Jez. He went around telling everyone that he knew nothing of its burial ground sanctity, or that it couldn't be used for a school. The school board was commonly the brunt of ridicule among local realtors who privately whispered among themselves, that "if you want to sell a piece of property for five times its value, sell to the school board." How had the institution of public education become such a public joke, Carlo wondered silently to himself? He lamented the destruction of the very principles upon which public education was built; its very foundation. He'd been so naïve during his teaching years.

One year, he volunteered to transfer to a black inner-city school during the first wave of desegregation. He'd really worshipped his principals and fellow teachers, all of whom were very professional. At his last school, university students who interned there, were hired, had a career, and retired from that same school. They'd taught generations within one family. It was the dedicated teachers who were the glue that held the entire system together. Yet, Carlo knew few of the top administrators believed that.

At the highest echelon, administrators were all self-serving. The most important decision of the day was where to lunch and with whom. The cronyism and nepotism had infected the school system like the plague. Carlo remembered having to learn to "play" the game by other rules without sacrificing his values, character, and integrity. Rather than act impulsively, he just watched and listened. He lived by the rule that when you're talking you aren't learning.

He also learned that there was no such thing as a secret in the school system. So he learned to keep his mouth shut to everyone. This way, the Nazi could never get a handle on whether Carlo was for sale. Hank Maine needed everyone to be for sale. He had to be in control; he craved the power. The power gave him the ability to rule behind the back of the superintendent who generally spent his time shaking hands, cutting ribbons, going to luncheons and rubbing elbows with community leaders. One of the Nazi's MO or modus operandi, was for he and Donna to entertain administrators in their home. Hank would make sure that his guests drank too much, ran their mouths, and he took all of it in, on tape. That's how he learned that Joe Nuñez resented R.V.'s charisma. Yet Joe was R.V.'s best friend!

Carlo sat at many of these social occasions drinking a Diet Coke garnished with a lime, and thought to himself, "This place is full of fake boobs and real assholes."Carlo was neither. But he was a gay man.

Thankfully, he was very secure in his identity. After all, he was in a long-term relationship with Orlando. They owned the 49th floor condo together in Miami Beach, and even had a financial interest in a very popular gay bar in Coconut Grove. Yet he still had to contend with the prejudices of not being closeted.

On more than one occasion, anonymous phone calls were made to the previous superintendent's office informing the secretary that Carlo was gay and shouldn't be around children. His enemies, even went so far as to suggest that he was a member of the Mafia. He'd chuckled when confronted by his principal, "Why because I'm Italian?"Carlo knew that the school system was rampant with closeted gays. Many a marriage, in reality, was nothing more than a mutual arrangement. Carlo always suspected R.V., and Nuñez were part of a troika of closet gays. The third member was Nestor Padron. Why did Carlo have these suspicions? Well, for starters, R.V.'s wife was as big as a freight elevator. In Spanish, the Cubans referred to her as "piano con tapete." Translated that means a grand piano covered with a Spanish shawl. It was rumored that the two slept separately.

Nunez's wife was widely believed to be a card-carrying lesbian. She was one butch piece of work!

Meanwhile, Nestor was a Mr. Mom, who somehow couldn't find an American woman to be his wife... so he brought one over from the Asia. This was just another reason that Carlo was disillusioned with the state of the school system's character. This was a dysfunctional government that put students last, and had little to do with the reality of public education, thought Carlo. As a principal, Carlo had found his true niche in education. He was a champion for students and teachers. Here he had a genuine impact upon the future of students, making their lives better through education. He saw to it that his teachers had anything and everything they needed to perform to their optimum potential. The beneficiaries of this policy were their students. Even his old laminate desktop was held together with Scotch tape... so that school money would go to the students first and administration second. A knock at the door to his office brought Carlo out of his contemplative state of mind. "Come in," he said.

The door opened slowly and one by one, his ranking top five staff members entered and sat around the conference table. They were aware of the rift between Carlo and Maine. Smug exuberance filled the air. Nobody wanted to be seen rejoicing in someone's death. But considering who had been murdered, they could hardly contain themselves. Carlo felt a smirk come over his face while desperately trying to hold back a smile.

CHAPTER #16

"Detective Gonzalez!" The person shouting was Hal Davis, the Miami police detective who'd been put in charge of the Nazi's murder probe. "What is it?" González inquired, as he continued reviewing the transcript of his taped interview with Maine's primary secretary, Betty Pardue. "We have a problem... and we have a lead. Which detail do you want first?" Davis stood still, waiting for González to respond.

Detective Hal Davis was grinning like a kid at Christmas. He loved to torment officers from other departments, even if they were his equals. In Davis's mind, there was no better police department than the Magic City's very own and he wasn't about to let some pipsqueak cop from a minor league department, one up him. "So here's the deal González. The good news is that the Medical Examiner has wrapped up his autopsy of the famous Dr. Hank "the Nazi" Maine. The bad news is the M.E. can only say that he died of a stab wound. The Tox Screen is being rushed, but at best we still won't know much more for at least a week."

"Gee thanks Davis. I'm not sure I could have figured that out without you and the M.E.!" González was pissed and that meant he was getting sarcastic. "Tomorrow, you and the M.E. can announce that Lee Harvey Oswald killed Kennedy!"

"I don't think so, González. I'm going to be too busy chasing down leads on the blue lace garter we found in another school administrator's desk! And it's another male chieftain here on the sacred reservation of learning! Forensics has identified it as a match to the Nazi's naughty undies! I wonder why Maine didn't wear the full set?" Davis was now chortling at his own humor. González suddenly thought of Betty Pardue's comment... 'it's like working in a brothel.' The school detective stared at his Miami counterpart for a moment. "What is going on in this place, Davis? Is this a school system, or Sodom and Gomorrah?"

"I honestly don't know man, but whatever it is, it's attracting the attention of the media cockroaches. I just got a call from headquarters. The national tabloid press has just landed and they're not here to soak up the sun on South Beach!"

******

There was a phone ringing in Jez's dream. She screamed at it to stop, but it just kept ringing. Suddenly, Jez awoke from her dream and realized it was her phone that was ringing. The deep sleep she was in was a result of her late night surveillance at the parking garage. With half an eye open, she saw the clock on her bedside table told her it was 9:00 am. She grabbed for the handset, silently admonishing herself for forgetting to turn the ringer off before falling into bed at 5am. "Hello." Her voice had that morning husk to it and she wasn't even trying to hide her sleepiness from the offending caller.

"Late night Robin?" The caller chuckled slightly. "I hope he was worth it!"

"About a billion dollars' worth, Batman," she replied.

Those were the code names this particular school district source had chosen for the two of them.... Batman and Robin. The crime and corruption fighters from Gotham City were now battling the evil educators in the Miami school system. It was corny Jez thought, but appropriate."What is it Batman?" Jez asked.

"I thought you'd want to know that you have some national competition to contend with. The USA GOSSIP and NATIONAL BIZZY BODY just flew in teams of reporters to cover Miami's latest murder mystery," Batman informed Robin.

"That's not competition winged one. Those are just the turkey vultures that winter here annually, hoping to gather some scraps." Jez ran her fingers through her hair as she moved from her prone position to sitting up straight. Both eyes were slowly opening.

"All Batman knows, is that the early vulture usually gets the worm, Robin. They're circling at district headquarters as we speak." Batman let his information sink in. "Well, they're about a day late and a dollar short." Jez stopped abruptly. "Make that one billion dollars short!"

"What are you saying?" Batman had a sudden urgency in his voice.

"Meet me at noon at the Lamplight. Park the bat mobile a block away and walk up to our green SUV, which I'll have parked out front. Open the back door and get in. I have some videotape you need to see. Bye now!" Jez clicked the phone off and smiled. She knew Batman was dying of curiosity. Jez got out of bed, opened her front door and grabbed the morning paper. She walked into the kitchen and was immediately blinded by the sun that was drilling its way into her 32nd floor condo, as it rose in the East. Out of habit, she grabbed a pair of sunglasses and put them on. Having a due East view of the Atlantic Ocean didn't have many drawbacks... at least not until after 10am when you didn't have to wear shades to read the morning paper! The rest of the day, the scene outside was a near unobstructed view of the magnificent hues of blues, aqua' s and greens... splashing about in one of God's wonders... the waters of the southern Atlantic. Jez had always wished she could paint some of the jaw dropping scenes she witnessed from her balcony. How the clouds captured the pink and orange of a western sunset on the glass balconies of her neighbor's windows, turning the colors into a drink spun with the gold of a blazing sun, or how purple often streaked its way through the blue sky. Her favorite was when the sun and the white sand off shore, combined to turn the water a neon sea foam green. That color always made her smile. It was just so brilliant and sparkling, all because of the pure white sand that treaded water underneath the surf. It's only purpose, besides softening the walk of beach goers who wanted to wade into the ocean's embrace, was to give color to lives that lived in shades of gray.

She'd never seen a color like it. Certainly not in her 64 pack of Crayola crayons! And certainly not growing up on the plains of Southeastern Kansas! But when she bought her condo, she made sure she installed carpet that was as close a match to that color of the ocean as she could find. Not many people would put aqua carpet in their home... but Jez was all about vibrant colors. Besides, everything else in her home was white... so it worked quite nicely she thought. As Jez poured her morning fix of Diet Coke, she flipped through the paper tossing out the classifieds and sports sections. Next she turned to the horoscopes and read hers. Stupid! But she said that every morning and yet it was always the first thing she read. Next she scanned the front page of the business section for anything of interest. Often she got ideas from the business news, but not today.

Today, the only news she cared about was the murder of Dr. Hank Maine and a billion dollars on the move! She grabbed her drink, tucked the two sections under her arm and headed for her bathroom. She put her diet coke on the vanity along with the newspaper, clicked on her bathroom TV, and then turned on the water in the shower stall. She was just about to step in... when she heard the words "We have breaking news about the murder of a top school administrator." Jez turned the water off and held her breath.

"11 news has learned that the Medical Examiner has ruled Dr. Hank Maine's death, the result of a single stab wound." The Barbie Doll anchor then stopped and smiled, as if bursting with pride that she'd read a whole sentence without tripping over a word. "No shit Sherlock!" Jez said out loud. She didn't know what she was more disgusted by... the fact that some big-boobed, 23-year old named Boofy, who'd just graduated from college less than a year ago was anchoring a morning newscast in a top 20 TV market... or the fact that everything in the news business was now "Breaking News!"

Jez turned the shower back on and began soaking under the heat of the rushing water. She remembered a time when an announcer's voice said there was a special report, or breaking news meant you dropped what you were doing and ran to the TV, trembling with fear and anticipation. That pronouncement told you that something hugely important had happened... President Kennedy had been shot... Saigon had fallen... or that masses were tearing down the Berlin wall. Now when people heard those words, Jez doubted they even stopped chewing their Cheerios. Breaking news could mean anything from the start of the war in Iraq, to a highway crash or tire fire. Jez should know. She'd once been asked to adlib a tire fire at the breaking news desk. "Tires are burning, no one is hurt, and the smoke is really black. Back to you Dean!" That's what she'd wanted to say. It was a five-second information bulletin at best. But no! Her boss wanted her to keep talking about the tire fire for nearly a minute! How was this relevant to the people in our community, Jez had wanted to ask. What's the story here? Where's the news value? Were viewers really as dumb as news managers appeared to believe them to be? Jez had to wonder. The dumbing down of news had now come to this: "a man who was stabbed in the chest with a Marine collector's knife had died of a single stab wound. Now back to regular programming." Jez wanted to throw up. As she rinsed the shampoo out of her hair, she wondered just how long she could stay in a business that was so hopelessly and totally useless to the public it was supposed to serve. By 10:15, Jez was out the door and headed into work. She'd use the 30-minute drive to phone her sources and make sure Emeril was ready to roll as soon as she got there.

CHAPTER #17

By Friday morning, the crime scene tape around the lobby of the school board auditorium had been removed. The hundreds of staffers who worked at headquarters, desperately needed that bank of two elevators. For two days they'd been restricted to the three remaining elevators to get to and from their offices. Because the headquarters building was a series of add-on wings to a basic building… getting from point A to point B, often took even the most seasoned employee a good bit of navigating to get where he or she needed to go. Having two of their elevator cars blocked at the lobby level had made Wednesday and Thursday hellacious for the school board employees. Board member Dr. Moses Moorehead had even had to wait his turn to get up to his 9th floor office. The 9th floor was the top floor, where board members and the superintendent and his executive staff all had their offices.

The fact that Moorehead was in the headquarters building at all, immediately sent a message to every employee that the situation following the Nazi's death was dire. Moorehead was not just the "Stealth Superintendent," he was also the "phantom board member." It was a rare sighting to see Moses at his school board office. He either didn't care or did the bulk of his work from home.

His trusty aide, Franklin Elder, got paid the big bucks to handle things for Moses Moorehead, or "Big Mo" as the little people called him. But on the Friday following Maine's murder… "Big Mo" was on deck, in his office and engaged in something. What, even his secretary of five years didn't know. Suzanne Quintana, or "Suzy Q" as she was called… didn't know if she should make coffee, or run out for a liter of Bourbon… Mo's favorite spirit! It was so rare to see her boss actually sitting at his desk! What would he want or need, she wondered? Her guessing was short lived. "QUUUUUUU!" Moorehead bellowed in his southern, Mississippi hick, southern dialect. How a single letter ended up having a six-syllable sound to it puzzled the statuesque, former black beauty queen.

Suzy Q had long concluded the man acted as dumb as a mule, to conceal the fact that he was smart as a fox. "Yes Dr. Moorehead," Suzy Q replied.

"Get Sil on the phone. Tell him I want his ass in here now!"

"Yes Dr. Moorehead." Suzy Q left to do as she was instructed. Sil was Silver Redstone... the first Chief of the Miami School Police Department. Although "Sil," as his friends called him, had retired a few years earlier, he was a force to be reckoned with, because his influence over the street cops of the department was still immense! While Moorehead waited for a response from Silver he dialed Joe Nuñez, the superintendent's number three guy, who'd now advanced to the number two spot since the death of the Nazi.

"Hey Mo, what's up?" Nuñez inquired.

"Lots, Joey," said Moorehead. "I want to see you right away."

Mo knew better than to ever discuss anything on the telephone. It was a lesson he learned when a former superintendent was bugged in the office and at home by the FBI. Because of that, he only made calls from a secure line at home. He had a guy who swept his home and his office for bugs every two days. Joe walked into Mo's office, closed the door and sat down.

"Donna is calling me." Moorehead said.

"Well, other than sympathy and comfort, what does she want? asked Nunez. Maybe she's calling about funeral arrangements. Perhaps she wants you to deliver the eulogy." Then Nuñez held his breath.

"Joe, don't act as stupid as you always make me think you are. You know what she wants. You know what she expects. For God's sake! Give me a break! You know what she knows!"

"I don't understand how she thinks that the Hank's death is relevant to her future fortune." Nuñez appeared clueless... at least as far as Moses Josiah Moorehead could tell.

"Let me lay it out for you Jooeey." Moorehead was fondling his banana flip hairdo. Getting the "THAT GIRL" Marlo Thomas, flip couldn't have been an easy look for an African-American male to achieve. But somehow, both he and the Reverend Al Sharpton managed to attain the same appearance... no doubt believing it was a good-looking hairstyle. "Donna's lookin' to cash in on Hank's piece of the action, you moron."

"No way Mo! How would that work?" Nuñez replied.

"It's not gonna work!" Moorehead barked. "I'm gonna have to take care of it. If that bitch thinks she gonna get a bite of our apple, she gotta another thaing com'in. Besides she is going to come into a big chunk of change from Hank's life insurance."

"What are you going to do, Mo?" Nunez was suddenly nervous sitting there watching Moorehead smooth his gray flipped hair.

"Just know that I'll take care of it. In the meantime, you don't take any of her calls. Do you hear me, Joey?"

"I hear you, Mo." Joe Nunez was only too happy to be dismissed. Just as he opened the door to flee... he ran into Silver Redstone. The two men didn't speak, as Redstone passed him on his way into Moorehead's office.

Behind closed doors, Dr. Moses Josiah Moorehead plotted strategy with the former police chief he'd bought and paid for.

CHAPTER #18

Det. Rogelio Gonzalez replayed in his mind the events of the past few days and his interview with the Nazi's widow. But what struck him was what he had seen at the Maine's home when police arrived to search the place. An entire room in the Maine's condo was filled floor to ceiling with pornography. There were porn magazines, videos, and DVDs. How could a wife tolerate such a room in her home, Gonzalez wondered? Was there a clue as to who murdered the Nazi in his collection of smut? Gonzalez didn't have to wonder very long. Walking towards him was Capt. Sheila Cohen, the head of homicide at Miami PD.

"I'm glad you're sitting down," Cohen declared as she approached Gonzalez's desk.

"Why?"

"Because I won't have to pick you up off the floor when I tell you about Maine's collection of filth," Cohen said.

"How bad?" Gonzalez leaned forward as Cohen took a seat in a chair next to his temporary desk at Miami Police headquarters.

"The sick son of a bitch not only had straight porn, but gay porn and child porn! And that's just what we've gleaned from the magazines... all 2,367 of them... and the 592 VHS tapes. My guys are just now starting to review the DVD's. Rogelio, we've got a tiger by the tail here and I'm not sure where this murder investigation ends and other crimes begin." Cohen watched as Gonzalez absorbed the bomb Cohen had just dropped on him.

"What in God's name are we dealing with?" Gonzalez said, almost to himself. This guy could have been the top educator in this county, and he's collecting child pornography right under his wife's nose?" Gonzalez was disgusted. "What are the chances any of the kids are local?"

Cohen got up. "About 100%. I'm trusting you with this information, only because you used to be one of us. If you were any other school cop, we wouldn't even be letting you sit in this office! We've been able to identify some of the videos as surveillance tapes from at least one local school bathroom." Cohen stopped.

"How do you know it's a local school?" Gonzalez was starting to get a sick feeling in the pit of this stomach.

"Rogelio, one of my officer's reviewing the tapes, recognized his son at a urinal. It took three of us to restrain him. If Maine wasn't already dead, I guarantee you, Officer West would be our chief suspect."

CHAPTER #19

"Dammit Jez, we need you live at noon!" Jez's news director was bellowing at the top of his lungs. Even though the door to his office was closed, Jez was certain the conversation was being heard throughout the newsroom.

"No! You need me getting another exclusive to promote for tonight's 6 & 11 newscasts," Jez shouted back with equal volume. "Just have Boofy re-track my story from last night with any updates. Do you have any updates? Or did the assignment desk forget to call the cop shop?" Jez was getting surly. "Don't be a smartass Jez. The desk knows how to do its job. And no, there are no updates as yet."

Boris Danken was fuming. He might have been ten years younger than his Chief Investigative reporter, but he wasn't a rookie and he was her boss after all. How dare she talk to him as if she knew best! Problem was, Danken knew she did. How to let Jez do what she did best, yet not let her think she was in control, was Danken's biggest challenge each and every day. He was turning pre-maturely grey because of this broad, he thought.

"Boris," Jez said softly, trying to ramp down the volume and hostility. "It's the noon news. Is it our number one rated newscast? No. If the cop shop has no updates, neither will any of our competitors. You know as well as I do, that there isn't another reporter in this town with the sources I have inside the school system. One of those sources is willing to meet with me at noon today. It concerns some of the video we shot on stakeout last night. If this is what I believe it to be… then we are going to rock this town! Think news, Boris. Think exclusive! You are always telling us to own our stories. I'm just trying to do that."

Jez was spinning her boss like a Washington D.C. political flack. She could tell Boris was beginning to break. Every time he picked up his squeegee ball and, well, squeezed it, over and over again, she knew he was on the verge of caving. And at this very moment, he was squeezing the squeegee ball to death!

"What stakeout? I didn't know you were on a stakeout last night. What for?" Boris was trying not to lose all his authority.

"I believe you authorized me to follow up on a lead that the superintendent of schools and his top flunkies were moving money around in ways the Feds would take issue with," Jez responded.

"What does that have to do with Maine's murder?"

"I don't know Boris. It may have nothing to do with it... or it might be the reason he was killed. Let me at least pursue it. And that means meeting with my source, instead of regurgitating last night's warmed over headlines."

Jez decided it was time to show a bit of humbleness before her chief news god. "Please, Boris. I wouldn't ask this if I didn't think it could be huge for this station." The two stared at each other, for what seemed like an eternity. Jez broke eye contact with her boss for only a second, long enough to see the saying on the terracotta jar on the shelf behind his desk. She'd given it to him for Christmas a few years ago. It said, "Be sensible. Do it my way."

Boris sat in his chair. It wasn't because he was admitting defeat... it was just that he always got tired of fighting with Jez standing up. That woman could go toe-to-toe with Saddam Hussein he thought and Saddam would need to sit down as well. "I'd better have the best exclusive this story can generate by 6:00... or," Danken was at a loss as to what to threaten Jez with. If he fired her, she'd just take her solid reporting across the street to another station, and he didn't have the firepower to combat her sources. If he threatened her with a demotion he'd be stuck paying her an outrageous sum of money to cover fires and town council meetings.

Sensing her boss' self-induced trap, Jez decided to help him out, picking up his sentence where he left off. "Or you'll force me to bake you cookies for an entire month. Got it. I'll go broke feeding your sugar habit, and you'll be happy."

"Yeah! Now get out of here and don't come back until you have a story that rocks this town!" Boris knew he'd lost the battle. So did Jez. But she had the courtesy to let him think he'd won. "You got it boss! By the way, do you know you scare the hell out me when you yell." Jez flashed a smile, then turned and left her boss' office. Jez grabbed Emeril as she flew through the newsroom and told him to bring his news car around front. She said they needed to be parked in front of the Lamplight by noon.

Across town, Carlo had wrapped up his staff meeting and was getting into his car. He'd been summoned to the superintendent's office. This can't be good he thought.

At Miami Police headquarters, Det. Hal Davis was dealing with Mrs. Hank Maine's attorney. She'd lawyered up after cops confiscated the Nazi's personal items.

And soaking up the sun, on the white sands of Miami Beach, was the person who'd bludgeoned the Deputy Superintendent of Schools to death. Never one to care much about medical warnings that the sun's rays could cause cancer, this beachgoer decided to really tempt fate and lit a cigarette. A copy of the Miami Herald fluttered in the breeze as the killer read every detail about Maine's murder that was printed. It's been 48 hours almost, and not one word about a possible suspect was in print.

"Good." The killer lay back on the oversized beach towel and began applying SPF 30… just to be safe!

CHAPTER #20

Carlo found a parking spot right in front of the school board administration building. He wasn't sure how many quarters to put in the parking meter. Would this be an all-afternoon tirade by R.V., or a quick and dirty, 20-minute lecture on the importance of keeping the district free from scandal. Yeah right! Like a stabbing murder wasn't scandal enough, Carlo chuckled to himself as he popped three hours' worth of quarters into the meter.

"Well hello Mr. Ferrini!" Carlo was greeted immediately by Charlie Hopkins the Monday through Friday security guard, who handled the Northside front entrance to the administration building. "Hi Charlie," Carlo responded. "I've been summoned to the 9th floor."

"Which evildoer needs to see you today?" Charlie inquired.

"R.V."

"No shit!" Charlie pointed to the sign-in sheet as he grabbed a 9th floor hall pass for Carlo Ferrini. "I remember a time when you didn't need one of these," Charlie said with a hint of nostalgia in his voice.

"So do I Charlie." Carlo took the badge and clipped it to his lapel. "I see they got the blood stains out of the floor." Carlo was standing almost exactly where he was when the Nazi had fallen into his arms two days earlier.

"Yes sir, Mr. Ferrini. A team of maintenance guys came over as soon as the cops cleared this place. They must have used a gallon of bleach and God knows what else to get the stains removed. I swear I still can't believe what happened here on Wednesday."

"You and me both, Charlie." Carlo pushed the "up" button on the elevator… and resisted looking again, at the floor where the Nazi had lost his life.

"Carlo!" Superintendent Rod Vascoe embraced his former chief of staff. "Come and sit, old pal." R.V. was in a friendly state of mind. Carlo wondered why.

"You've been through a lot these last few days, my friend," R.V. said.

Carlo was having none of it. He knew R.V. was in a corner, and he wasn't going to be the one who bailed him out.

"Rod," Carlo said his name with a good measure of cynicism and smirk. "Is it really necessary for you to pull me out of my school and away from my duties as principal?"

"Shut up!" the superintendent snapped. "I've had just about enough of your "holier than thou" attitude. The situation at hand is serious, and you don't exactly have a "get out of jail free" card." Superintendent Vascoe glared at Carlo.

"R.V. you are so right," Carlo smirked. "I can no longer keep the shit you and the boys have done in the name of education, to myself. That's why I'm going to share everything I know with Jez Underwood." Carlo stared at R.V. "Rod, why did you let this thing get away from you? How could you believe that hype that was fabricated by Hank? When you and I worked together, I admired your honesty, and the second-hand furniture we had, and hand-me-down computers." R.V. was turning purple. Of all the people he thought would betray him, never had he suspected Carlo Ferrini.

"Jez?" R.V. was sputtering. "Why would you… how much does she… Carlo!"

Vascoe grabbed at his left arm…. then dropped to the floor.

For the second time in three days… Carlo Ferrini found himself holding a colleague in his arms. In a flash… he remembered his devotion to this man, how he expedited R.V.'s meteoric rise to ultimately become superintendent. The espresso machine he'd bought, so R.V. could serve his guests Cuban coffee in the traditional demitasse cups. Those touches ingratiated him to the Cuban business community and the school system's influential power structure who'd never thought of Rod Vascoe as superintendent material.

Carlo suddenly shook himself from memory lane, and realized Superintendent Rod Vascoe was dead.

CHAPTER #21

Jez and Emeril were parked in front of the Lamplight Restaurant, waiting on Batman. "Jez, what do you sink dis guy can help ju wis?"

Jez translated in her brain. "Jez, what do you think this guy can help you with?"

"Emeril, the superintendent and his flunkies just moved one billion dollars, in violation of no less than 20 Federal statutes that I can think of off the top of my head, and you want to know how Batman can help?" Jez was getting testy.

"Chill blondie." Emeril tolerated Jez's outbursts. He was such a sweet, even keeled human. Jez knew how lucky she was to work with Emeril but sometimes she'd forget and treat him like she did most of her boyfriends... hence her single status at age 46! Before she could continue contemplating her "old maid" status, the back door to Emeril's news car opened and Batman jumped inside.

"You'd better have something WHAM! BAM! for me," Batman exclaimed.

"Name a date and time I've ever disappointed you, crime fighter," Jez responded.

"OK blondie," Emeril interjected. "Show the guy what he came here to see and cut the beach stuff."

"It's bitch stuff, Emeril!" Jez was verging on a chuckle.

"Whatever it is, just show it to me." Batman was nervous, and wanted his date with Jez to end sooner rather than later. Emeril loaded the portable playback machine with the tape he'd shot the night before.

Jez began a narration. "Here we are shooting inside the superintendent's office. It's about 11:45pm. R.V., Padron and Nuñez are hovered over the superintendent's computer screen, looking at different accounts or reviewing them. We think they moved $10 million out of Title One funds into operations to cover a temporary deficit. This has been their routine recently. Now fast forward Emeril."

As instructed, Emeril hit the fast forward button on the video machine, and waited for Jez to tell him to stop. "Stop!" Jez wasn't even hiding her excitement. "Look Batman! It's Big Mo!" The time stamp on the tape said 12:21a.m. "Now, if you're as good as Emeril, you can read Big Mo's lips and know what he's saying." Jez was baiting her source.

"Transfer one billion dollars... something bank." Batman looked at Robin.

"Very good, Batman. Now tell me why the most powerful man in the nation's fourth largest school system is instructing the superintendent to transfer $1 billion dollars to a Cayman Bank?" Jez waited for a response.

"Because, junior crime and corruption fighter, the State of Florida only audits the district every five years. The assholes know they've got another three years, as of right now, before they have to correct all their shady money moves. They use the capital money to earn interest in their offshore bank accounts. They keep the interest, say, on a billion dollars, transfer the billion dollars back to the capital fund... and nobody is the wiser." Batman shut up so his information could be absorbed.

"Fuck me running!" Jez exclaimed. "Yeah! Fuck me runzing too," Emeril said. "How can we prove this Batman?" Jez inquired.

"With this Cayman bank account number." Batman then handed Jez a piece of lime green paper with a ten-digit number, and the name of a Cayman bank. "What I am about to tell you, along with that bank account number could get us all killed." Batman took a deep breath before he continued. "But I'm sick to death of the corruption in this school system. So I'm going to share something with you I've never told another soul... not even my beloved mother."

For the next 15 minutes, Batman outlined, in great detail, how Big Mo and a few of his close associates, collected, disbursed and transferred kickback money and stolen district funds. Jez and Emeril listened in silent shock. Jez, of course, was taking notes like a seasoned stenographer.When Batman was finished baring his soul... Jez had just one question.

"How do we prove all of this?" she asked. "This is such an inside operation, I don't begin to know how to infiltrate and get the proof we need."

"I'll do it," Batman announced in a hushed tone. Jez and Emeril looked at one another, astounded by what they'd just heard.

"How Batman?" Jez asked quickly.

"I'm on the inside, Jez. I've been a part of the scam. They have no reason not to trust me."

"Batman!" Jez was stunned.

"You two get me the hidden cameras, microphones, or whatever is necessary to prove this scandal, and I'll get you the goods." Batman went silent.

For a few seconds no one in the news van said a word.Jez finally broke the silence. "When will all this go down next?"

"Sunday," Batman informed them. "After I get this for you Robin, I'm dead to you. Understand?" Jez nodded that she understood. Batman then unlocked the back door of the van and got out. As he pushed to close the sliding door,

Jez grabbed his hand. "You know I've always loved you in my own way."

"Yes, replied Batman, "but I never had your heart in the way I wanted. We'll talk soon." Batman slammed the door shut and was gone.

CHAPTER #22

"Jez?" Carlo had dialed the reporter on her cell phone.

"Hey Carlo! How are you holding up?" Jez asked.

"Not so… I… um… oh God!"

"Carlo? What is it?" Jez was now very worried. She and Emeril were racing back to the station after their meeting with Batman. In spite of her excitement at the news Batman had just dropped in her lap, she realized her other important source sounded incoherent. "What's going on Carlo?"

"Jez, I'm on the 9th floor with R.V. and he isn't breathing."

"Carlo… stay put. Don't move. Emeril and I are on our way. Call 9-1-1. But only answer the phone if it shows up on caller I.D. as the front security desk. Authorize the two of us up to the 9th floor. Carlo? Are you with me? Do you understand what I just told you?"

"Yes, Jez. Please hurry," Carlo pleaded.

"It will be o.k." Jez said, trying to reassure her friend. Jez then turned to Emeril and said, "the school board building… and fast!"

"Blondie, you drive this old Cuban crazy!"

"You're damn straight! Now move it! Our 6:00 lead is waiting for us on the 9th floor at the school board building." Emeril hit the gas, and they were off.

******

"Why do you let her run all over you like that?" The assistant news director was in Boris Danken's office trying to talk some sense into him. Jez Underwood rubbed Allison Wheeler so raw she could hardly stand to be in the same universe with her. "You're the News Director, Boris. If you want her live at noon she goes live at noon!" Allison had sensed a weakness in Boris Danken, and was going in for the kill! She'd exploit Underwood's defiance of her boss's wishes, and hope that Danken would fold, thus undoing his permission for Jez to work her sources, and come up with some super exclusive. Allison got a bur up her butt every time Underwood went off and did her own thing. She'd always loathed the fact that Jez didn't report to her, but directly to Danken. It was a perk Jez had negotiated in her contract. She'd paid her dues in this business, and at this point in her career, Jez had made a big deal out of not being left to the whims of the assignment desk. She wouldn't sign her contract unless she was allowed to be an independent player.

Wheeler, on the other hand, enjoyed barking orders, and resented not being able to tell Jez what to do. In Wheeler's mind... reporters were just actors on a stage and they moved wherever and whenever the assignment desk instructed. They were "talent," meaning Allison believed she was superior to the "on camera" folk. This misplaced competitive streak had compromised the 11 News product on more than one occasion. But Danken wasn't willing to throw his chief "yes person" overboard. Not yet anyway.

"If she brings in a super exclusive, what do I care whether she was in the stupid noon show or not?" Danken asked Allison.

"That's not the point. She defies you without repercussion!" Allison was fuming.

"Yes, and she usually does so with good reason, Allison." Danken hadn't quite finished his sentence when his Nextel buzzed. It was Jez. "Allison," he inquired. "If you care to find out why I let her get away with the crap that drives you so insane, might I suggest you take a seat and listen.

"R.V. is dead!" Jez screamed into the Nextel.
Boris and Allison looked at each other as if they hadn't correctly heard what Jez had said.

"Repeat!" the news director shouted.

"Superintendent Rod Vascoe is dead! Copy?" Jez was breathless.

"How do you know, Jez?" Boris Danken was standing now waving his arms and mouthing to Allison to find an anchor, any anchor, to head to the breaking news desk."Because I'm here on the 9th floor where he's laying without a pulse! Capiche?" Jez mimicked her boss's basic Italian, even in her excitement. "We think it's a heart attack, aneurysm, diabetes... who the hell knows! But he's dead!"

"Do you have videotape Jez?" her boss half screamed.Jez looked at Emeril and rolled her eyes.

"Video, boss? What's that? I thought I worked for radio. Of course I have video Boris!" Jez was almost beside herself with her boss's stupidity.

"Cut the shit Jez! We've got a live truck headed your way... but first you're going to do a phoner with an anchor at the breaking news desk." Boris Danken was now running out of his office into the newsroom, where chaos was in progress.

"We don't have any live truck operators in house until 2pm!" screamed Allison Wheeler from the assignment desk. "This is exactly why I've been begging you to insist on making sure engineers were on duty 24/7, Boris!" Allison wasn't holding back. "I'll call the Chief engineer and tell him he has to drive a live truck himself," Boris shouted. "Where is our anchor?"

"We don't have one of those either, Boris." The assistant news director was turning purple in the face. "The noon show people are gone, our main anchors won't be here for 30 minutes and I can't find one reporter who is lunching in the building."

Boris was about to spin into orbit at his lack of staff when he heard his Nextel beep."Jez, stand by," he roared.

"Do you care that I have an exclusive interview with the man who held the superintendent in his arms as he died? He also happens to be the same man who held the "Nazi" in his arms when he died!" " Jez no longer sounded out of breath.

"What??????" Boris Danken momentarily thought he might have his own heart attack.

"When I promise you an exclusive boss, I deliver! Now get two more crews down here, another live truck and put Chopper 11 up." Jez was calling the shots, and all Boris could do was stare at his Nextel and his empty newsroom.

CHAPTER #23

"This can't be happening," thought Det. Hal Davis. He'd just received word of a 9-1-1 call regarding the Superintendent of Schools having a medical emergency. He was in his under-cover cop car with lights and sirens running, in hopes of get-ting to district headquarters before the demise of another top school administrator. No such luck! Det. Davis arrived at the same time as his school police counterpart, Det. González. By the time both men got to the 9th floor R.V. was dead. His cold body lying on the floor.

"Is murder your new profession Ferrini, or do you just like to hang out with dead bodies?" Davis inquired.

"Neither Detective Davis," Carlo responded, incensed by the detective's humor.

"Then you won't mind explaining why the top two educators in this town have dropped dead in your arms, will you Ferri-ni?" The two men stared at one another.

"I am the one who made this man superintendent material. He was like a mentor. At the very least, he was a nice, inef-fective, clueless, glad hander. If you think I get any joy out of his death, then you don't know me!" Carlo was beside him-self pacing the floor outside the office where Superintendent Rod Vascoe lay."I am not Col. Mustard with the candlesticks, Detective!" Carlo was visibly shaking.

The constant screaming of police cars and ambulances… quickly got the attention of most every employee at the school's administrative headquarters. Already jittery because of the murder two days earlier, employees rushed to win-dows and dialed the security guards in total panic. Word of the superintendent's sudden death, spread like wildfire. Of-fices with TVs went silent, as employees listened to the Spe-cial Bulletin being broadcast on Channel 11.

A static photograph of reporter Jez Underwood filled the screen as she phoned in a report to her news director, who was now substituting as an anchor, about the sudden death of Miami's School Superintendent Rod Vascoe. "I'm on the hallway of the 9th floor, where the superintendent's office is located. He was in the middle of a meeting with Principal Carlo Ferrini, when he collapsed and died."

"Jez, isn't Mr. Ferrini the same man who was with Dr. Hank Maine after he was stabbed to death two days ago?" Boris, doing his best impression of a diva anchorman, was peppering Jez with questions.

"Yes. He's the same person. And you can bet the police have a lot of questions for Mr. Ferrini." Jez didn't want to appear too sympathetic when talking about her key source, fearing it might reveal to anyone listening closely, that Jez was anything but impartial when it came to Carlo.

One person listening closely was Moses Moorehead. Like most of the other board members in their 9th floor office they'd been put on lock down by the cops. Few spent enough time in their offices to bother with a television set. So they'd gathered in the president's office, where Jewel Haynes had a 50-inch flat screen Plasma TV on the wall.

Boris was back on camera now with another question for his reporter. "Jez, were you in the superintendent's office when the police and rescue personnel arrived?" "Yes, I was." Jez slowed her toned delivery in order to sound somber and respectful, not joyous with an exclusive. "And coming up very shortly, we will have exclusive video from inside the dead superintendent's office right…" Jez stopped mid-sentence. The next thing Boris heard her say was "who the hell do you think you are?"

"Jez?" Boris asked. "Jez, are you still with us?" There was no response, except the faint sound of Jez as he heard her screaming something about taking her cell phone and denying her a right to communicate. Then there was nothing but dead air.

"We'll take a break and be right back with breaking news from the Miami School board's headquarters," Danken informed viewers as a commercial began to roll. Inside Jewel Haynes's office, Moses Moorehead was fingering his flip hairdo. He glanced around at his fellow board members, at least the ones who'd been present in their offices when word of the supt.'s death circulated. President Jewel Haynes looked visibly shocked and horrified. So too did Amelia Salas. Vice-President, Dr. Cecil Raymond was unreadable and Moses knew why. Meanwhile the ditzy moron of the group was Bitzy Champlain. She was crying and sobbing and shaking and generally being a hysterical female!

No surprise, thought Big Mo. He then began to wonder where the other board members were and what their reaction would be. He'd find out as soon as the authorities decided to let them off the 9th floor. But that would be awhile... and for good reason.

Batman was just pulling into his condo driveway when he heard the news bulletin on the car radio. "According to reports from Channel 11 news, our news partner, Miami's school superintendent, Rod Vascoe is dead. Speculation at this time is that his death is due to natural causes, but police have the school board building in lock down. According to 11 News Reporter Jez Underwood, who was in the Superintendent's office right after he died, Rod Vascoe died in the arms of Principal Carlo Ferrini... the same man who held the Deputy Superintendent Hank Maine in his arms, after he was slain with a knife like dagger in the lobby of the district's headquarters on Wednesday. Underwood has exclusive video of Superintendent Vascoe's death... so stay tuned to Channel 11 for her report.

"Batman turned off the engine.... put the car in park and sat like a mummy in the driver's seat. Batman was trying to playback the timetable in his mind. He'd met with Jez and Emeril at noon. They'd looked at the tape, and talked for about a half hour. Jez had to have been headed back to the station around 12:30-12:45pm. That meant, that while Batman was divulging deep dark secrets to his favorite newsperson, the superintendent had died.Batman didn't believe in coincidences, at least not where the school district was involved. He knew that it was no coincidence for example, that a man who was hired to oversee compliance with the building code of several schools, just happened to be on the board of the construction company that was building some of those same schools. Batman knew why.

For years, kickbacks had been the name of the game for Moses Moorehead. He'd had to tell Jez to take a chill pill, when she'd finally gotten a line on a man who'd been propositioned by Big Mo and his associates to do the kickback thing, but the guy refused to talk, fearing, rightfully, for his life. It was Mo's typical vendor scam. A new vendor, wanting to do business with the district, was told to meet with Dr. Barbara Ross, head of procurement. She fielded all vendor proposals. If she thought any of them had merit, she then informed them that they would have to do business with a "special" company. In fact, Big Mo and Dr. Ross were silent partners in that company, meaning their involvement was untraceable. In the case that Batman knew of, Mo and Ross were demanding that the vendor use their trucking company to transport his construction materials from Georgia. Violating Interstate transportation laws was a federal offense... so this person got cold feet. But not before Jez had learned that he'd paid Big Mo's low-level henchman a $500 cash bribe. She'd met with the man over lunch one day, and could barely swallow her food, once he began telling her what he knew. But he was adamant. He would not talk. It was a typical scenario. People always wanted to talk to Jez about what they knew but rarely did they want to come forward, even if she put a bag over their head! It was this frustration that prompted Jez to put Moses Moorehead under surveillance.

Although his address on his election filing papers said he lived with his ex-wife in District 1, Jez had followed him for over two weeks, and every night he went home to a house that was, most certainly, not in his district. On top of that, she and Emeril had videotaped a former NBA basketball star, living at Big Mo's house. The guy had fallen on hard times, and Jez learned that Moses had gotten him a job with the district. It was so typical of the cronyism that infected the school system. Batman, of course, had known all of this. But he had to know how dedicated Jez was to the truth. So he let her spend her time learning stuff he could have just told her. It, at least, gave him plausible deniability.

CHAPTER #24

It hadn't been easy getting away to the beach. But the Nazi's killer was determined. Perfect Chamber of Commerce days like Friday didn't come along as often as the Chamber of Commerce wanted tourists to believe. But the sun was high, the wind cool, and the clouds invisible. That's why a murderer was on the beach. Fortunately, a radio nearby on the beach had broadcast the latest disaster at the school board building. As the killer listened to the report, a thought occurred to him. That should take the heat off my offense, thought the killer. I couldn't have planned this any better if I'd tried! The killer's smugness was oozing from every pore. Killing Deputy Superintendent Maine, had not been a rash, or rushed decision. Maine had deserved it, thought the killer. He deserved worse, but killing him was all I could do.

It had been three years since Maine's killer had been given the only reason needed for the Nazi's murder. That's when Hank Maine had first introduced his killer to the Royal Poinciana Ranch... otherwise known as the "sex house." The house was a ranch style home, surrounded by a concrete wall that encircled the home's two acres full of Royal Poinciana trees, in what was called "farm country." It's out of the way, secluded location made it a perfect place for all kinds of things to be done by all kinds of people who wanted privacy... no questions asked. Maine had taken great pains to make sure his "guest" was comfortable. Maine had introduced his guest to some of the "players" in the house. A few were well known to Maine's arm candy... others were not. It was a jaw dropping experience. Never had this person seen such debauchery! It wasn't as if the sex was shocking. Hell, half the clubs on South Beach were sex houses, where men and women, or a man and two women, openly screwed in front of voyeurs. At the gay clubs, the scene was the same. But knowing who some of these people were... that was the shocker!

There was a local Mayor, one county commissioner, and two city commissioners from different municipalities in Dade County. There were at least 10 of the school district's top brass... including two school board members... and a smattering of lobbyists, politicos and various members of Miami's business community. The killer remembered wondering why so many important people, would put so much at risk for sex. Clearly, the people who ran this place made sure that risk was at a minimum. The killer had noticed four unmarked cop cars parked outside the compound when Maine had driven in. The Nazi had bragged that he handled security, so the killer had assumed the cops worked for the school system.

"What the hell is this place?" the killer quietly asked Hank Maine.

"Our own personal paradise, good looking," Maine replied with a lustful looking grin under his Hitler-like mustache. Just then, a well-known, sitting Mayor had walked up to Maine's guest. The Mayor dragged his skinny, limp hand down and around the killer's face, caressing it tenderly. It sent a chill down the killer's spine. Maine reached up to stop the caress. As he did so, Maine leaned in and kissed the Mayor passionately, as if no one was within a mile of seeing what was going on. This was the picture stamped in the memory of Maine's killer… a memory that would ultimately lead to murder.

CHAPTER #25

Lee Molina walked into his oceanfront Miami Beach condo wondering where his wife Lily was. He'd just heard on the radio about R.V.'s death, and was rushing to turn on the TV when his wife stepped out of the bedroom wrapped in a lush, white terry cloth robe. She was almost golden brown from sitting in the sun all day. Even though Friday was technically a workday, Lily Molina rarely kept standard office hours. She basically came and went, worked and didn't work when she pleased. Although her disappearances were legendary in the school system, no one dared report her absences because of who she was. As the wife of an out of control, power hungry principal and Big Mo's lover, Lily was untouchable, or so she thought.

"Have you seen the news?" Lee quizzed Lily.

"No. Why?" she asked.

"R.V. is dead, that's why!" Lee Molina was almost screaming.

"Rod?" Lily was clearly shocked.

"Yes Rod. Rod Vascoe, Superintendent of Schools, Lily. The man who appointed us and protected us! He's dead!" Lee was pacing waiting for the TV to power up.

"But… how?" Lily stood dumbstruck.

"I don't know! That's why I'm turning on the news you idiot bitch! You think I was going to show up at headquarters asking questions? I'm staying as far away from that place as I can. I heard on the radio that it's in lock down again! This is getting old and scary!" Lee Molina walked over to the condo's bar and poured himself a stiff Scotch… no water.

Lee Molina was a pig of a human being. He was tall, but fat, in his gut mostly. He had hair that resembled a bad rug, and breath that could make elephant poop stand up and run away. He chased anything in a skirt, and treated everyone, men included, as if they were beneath him. How he'd ascended to the position he currently held, boggled even the dumbest of minds. But "Teflon Lee," as his wife called him, had a knack for ingratiating himself with the powerful and "powerful wanna bees." A betting person would have laid odds that this human scum would have self-imploded by now, but not Lee. Even after Jez had exposed him doing a strip tease at a professional conference two years earlier, "Teflon Lee" had managed to survive somehow.

Lily Molina walked barefoot over to the couch and sat slowly. She looked at her husband, pouring himself a drink at the wet bar, and wanted to vomit. What had she ever seen in this pathetic excuse for a man, she wondered. He turned her stomach. The idea of him touching her in any intimate way, made her skin crawl. His breath was so foul it would gag a maggot. How could she kiss that? How could his female flings get close to him? Ugh! Lily may not have been the "cat's meow" today, but once upon a time, she'd been a looker and a pretty hot Latin babe in the school system. Lily firmly believed that it wasn't what you know, but who you blow, that would get her ahead and so she'd put on her knee pads for lots of extra-curricular work, in hopes of getting ahead. It had led her to Lee, and for now, she was stuck with him. Why she couldn't get herself out of her predicament was a secret she kept to herself. The fact was, that between the two of them, they had more on each other than Carter had pills!

The TV came on as Lily recounted the first time she'd met Lee Molina. She had recently divorced her husband, the father of her children, and was working in the school board building for a summer school session. Lee also worked there. That was the start of the romance. He was married at the time. His wife was from a very prominent old guard Miami family. The affair started as a lustful secret, but quickly worked its way into the kind of attention that couldn't be kept a secret.

Back then, Lee Molina was tall, handsome, and a real charmer with women. He'd had lots of practice, as Lily now knew. Lee was channel surfing looking for a local newscast with any word of what might have happened to the superintendent. Suddenly, he locked on Channel 11. A man they'd never seen before was standing in the newsroom appearing to act as an anchorman.

"Viewers, my name is Boris Danken, the news director here at Channel 11. I'm temporarily filling in for Dean Sands, who should be here momentarily. But in the meantime, we felt it was important enough to bring you the news of the most recent death in the Miami school system. According to our reporter on the scene, Jez Underwood, we can confirm that Superintendent Rod Vascoe is dead." Lee Molina threw his drink back deep in his throat... Lily gasped.

Both Molinas stared at one another their eyes secretly communicating their thoughts.

"I don't... I just can't... How can this have happened, Lee? Not now! Not now!" screamed Lily.

"According to our reporter on the scene..." the Molinas were now hearing the TV again. "Supt. Vascoe was meeting with Carlo Ferrini, a Principal, and the same man who held the dying body of Deputy Supt. Hank Maine, right after he was stabbed in the lobby of the school board building only two days ago. Although the building remains in lockdown, we are hoping to have a live report from Jez Underwood in the next few minutes, so please stay tuned to Channel 11 for all the late breaking developments. I'm Boris Danken, filling in for Dean Sands.'

Lee and Lily Molina stared at the TV as Judge Judy popped on in mid-sentence.

CHAPTER #26

"Blondie!" Emeril was yelling at Jez. "Out the window!" His tone told her there was an emergency. Jez ran to the only window available to her in the lockdown/incommunicado mode the cops had put everyone in on the 9th floor. It was a tiny window facing east… but it was all she needed to see Carlo Ferrini being hauled away by the Miami Police Department.

"Are you getting…" Jez didn't even have to finish her sentence. She looked up to see Emeril with his camera hoisted on his shoulder clearly taping everything that was happening down on the street level. She also knew what a chance he was taking. So she decided to run interference for him. Jez marched out of the small room where they were being held and screamed… "I demand to see whoever is in charge here." She began pushing past the guards at the door who were helpless to hold her back. Most of them were avid fans of Jez, and keeping her from doing her job was not in their makeup. "Who is in charge here?" Jez demanded. " I am a journalist, and will not be held one minute longer without some explanation." The ruse was working. All guardian eyes were off the room where Emeril was videotaping.

Moments after Carlo Ferrini was whisked away in a patrol car… Emeril felt empowered! So he turned his camera toward the scene outside the door. He was now recording every second of Jez's outburst and the resulting turn of events.

"Where the hell is she? And why can't we raise her on the Nextel?" screamed Boris Danken? "The live trucks are at school headquarters, but not one of them has seen Jez for a feed." Danken was ready to blow his famous stack. He'd watched as the other news stations had broken in and reported Jez's information as if it was their own.

Meanwhile, his anchor, Dean Sands, had arrived and was immediately dispatched to the news set to begin handling the coverage. Boris was more than relieved to be finished playing "anchorman." Unfortunately for Sands, he didn't have much to work with, and was reduced to ad-libbing live on the air, without any hint of a story from the only reporter who really had the story. Danken desperately needed Jez on the air, to dispel any myths that the other channels had a scoop. "Unit 60. Any sign of "Underhanded?" Danken yelled. He was using his nickname for Underwood. He nicknamed all his news staff. No one knew why, except he thought it was cute… sort of like when he spoke Italian!

"No sir," came the reply from Unit 60. "In fact, I haven't seen one person leave this building since I got here, except for the guy they took away in a patrol car." The live truck operator was emphatic. "Sir, I don't think anyone is being allowed out. Copy?"

"Yeah, I copy 60!" Danken was beside himself. Then he had an idea."Do you have a mast cam Unit 60?"

"Yes, sir," replied the live truck operator. "Put it up and get a signal. We're going to take it live. Just give us what you can. Copy?" Danken was reinvigorated.

"Copy," replied Unit 60. The engineer then began pushing buttons and twisting dials to make the large TV mast with a camera on top, rise and become operational. As soon as Unit 60 got confirmation from the feed room engineer back at the station that his signal was good, he asked, "Is there anything you want me to focus on?"

"Zoom in on the 9th floor," the News Director commanded.

He then punched a button and spoke into the anchor's earpiece.

"Dean, throw to a live feed from outside the school board building. We haven't located Jez, but Unit 60 has its mast cam up and he's zooming up to the 9th floor. Tap dance through this until we can locate Jez."

Danken then turned to the feed room engineer, and ordered her to roll videotape on everything the mast cam was beaming back to the station.

Back on the Nextel, Danken clicked Unit 60; "We're taking you live. What do you see?"

As the live truck operator guided the mast cam upwards toward the top floor of the school district's headquarters... he suddenly stopped. At the 7th floor, a window was open and a woman was standing on the ledge outside the open window. Before the engineer could click his Nextel... the woman jumped to her death... all of it broadcast live on Channel 11.

CHAPTER #27

"What the fuck!" Boris Danken was standing in the feed room watching the live feed come in from Unit 60. Even during the attacks on 9/11... Channel 11 had not aired the suicide leaps of the desperate people fleeing the fiery World Trade Center towers. Now, by happenstance, they'd aired the suicide jump of a woman from the school board's administrative offices. Danken was beside himself, as he started screaming orders to everyone in the newsroom to get moving.

A third death at the school board building meant wall-to-wall news coverage. Every employee was ordered to stop what he or she was working on, and get on this story. Meanwhile, up on the 9th floor, Jez was going crazy trying to find a way to contact her station, ever since the cops had taken her cell phone, disconnected the office phones, and confiscated Emeril's Nextel. Word had just come, that Associate Superintendent Barbara Ross had committed suicide by jumping from her 7th floor office. But Jez had no way to get word to her boss.

Carlo Ferrini sat in the back of a patrol car on his way to a police interrogation room. All he could do was wonder how this had happened to him. His day started out normal. He awoke around 4:00a.m... took his dog Samba for a walk... then returned to his condo to make cappuccino and a light breakfast. He'd gone to work and was trying to conduct business as usual, until the call came from R.V. to come downtown. Carlo's head fell back against the stiff, cheap upholstery of the police car he was in, trying to absorb the events that had led him to this moment. Instead, all he could remember were things he'd been trying for years to forget. His mind raced like the reputed adage that when one is dying, the events of his life flies through his mind. Some were his experiences with administration. He had been asked numerous times to hire incompetents who were well-connected to board members, top administrators or other outside elected officials/politicians who were currently having affairs with them. He had to supervise principals who were very well protected. Then, working closely with Rod, he was bombarded with requests to arrange fundraisers for politicians that could in some way, further Rod's path to the superintendency.

The instructions were to get everyone on the "inside track." Take 20 tickets to sell for some political fundraiser. The result? A pyramid scheme of pressure to deliver, or be banished from favor. The pressure was great and it filtered all the way down to the security guards, custodians and everyone in between.

He paused for a moment and remembered a phone call from a Miami newspaper reporter, interrogating him about the common practice. He was astute enough to diffuse the situation and nothing resulted from the interview. Rod Vascoe praised him for the way he handled the situation... since it all led to the top. Carlo knew he had tremendous power, but he never abused it. Unfortunately, Carlo had been forced to sit on many a fictional interview committee. He knew the application and interview processes for principals and assistant principals were a scam. But that was a top level secret. The position was always filled, he knew, before it was created and then advertised with the intended's qualifications to limit the number of applicants.

The "inside track" people were selected for the interview committee, and presented as if they were kings and queens being anointed. Applicants who were qualified, but not "chosen," were left clueless and never got the promotion. Carlo remembered the lamenting and sorrow of rejection of some of those applicants, their self-esteem decimated. But there was nothing he could do... not if he wanted to keep his job.

The school system was an operation of smoke and mirrors. The losers were always the kids and the taxpayers, Carlo thought to himself; his eyes closed remembering the scams that piled up like sand on Miami Beach. For example, he knew how administrators used to manipulate adult and vocational education classes. Funding for these schools came from the state, based on the number of students enrolled during critical attendance weeks, usually four times a year. The State Legislature finally put an end to the practice of counting "asses in the classes," as it was commonly referred to. Instead the adult centers had to prove student achievement and performance in order to receive state funding. When enrollment was low, many times Carlo heard the top district officials advising someone to visit the cemetery and get some names to increase the enrollment. Other examples of this type of fraud were to use jail inmate's names, or those of comatose senior citizens in nursing homes.

This did harm on so many levels he thought. Taxpayers paid for students who didn't exist, so crooked principals could keep their jobs. And teachers who taught these ghost classes, filled with the "learning dead," further sucked the taxpayers of money.

Then there was the fact that under-enrolled adult school facilities, that should have been closed, weren't... denying the severely overcrowded Kindergarten through 12th grade schools any relief from the sardine packed classrooms.

In defiance of board rules, some administrators even supervised their own relatives, signed their payroll, evaluated them, and often lavished them with overtime hours to ultimately boost their retirement income. In one school, Carlo recalled, the principal was so brutal with her staff and faculty that some of them who fell from favor were relegated to broom closets as classrooms. On one occasion, this particular principal, who was widely known to be sleeping with a married state legislator, was yelling so fiercely at a custodian that the man began to pee himself.

These were the people in charge of our children's education! These were the type of people who Jez attempted to expose, and Carlo attempted to survive.

Now, here he was, Carlo the survivor, under suspicion for two murders. Suddenly, Carlo was jerked out of his thoughts by the sound of hysterical chatter coming from the police radio. It was hard to hear because of the plastic divider between the front and back seats in the patrol car... but he could swear he heard something about a woman jumping from the school board building. He watched as the cop who was driving him to headquarters furiously clicked away on his walkie-talkie. The Plexiglas barrier prevented Carlo from talking to the officer, so Carlo banged his fist on the divider, "Did

I hear something on your radio about a suicide at the school district?" Carlo shouted.

The officer responded, "They're calling for rescue. Apparently they have a jumper."Jumper was the term cops and the media used for people who killed themselves by jumping to their death. Floater was the term used for drowning victims… and toasted marshmallow meant a fire victim. It was sick, but gallows humor was what got these humans through the tragedies that confronted them in their jobs almost daily.

"Who jumped?" Carlo pressed. "Did they say?"

"A woman. That's all they've said," the officer informed Carlo. Once again, Carlo threw his head back against the seat. A woman? Who could that be, he wondered? At least she didn't land in his arms! For once he was glad he was in the back of a police cruiser. They couldn't accuse him of having anything to do with the system's third death. Or so he thought.

CHAPTER #28

The City of Miami was in full-scale pandemonium. Three deaths in as many days at the school district had turned the spotlight on a closed, insular and secretive culture. It was the equivalent of a Category 5 Hurricane inside a bureaucracy that was unaccustomed to public scrutiny or attention.

Like most school boards, Miami's functioned in a bubble. Rarely was a mirror put to the face of those who held the education of young people in the palm of their hands. The public had always believed that their school boards were the mom and pop of bureaucratic shops. The public, long ago, had stopped watching or caring. Few voted for school board members, and those who did, paid little attention to the man or woman they voted for. So, while the public was sleepwalking through school board elections, school boards were silently and stealthily growing into gigantic corporations, with budgets the size of some third world countries. It was against this backdrop, that cops, the media, the public and especially those who worked in the school system, struggled to make sense of what had happened in the last 72 hours.

******

"Ferrini! Now!" Detective Hal Davis was shouting at the top of his lungs.

"Yelling isn't necessary," Ferrini insisted.

"Fine. Let's sit and talk," Det. Davis said as he motioned for Ferrini to take a seat at the massive conference table." Carlo?"

"Davis?" The two men were locked in a conversational stalemate. Minutes passed as they stared at one another. Finally, Davis had had his fill of this dramatic bit."Why were you in the superintendent's office this afternoon?" Det. Davis paused.

"Because he summoned me." Carlo stared at the detective.

"Do you know why he summoned you?" Davis pressed on.

"Not a clue!" Ferrini was indignant. He knew where Davis' line of questioning was leading.

Davis responded in kind. "The superintendent summons you to his office, two days after his deputy has been murdered and died in your arms, and you don't have a clue what he wanted to talk to you about?"

"God, you are quick Detective!" Ferrini was dripping in sarcasm.

"You have no idea how quick, Ferrini." Immediately, Det. Davis yelled for uniform officers. "Take him to interrogation room 3." Davis glared at Ferrini, who was not too shocked by these developments.

"Davis, you'll live to regret this," declared Ferrini. "I put Troy White on retainer the day after Maine was killed."

Troy White was, without a doubt, the best, and most expensive defense lawyer in all of South Florida. Just to get a meeting with him cost $50,000! But he was more than worth it, if you needed high-powered legal representation.

"Only guilty assholes put Troy White on retainer," Davis sputtered.

"Want to put a bet on that Davis?" Ferrini responded. Davis shook his head and left the room. Miami police officers led Carlo Ferrini away.

CHAPTER #29

On Friday afternoon, Carlo Ferrini was in an interrogation room at Miami Police headquarters waiting on his hot shot "attorney to the stars," Troy White.

Jez and Emeril were stuck on the 9th floor, unable to report, but able to document everything that was happening that no one else had access to. Det. Davis was pulling his hair out.

School board members were hunkering down, lip locked, for fear of saying anything, but monitoring the wall TV in Jewel Haynes' office.

And in the halls of power at Channel 11... a news director was forced to impersonate the most high profile of all his anchors, because he was too cheap to pay for a workday schedule that had the anchor desk covered 24/7!

What could be funnier? It was the ultimate collision of sanity and insanity... life and death... comedy and tragedy. It was SO Miami!

******

Carlo Ferrini had never seen the inside of a police station or a jail. But he was seeing it now. He'd finally been joined in the interrogation room, by his lawyer. Detective Hal Davis and Capt. Sheila Cohen handled the questioning.

"What was your relationship with Superintendent Vascoe? When did you meet? Where did you meet?" demanded Detective Davis.

"You don't have to answer that Carlo," his attorney advised him.

Carlo explained that he had nothing to hide, and began explaining how he and R.V. had first met when Carlo worked in a department that was under R.V.'s supervision.

"I impressed him," Carlo exclaimed. "So he hired me on as his "right hand man." Carlo told them how he had handled everything for R.V. "He was helpless without my assistance." Carlo proclaimed.

"Why?" asked Capt. Cohen.

"Because he was in over his head!" Carlo just stared at the two detectives.

"So you thought you were better than him"? said Davis.

"No, I didn't think it, I knew it. But that didn't matter. My job was to make him look good, and I did just that!" Carlo folded his arms across his chest.

Carlo then relayed how his relationship with R.V. pretty much cooled, once he was no longer needed. He described how, as R.V. became increasingly more powerful, the expectation was, that a higher-level administrator would handle what had been so carefully and conscientiously taken care of by Carlo.

"So you were vengeful?" Cohen asked.

Carlo retorted, "I didn't hate or dislike R.V., I just had very little contact with him after he became so important and powerful on his ascent to his final aspiration – Superintendent of Schools."

Davis, in his rough tone, asked, "Were you in frequent contact with the superintendent?"

"The daily phone calls from R.V. fell off gradually, until there were no more," replied Carlo.

Davis pushed. "So you felt spurned?"

"No, not really. If he was in the vicinity of my school, he would drop in for a visit." Carlo remembered those visits. "Everyone in the school, but I, was impressed. Generally speaking, R.V. just wanted to show off his new car and all the high-end technology installed in it at taxpayer expense."

"So you were jealous?" asked Cohen.

Carlo thought for a minute, remembering how R.V. would make a disparaging remark about something or another at the school. Never was Carlo given praise or credit for the increase in test scores and achievement, morale, the lack of union grievances, or "no unlocated property" on his property audit.

"Not at all," he finally said. "Being Superintendent was never a job I would seek. Only at a school can one make a positive impact on students."

Davis replied, "So you thought you were above the district administrators?"

"Frankly, I never needed accolades, and I rarely got any from the higher ups! I can think of only one time I was 'complimented.' Carlo uncrossed his arms, leaned back in his chair and continued.

"Jez Underwood made a surprise visit to my office, questioning the admissions of foreigners into the school who were not residents, but weren't paying the required fees for their education. In she came with the cameraman and camera rolling. I was very skilled at diffusing the situation, and did so by commenting in the final statement, since the early beginnings of this country, immigrants have learned to circumvent the system, and that is precisely what has led them to success – perseverance and determination!'" Carlo continued, "The following day, after viewing the telecast on the news, R.V. called to, applaud the manner in which I handled the reporter."

Cohen asked, "Do you know why the superintendent wanted to see you today?"

"He didn't say, and I didn't ask. When the boss summons you to his office, you drop everything and you go," said Ferrini.

"Take it from the top again, tell us exactly what happened when you arrived," Davis ordered.

Carlo smirked. "Fine! Let's take it from the top!" Carlo crossed his arms again, and looked mockingly at them as if to say, you may think my story will change, but it won't because this is the truth. And so, Carlo began again, repeating everything he'd already told the cops twice before.

Carlo Ferrini concluded with an observation about the late superintendent, "R.V.'s downfall, was believing his own PR."

"Enough with the editorializing," Davis insisted.

Cohen asked, "Can you give us a reason why we shouldn't charge you for both the deaths of Hank Maine and Rod Vascoe?"

"Don't answer that," his attorney insisted, but Carlo wasn't listening to his legal advisor.

"Because I had nothing to do with them, and you know it!" Carlo was starting to get angry.

"When was the last time you saw Supt. Vascoe before Dr. Maine's murder?" asked Cohen.

"It was at the opening of schools meeting for administrators, and afterward he phoned me from the car to get my opinion on what a great dog and pony show he put on. I told him to watch his back with those jealous people. His response was to tell me to "Shut up right now. If you say one more word, you'll regret it!'"

Cohen retorted, "Why would he say that?"

Carlo replied, "I think he was in the car with Dr. Maine, and had me on speaker phone.

"Why did you think that?" Davis inquired.

"Because the only time that fool acted like a hard ass, was when Hank Maine was around! It was like R.V. was trying to impress the Nazi by talking tough. I never understood why, but I certainly knew when R.V. was not being himself... and that was every time Hank Maine was present." Carlo stared at both detectives.

"What's your take on Hank Maine's murder?" Davis asked.

"He's dead," Carlo replied, dripping with sarcasm.

"Try being less cute, why don't you," insisted Capt. Cohen.

"I don't have a take on his murder, except for the fact that his bludgeoned body died in my arms." Carlo was on a roll.

"Hank Maine did everything in his power to get me out of the way so that he could exert full control over R.V. I was the one who covered R.V.'s back and ass."

"Covered his back and ass from what?" Davis asked.

"Hank Maine had blackmailed two superintendents before Rod Vascoe, and I have no doubt that he was doing the same thing with R.V. It was Maine's 'modus operandi.'"

"How do you know that?" Capt. Sheila Cohen stood up from the interrogation table.

"I had a visit from a legislator who was upset that R.V. had dumped me for Maine. He was aware, that as the driver for the last couple of Superintendents, Maine had overheard most of his boss's very confidential conversations with a number of elected officials. Those superintendents were all so stupid, not only to trust Maine, but to use the speaker phone!"

Davis and Cohen were silent, absorbing the picture Carlo was painting of the inner dysfunction of their community's public school system.

"So Maine was a blackmailer," declared Cohen.

"And a crook!" Carlo shouted.

Davis demanded, "Can you give us examples?"

"There were contracts awarded to vendors and 'consultants' without bid and in flagrant violation of board rules," Carlo began. "Maine was the deputy overseeing all the technology systems. One day, we were told that we would be getting a new phone system. I can tell you that we had no problems with the former system. But Maine didn't care! He and his associate superintendent signed up a new telecommunications vendor, one who was willing to pay the Nazi and his henchman, a kickback!" Carlo continued. "I can tell you that new, piece of shit, phone system was the subject of many sidebar conversations at principals' meetings because the majority of the system's mainframe e-mails were reporting phone outages. The new system that cost many millions was a total joke, and I'm being kind!"

"How do you know there was a kickback involved in the deal?" asked Capt. Cohen.

"Because the associate's mouth is as large as his gut!" Carlo was on a roll. The idiot bagman, bragged to someone with whom I am friendly."

The two detectives just stared at Ferrini.

"There are lots of secrets in the school system... some are better kept than others," Carlo announced. "Capt. Cohen," he continued, "this place has been a cesspool of corruption and mismanagement for years and no one at your police dept., the district attorney's office, or the F.B.I. has seen fit to investigate it. Now suddenly, everyone is interested in the school system because three people are dead? Brace yourselves, because those deaths will lead to investigations that will unleash untold corruption, immorality, and the vilest breaches of ethics on an unsuspecting public you have ever imagined! Now may I get a cup of coffee?"

Capt. Cohen asked, "What's to keep me from booking you? Because it's apparent that you resented your treatment by those who've died. Revenge could be a solid motive."

Carlo replied, "Because you know that I had nothing to do with those deaths. Juvenal, the great Roman satirist, wrote,

'Revenge is the weak pleasure of a narrow mind.' Capt. Cohen, I don't have a narrow mind."

CHAPTER #30

Into the still quiet of the chaotic situation at the school administration building, Jez and Emeril suddenly had their phones returned to them. The lock down had been lifted at 4:35pm. She'd grabbed Emeril's Nextel, clicked it, and then screamed, "Unit 60! Power up. I'm on my way down! Tell the feed room to clear all other traffic. We have unbelievable videotape! I want on the air the second you can cue up the tape I'm bringing." The operator in Unit 60 sat straight up. After spending the afternoon locked down inside the school board administration building... Jez was now running free through the North exit door. As she bolted outside... she saw an entire block lined with live broadcast trucks, and a line of reporters with microphones in hand, and cameras on tripods.

There were the four English language stations in Miami, and two Spanish language stations. Then there were the "other" stations, whose call letters and language no one in Miami even knew. That's what was so incredible about this town, she thought. Just buy a live truck and call yourself a TV station and you were part of the media. Quickly, Jez spotted Channel 11's truck and ran toward it waving the videotape in her hands.

Unit 60 saw her coming. "This is Unit 60 to base. Jez is out and on her way to the truck. Please stand by for videotape."

"QSL," came the response from the feed room engineer. The Miami media had long ago adopted the cops "Q" code. It was like, but different from, the "10" code most other police departments used around the country. QSL was the equivalent of 10-4... meaning "got that."

"Andy!" Jez hollered at her live truck operator. "Rewind all the way... Emeril says everything we want to see is on this tape. Tell the station to take the feed live and I'll do a walk and talk phoner until Emeril can get his gear set up for a live shot."

"No need, Jez. Ryan McDaniel is already set up on the sidewalk, just waiting for you to stand in front of the camera," Andy informed her as he slammed the tape in a video machine. "We've got five teams set up down here. There is no other news today, as far as Boris is concerned, especially now that he's debuted as an anchorman."

"Yeah, now he's officially a News God!" Jez said, dripping with disdain.

Jez had some idea what video Emeril had shot… but she was now asking the station to trust that she could narrate the raw, or unseen, unapproved video, without putting them at legal risk. It was at moments like this, that management often had to trust it's most seasoned employees, and when those employees had to deliver. Jez knew she was up to the job; she just didn't like knowing what the pressures were.

"Do you have IFB?" Andy asked her, referring to her cus-tomized earpiece that would connect her to the producers and directors in the control booth back at the station. It also allowed her to hear "on air" audio.

"Somewhere in the bowels of my purse, I do." Jez then turned her purse upside down and dumped its entire con-tents on the floor of the live truck. Andy winced when he saw the stuff pouring out of her black bag. A huge pink wallet, a baby blue makeup pouch the size of most small handbags, a bottle of water, checkbook, hairbrush, hairspray, hairclip, hair scrunchy, lotto tickets, a small umbrella, hand lotion, a cell phone, grocery coupons, pens, highlighters, a thin reporter's notebook, nail clippers, car keys, a can of Slimfast, a power bar, business cards, gum, breath mints, a pack of cigarettes opened, and one that wasn't.

"Got it!" she screamed as she jammed the IFB in her ear… and Andy plugged it into the audio box carefully eyeing the mess on the floor of his live truck, as if he expected an alliga-tor to crawl out of her bag too.

"Jez! Oh my God! This is Sophie! Are you Ok?" Sophie the producer was, once again, violating Jez's eardrums.

"Shut up! Sophie. Whisper. Please!" Jez begged her eager and anxious producer as she pulled her earpiece out of her ear for two seconds, before putting it back in.

"Sorry Jez." Sophie was repentant.

"Just get me on the air, Sophie and roll the tape we just fed back," Jez ordered.

"Dean is finally on the desk, Jez. We should be coming to you in 30 seconds."

"Hopefully before the competition steals our video out of the sky!" shrieked Jez.

She knew how competitive and cutthroat the Miami TV market was, especially when there was major breaking news. She didn't doubt that her competitors would try to swipe her exclusive any way they could."Is anyone in need of an audio check?" Jez asked sarcastically... knowing full well, they were all but ready to go live and no one had checked her microphone.

"I'm officially requesting audio for this live shot!" Jez added.

Some days it seemed to Jez, as if you needed a requisition order for basics such as audio, at the number one station in the 16th TV market. It had become a joke among the crews, "Did you request audio?"

In her earpiece she heard Janine, the audio person say, "Sound test of diva talent is complete."Jez just rolled her large hazel eyes. At this point, they could call her Leona Helmsley, she didn't care. She had the big story! Besides, if it took sarcasm to make sure her microphone was turned on; she'd do it ten times a day.

"Five seconds," Jez heard Sophie whisper softly in her ear. Ryan's left hand was up, all five fingers spread erect. Then one second at a time, each of his fingers curled into his palm until he pointed to her, indicating she was "on."

CHAPTER #31

The body of Barbara Ross had been covered with a white tarp and yellow crime scene tape encircled a broad area around her broken and lifeless body. She jumped from the East side of the building, where most of the live trucks usually set up. But as soon as the cops got on the scene, they forced all the stations to move their trucks to the North side of the building. A perimeter had been set up that pretty much kept the prying eyes of the media out of range, as detectives worked furiously to secure forensics, take photographs and generally process the scene. After Jez's first live shot with the video inside the dead Superintendent's office, she had a chance to catch her breath and realize the massive effort the station had mounted to cover both deaths.

Another crew had been assigned to handle the suicide. Jez was grateful for that! She was already spread pretty thin. But because most news organizations had policies about not covering suicides, most of the live hits for the next 90-minutes were going to be on Jez's shoulder, instead of the other crew on the Barbara Ross story.

Jez hadn't even had a moment to contemplate the implications of Ross' death yet. And she was too busy going live every five minutes to call some of her school district sources for information. Ross and her rear window exit from the world would have to wait!

******

Detective Hal Davis was not going to make it home for dinner. Although Friday night was supposed to be his sacred night with the family, the school system's deaths were now his paramount concern primarily because they were the Chief's and the Mayor's paramount concern. Currently, Davis was waiting on a Tox screen from Dr. Maine, an autopsy report for Supt. Vascoe, and now he was waiting on the Medical Examiner to arrive because Barbara Ross had been a lousy window cleaner. Shit! He thought. Then there was the video of child porn involving an officer's son. How could he forget that complication? They don't pay me enough to handle this much crap, he thought to himself.

Although the lockdown had been lifted for the rest of the building, those who had offices on the 9th floor were still being questioned, one by one, by police. The school board members had kept themselves entertained by congregating in President Haynes' office as she channel surfed the various news stations. But not Big Mo. He'd retreated to his office and closed the door.

Behind that closed door, Moorehead and his trusted aide, Franklin Elder, sat looking at one another. It was as if they could read each other's minds without speaking. It's the kind of kinetic thing that happens when people are very close, have lots in common or know too much about the other, to let the "other" forget how much they know. "Mo," Franklin spoke first. "You can't show no emotion, no matter how hard it is for you to do."

Moorehead nodded yes, but still couldn't speak. It was uncommon for the district's most powerful board member. Even if he spoke slowly, he generally always spoke. "Mo, there is a lot we have to take care of," Franklin Elder implored. "I need your full attention and help. I can't do, what has to be done, on my own." Franklin waited for some kind of response from his boss.

"She came to me this morning at about 10:30," Moses Moorehead said without looking up. He knew Franklin would know he was talking about Barbara Ross.

"She wanted out. I told her, no way!" Moorehead finally looked Franklin Elder straight in the eyes. "I told her I'd kill her before I'd let her out of our arrangement." Franklin stared at Mo with a steely look. "She threatened to go to the media if I didn't let her out!" Dr. Moses Moorehead was handling his hair, flipping the flip, which was his signature.

"She was an idiot playing with fire," Frank Elder insisted.

Moses Moorehead was compulsively playing with his flipped ends as if hypnotized by his predicament. "But she was my idiot!" Mo was softly screaming, almost verging on tears. "I gave her the world and this is how she thanks me? Jumping out a window, bringing police, the media and public scrutiny to my doorstep? Do you know how hard I've worked to avoid all of that over the years?"

Of course, Franklin Elder knew. He had been involved from day one. Moses Moorehead was standing now, wild with rage."Mo, of course I know," said Elder.

Moses Moorehead was pacing his small school board office like a caged tiger. "She's screwed me and I didn't even get to enjoy the fuck!"

Suddenly, Moorehead bent over... threw his precisely coiffed hair over his lap and ripped the wig from his head heaving it across the room... revealing wisps of kinky gray hair that barely dotted the landscape of his bald head. Franklin Elder stood, looking at his boss in shock. He thought he knew everything about his boss. But he had no idea that Moses Moorehead's famous flipped locks... were actually a wig!

CHAPTER #32

Donna Maine hadn't gotten out of her bed since her husband's death. The day the cops had carted out the contents of his home office, Donna had crawled under the covers and let her in-laws plan Hank's funeral. Donna Maine had never been a woman of independent mind or body. Hank bought her clothes, told her what to wear, what to say, and how to say it. He paid the bills, drove the car and even fed their pet cat "Goldie." Donna was arm candy for Hank, and it had never occurred to her to object to her status. But sheltered under the covers of her marital bed, Donna was starting to re-examine her life.

The sobs came in waves. Donna had set a box of tissues next to her, so she wouldn't have to get out from under the covers to blow her nose. The only thing that got her out of bed was the urge to pee. And even that was diminishing, since she'd stopped going to the kitchen for any form of hydration. Donna, quite frankly, wanted to die.

She'd called the few people she believed knew what her husband was up to, in hopes of getting a piece of his action, but she'd been summarily rebuffed. A stronger woman might have crawled out of bed, gotten dressed to the nines, stormed into those assholes offices and blackmailed them to the hilt. But not Donna. She was the flan dessert at Cuban restaurants… tasteless, pudding like, unmemorable and bland. Donna's wailing, was accompanied by bouts of body jerking hiccups. Crying and hiccupping at the same time was such a difficult task, kind of like patting your head and rubbing your belly at the same time. This condition had plagued Donna Maine for two days. But suddenly, in the middle of a hiccup and gulp, it dawned on her… Hank had done what he'd done for a reason. His secrets, his duplicity, it was all part of his game plan to achieve power and dominance. Donna's hiccups started to subside. She blew her nose. She wiped her eyes and suddenly she could see clearly what she had to do.

******

Jez had blown away the competition with her video of the dead Superintendent of Miami Schools and the video of Associate Supt. Barbara Ross jumping to her death. Almost lost in all of the spectacular video, were the shots of Carlo Ferrini being shoved into a patrol car and led away for questioning. Jez had just finished doing 9 live shots in 90 minutes. She was exhausted as she yanked her earpiece from her ear. "Is food in our future Emeril?" Jez asked her photographer.

"Not in this neighborhood blondie." Emeril was referring to the slum neighborhood they were standing in.

The Miami School System Headquarters was located in a fringe neighborhood near downtown. It was suspect during the day and downright frightening at night. It's one of the reasons Dr. Hank Maine had insisted on hiring so many security guards for the headquarters building. It's about the only thing the Nazi had done right, Jez thought. "Base to Jez." The sound of Boris' voice made the rumbles of Jez's starved stomach grow even louder.

"Jez here. What's up?"

"You are planning on working a double shift aren't you Jez?" Her news director always made a question sound like an edict. "No, Boris. I'm going home now to rest my weary bones and have a drink," Jez quipped back. "I worked a double on Wednesday, a double shift yesterday... I am incapable of doing so again."

"I'll give you three comp days next month! Take a vacation! Go somewhere fun!" That was known as "The Boris Bribe."

Jez knew better. Management promised comp time because they were too cheap to pay overtime, then they found endless excuses that comp time wasn't available. Jez, and other reporters, had stopped accepting their comp time offers. They knew it made them targets for firing or layoffs, but life was too short and Channel 11's middle age reporters and anchors wanted more time for family and rest.

"I'm spent, Boris. I'm going home." Jez was firm.

"Not an option," Boris announced."Tell my feet that!" Jez got so tired of news managers just assuming she had no life and could work 24/7 because she was single. The fact that she had no life was none of their business! Sometimes she just had to stop their insanity by faking a real life and then threatening them if they dared to upend it. Boris was now tacking against the wind. He was cleaver enough to know when to change course, and so he did.

"Underhanded," he whined like a 16-year old girl. He always used his nickname for her when he really wanted something.

"This is your story… your exclusive… your big scoop! No one at this station or any other in town can do it justice. You know how important the 11pm news is. We really need you on this story. It's yours. No one else can own it or should own it." Boris was playing her, and he knew it, but so did she.

"You're right Boris, I do own this story, that's why I'm going home to work this story for tomorrow, instead of burning myself out, making you happy." Jez was defiant.

"Jez!" Boris was screaming."I'm going to dinner Boris. You have one of your cheap, big-breasted, future stars handle this at 11. After all, isn't that why you pay them the small bucks?" Jez clicked off the Nextel, looked at Emeril and asked where he'd like to have dinner.

"In a county far away from Miami, blondie!" he replied, dreading his return to the station. She really pushed people's buttons he thought, and I'm sure to be guilty by association!

CHAPTER #33
SATURDAY

Carlo Ferrini woke up on Saturday morning holding his head, trying to process what had happened in the last two days, what had happened to him, to the top three people at the district and what was likely to happen. He was frantic that there would be more police questioning, even though he didn't know a thing about any one of the deaths... not Maine's, not Vascoe's, not Ross'. He was relieved that the police let him go after the interrogation, and that he was waking up in his own bed, and not a jail cell cot.

Meanwhile, at the cop shop, detectives were getting an early jump on all the forensics the Miami CSI unit had uncovered. "Vascoe had a heart that was plugged with bubble gum!" reported Detective Hal Davis. "His arteries were so clogged, draino wouldn't have cleared them. So I guess we can rule out foul play in his death."

"Maybe he was scared to death?" Det. Gonzalez was offering an idea.

"Scared of what?" asked another cop. "Carlo Ferrini?" He started laughing.The handful of detectives who had shown up at daybreak for work looked at one another, then at Gonzalez then at one another again, and joined in the laughter. Detective Davis waved his hands telling them to stop.

"Let's look at any clues we can get from Ross' suicide note. And let me remind you... as of this moment, the press knows nothing about a suicide note. If I hear one whisper about it... everyone in this room will be under suspicion. QSL?" The entire room was nodding in the affirmative. Nine out of ten were also trying to think up inventive ways to let Jez Underwood know what was happening.

There wasn't a homicide detective in the City of Miami that wasn't on the clock on Saturday. The Chief had made sure of that. As was the case in all bureaucracies, shit ran downhill. The police chief was getting pressure from the City Manager, who was getting pressure from the Mayor, who was getting pressure from the commission and the public to resolve the unprecedented number of deaths at the school system. Worse than that, was the media. The Mayor was being hounded by the news hounds for answers and he didn't like, not having any. Waiting on the cops to do their job was infuriating. "I'm getting calls from Larry Fucking King, for God's sake!" screamed Miami Mayor Javier Castillo... to his pitiful staff who'd dragged themselves into City Hall on a Saturday morning.

"Sir?" began his PR aide Carmen Rico. "This is a really simple situation, if you'll just let me explain." Carmen Rico was Hispanic, but she wasn't Cuban, and in Miami, that was the equivalent of the seven deadly sins! Why Mayor Castillo had chosen her to be his spokeswoman didn't exactly boggle the mind. Carmen was a plastic surgeon's college experiment... big tatas, flabless thighs, puckered lips and long, flowing black hair... compliments of her hairdresser and his designer hair extensions.

Now Carmen was going to try and advise her mayor on how to handle a media disaster. Life was funny, thought Mayor Castillo. He could listen to his Puerto Rican chica or just pretend her mouth was moving and she wasn't really saying anything! What a choice he thought. Javier Castillo was no John F. Kennedy. He wasn't about to let Carmen whisper in his ear during pillow talk, "Ich bin ein Berliner..." as Marilyn Monroe had, so famously, and allegedly done, with JFK. But Castillo needed an ear, and Carmen's was the only one close enough at the moment. "So what do you suggest, mi amor?" the Mayor asked.

"Blame all these needless deaths on the FCAT, my prince!" Carmen sighed as if sexually satisfied. "Hear me out Javier! The pressure for our school children to perform in a patterned way is enormous. That pressure starts at the top of the food chain and bubbles down to the kids, who throw up and can't sleep days before the damn test! Expecting educational proficiency is an admirable goal, but the way this state is going about it, is retarded and feckless." Mayor Castillo was astounded. He wasn't sure he'd have won if someone had bet him that Carmen knew the meaning of the word "feckless."

"Spineless? You're saying the state is spineless?" the Mayor queried his aide.

"Of course! I know what feckless means." Carmen was getting huffy.

"But how does that translate into three deaths at the school system my darling?" asked Mayor Castillo. Carmen Rico stood, straightened her very short A-line skirt, and pushed up her pointed, starched collar. "If you want to be Governor someday, this is what you have to say. R.V. likely died of natural causes triggered by the pressure to see his district perform up to state standards... standards we all know this district cannot meet because of the transient nature of the community and the sheer numbers of immigrants that the rest of the state does not have to cope with. Make the Governor and his FCAT the hit men who killed these three honorable public servants!" Carmen paused for effect. "Barbara Ross succumbed to the pressures of FCAT as well, only her method of coping with the pressure was to commit suicide. Javier, you have to say the words... 'commit suicide.' Anything less, won't play. Don't dance around the 800-pound elephant in the room. And as for the Nazi, you will explain how his tough stance on this failed experiment by the state, i.e., the Governor, set him up to be the "bad guy." You'll outline all the reasons parents and teachers and principals would have wanted him dead, because he was the FCAT enforcer."

Castillo stared at his raven-haired PR bimbo, and felt as though he'd suddenly found God!

******

Carlo took his dog Samba out for her Saturday morning walk, just as the sun was peeking over the edge of the ocean, as if to challenge the powder puff clouds that also wanted to frame the Atlantic Ocean's horizon.

Across town, Jez Underwood was fighting the urge to open her eyes, even though the sun was starting to bleed into her bedroom like a laser.

And sitting on the beach, enjoying the morning sun was the Nazi's killer. An early breakfast at an Ocean Drive restaurant on the veranda usually meant a good day all around. The killer was hoping luck hadn't changed. "Will there be anything else?" asked the breakfast server.

"Just my check," said the killer.

"We have a fresh pot of coffee if you'd like a refill." The waitress watched for a reaction as she picked up the killer's breakfast plate.

"No thank you, one cup is my limit," the killer responded. "I get too jittery if I have more."

"Caffeine is such a kickypoo drug, don't you know!" The waitress, who was British, was laughing as she hauled away the killer's breakfast plate.

If only she'd known what a platter of DNA evidence she held in her hands, the killer thought, then chuckled and calmly signed the credit card receipt, got up and walked to the beach. It was time to work on a golden tan.

Over at Channel 11, Emeril was in the photographer's equipment room, rigging up the hidden cameras that would be used the next day for the sting involving Dr. Moses Moorehead.

After some discussions with Batman, Emeril had decided they'd need three hidden cameras. Batman would wear the "glasses cam," meaning his eyeglasses would act as the camera and allow him to get "dead on" video of whatever, or whoever he looked at. He would also have a second sneaky camera in his briefcase, which he would leave in a strategic place in the church to get the wide shots. A female producer would carry the "purse cam" which Emeril was mounting inside the buckle of the purse's shoulder strap. It was no small task making sure each camera lens was positioned correctly and wouldn't jiggle loose with movement. He had to make sure each recording device was working properly and had fully charged batteries. He also needed to make sure that there were plenty of tapes for the briefcase camera. The other two recorders were digital and didn't require tape, but their batteries also didn't last as long as the tape based recording devices.

In an hour, the producer and Batman would arrive at Channel 11 to rehearse with this very sensitive and often unpredictable equipment. Emeril was suddenly startled by a voice behind him. "Sneaky cam set up, huh? Must be a big shoot for "Underhanded!"

Emeril turned to see Ryan McDaniel, a fellow photographer, standing in the doorway. "So whose life is she planning on ruining now?" McDaniel asked.

"If I tell you..." Emeril began.

"Yeah, yeah, yeah... I know, you'll have to kill me," responded his colleague. "Listen, you'd better warn her that Boris may be about to ruin her life if she doesn't cool it. Some people who were in his office last night when she hung up on him and refused to work the 11:00 news, told me later that they'd never seen him so pissed! And Allison was, of course, egging him on. They're gunning for her, man."

Emeril looked at Ryan with concern. "I can talk to her, but ju know as well as I do, that she rarely listens, and frankly, she's jusually right. Boris and Allison are on a power trip."

"I don't disagree," said Ryan, "but he is the boss... like it or not."

"I'll bring it up. We're going to be on a long surveillance tomorrow and will need sometinkg to talk about." Just as Emeril started to turn his attention back to his cameras... he stopped, looked around at Ryan and said, "Hey Chico... thanks."

CHAPTER #34

Detective Bob West had hardly let go of his young son, since getting home on Friday after seeing the chilling video of his son at a school urinal. He'd even slept with his son that night.

West was a single dad, who often worked long hours, and carried with him, the guilt of not always, being able to spend time with his son. Thankfully, the detective's mother lived with them and was able to care for Bobby Junior. West had gone berserk when he saw the grainy videotape. Several of his fellow officers had to restrain him from tearing the room apart. After they'd calmed him down, one of the police psychologists had come in to talk with Det. West about the best way to handle the topic of possible molestation with his son.

They'd agreed that the psychologist should facilitate the discussion with the boy and that West should not be in the same room. They'd agreed to meet at the station and use one of the children's interrogation rooms, which would allow West to monitor the questioning through a one-way mirror. He was well aware that he was incapable of containing his anger, but didn't want to scare his child if he blew up at what he heard.

After lunch, West told his son he needed to go to the station to do some work, and asked if he'd like to come with him. The boy was elated! Even at age 7, Bobby Jr. knew he wanted to be a police officer, just like his dad, and loved it whenever his father took him to the station where he could see all the police cars. Bob and Bobby Jr. left their home around 1pm on Saturday, headed for what Det. West knew, might be the most difficult day of his life to date. They arrived at the cop shop and, after Bobby Jr. spent a few minutes in the parking garage begging his dad's colleagues to flash their lights and turn on the sirens of their patrol cars, his dad walked him into the station and up to the 3rd floor, where Dr. Marlene Mancuso was waiting.

"Hey son," Det. West had picked up his little boy and was holding him in his arms. "Dad has some really important paperwork to finish and I need some uninterrupted time. But this nice lady Marlene has agreed to play with you while I'm busy. She has this really nice room with all kinds of toys and games! Do you mind keeping her company while I do my work, Bobby?"

"O.K. dad," Bobby Jr. replied as he looked at Dr. Mancuso.

"Come with me Bobby. I have this really cool room where you can color, play video games... you name it." Dr. Mancuso took little Bobby by the hand and led him off to the playroom/interrogation room. Detective West and his Sgt., Jay Leventhal quietly slipped into the adjoining room with the two-way mirror. On the 6th floor of the police station, detectives were continuing to pour through the smut they'd carted away from the Nazi's home. It was such a massive collection, and had the despicable potential to be part of a bigger porn ring that the cops had decided to call in the FBI, and the United States Postal Inspectors, in hopes their vast databases would help the Miami P.D. get a lead. "I'm not sure how much more of this I can watch without throwing up," announced Det. Ricky Ingersoll.

"Ditto that!" It was Capt. Sheila Cohen, his boss. The two of them had been trapped in a room for almost 48 hours, watching the handiwork of society's underbelly sickos. They'd seen just about every conceivable kind of pornography, but what bothered them the most, was the stuff they suspected came from children of the Miami Public School System. How many parents' hearts would be broken soon? How many children would need a lifetime of psych services? How many of these children were already dead? And who else in the district, besides "Mr. Victoria's Secret..." had possession of the same type of material? Those questions gave every detective on the case a raging headache.

Capt. Cohen inserted one of the last DVDs. "Two more guys, and we're done."

"I'd praise God, but after looking at this shit for the last 24 hours, I'm not sure there is a God!" Detective Ingersoll informed his colleagues. A group of five of Miami's best Detectives from the special crimes unit watched as the video came up on the screen.
"What the hell is this?" demanded Capt. Cohen.

"Not child porn!" chuckled her guys. "It looks like a wedding of some sort."

"Then why does the bride look like a man?" asked Cohen.

As they all stared at the moving pictures on the screen Ingersoll gasped. "That's no bride," he announced. "That's Dr. Jesse Joe Crandall!" He was craning his neck to look around at all the other detectives in the room.

"You mean the school board member Dr. Jesse Joe Crandall?" asked Cohen.

"Damn straight!' Ingersoll screamed. "Zoom in on a close up Vic." He was now talking to the department's video guru, who could do just about anything with digital or videotape.
As Vic Waters maneuvered the buttons on his computer, the image of the bride got bigger and clearer. Suddenly, the video screen was filled with an image of a tall, oversized, bearded, black man, dressed in a long, flowing, and billowy white wedding gown, complete with a sprawling net veil on top of his grey head. It was school board member, Dr. Jesse Joe Crandall... in drag!

"Well, I'll be damned," Capt. Cohen, uttered as the room erupted in laughter.

"Isn't he a preacher"? asked one of the detectives.

And a former cop," added Capt. Cohen.

"I guess he traded in his white hat for a white veil!" chuckled Det. Ingersoll. "Vic, let the video roll, now that we know who the star of this show is!"

Vic Waters hit play, and the room full of cops watched as the bearded bride, took the arm of the groom, who was Mrs. Crandall, also dressed in drag, as a man in a tuxedo. Suddenly, the camera pulled out wide, revealing a crowd of about 30 people, all of whom were men dressed as bridesmaids, and women dressed as groomsmen.

"What the hell?" Det. Rogelio Gonzalez was the only officer from the school system's police force in the room. It's the reason he immediately recognized so many of the faces of those who were gender bending.

"Most of those people are some of the system's top administrators," he announced. He got up, walked over to the viewing monitor and began pointing to men/women and women/men, naming each of them. Among those he recognized, the Superintendent of Schools, Rod Vascoe, Dept. Supt. Hank Maine, the Dept. Superintendent of Personnel, the Dept. Supt. of Federal Grants, and Associate Superintendent Lily Molina was there with her husband Lee. He was one of about seven school principals Gonzalez recognized.

On the videotape, the crowd was escorting the bride and groom into the entrance of a church. As the camera panned up to a sign... Gonzalez exclaimed, "That's Jesse Joe's church! They're holding this god damn drag wedding at his very own church!"

Laughter and off color comments erupted throughout the room... as the cops watched the Reverend Crandall fight to keep his wedding veil from blowing away.

Finally, Capt. Cohen stood up, "Enough with the locker room humor! Can we please restore some order here guys? I know we all needed some comedic relief but we still have a job to do."

"Yeah," shouted Ingersoll, who stood up and began prancing around, imitating the Reverend as a bride in the wind. "Like finding out where I can get a wedding dress as beautiful as Jesse Joe's!"

Things were out of control, as hysteria took over the exhausted cops who joined their friend merrily prancing about the room... as if they were a bride about to lose her veil to Miami's tropical winds!

******

Meanwhile, the sun on Miami Beach was blazing hot. There wasn't a cloud in the sky. The only thing saving the killer from heat stroke was the cool breeze blowing in off the ocean. A frozen water bottle was quickly melting nearby the lounge chair in which the killer lay. Cold water would soon be hot water, if the killer didn't seek out some shade.

Gathering up a beach bag and towel, the killer headed to the nearby Palace Bar on Ocean Drive and 12th Street. A hint of sunburn began to sting the killer's skin, who hoped a cold cocktail would cure the burning sensation. What sensation had Maine felt, the killer wondered, as I jammed a knife into his gut? Was it a burning, painful feeling? Or did the shock of it all, leave him without any feeling?

Too bad I can't ask him, the killer thought... as the chill of a frozen drink, melted going down the killer's throat.

CHAPTER #35

Bobby West Jr. was sitting in the Miami police station's children's playroom. It looked just like a daycare, only it wasn't. Bobby was there with Dr. Mancuso, the department's psychologist.

Watching from an adjoining room was Bobby's father, Sgt. Jay Leventhal and Capt. Sheila Cohen.

"Where do you go to school Bobby," Mancuso asked, trying to get to know the boy.

"Sandy Pointe Elementary. I'm in first grade!" Bobby announced proudly.

"Do you like school?"

"Yeah!" The boy was a tad hesitant.

"Is there anything about school you don't like," Mancuso gently prodded.

"Reading!" he blurted out.

"Why is that, Bobby?"

"It's hard for me. Harder that it is for most of the other kids," he said. His head hung down, as if embarrassed. "And I don't like that teacher."

Mancuso knew she needed to tread carefully. "What teacher is that, Bobby?"

"The one who comes to our school sometimes and makes us go to the bathroom before we can sit in our reading circle. He makes Mrs. Cordell leave, and he takes over."

"Why is that?" Mancuso asked.

"I don't know. But it's weird." Bobby's head still hung down as if he was afraid to look Dr. Mancuso in the eye and he was fidgeting with one of the buttons on his shirt.

"Does this teacher have a name?"

"He told us to call him Doctor," Bobby informed her. "But I don't think he looks like a real Doctor. Doctors are supposed to be nice and kind. This doctor is mean to us."

"How is he mean?" Mancuso was trying hard to keep her voice even and steady.

"If we didn't read all the words just right... he made us... he... he... he made us... pull down our pants."

"Did he say why he made you do that?" Mancuso braced herself.

"Not really." Bobby went quiet. Mancuso just let the silence hang in the air, and prayed his father wouldn't come barging through the door!

Bobby began to color in the coloring book on the table in front of him. Marlene Mancuso joined him. After about five minutes of silent coloring... Bobby looked up. "Dr. Mancuso?"

"Yes, Bobby."

"Why would he take pictures of us whenever he made us pull our pants down? What does that have to do with reading?" Bobby was finally looking her in the eye.

"I'm not exactly sure why he'd do that honey, but it was wrong." Mancuso knew she needed to press her young friend. "Bobby, I need you to tell me everything you remember about those reading classes with the Doctor, and I need you to draw a picture of him. Can you do that for me?" she asked.

"Sure!" The child was suddenly ecstatic. My grandma says I'm a good artist!" With that, the child began to draw a picture of a monster.

CHAPTER #36

By late Saturday afternoon, Batman and the producer had arrived for their dress rehearsal with Emeril and his "sneaky cams."

Batman put on the "eye glasses cam" and began walking around the second floor of Channel 11 writing down notes of the things he was looking at, so they could compare what he intended to shoot, with what turned up on the video.

The producer basically did the same thing, only she had a bit more of a challenge, in that she had to constantly re-adjust her aim, meaning up, down or sideways, since her camera was not set up to be trained on what she was looking at.

Emeril had them shoot for an hour, and then he made them both practice changing batteries and re-starting the videotaping. Emeril would start things for them before they walked into the church, but once inside... they needed to be experts at doing it themselves.

It was no easy task, as Batman quickly found out. The digital recorder was super sensitive. When he re-started the recorder after changing the battery, he accidentally put his thumb on the stop button. For the next ten minutes, he recorded absolutely nothing! Emeril realized he had to come up with a way to "dummy proof" the damn device.

Meanwhile, Louise, the producer, was having a tough time getting the hang of focusing the camera on what she wanted to shoot. She was too close, too far left or too far right. Emeril was ready to pull his hair out! What little hair he had left, that is.

Emeril was getting close to retirement age. His receding hairline and paunch around his waistline reflected the fact that he'd covered a lot of news stories, from the early days of bulky film canisters, to now, when some broadcast TV cameras shot video on a tape, no bigger than the size of a pack of cigarettes.

He'd traveled the world tracking news stories for Channel 11. In the old days, there was lots of help. A cameraman traveled in a pack of four including the reporter, soundman and grip, the person who lugged the unwieldy cables around and generally watched everybody's back. Today, Emeril, like all the photographers, carried all his gear, including a camera that weighed about 50 pounds. In Miami's sub-tropical heat, such a physical job took a toll on the young men, never mind the "old timers" like Emeril who'd hung in the business, even as it changed faster than his hairline.

Now here he was training a 22-year old assistant producer on the nuances of a hidden camera, and a guy who was a 57-year old orthodontist!

"Ju two aren't leafing this place until ju are perfect with these thinks!" Emeril began putting them through their paces again.

CHAPTER #37

Children can be great artists. They can also be bad ones. Dr. Mancuso held her breath, not knowing which kind of artist Bobby would be. But she was pretty certain he'd capture the essence of the man called "the doctor."

Ten minutes, thirty minutes, fifty minutes had passed and still young Bobby was drawing often erasing what was a pencil sketch. He'd sometimes stop for minutes at a time to look at his handy work. Mancuso had never seen a child so obsessed with details.

After an hour, Mancuso decided to probe.

"How's it going Bobby?"

"Good." He replied. "But I'm having a hard time getting his weight just right."

"Oh, I thought you were just drawing a picture of his face! No wonder you are being so specific." Mancuso paused.

"What's specific mean?" asked Bobby.

"It means precise, exact..." Mancuso struggled for a word a young boy would perhaps understand. "It means perfect," Mancuso declared.

"I like to be perfect," Bobby responded. "My dad says it's important to be perfect." Bobby then resumed his drawing.

Twenty minutes later, he put down his pencil, looked up at Dr. Mancuso and said, "I'm finished ma'am."

Slowly, he pushed his drawing across the table toward Marlene Mancuso, until it reached her. She turned it upright and stared in horror. Young Bobby West had drawn a demon! The image was half human, half devil, as best she could figure. He had pointy ears, a forked tail, a large nose... but his face was a face no adult born after 1900 wouldn't recognize... it was the face of Adolf Hitler. It was the "Nazi."

"Hitler! He drew Hitler?" Detective West was puzzled beyond all reasoning. How would his 6-year old know about Adolf Hitler?

Capt. Cohen had arranged for a couple of uniformed guys to keep Bobby Jr. entertained in the squad room, while she and his Dad met with Dr. Mancuso.

As she took her first glance at the child's drawing, she quickly agreed. "It does look like Hitler. But so did Hank Mai..." her words vanished just as her head whipped around to look at Detective West.

"Hank Maine!" they both screamed simultaneously.

"The school official who was stabbed to death?" Dr. Mancuso asked, feeling as if she was a bit out of the loop.

"The very one," Det. West replied as he combed his fingers through his wavy chestnut colored hair and began pacing.

"Dr. Hank Maine was the Deputy Superintendent of schools," Capt. Cohen went on to explain. He was the 2nd in command of Miami's public education."

"Did you say Dr.?" Mancuso asked, suddenly sensing she was now in the loop and might even be a few steps ahead of her cop pals.

"Not a medical doctor, but a PhD.. doctor," Cohen responded.

"Oh, my God!" Det. West blurted out. "Bobby said the man told the kids to call him Dr.! We were all thinking the white-coat, stethoscope kind of doctor. But it would make sense that Maine wouldn't tell the kids his name. And the kids would naturally think of a medical doctor. It's the only kind of doctor most 6-years know about!"

"It would also explain how he could commandeer a class-room without raising suspicions," Capt. Cohen added. "What teacher in their right mind would challenge the second most powerful person in the school system's chain of command."?

"I'll kill him!" Det. West screamed as he jammed his fist into the wall.

"Sorry, Detective. Someone else has already done you the favor," Capt. Cohen said as she walked over to him and gently sat him in a seat at the small table they'd been standing around.

"Jesus Christ!" A light bulb had just gone off in Bob West's seasoned investigative mind. "And I'm on the task force that's supposed to find the person who killed the man who molested my little boy? Who stripped him of his innocence?"

Mancuso and Cohen just looked at one another, as the irony began to dawn on them as well.

"I'd rather pin a medal on the son-of-a-bitch, than cuff him and put him behind bars!" Detective West was shouting at the top of his lungs now.

"I don't think that will be your assignment anymore Bob. In fact, I can guarantee it won't. Now go get Bobby Jr. and take him home. It's been a long day for both of you. I'm ordering you to take the next week off."

With those words, Capt. Cohen walked over and opened up the door, holding it for a few minutes, as West tried to compose himself for the drive home with his little son.

CHAPTER #38

Around 6pm on Saturday, Jez had called Carlo to make sure he'd survived the great "police inquisition."

"I'm fine, just tired." he said. "But I think they now realize I'm not a party to all this madness. I certainly gave them enough information to keep them busy pursuing leads for the next two weeks," Carlo informed Jez.

"Carlo? What did you cough up?" Jez asked.

"Stuff," he replied.

"Like stuff I haven't yet reported on?"

"Sort of. Jez, I had to. They were ready to book me for murder! I had to tell them what I knew. I'm innocent." Carlo was adamant.

"I know, I know," said Jez. "I just wish it hadn't come to this, but I understand you had to do what you did. Let's just consider it water under the bridge. Are you going to be ok?" she asked.

"Troy White, my attorney thinks I'm in the clear," Carlo said with great confidence.

"I'm not talking legally, I'm talking about your emotional state of mind, Carlo."

"Jez, innocent people can sleep like babies," Carlo insisted."

"Then do so, my friend. I've got to go. I have an early call and a long day of surveillance tomorrow," Jez informed him. "I'll check in on you when I can."

She clicked her phone off, set her alarm clock and began her struggle to sleep.

As she drifted off... the nightmares began. She was in her childhood neighborhood in Kansas... sneaking around the back yard of huge mansion down the street from her house.

There were fountains, and ponds with beautiful lily pads... scads of rose bushes... and a small creek.

It was always Summer in her dream, so the creek was low... yet every night as she went to put her bare foot in the stream of trickling water... a monster always reared its head and tried to attack her. Some nights, the demon, which was a cross between a dragon and an alligator, only nipped at her toes. Other nights... it managed to pull her into the shallow water, where she flailed, trying not to drown.

The next thing she knew, she was running from someone on horseback. As she got to the main street... her grandmother, driving a red Lamborghini, pulled up and urged her to get in. But as soon as they stopped at the next stoplight, Jez leaped out of the car and was running... with the monster close behind her.

This is the moment when she'd wake up sweating and breathing so hard, she always thought she might hyperventilate! But on this night... she didn't wake up... until the monster had caught her and was starting to eat her alive.

She heard herself screaming, "No! No! No!" And then vaulted from her bed and began flipping on every light in her condo.

CHAPTER #39
SUNDAY

Sunday services at the Church of the Great Believer didn't start until 9:00am. So Jez and her undercover crew had decided to meet at the TV station at 7:00am.

Because Jez wasn't planning to be on camera, she didn't have to get made up. All she did was throw on a pair of jeans, a tee shirt, and a ball cap.

Batman was right on time, but Louise, the producer, was nearly 20 minutes late. Emeril was beside himself, and let the chica know it.

"OK," announced Jez. "I want a final technical run through. There is no margin for error today... no "do overs!"

For the next 20 minutes, Batman and Louise played and worked with their undercover, sneaky cams, while Emeril and Jez watched, coached and generally vomited advice.

At 8:20, the four of them headed off for the 10-minute drive to the "Church of the Great Surveillance" as Jez called it.

Mrs. Hank Maine was also on her way to church! After she'd crawled out from under the covers of her king size bed... she'd decked herself out in her finest St. John knit suit, a lilac color and called for her car. Her plan was to confront her husband's business, or blackmail partners, and demand the same cut Hank was getting. Donna Maine decided she'd played the role of the "dumb housewife" long enough!

Hank had been a pig of a husband. She'd tolerated his infidelities, his corruption and narcissism. But now, with him dead, she'd decided it was her turn for a small portion of the action, which she knew was vast. All she wanted was her small slice.

It never dawned on Donna Maine, that cutting into the gang's action, could get her knifed, just like her husband.

As she parked her car at the Church of the Great Believer, she checked her makeup in the rearview mirror and decided she looked good enough to play the game of "one-upsmanship."

Three cars away, the Channel 11 news crew was parked... and Emeril was wiring his two undercover operatives with their respective "sneaky cams." It was 8:50.

"Showtime," Emeril announced.

"Be careful," Jez cautioned her crew. "Be very careful."

******

Inside the Church of the Great Believer, Dr. Moses Moorehead was holding court at a conference table in a second floor room that was off limits to everyone, but the church's pastor, Reverend Daschle Hamill... or "Rev. "L" as his parishioners referred to him with affection. Sitting around the table, were Big Mo's five cohorts in crime.

"This is our final Sunday for a while till things settle down," Moorehead declared.

"Why the jitters, Mo?" asked Rev. "L." We've been at this for years and no one is the wiser!"

"Don't kid yourself "L," Moses Moorehead responded. "That bitch Jez Underwood has got the whole damn community focused on the school system. I can't buy a peach at the Publix without hearing someone talking about her latest report on our alleged corruption, mismanagement etc."

"So, who the fuck cares what they say at the grocery store!" Thaddeus Brown pounded his fist on the table.

"Who cares?" asked Moses. "You should care, that's who!"

Big Mo didn't have to stand to make a point. The tone in his voice said it all and his tone was telling Thaddeus that he was an idiot.

"Thad, she videotaped you selling French Champagne for a handful of cash, out of the trunk of your car behind some dive grocery mart in Liberty City, for God's sake! And might I remind you, that she got your time sheets and proved that you were on the taxpayer's nickel while you indulged in some debasing free enterprise! It cost you your job! The TV station didn't stop playing that video for over a week!" Big Mo was a black man turning purple with anger at his clueless friend. "You should care, moron! That's who!"

Thaddeus Brown hung his head. He knew when to shut up and take his licks. He knew Mo had a point, but Thad was chaffing at the idea that the group's little "cash cow" was going to dry up after today's Sunday service.

"So what's the game plan, Mo?" The question came from the man known by his nickname "The Transporter." He'd been given that name because it was his job to transport the money they collected at the church, to the Cayman Islands.

Big Mo didn't trust wire transfers. He insisted the cash be carried by one of the group, and personally deposited into the offshore bank account. After several years, that job had become the sole duty of "The Transporter."

"There's no game plan," Mo insisted. "We simply do the same thing we've done a million Sundays before today… only today will be our last hurrah!"

"Why?" It was Batman asking the simple question.

"Why? Because I say so!" screamed Moorehead. "And if anyone of you at this table have any more stupid questions, might I suggest you save them for your interrogation by the po-leece."

On a credenza opposite the Reverend "L's" conference table, sat Batman's briefcase. Inside it, a videotape was rolling.

****

"Praise Jesus! Amen! Hallelujah! Amen! Praise God! Amen! Hallelujah!"

Louise was black, but she hadn't been to a black church service in almost 10 years. She'd forgotten how devout and passionate African-American parishioners could be.

Louise was a 28-year old assistant producer at Channel 11, who'd gotten her big break at a paying TV job, after an internship at the station.

She really liked sports and wanted desperately to cover the Miami Heat, Marlins and the Miami Dolphins, but circumstances had placed her in special projects, in the investigative unit under Jez Underwood. Louise was in awe of Jez and the job she did, but working undercover was scaring the shit out of Louise.

"Turn to page 17 in your hymnals and join me in a rousing rendition of "Jesus Loves Me!" Reverend "L" stood and implored his flock to follow his lead.

"Jesus loves me yes I know, for the bible tells me so…" Louise cringed as she recited the words to what she'd always considered a children's song, but somehow, someway, today, an entire congregation of adults were belting out the same tune and making it sound like they were laying down the red carpet for the second coming of Christ!

She was suddenly aware of her purse cam, and began fidgeting with it, in hopes that she was getting videotape of the men who were now passing the offering plate.

Batman had told Jez, how Mo's group of deacons, of which he was one, passed the offering plate in order to make sure they maintained complete control of the money at all times.

He'd given her complete details of how Mo's group of thieves collected kickbacks from vendors and stole from taxpayers.

As fraud schemes went... Dr. Moses Moorehead had managed to create one of the biggest. It was basic at its core. He set up front companies, blackmailed vendors to do business with his phony "companies" in exchange for real business with the school district... and then made sure he got kickbacks from all vendors. Plain and simple! He cashed in on Sundays at church, odd, as that may seem. It provided him the cover he required. Moorehead wasn't a sophisticated man, but he wasn't stupid either. He'd survived for over 40 years, by making sure he kept his friends close and his enemies closer. Sure, he'd made mistakes. He'd occasionally trusted people he shouldn't have.

He'd allowed the media to get the best of him and show him in a bad light... like the time that Jez Underwood had chased him around the school administration's lobby with a microphone and a camera. He'd looked like a total ass when he'd just stared at her. He'd vowed that would never happen again.

He needed the public not to turn on him and Jez was doing a good job of making that happen. So Moorehead had tacked in a different direction, just like a sailor trying to grab the best wind.

Instead of running from her or engaging her in another "stare down," he spoke to her if she caught him, but he said as little as possible. And he acted as if this didn't make him nauseous. It had worked, to a degree.

You see, Jez had made a private vow to herself that if Moorehead ever granted her an interview, she'd stop using his middle name every time she said his name.

Jez had learned from ancient school documents she'd gotten her hands on, that Moses Arly Moorehead was christened, Arly Moses Moorehead. For whatever reason, he'd flipped his first and middle name, around the time he went to college, and was forever known as Moses. That is until Jez began using his second name as if it was painted on him. He hated it, and she knew it. Her sources told her so. It was her subtle way of irritating him... that wouldn't be obvious to her viewing audience.

But now, with three of the top district people dead, Moorehead knew he'd be put in the white, hot spotlight, not only by Jez Underwood, but also by the police. How he handled that could mean the difference between jail and no jail.
Batman had also told Jez how the group stole from Dr. "L's" parishioners, with the full knowledge and cooperation of the righteous Reverend.

Why church members never wondered about their church always being in a chronic state of disrepair, in spite of the money they generously gave each week, had constantly amazed Batman. He figured Reverend "L" did just enough to keep suspicions at bay. After all, who'd question a man of the cloth?

And since those in charge of the church's business affairs, were the same scheming thieves passing the plate each week, how would the mostly poor, undereducated, and trusting members of the faithful flock, know anything?
If this horrible scheme wasn't an argument for education, Batman didn't know what was.

After the offering was collected, each deacon headed upstairs to the pastor's conference room to count the day's spoils. Adding to the cash from the parishioners, was "The Transporter" and Thad Brown.

Both spent each week collecting, or rather extorting money from frightened teachers, janitors, bus drivers, cafeteria workers, principals, assistant principals, department directors, vendors and contractors, all of whom, knew that it was better to pay Big Mo than to piss him off.

That extortion money was then co-mingled every Sunday with the spoils from the collection plate. Upstairs, Big Mo and his group divvied up the cash. $1,000 was put in each man's pocket on the spot. The rest, usually in the tens of thousands, was handed to the Transporter, who would hop a flight to the Cayman's first thing Monday morning, to fatten the group's bank account.

Only this Sunday, the practice of picking the pockets of the parishioners was being videotaped!

Louise had done her best to position her "purse cam" to capture the faces of the deacons doing their "thing." Batman had left his briefcase near the alter for a wide shot of the crime... and he wore the glasses cam that he hoped had been rolling when the group of thieves gathered in the upstairs conference room to pass out the cash. He hadn't had a chance to double-check his equipment after arriving at the church. He was mostly busy watching the clock so he wouldn't forget to replace batteries. He was now just five minutes away from needing to do that. Shit! He thought.

Outside the church, in a parking lot across the street, Jez sat in the news van with Emeril. They hadn't talked much. Nerves were the great silencer on a stakeout.

"So, blondie, do ju sink they managed to get us some goot video?" Emeril smirked.

"If they didn't, I'll kill them myself!" Jez was nervous as a cat. She reached into her purse, unscrewed a prescription bottle, dumped a tiny peach pill into her hand and threw it toward the back of her throat,

"Taking a chill pill?" Emeril asked condescendingly.

"Yes!" Jez replied. "Want one?"

"No, chica."

They sat in silence for another 10 minutes, when Emeril decided to broach the subject of their boss, Boris Danken.

"Jez, ju know I love ju and would do anytink for ju, right?"

"Of course," Jez replied, as she picked at her nail cuticles... keeping an eagle eye on the front of the church.

"Then let me offer ju a bit of advice." Emeril turned in the driver's seat to look directly at her.

Jez, sensing a seriousness in Emeril's voice, looked over at him and said, "Sure, what?"

"Blondie, Boris is gunning for ju. That stunt ju pulled the other day, talking to him likes ju did and then clicking him off... well, I have it on goot authority that he went crazy! Crazy like nobody has ever seen him get. And that totie of his Allison, is jegging him on." Emeril paused to let his comments sink in.

"It's egging him on," Jez corrected Emeril.

"Jez, he's looking for a way to fire ju."

"I know Emeril." Jez turned back and stared at the front of the church for a second. "E," (that was her nickname for him) you know that in this business, you're only as good as your last story, and as long as I keep giving him good, no great stories, he'll tolerate me. He won't like it, but he'll do it. My good stories mean he has hopes of keeping his job... and I have hopes of keeping mine."

"I hope ju are right, Blondie. I hope ju know what ju're doink." Emeril turned back in his seat and began staring at the church again too.

Without looking in his direction, Jez quietly said, "Thank you for caring Emeril. It means a lot to me."

CHAPTER #40

One thing about black church services… they weren't short! After nearly three hours, parishioners began leaving the church. Louise cautiously approached the van, trying to act normal.

The minute she was in the backseat… Emeril put the pedal to the metal, shouting, "Outta here!"

Emeril, Jez and Louise drove about six blocks away from the Church of the Great Believer before they pulled over and parked. Jez phoned Batman and told them where to join them. He arrived a few minutes later.

He parked a safe distance away from the unmarked 11 News SUV, looked around, realized the coast was clear and then called Emeril, and gave him the OK to approach his car.

Emeril got out of the driver's side of the news van and sauntered over to the passenger side of Batman's car. Batman was hoping that anyone who might be observing this would think of it as nothing more than a drug deal going down.

Emeril got into the car and Batman immediately locked the doors.

"Please tell me ju got pictures," implored Emeril.

Batman was already stripping himself of the hidden camera gear and sighed, "God I hope so! I don't think I hit any wrong buttons."

Emeril rolled his eyes at Batman, as if to say, "You'll need more than hope, Chico!"

As Emeril took the recorder attached to Batman's glasses cam to check for video, he mumbled under his breath, "cos if ju got notink, Blondie is going to make you sink soprano."

"Thanks for the warning," Batman responded sarcastically.

Batman listened, expecting to hear a recorder in rewind, but digital video didn't do that. He was trying to read Emeril's face, but there was nothing, no reaction.

Suddenly, Emeril hit a button. At that very moment, Emeril looked up at Batman. He stared, as if boring a hole through Batman's brain.

"Well?" Batman questioned with a great sense of urgency.

Emeril wrinkled his forehead. "It's a little dark and shaky."

Batman realized his breathing was in limbo... hanging on Emeril's every word.

Then, without warning, Emeril burst into giggles of glee and began screaming, "Ju got it! Ju got every single think! My Got, I couldn't have jung it better myshelf!!"

As the two men realized that Batman had operated the camera equipment perfectly... they began "high fiving" each other. Immediately, Emeril motioned for Batman to come and see how his eyes had managed to document every aspect of the crime in the church.

CHAPTER #41

Donna Maine sat frozen in her car. Although she'd gone to the Church of the Great Believer to confront her dead husband's corrupt cronies... once she got to the church, she realized that she was conspicuously out of place, dressed to the nines in the wrong part of town.

"Shit," she muttered to herself.

She decided to re-group and re-think her plan.

Three hours later she was still sitting in her car, having decided the best plan of action, was to wait for Dr. Moses Moorehead to leave the church.

Although most of the parishioners had already filed out, Donna had still not seen Moses Moorehead.

"What is taking him so damn long," she said to no one in particular. She squirmed in her car seat, having realized just how full her bladder was and how badly it wanted to burst.

As she contemplated how long it would take her to get to a safe part of town to find a suitable place to crash into a ladies restroom, she glimpsed Moorehead's profile as he left the side entrance to the church and got into his large maroon Lincoln Town car. As he drove away, Donna peeled out after him.

"Oh, shit!" Donna Maine suddenly realized she was tailing a person like the cops did in those TV shows, and yet she knew nothing about tailing.

"I don't know where I am. I don't know what I'm doing, I must be crazy!"

Not knowing how to follow a car, she found herself too far back and ended up running two red lights to keep up with him.

"Fuck!" she shouted as she blew through the second stoplight.

Visions of a cop handcuffing her and hauling her off to jail in her Lilac St. John's knit suit, popped into her mind.

"Well at least I'll look good in my booking photo," she thought, as she followed Dr. Moses Moorehead through Miami's inner city.

Eventually, Big Mo, in his big Lincoln, pulled into the parking lot of the Outpost Lounge. It was a popular place for Miami's black elite, even though it's façade looked like a condemned building, stripped of exterior paint by hurricanes, windows replaced by sheets of plywood... roof tiles missing, a neon sign dangling from the side of the building and not one tree standing to provide any shade for a parking lot that was nothing but pea rock mixed with gravel.

Donna pulled into the parking lot and was somewhat taken aback at the number of luxury cars parked there on a Sunday afternoon.

She saw Big Mo park and leave, his car lights flashing as he locked the vehicle by remote. Quickly, she seized the moment and raced towards him, forgetting to lock her own car doors.

"Moses! Moses!" she called after him. He stopped in his tracks and turned around to see her running towards him, tottering in the gravel in her spiked lavender designer high heels.

"Donna, what a pleasant surprise. How are you? You know how badly I feel for our loss of Hank."

Instantly, it dawned on Moorehead to wonder, "How the hell did she know I was here?"

"Moses, we need to talk," Donna announced determinedly.

Mo's mind was racing. She must have followed me! And if this idiot woman can do so, so easily, who else can? His mind was spinning as if it was a tilt-a-whirl.

A master at playing dumb… Mo looked at her and replied, "Donna, my dear, whatever is on your mind? You know I'm here for you, but this really isn't the place, the parking lot of a club."

To which Donna replied, "Moses, I need to use the ladies room. Would you accompany me inside?" He put his arm out and she placed her hand on it, in a demonstration that made it appear as if they were a couple.

Once inside, he directed her to the ladies room, where she peed like a racehorse! Finally comfortable for the first time in three hours, Donna Maine walked over to the mirrored sink where she checked her flawless makeup.

When she emerged, she finally had the empty bladder and clear head to look around the place. She quickly came to the realization that the "club" was full of black men and a few women who looked as though they were… well… not exactly "church ladies." OK, she thought, they're goddamn prostitutes!

Mo was at the bar talking with one of the "painted ladies" and another man when she returned. She approached him and repeated, "Moses, we need to talk." This time she was half whispering.

"Sure darl'n, but first you need to quench your thirst and chill a bit. It's on me." Big Mo handed her an ice filled highball cocktail.

Parched after sitting in her car for hours, and finally having relieved her bladder, Donna suddenly realized how thirsty she was. So, instead of sipping, she all but drained the glass in a quest to wet her dry throat. It would be the last thing she'd remember.

CHAPTER #42

Sunday was anything but a day of rest for cops at the Miami Police Department.

Capt. Sheila Cohen was in house, as were all the members of her investigative team working on the Hank Maine murder.

"What are we going to do about all of this child porn?" she asked out loud, rubbing her temples to try and stave off an emerging migraine.

Detective Gonzalez didn't hesitate to respond. "I'll get right to the point Captain. We have to call in the FBI." He allowed his words to hang in the air. Capt. Cohen didn't respond, so Gonzalez pressed on.

"Can you imagine if this hits the media? You can forget about Miami's overcrowded classrooms, because parents won't let their kids even go to school! The Feds have a much tougher "no comment" policy, and besides, child porn is really more their jurisdiction, since it probably involves crimes committed across state lines or even across continents."

That reality had already dawned on Sheila Cohen while she tossed and turned trying to sleep the night before. It's the reason a migraine headache was creeping up on her now.

"Who's got the off-hour phone number for the Special Agent in Charge?" she finally asked.

"I do," Detective Gonzalez, volunteered.

"Call him," Capt. Cohen ordered. She then left for her private office.

On the street corner, just outside Cohen's corner office, a member of her investigative team was punching in a number on his cell phone. As he did, he ordered a hot dog from the street vendor. After putting gobs of mustard and relish on his hot Sabrette… he walked off and hit dial.

A woman answered. "Investigations. This is Jez."

Emeril, Louise and Jez were back at the station dubbing the surveillance tape from the church onto broadcast quality videotape.

It was afternoon, and none of them had eaten since very early in the morning, so the conversation had turned to ideas for lunch. That's when Jez's cell phone began to ring.

Smart people never separated starving news people from their food, which was why Jez was so grateful for caller ID. Another reason she loved that feature of modern day communications... it told her when someone really important was calling. The number she saw meant an important source was on the line.

"What's up?" she asked... without the pleasantries of courteous phone manners.

The voice on the other end was the familiar one she expected to hear. "They're taking everything to the FBI."

"When?" Jez asked.

"Pretty darn soon."

"It must be bad," she inquired.

"You have no fucking idea!"

"I don't need the full Megillahcuty, darl'in, I just need enough to lead tonight's 11pm news. Can you do it?" Jez held her breath.

The pregnant pause on the other end of the line sent chills up her spine. Was her source going to wimp out?

"I noticed your front tires were low. Go get some air at the Shell station at 36th and Biscayne in an hour. Tell Phillip you need a dollars' worth of quarters for the air machine. Got it?"

"Got it," Jez replied. "An hour. Thank you so much!" Jez heard a click and the phone went dead.

CHAPTER #43

Sunday was opening day at Flamingo Gardens Race Track, and it could not have been a more perfect one, for the start of pony season. The sky was a gleaming blue and cloudless, the temperature was a perfect 74 degrees, the track conditions were "good," and the first race of the season had a $250,000 purse.

The first race at Miami's historic track was just 20 minutes away and Lee and Lily Molina were studying the racing form as if it was an SAT prep paper. They were sitting in the superintendent's private box at the racetrack, along with Dr. Moses Moorehead, School Board President Jewel Haynes and her husband Turo.

"I'm not listening to any of your racing advise after last season, you asshole!"

Lily Molina was still ticked that her husband's advice on winning money at the horse races last year had cost her $20,000. Technically, the money came from her personal checking account. But it was always replenished with money she took out of her department's budget. It was a simple matter of a phony purchase order here and there, bogus mileage, or some dummy receipts from principals special purpose accounts. School principals who wanted to stay on her good side knew they had better help her out.

"Fine!" Lee Molina just wanted his screeching wife to go away. "I don't care how you bet, Silly Lily. Just shut up and do it!"

"Did you see the name of the 5th horse in this race Lee?" Lily was pointing to the racing form as she shoved it under her husband's nose.

"I wear glasses Lily, I don't need to have you shove the small print in my face," Lee barked, as he took a swig of scotch. It was his third one, and the races hadn't even started yet. At that very moment, he saw what Lily was pointing at.

"HIGH IQ." That was the name of horse number 5 in the first race... and the reason for Lily's incessant chattering.

"It's a sign Lee!" Lily screamed! "A horse with an educational name. We have to bet the farm on this one!"

"Lily, we don't have a farm, and even if we did, I wouldn't allow you to bet it on a horse, never mind one that was 50 to 1 odds." Lee Molina shook his head in disgust.

"Fine! I'll only bet $200 on number five to win." Lily was undeterred.

"It's your money, honey," Lee muttered as Lily marched off toward the pari-mutuel windows. "Or rather your district money," he said quietly under his breath.

On the track, the tractors had moved out to begin grading the dirt, behind them the watering trucks followed. The tractor pulling the starting cages was not far behind. Suddenly, the driver in the first tractor screamed and slammed on the brakes.

Twenty feet in front of him was the body of a blonde woman in a lilac colored outfit, dumped in the dirt and muck of the racetrack at Flamingo Gardens.

CHAPTER #44

"Hey Phillip! I think my goddamn front tires are low. You know these fancy foreign cars better than me. Can you help me gauge the air in my tires?"

Jez was putting on her best helpless female act. Fortunately, she was debasing herself in front of someone who knew her better than to think she was a vacuous, dumb blonde, who didn't know a tire gauge from a gas gauge!

"Sure Jez," replied Phillip Rose, owner of the Shell station where Jez had been told to get the drop from her source.

Phillip was a robust guy, with a big heart and kind soul, who'd carved out a very good living running service stations around Miami. He was a "huge Papa Bear," who nurtured his kids like "Mama Bear" when his ex-wife went nuts on him, and left town.

Jez had known Phillip long before he'd bought one of the most profitable gas stations in all of Miami. When she'd live on Miami Beach, it was his station where she had her car serviced, gassed up and basically taken care of.

"I only have dollar bills Phillip, and the air machine takes quarters. Can you give me change, please?" Jez wondered how her source knew about her friendship with Phillip, and why he was being used for this secretive purpose.

"Here Jez," said Phillip, "four quarters for a dollar."

Phillip, who was standing behind the cashier counter, took her one-dollar bill. He then handed her four quarters and hooked a plastic bag on her index finger.

"That should take care of you Jez." Phillip gave her a look that made Jez think he wanted her out of there as fast as she could move, so she did just that.

"Thanks," she said, and was gone.

Jez took about 60 seconds to get from Phillip's gas station back to Channel 11. As she raced inside, she suddenly came face to face with Boris.

"What the hell are you doing here on a Sunday, Boris?" she asked.

"Same thing as you Underhanded. I'm working."

"You're working on your resume tape, too?" Jez, sassed back, biting her lip to keep from busting a gut.

"No, I'm here trying to cut you out of all the promotions of our newscasts!" Boris wasn't usually that quick on his feet. She gave him a A- for the comeback.

"Why? Because I'm not a size 2, with 38 DD breasts, and am pushing 50? Shame on you Boris! I think that constitutes dis-crimination!" Jez winked at her boss on the outside, but was fuming on the inside.

"So sue me Jez!"

"Boris, I would, if I didn't know what a big waste of my time it would be to target such a panty waist..."

As Jez opened her mouth to spew more vindictive venom than Boris had ever heard, she suddenly turned.

"Hey blondie. Get your ass upstairs. We have an exclusive to prep for tonight's 11pm news."

It was Emeril to her rescue.

"What exclusive?" Boris was now more interested in what she could do for him than what she was saying about him.

"It seems that Dep. Supt. Hank Maine had an addiction to pornography, including, but not limited to, child pornography." Jez stopped talking.

"How do you know?" Boris had quickly put his news director hat on... forgetting all about Jez's verbal insubordination.

"Because I have videotape proof." Jez raised her right arm. In her hand she held the videotape of one of Dr. Hank Maine's porn videos passed to her by her cop source.

"Why are we standing here?" Boris screeched! "Get that videotape to pre-production, promotion and all the news editors. I want clips of it on the air every commercial break from now until we lead with this at 11pm!"

Jez couldn't believe that her boss, the editorial Czar of the newsroom, wouldn't even ask to see some of the video himself. It appeared as though he was going to allow "his people" in the newsroom to handle everything.

Jez was shocked and nervous. Could this be his way of setting her up, she wondered? Maybe he was smarter than she gave him credit for. No. She was being paranoid, she thought. Boris was a news director. Smart had nothing to do with his job title!

It was simply the way the news business operated in today's world. Fact checking had gone the way of the dinosaurs. In the new millennium, it was all about "get it on," worry about the fallout later. So far, Boris had operated in the "Instantaneous Zone" without repercussions. Jez thought it was time he was called on it.

As Boris walked away, Jez turned to Emeril and said, " dub the worst stuff of that tape for the editors "E." We'll show Mr. Danken what happens when he takes his eyes off his newscasts, and leaves the editorial content to his pathetic minions."

"Blondie, you can't..." Emeril was horrified at what he knew Jez was proposing.

"Watch me poor refugee!" Jez was adamant. "I'm going to teach that son of a bitch a lesson about life and news gathering in his hyper-active video world, even if it gets me fired!"

Jez grabbed Emeril by the hand and led him off toward the video room where the worst of the terrible tape was cued up.

It ws the tape her source had hand fed her. The tape that she hoped would bring her dastardly boss to his knees.

CHAPTER #45

Carlo loved horse racing! So he always made sure his cal-
endar was clear for the first day of races at Flamingo Gardens. The ponies were a secret indulgence he allowed himself, as long as his losses didn't exceed his gains by more
than 10%. He was so disciplined, that he could just walk
away from the track if his self-imposed limit was breached.
No track was going to make a killing bilking Carlo Ferrini, he
swore. His partner, Orlando, accompanied him and it gave
them some quality time together.

As he stood in line outside the betting window, preparing to
bet a Quinella on the first race… he heard a voice over the
loud speaker.

"Ladies and gentlemen, may I please have your attention.
Due to unforeseen circumstances, the races scheduled for
today at Flamingo Gardens have been cancelled. We apolo-
gize for this departure from our normal routine, and hope that
you will join us tomorrow, when Florida's most prestigious
racetrack features a day of races for 3-year olds only! Thank
you for your business and your patience."

"What the hell?" thought Carlo, just as the thousands of people at the track screamed in an uproar!

Separating a player from his or her ponies was not a smart
move for any track owner, so Carlo knew something really
bad had to have happened to get track officials to end the
day before it began.

The sounds of people clamoring for their money back at the
pari-mutuel windows, was exceeded only by the fury of
those who'd planned a full day of fun at the track, and hadn't
even had the chance to win the price of a hot dog!

"This is insane," grumbled a white haired man in a Hawaiian
shirt standing next to him.

"I don't get it either," Carlo responded.

"Yo! Baldy!" shouted a punk two people over. Carlo turned. "You ole timers know what da fuck is going on here?"

Carlo shrugged, hoping that a failure to communicate would get the guy to go away.

"Pops!" Carlo turned again. "I'm talking to you! Don't diss me like I'm some kind of used Kotex!" The punk kid was a character right out of some bad "C" rated mob movie, and Carlo wanted no part of him.

"I believe the police sirens I hear approaching the track are "da" reason for "da" inconvenience you are experiencing." Carlo hoped the junior "wise guy" didn't understand his mocking imitation of the low life.

"No fuck'n way!" With that declaratory phrase, Carlo watched as the punk ran off... leaving Carlo to ponder the reason for the sirens that grew louder with every second.

It was at that very moment, he glimpsed the profile of Dr. Moses Moorehead scurrying toward the exit, followed by what could only be described, as Big Mo's posse.

Because an ambulance was always on call at the track and was always bringing up the rear once the horses were racing... it was pretty easy for the track bosses to get emergency personnel to the woman in lilac.

"Somebody did a shitty job of burying this poor gal," one of the Emergency Medical Techs commented as the other furiously tried to read her vital signs, that is, if there were any.

"Shut up and put the cuff on her." The EMT was referring to a blood pressure cuff. He'd already felt a faint pulse in her neck, and was pretty certain she wasn't dead... but how close she was to final prayers, he wasn't sure.

The first EMT decided to try and administer mouth to mouth. No sooner had he started trying to breathe fresh oxygen in her lungs, than the woman in lilac began huffing and coughing and screaming, "Get off me you fucking wack job! I'll sue your ass ten ways from Sunday if you don't get your tongue out of my throat!" She abruptly sat upright.

"Ma'am, I'm with the ambulance service. We thought you were dead," the EMT informed her. He was a simple WASPY country boy from North Florida, who'd always been taught to respect his elders, but this woman was making it hard for him to do just that.

"So does that give you any right to kiss a dead woman?" Donna Maine was back to her old self again... sort of.

"No ma'am, I wasn't kissing you..." but before he could finish his sentence the widow Maine was thrashing him with her fists and screaming something about her ruined designer suit.

"Who are you?" she screeched, just as the EMT's put her on a gurney and up into the ambulance.

"We're here to help you ma'am," responded one of the EMT's.

"Help me? Where am I? What's going on here?" screamed Donna Maine, just before they injected her with a sedative. The last thing they heard her say before she went unconscious was, "Do you know who I am? My name is Mrs. Hank Maine," she slurred as her eyes shut.

The EMT's slammed the ambulance doors, turned on the siren, and sped away to the nearest hospital, followed by several police cars that had just arrived with lights and sirens running.

As the crowd poured out of Flamingo Gardens Race Track, Moses Moorehead was making a quick getaway, observed by Carlo Ferrini.

CHAPTER #46

"Stand by," yelled the floor director at the Channel 11 news studio.

"Five, four, three, two, one."

Dean Sands postured in his anchorman sort of way, and began reading from the teleprompter, a script that had been revised up until the moment he sat in his anchor chair. It was the first Sunday of a major ratings period, and Sands seven figure contract depended on viewers trusting his every word.

Sands sat upright. His demeanor either conveyed authority, or a broom up his butt.

"Tonight," Sands began, "11 News has shocking details of a secret life. A life led by Deputy Miami Schools Superintendent Dr. Hank Maine. A life filled with secrets, uncovered by our Investigative Reporter Jez Underwood. She joins us now with a very disturbing report. Jez?"

"Dean," Jez began... "If anyone watching this newscast is under the age of 21... we ask that you turn us off. That is hardly a request a news station would ever ask of its viewers. But we are very serious in our need to caution anyone who is currently tuned in to 11 News. What you are about to see is offensive at best, horrific at worst. Even adult viewers should be warned, the video you are about to see is alarming."

Jez knew viewers were like children... tell them not to do something or look at something and, of course, they would!

"It's like a train wreck, boss. Nobody wants to look, but they do."

It was a difficult sell convincing Boris to actually ask viewers to turn off a newscast that was in the ratings dumper, but after she'd explained her version of reverse psychology, Boris had reluctantly agreed to try the idea. He knew they'd have to warn viewers anyway, so he'd let Jez have her way. But he made it perfectly clear that if her idea bombed, she'd shoulder the entire blame.

"And what if it succeeds?" Jez had asked him.

"Then I'm a genius and you aren't jobless!" What a prick, Jez thought. Just when she didn't think she could dislike him anymore than she already did, he found a way to make himself more despicable.

As Jez's videotaped story began to play for viewers, she momentarily tuned out the audio in her ear and began thinking about the sounds of channels changing to 11 News.

She was confident that she could hear the sound of school board employees grabbing their telephones and calling all their friends, relatives and colleagues to turn on Channel 11. Jez knew the rumor mill was already working overtime, mostly because she'd made a few "heads up" phone calls to some top school officials and sources. She'd also been obligated to phone the system's spokesman for comment, and she'd tried but failed to contact Donna Maine.

Switching back to reality, Jez began listening to her report, and observing the reaction from the anchors and studio crew. She'd learned long ago that they were always a good barometer of what the public's reaction might be.

Jez Underwood stood in front of the video monitor located in the main news studio at Channel 11. It was a gigantic TV screen, the likes of which, any man, woman or child would want in their home.

Meanwhile, on TV screens of all sizes, videotape of child pornography was coming into viewer's homes.

Jez heard her audio track.

"The stabbing death on Wednesday of Dr. Hank Maine, has unleashed a torrent of evidence of a disturbing, secret life, few in this community could have imagined was being led by the second most powerful administrator in the Miami School

System. In addition to our reports on the ladies lingerie Dr. Maine was wearing at the time of his death… 11 News has obtained one of the thousands of pornographic items, confiscated from Maine's home. You will only see this videotape on 11 News. We have disguised the faces, but you can clearly see young boys relieving themselves at urinals, in what appears to be a school bathroom. The children appear to be as young as five or six years old. The video camera used to tape these images, was set up in a manner so as to capture a full frontal view of the boys genitals.

"Jesus Christ!" Jez heard one of the camera guys say. "What a sick bastard."

"Jez!" Dean shouted at her across the studio. "Is this in a Miami school?"

As if to answer him, her audio track continued.

"We cannot say for certain if this is video from inside a Miami school. Police sources would neither confirm nor deny the location. But viewers may remember another 11 News exclusive we broke last year. It too, involved Dr. Maine's use of videotape. We uncovered how he used hidden surveillance cameras to spy on board member's offices, including cameras set up in the administrative bathrooms at district headquarters. In addition to the scenes in the bathroom with the small boys, are scenes from inside what is clearly a school classroom."

The video switched to a scene of five children lined up in front of small school desks, as if they'd been ordered to the front of the classroom, except all the desks behind them were empty of classmates.

Jez's report continued.

"Again, we have purposely disguised the faces of the children. In this clip, the kids, both boys and girls, begin to undress. Pacing in front of them is the image of what appears to be an adult male. The angle of the camera is only able to capture images of the adult from the waist down. The kids appear reluctant. Here you can see the adult banging some kind of cane or large stick on the floor, which prompts the children to speed up the removal of their underwear. The next image shows the adult's hand reaching toward the first child, a boy, and grabbing his genitals."

For two brief seconds, the video shows a large hand massaging the boy's penis. Then the video freezes.

Jez continued.

"We will spare our viewers the rest of what is a most disturbing tape. Instead, we have frozen the video here, so we can show you a close up view of the adult's hand."

The video began to jerk as it zoomed in ever tighter and tighter on the hand.

"What you are looking at is a large ring on the index finger of a man's right hand." The video then zoomed in even closer to the top of the ring.

"11 News can confirm that this is a male class ring, that at one time, was the style of class rings ordered by graduates of Miami Community Junior College back in the late 60's. The raised letters MCJC can be seen. This appears to be a very similar ring to the one worn by Dr. Hank Maine on his right index finger. Maine graduated from MCJC in 1969. For a closer comparison, 11 News went to our archives for videotape of Dr. Maine from last year. Viewers may recall the tussle I had with Dr. Maine, when I tried to interview him about the hidden cameras in the administrative building... and he reached out and grabbed the microphone from me. Again, we have frozen the moment when he put his right hand on the microphone. And we have zoomed in on the ring he was wearing on his right index finger at that moment."

Suddenly the screen split and the image of a man's finger on a microphone appeared on one side of the screen, the image of a man's finger on a child's penis was on the other side.

"It will be up to authorities to decide if this is the same hand and the same ring in both videos. But, as you can see, in both images, a similar looking hand is wearing an MCJC class ring on his right index finger."

"Stand by," the floor director shouted to his stunned crew and the news talent in the studio.

Jez was back live on camera.

"11 News was unable to reach Dr. Maine's widow. Donna Maine did not return any of our numerous phone calls. As for the school system, their spokesman declined to comment on a videotape they haven't seen. Instead, he referred our calls to the Miami Police Department. Dean, back to you."

Dean Sands sat at the anchor desk as if mummified by what he'd just seen on the air. As he stammered to collect his thoughts, upon seeing the red tally light on the camera, indicating it was on him, he only managed to speak the words "We'll be right back."

As Channel 11 faded to black and went to a car commercial, the phone lines inside the newsroom lit up like neon signs on South Beach.

CHAPTER #47

The phone in Boris Danken's home was also ringing.

"Hello," he answered.

"Are you fucking crazy?" screamed the male voice on the other end of the line.

"Be in my office in 30 minutes!" As Boris heard the phone connection go dead, he realized the voice screaming at him was his boss, the station's General Manager, Tab Tanner.

"Shit! Shit! Shit!" Danken had heard Tanner get mad before, but never like this. There was a tone in his voice that was almost demonic sounding. Danken quickly threw on a pair of jeans and a tee shirt... one that said "11 News" in big bold letters. If he was going to be fired, he'd do it with his uniform on.

"I've been summoned to the station by Tanner," Boris turned to inform his overnight guest. "I don't know when I'll be back, or if I'll ever be seen alive again."

"Why?" his friend asked. "I thought the story was huge!"

"So did I," Boris commented as he zipped up his jeans. "But I guess the boss sees it as a huge mess." Just then, Boris' Nextel clicked. It was the newsroom calling.

"Boris! Boris!" It was his executive producer.

"I'm here Warren."

"The phones are going crazy!" Warren Fletcher was screaming at the top of his lungs, much like Tab Tanner, Boris thought. "We can't begin to handle all these calls man. Will you authorize overtime so I can get some people in here to help with this mess?"

Mess. There was that word again, thought Boris. Suddenly, his heart was palpitating and he had the notion that he might mess himself. There was that word again!

"Yes! Yes! Do whatever you have to, to deal with this mess. I'm on my way in. Tanner wants to meet with me."

"That can't be good," Fletcher responded.

No shit braniac, thought Boris. "Yeah! Thanks for stating the obvious Warren."

The Nextel clicked and went silent.

CHAPTER #48

From the time Donna Maine had arrived at County line Hospital, she'd been surrounded by cops. The uniformed guys had been instructed not to let her out of their sight by the homicide detectives, investigating her husband's murder.

After being wheeled into the emergency room following her transport from the racetrack, Donna Maine had finally been moved to a private room, largely because the police needed her under guard. The widow of a stabbing victim who was found dumped at a racetrack as if she was a dead person, had triggered all kinds of bells and whistles with law enforcement.

While authorities looked on, doctors had drawn blood for a Tox screen, hooked Mrs. Maine up to an I-V, taken her vitals, and generally let her sleep off the sedation the EMT's had informed them they'd been forced to give the hysterical woman.

Capt. Cohen didn't waste any time rushing back to Mrs. Maine's hospital room. In light of the unauthorized release of one of their evidence tapes, meaning the video of the kid at the urinal, that Jez and shown, Cohen was determined to handle the situation herself. Her determination was partly motivated by an hysterical phone call from her police chief following the promotions of Jez's report at 11pm.

As Sheila Cohen slowly pushed open the hospital door to Donna Maine's room, she was surprised to see the widow Maine sitting up, instead of passed out in the reclined position.

"Mrs. Maine, I'm Capt. Sheila Cohen of the Miami Police Department. I'm going to need to ask you some questions. Is that ok?"

Donna Maine might have been sitting up, but she was anything but coherent. As her head fell from one side of her shoulders to another, Donna Maine slurred some incoherent words that sounded somewhat like, "I'm Donna Maine. Do I know who I am? I'm Donna Maine. Who am I do you think you are?"

Oh, God, thought Capt. Cohen. This is not a woman ready for a police interrogation. She turned to the uniformed officer sitting near Maine's bed and told him to call her when she was alert and sane!

"Will do," the officer replied.

Capt. Cohen then turned, grabbed the door handle, only to be startled as the door pushed back at her before she could pull it open. Standing in the doorway was Dr. Moses Moorehead, the "stealth" superintendent of the Miami School System.

In his well-known raspy voice, Moses Moorehead apologized for startling the police Capt.

"Puhleeze forgive me Capt. I was just so anxious to attend to the needs of my dear friend's widow. I did not mean to startle you."

"Not a problem, Dr. Moorehead," Capt. Cohen insisted.

"How is our dear Donna?" Moorehead asked.

"Still a bit out of it," responded Cohen. "And I'm afraid she is not able to receive visitor's sir." Cohen suddenly realized she was in a stare down with the powerful Moses Moorehead.

"Reaaaly?" he said in that southern drawl of his.

"Really." Cohen responded in a short and succinct one-syllable reply.

"That's a tuurrible shame," Big Mo responded, trying to hide his growing anger.
"Becuz we at the school board try to look out after our ooowwen."

"That is so wonderful Dr. Moorehead. But we at the police department try to look out after our investigations. As a result, you are not welcome here right now, sir." Cohen held her ground.

"Of coouurse, Captain." Big Mo knew when to retreat. He was corrupt, but no dummy.

"I'll come back to see Donna when you wonderful law folks have decided she can see old friends. You will let me know, won't you Captain?" Big Mo wasn't budging.

"I will personally let you know, Dr. Moorehead. Thank you for your cooperation."

With that blow off, Moses Moorehead turned on his heels and walked off down the hospital hallway, playing with his flip hair as he left.

Capt. Cohen, still holding the door open, turned to the uniformed officer and said, "Don't you dare leave this room, or let anyone but a cop in here. I'm immediately putting three more uniformed officers on guard duty to help you out and cover her door. Until then, guard this somnambulist as if she was the President of the United States."

Sgt. Cohen then turned and exited.

CHAPTER #49

Carlo Ferrini hadn't stopped talking on the phone, ever since Jez's story had aired at 11. His call-waiting beeped incessantly, and conversations on his home phone, were repeatedly interrupted by his cell phone ringing.

Carlo wanted desperately to call Jez, but he couldn't get off the phone to do it.

"My God Carlo, did you see Jez's report?" It was his mother, a huge Underwood fan.

"Damn, man, Jez hit a home run tonight! Call me." It was his secretary.

"Carlo, it's Penelope! I hope to hell you caught Channel 11's news a few minutes ago. Jez has got the entire district twisting in the wind. Call me."

And so the messages went, piling up like garbage at Mt. Trashmore, South Florida's famous or infamous landfill.

But the only phone call Carlo insisted on returning was the one from Donna Maine. She'd sounded drugged in the message she left him. She mentioned something about being under guard in a hospital room. She was slurring her words. Somehow, she'd managed to leave a phone number. Carlo called it immediately.

"County Line Hospital," a voice said.

"Donna Maine's room please," Carlo declared. There was a pause... and Carlo could hear the clicking of nails on a computer keyboard.

"I'm sorry sir, but that patient has a block on her calls." The anonymous voice informed Carlo that he could try again tomorrow, then wished him a good night and hung up.

Carlo was puzzled. County Line Hospital was at least 15 miles from where Donna lived, and wouldn't exactly be the first place she'd elect to go if she had a medical emergency. So why was she there? On the other hand, Carlo thought, County Line was just blocks from the racetrack where he'd spent part of his afternoon, before an announcement had ended his big day of betting.

He'd been wondering why the track had shut down. But after flipping channels until he nearly had carpel tunnel syndrome from working his remote, he'd not heard one word on any station about opening day's abrupt ending at the track.

Privately he wondered, did Donna's hospitalization have anything to do with the troubles at the track? He quickly dismissed the idea as too ridiculous.

Jogging him out of his introspective thoughts, Carlo suddenly heard the phone ringing again.

"Hello," he answered.

"Mr. Ferrini, this is detective Hal Davis. I've been informed that you just tried to call Mrs. Hank Maine. Sir, I need to ask you why you were contacting Donna Maine at such a late hour."

Carlo was stunned. Why were the police involved in Donna's hospitalization, and why did they know who was calling her.

"Detective, I was merely returning Mrs. Maine's phone call to me earlier this evening. Now can I ask you a question?"

There was no response on the other end of the line. "OK, forget your permission, why are you monitoring calls to Donna Maine, and why is she in a hospital?" Ferrini was determined.

"Mr. Ferrini, we'd appreciate it if you'd be at the hospital tomorrow morning at 9:00."

"I'll be there." Carlo Ferrini clicked off and then sat staring at his phone handset as if it would somehow speak to him about what was going on. It didn't!

CHAPTER #50

Boris Danken pulled into the station's parking lot exactly 25 minutes after he'd gotten the call from Tab Tanner. Boris parked his convertible BMW 740i in the covered spot that was part of his employment perks. He had the top down... hoping the wind whipping his head would somehow calm his ever-increasing jitters that he was about to lose his job.

As he was getting out of his car, he heard the screeching of tires and brakes and horns honking. As he looked up, he saw the sleek, ice blue Jaguar that Tanner drove, wheeling into the station's parking lot and coming to a dead halt in the GM's covered parking spot.

Slowly, Boris approached Tanner's car. He saw Tab with his head on the steering wheel. Had he knocked himself unconscious, Boris wondered?

"What the fuck are you looking at?" Tanner's voice was stronger than the visual of a man slumped against a steering wheel would have telegraphed.

"Nothing Tab. You asked me to be in your office in 30 minutes. By my calculations, we both have two minutes in order to be on time." Boris stopped talking.

"Always the smartass aren't you," bellowed Tab Tanner as he looked up from his steering wheel repose.

"Let's take a ride to the fifth floor, junior." And with that statement, both Tanner and Danken headed for the front door of the station. Tanner slid his ID card through the security machine... and both of them walked onto the elevator. Tanner hit the button to the fifth floor. Boris didn't move.

"You show video of a man's hand jerking off a kindergartener and call that news?" Tab Tanner was pacing like a caged lion, even though he was technically not caged at all, but in his plush 5th floor office.

"Tab... let me explain..." Boris could barely begin the semblance of an excuse before his boss began shouting again.

"Tab," the General Manager said, now mocking Boris. "I want to explain why I'm such a dunderhead! Why I let this station of great repute, become the laughing stock of the entire TV news industry, and why you, as General Manager, will be a broadcast outcast, from now until all eternity! Does that about sum up all your failings tonight Boris?" Tab Tanner was as red in the face as a sunburned snowbird from Canada.

"Tab... let me explain," Boris Danken tried again.

Tanner's high pitched mocking continued.

"Tab, I'm such an idiot News Director, I had no idea we'd be broadcasting child pornography to the world. I thought the tape would only air in Miami!" Tanner had now grabbed Boris by his crotch. "How does it feel to have someone squeeze your balls, Boris? Because if this feels uncomfortable, just imagine how your males are going to hurt when I drop kick them into Newfoundland!!!" Tanner gave one last squeeze and then let go of Boris's jeans.

Tab Tanner wasn't finished.

"Don't for one minute think you are going to shove this mess onto Jez. Whatever she did, good or bad, was done under your reign. You are the news director. You get the blame and the "atta boys." Right now there are no "atta boys" for you in my vocabulary." Tanner stood facing Boris, as close to him as if they might kiss.

Suddenly, Tanner reached for his crystal handled letter opener... pulled it up as if it was a dagger... and began chasing Boris around his desk screaming, "I'll kill you, you mother fucker! I'll kill you, you fucking motherfucker! Stand still so I can kill you mother fucking, mother fucker!"

Danken managed to reach the G-M's door and fled down the fifth floor hallway as Tanner ran after him... letter opener in hand.

CHAPTER #51

It was nearly 2:00a.m. before Jez got home.

First there were the phone calls that had flooded the newsroom as well as Jez's personal line. While she was trying to
handle the barrage of calls from friends and sources who
knew her private number, the newsroom staff was scrambling to answer the constantly ringing phones, not only at the
assignment desk, but it seems every human being who knew
one of the other reporters or any person on the news department's staff had decided to try and reach them on their
private lines.

The cacophony of different ring tones was more than Jez
could handle. So after about an hour, she got up from her
desk to go to the bathroom. As she was walking down the
hall, the stairway doors by the water fountain suddenly burst
open and Jez saw Boris Danken running for the lobby door.
Before she could open her mouth to say anything, she heard
screaming like a wild animal. Except the animal was screaming something about killing the motherfucker.

Jez had barely begun to process the scene in front of her,
when Tab Tanner came rushing through the same stairway
door. Jez froze in her tracks as she realized that Tanner was
running through the station's lobby with his crystal-handled
letter opener raised above his head as if he was planning on
bludgeoning someone to death. The scene was eerily remi-
niscent of a moment she'd had last year with Tanner in his
office. What was it with him and that letter opener, she wondered?

Her inner thoughts were quickly shoved aside, as she realized that her general manager was running after her news
director with a sharp object... threatening to kill him. Suddenly Jez was running too. Now the scene was officially the
Three Stooges, as Jez, a reporter, chased after her general
manager, who was chasing his news director shouting death
threats so loudly, that the population of Cuba probably heard
the dust up!

"Tanner!" shouted Jez as she exited the lobby door into the parking lot. No reaction.

"Tab!" No reaction.

She watched as Tanner ran in between cars, zigging and zagging, trying to catch Boris. Just when Jez had decided things couldn't get any worse than two grown men running serpentines, one armed with a letter opener, it did.

As Jez ran past the security guard's shack, she saw the "rent-a-cop" come out of her office with her gun drawn.

"No Izzy! No Izzy! Put the gun down," Jez shouted at the guard while also trying to keep one eye on Tab and Boris.

"Problemo, miss! Problemo miss Jez?" Izzy shouted at Underwood.

"No Izzy! No problemo! Just macho stuffo," Jez replied, knowing full well that this sweet woman waving a revolver spoke very little English. The native language of the United States of America was apparently not a job requirement to be a security guard.

"No, no. No, no Izzy! Jez make ok aquí! Comprendo?" Jez was trying to tell Izzy the guard that she'd take care of everything here. But her restaurant Spanish was undoubtedly an impediment in conferring that information. Shit! Thought Jez. I really should have taken that Berlitz Spanish class last year.

No sooner had Jez said "aquí," meaning here... than Izzy began racing toward the two men who were now tussling like two-second grade bullies on the playground.

Boris had obviously tried to get to his car to escape the letter-opener wielding general manager, but he'd clearly failed. Jez saw that Boris' driver's side door was open, but he wasn't in the car. Instead, Boris and Tanner were rolling around on the asphalt parking lot, struggling.

Jez tried again to bring the two alleged adults to their senses. "Tab!" she yelled.

"Boris!" Nothing.

"Tanner, stop it! You're the god damn general manager!" Nothing.

Frustrated and desperate to stop the insanity before any employees saw the pathetic fisticuffs Jez was watching, she realized more radical measures were needed.

"COPS!" she screamed at the top of her lungs. Suddenly, both men stopped cold, each still with a firm grasp on the others wrist.

"I called the cops. They're on their way, so get up and get out of here. I'll tell them something, but just please get out of here, both of you, I beg you!" Jez was shouting.

Boris scrambled to his feet and ran to his car. He peeled out of the parking lot before Tab could even sit up. Jez walked over and grabbed Tanner by the arm to help him stand.

"What in God's name are you doing "T?" "Jez used the nickname she'd bestowed upon him years earlier. "Are you out of your fucking mind? What if another employee had seen this madness? Do you have any idea how fast you'd be out of a job?"

Tanner was looking at Jez, as though he'd just come out of a trance and was trying to figure out where he was. His hair was messed up, his tee shirt torn, and his khaki shorts were streaked with black stains from the asphalt. There were cuts and bruises all over his head, arms and legs.

"It's bad enough that Izzy is a witness. The rumor mill will no doubt be on overdrive as soon as she finds someone who speaks Spanish that she can tell about what she witnessed! Shit Tanner!" Jez took him by the arm and all but dragged him towards his car. "Now get out of here, go home and come back tomorrow as if nothing happened."

Tanner fumbled in his pant pockets for his car keys. Finding them, he sat in the driver's seat.

"Tanner, go home!" Jez slammed his car door, waited for him to start the engine, and watched as he slowly drove out of sight.

Jez turned toward the guard shack. There stood Izzy, already on her cell phone chattering away in Spanish. Jez didn't need an interpreter. She was pretty sure she knew what "loco," meant, and Izzy couldn't stop saying it.

CHAPTER #52

When Jez walked into her condo, she saw her voice mail light blinking. "You have 45 messages," it told her.

"Jeez!" It was times like these when Jez missed her two cats, "Scotch and Soda." It was also times like these she was glad they weren't around. There were 45 people who had her home number and were calling because they were either angry as hell, or giggling hysterically about her report that night. It always worried her when she had her sweet pets, that one of her enemies might do harm to them, to get to her.

Jez wasn't sure she had the energy to listen to the messages and decide she'd do selective checking. Her voice mail loomed as just another source of anxiety.

The only numbers Jez wanted to see was Batman's and Carlo's. So instead of listening to messages, she headed straight for her caller I.D. reader.

There it was, Carlo Ferrini, caller number 40 at 1:31a.m. "I guess I don't have to worry about waking him up," she said out loud, as she poured herself a glass of wine and lit a cigarette. Plopping on her living room couch, she dialed Carlo's home number.

"Hello," he said.

"Please tell me nobody has put a hit out on me yet," Jez responded.

"Oh, my God Jez! Of course not. Teachers think you're a saint!"

"Thanks, but an equal number of people think I'm the devil incarnate, including my bosses." Jez took a sip of wine.

"My phone hasn't stopped ringing since 11:05," Carlo announced.

"Mine neither." Jez inhaled a puff on her cig. "And I can't bring myself to listen to half of what those callers are saying, if tonight's spectacle in the parking lot is any indication of response."

"What are you talking about?" Carlo asked.

"Oh, nothing really. Just another night in the whacky world of local news. You know, the general manager loses his mind and tries to kill the news director by chasing him around the parking lot with a semi-lethal weapon, while a Spanglish speaking "rent-a-cop" threatens to shoot anyone who is moving."

"Huh?" Carlo was mystified.

"Forget it. I'm tired and babbling. Now tell me what you've heard from all your phone callers." Jez desperately wanted some good news.

"Well, the word is that the teacher's union is going to call for the firing of all the top deputies, and if that doesn't happen, they're going to threaten a strike. There's also a rumor that the president of the school board boarded her private plane at midnight, claiming a previously scheduled vacation. And if that doesn't get your juices flowing, I can tell you that the police have Donna Maine under guard at County Line Hospital!" Carlo was beside himself with glee.

"What? Donna Maine is where? Under guard? Why?" Jez took a big swig of wine.

"I don't know," Carlo informed Jez. "But the red-headed, gold digger called me, sounding like a dumb blonde."

"Carlo, don't you think that if Donna Maine was hospitalized and under police protection, the news media would know about it." Jez stopped.

"I agree. It's the reason I've been flipping channels like one of my attention deficit disorder students. But when I returned her call, the cops got in touch with me. I'm supposed to be there at 9:00 tomorrow morning."

"You're going aren't you?" Jez asked.

"Of course."

"Good. Call me the minute you can. I'm dead, Carlo. If I can hit the pillow in the next 30 minutes, I might get three hours of sleep." Jez yawned. "I love you friend. We'll talk tomorrow."

"Hey Jez."

"Yeah, Carlo."

"Bomb," he said.

"Huh?"

"You are the bomb, Jez. That's what everyone was saying about you tonight. That you're the bomb! I just thought you'd want to know."

Jez was overcome by such a simple statement. She was tired, stressed, anxiety ridden and scared. But those words from Carlo brought tears to her eyes.

"Thank you so much Carlo. I did need that. Be safe my friend. We'll talk tomorrow."

Jez clicked her "off" button, inhaled another puff from her cigarette and started to sob. Emotions were not something she shared with anyone. But tonight she wished "Scotch and Soda" were there to lick her face and snuggle with her, as she cried herself to sleep.

CHAPTER #53
MONDAY

It was Monday morning, and Miami's top detectives were huddled around a conference room table at police headquarters. In front of them were dozens of boxes of documents taken from Dr. Barbara Ross' office, following her suicide leap.

"We know a few things for certain," the Chief of Police began. "Big Mo and Dr. Ross were tight. How tight, and what bonded them, we don't know. But one sure fire way to try and find out, is to go through every document in this room."

Groans from his detectives were audible. These cops liked solving crimes. What they hated was the paperwork that sometimes produced results, and sometimes didn't.

"If I wanted to be a paper pusher, Chief, I'd have gotten an accounting degree," Detective Gonzalez moaned.

"If I'd wanted to be a nursemaid, I'd have gone to work at a daycare center," the Chief snapped back. "Now get cracking. Think of all the overtime you'll make tonight. You might even be able to upgrade that 1970's kitchen your wife is always bitching about, Rogelio" The Chief turned and walked out of the conference room.

Before the door slammed, Gonzalez's colleagues were taunting him.

"Oh baby! A new refrigerator!"

"I always wanted to take Microwave cooking lessons, sweet pea!"

"Honey bun, now you don't have to take out the trash, we can compact it, thanks to the hundreds of hours in overtime you worked solving the crime of the century!"

As his fellow officers began to imitate a woman sobbing with joy, Gonzalez drew his gun from his holster and pointed it at the ceiling.

"One more word from you mother fuckers and I swear I'll blow your heads off!"

"Yeah, yeah, yeah," they all mumbled as each one reached for a box of documents and began the task of searching for answers in the mounds of papers.

At 8:55 a.m. Tab Tanner pulled into his private parking spot at the station. He pulled his suit jacket off the hook in the back seat, threw the jacket over his broad shoulders and walked toward the front lobby.

At the same time, Carlo Ferrini was parking his car in the garage at County Line Hospital.

As he'd driven past the hospital's front entrance to get to the parking garage, he'd noticed the line of Miami Police cars parked in front of the main entrance. "Holy shit!" he said out loud.

He realized he had no idea what he was getting himself into by visiting Donna Maine. But he was already there, and he may as well find out. Hell, nobody was expecting him to clock in anywhere. But Jez was expecting him to get information, so he'd do what he could.

At Channel 11, management was watching the clock tick as if it might explode. Their anxiety was focused on the ratings from last night's 11pm news. The numbers were almost always delivered by the ratings service, straight up at 9:00a.m. It was already 9:03 in the morning, and the station's management was sweating bullets.

Tab Tanner was hung over and angry. Boris Danken was angry and indignant. The rest of the station's executives gathered around the conference table were scared and very silent. Everyone was staring at their laptops waiting for their computers to ding.

Time stood still for the nervous crowd until 9:07. Laptops chimed simultaneously.

Instantly, hands were on the mouse pad scrolling down to the 11pm newscast.

Someone screamed "Oh my God!" The others looked up from their computer screens; mouths hung open. Tab and Boris stared at one another. Then suddenly, the station's conference room erupted into bedlam. The ratings for Sunday's late news were on par with the Super Bowl.

Everyone was jumping up and down screaming, "high fiving" and hugging whoever was next to them.

"We hit it out of the ballpark!" shouted the General Sales Manager.

"I haven't seen numbers like this since 9-1-1!" said a stunned Program Manager.

It was then that each executive began to notice that the only two people in the room, not celebrating victory, were the news director and the general manager. Their eyes were locked in a visual version of arm wrestling. Silence hung in the air once more, as the station's top brass slowly sat themselves back down in their chairs and waited for Tab and Boris to blink.

CHAPTER #54

Carlo entered County Line Hospital and proceeded to the reception desk to inquire about Donna Maine's room number. Carlo watched as the elderly receptionist made a phone call. Whatever happened to Candy Stripers, he wondered to himself. Now, folks who had one foot in the grave serviced every hospital. Maybe it gave them comfort knowing how they would go. Or maybe they thought it would buy them better hospital care, since they worked for the hospital. If that was their reason for doing a job where sick and old people died, then all the power to them, Carlo chuckled to himself.

"Your name sir?" she asked.

"Carlo Ferrini."

He watched as she repeated his name then hung up.

"Mr. Ferrini, someone will be down to escort you in a moment. Please have a seat," she informed him.

Carlo turned and headed for an oversized chair in the lobby. His mind was whirling. What could all this be about? Why did he need to have someone escort him to Donna's room? Why was Donna in the hospital to begin with, and why was she phoning him of all people? His mind raced.

Within a minute, a uniformed Miami Police officer arrived and asked that Carlo follow him. The men walked down the hall to a secluded office where Capt. Sheila Cohen was awaiting Carlo's arrival. She thanked the officer and asked him to remain outside of the door.

"Mr. Ferrini," Capt. Cohen began. "I need to have a private, and hopefully, confidential conversation with you." She sat down in a chair beside Carlo.

"I had a good feeling about you and your credibility when we interrogated you last week. I want to know if I can rely upon you for complete honesty as we investigate Dr Maine's death. Will you agree to that, Mr. Ferrini?" Carlo uncrossed his legs, and leaned forward.

"I will do whatever I can to assist you, Capt." he replied.

"Do you have any idea why Mrs. Maine called you from the hospital?" Cohen inquired.

"I have no idea, Capt." Carlo admitted he was flabbergasted to receive her call on his answering machine. He knew that Donna didn't have much of a life, largely because Hank did the thinking for her. He explained that Maine's wife was nothing more than arm candy for the dandy deputy superintendent!

"Capt., this is a woman who couldn't even select her own wardrobe!" Carlo leaned back and crossed his legs again.

Capt. Cohen then began to outline the events that had occurred on Sunday with the discovery of Donna Maine's body at Flamingo Gardens Race Track. Carlo sat in total shock as she explained about the body dumped on the actual dirt track, the ambulance trip to County Line General, and then she dropped the bomb.

"Do you know anyone within the school system who was especially close to Ms. Maine? I mean someone who would know she was in the hospital without specifically being notified, and arrive unannounced to pay her a visit?"

Carlo thought for a moment and then shrugged his shoulders. Sheila Cohen could tell from his body language that he was truly surprised.

"Mr. Ferrini, I need to ask you about a very sensitive matter." Capt. Cohen paused. "Can you tell me anything from your perspective as to what was going on at the school system's headquarters that might be construed as illegal activity?"

Carlo calculated his response very carefully. After a long pause, he said, "I have my suspicions, but I was never an insider on such dealings in the school system. Those close to the superintendent were always referred to as the 'palace guard.' Many things were done in the name of the superintendent about which, I hope, he knew nothing. The title of superintendent carries a lot of weight. Defy orders when commanded, and you could be banished to Siberia. Look what happened to me, for God's sake, and I didn't defy orders"

"Thank you Mr. Ferrini. Here's my card. If you think of anything, please don't hesitate to call me." Capt. Cohen then took Carlo to Donna Maine's hospital room. When they reached the door, he was shocked that the security was so tight. There were three officers posted outside of Donna's room.

When he entered, he noticed another uniformed officer in the corner. He greeted Donna, who was sitting up in a chair in the corner of the room next to the window. She appeared to have nodded off to sleep, but looked up and smiled when Carlo spoke to her.

"Carlo, I'm so glad to see you, and happy that you got my message. I really need to speak with you because I know you're honest, and that Hank screwed you over, but I know why he did it, I'm sure you also know why, and I know that even after that, you never changed with me. So, as I sat here, pondering what to do next, and whom to trust, you immediately came to mind. Carlo, please take a seat here by me." Carlo sat in an adjacent chair, but she asked him to pull it closer.

"I have no friends. You know Hank wouldn't allow it, and the school system people with whom he associated, are all either corrupt or self-absorbed. I already tried to approach one of them and that's what landed me here… almost dead!"

Carlo's mind raced. Who could that have been? What would she tell him?

"Donna, I always had a special place in my heart for you, Carlo began. "You're such a lady, and deserved better than the treatment you received… especially from Hank."

Donna looked so tired Carlo thought.

"Carlo, I don't know where to start, but I have to tell someone. That's why I called you." Donna shifted in her chair, looked down at her wringing hands, and then began to tell Carlo everything.

As she began to unburden herself of hidden secrets, she began talking very fast.

"Hank was robbing the district blind," she began. "And he wasn't the only one. You know how he loved to brag that he was so almighty powerful. Well, he got too cocky and greedy, and I think that's what was behind his murder. It was his arrogance, believing that he could get away with anything, just like most of the powerful people in this town. Carlo, he was also a sex addict, not just with school system women, but men. But what really chilled me to the bone was his growing addiction to child porn and pedophilia."

Carlo was trying to keep his shock from showing. "Donna, I don't know what to say. I had no idea your marriage had degenerated so badly,"

"In the end, our relationship was more like a convenience and sharing a home. He only wanted me as a trophy wife, and that is why I had to be glamorous all the time, regardless."

Donna stood and looked out the window. Carlo would later realize that she was mustering the courage to tell him an unbelievable tale, which, if Carlo didn't know the bastards who ran the school system, he'd think were tales of delusions.

"Carlo," Donna began, "Hank and some other top administrators, board members, school police, even some principals, were skimming money from the system, and taking bribes from contractors and vendors. Much of it was for 'no bid' contracts. That is why he was so obsessed with the Channel 11 reporter and her stories. She was on the right scent, sniffing out these things. He even knew that somebody had gone to the FBI, but after 9/11, the focus turned to terrorism, and all other investigations were apparently just dropped, frozen or forgotten."

Donna then proceeded to tell Carlo about her conversations with Dr. Moorehead, and of waiting outside the Church of the Great Believer because she knew what they did in there with the payoff money from vendors.

"You know Hank couldn't keep a secret." She actually laughed. "He liked to brag to me. So I know where all the skeletons are buried, so to speak."

She told Carlo how she followed Big Mo to the club. "I'm pretty sure he drugged my drink. But I guess we'll know for sure as soon as the police finishing doing all their tests. I was just lucky to be found, even if only half alive."

Carlo then realized why there was such a massive police detail outside of her room.

"That son-of-a-bitch tried to murder me!" Donna screamed as she turned away from the window to face Carlo. What should I do? You know how powerful Moses is. I'm scared."

Carlo got up from his chair and put his arms around her to comfort her. After a few seconds, he let her go, and began pacing the room… thinking.

"Donna, you have to speak with the police. Demand some kind of protection. And I don't mean uniformed officers, I'm talking the witness protection program. Demand to talk to the FBI. Make them a deal. Clearly, much of what is going on in the district involves federal money and that means the FBI. I know that you have enough information to put some people away." Carlo paused to let his words sink in.

"Donna, You must be willing to testify. The FBI may even want to re-open the original investigation that you said they scrapped in 2001. Donna, please let me ask Capt. Cohen to come in. Talk candidly with her, and see what she suggests. She must be very concerned about your safety to have assigned such a large police detail to you."

Donna nodded affirmatively. Suddenly, the proverbial light bulb went off in Donna's head.

"Carlo, Hank was also involved in a long term affair with a guy who works for the school system. At first the guy was working part-time at a school. Hank would call the guy's boss and ask for the kid to do some menial task for him, and everyone felt Hank would be beholding to them for releasing him during work hours." Then Hank brought him downtown to the headquarters building as a full-time clerk. I mean the guy was only 19 or 20 at the time. Oh, I wish I could remember his name, but he rose through the ranks with promotion after promotion quickly becoming an administrator, and all of this success with only a high school diploma! How in God's name does that happen in a school system, where credentials are everything?" Donna looked at Carlo.

"Well. It's not as if cheap degrees and uneducated people were unique in the school system, Donna." Carlo stopped to watch her reaction.

"I seem to remember that this guy lived with his parents, so Hank's trysts took place at a house owned by the school system. Hank was too cheap to set the boyfriend up in his own apartment.

"I can't remember the guy's name," said Donna. "I know that he started seeing a younger guy and Hank became furious that he was so brazen as to do so after Hank helped him so much with his new position, submitting the necessary memos to get his salary raised," Donna Maine paused.

Carlo had no response. What could he do since he actually knew who she was talking about?

"Hank called him a sociopath, psychopath, or something like that, many times." He used to say, 'To him, the end justified the means'. I know the guy had numerous sexual harassment complaints filed against him. Maybe they were for attention, so that Hank would intercede and make them go away. You know what they called it? 'Unsubstantiated.'"

Donna looked at Carlo for a response. "Hank said the guy bragged to people that he was in training to be the next Hank

Maine. Hank was incensed about it when the word got back
to him."

Carlo remembered thinking, the guy had the upper hand because he could blackmail Hank big time!

Then he thought, "Hell hath no fury like a lover scorned."

"Donna, you have to talk to the cops. Please let me bring
Capt. Cohen in here." He waited as Donna stared out the
window.

For the longest time, there was no reply. Finally, Donna
Maine turned, looked at Carlo and said, "Fine. Tell her I'm
ready to talk." Donna's words hung in the air.

"I promise," said Carlo, "it will be the best decision you ever
made."

CHAPTER #55

Batman had literally gone into hiding after his final Sunday at the Church of the Great Believer. He'd kissed his elderly mother and told her he was going on vacation.

"Tú mereces una vacaciones mi querido hijo,"You deserve some time off my darling son," she told him in Spanish.

Even after 35 years in America, she, like so many Cuban exiles, still spoke little, to no English. They'd always believed they were just days away from returning to their homeland. But days turned into weeks, weeks turned into months, months turned into years, and before they knew it, they discovered they were living and dying in the U.S.A.

Their homeland, Cuba, was lost to them, and they were lost as well. Batman's mother used to step out on their balcony and look up at the sky around sunset. She'd see cotton ball-sized clouds, hanging from the royal blue sky that sparkled with hues of pink and orange from the color of the sun as it prepared to set in the west. Sometimes, a particular cloud would shine; white hot, like a theater Klieg light was aimed right at it.

Mother Batman, loved to look at the sky each night, knowing that her native land and hometown, Havana, was seeing the same sparkling glow of the clouds that hovered over her accidental homeland in Miami, Florida.

"Mami," Batman said… using the term of endearment most Cubans used, regardless of their age. Most Anglos stopped calling their parent's mommy and daddy when they turned 10 years old. But Cubans called their parent's Mami and Papi, like Anglos said Mom and Dad.

"Si, mi amor," she responded.

"I have gotten myself in a big bowl of trouble, Mami."

She stared at him, slightly puzzled at the key English words she understood.

"I must leave for a while, Mami." Batman was choking back tears. "I've arranged for Bianca, next door, to take care of you, while I'm gone." He paused. "I know you adore Bianca, and maybe when I return, she and I can explore the idea of marriage."

Batman took his mother's wrinkled and frail hands in his, and kissed them. When he looked up, he saw a single tear sliding down the right side of her weathered face.

"Don't cry, Mami," he implored. "I'm doing something that is right, not wrong… just like you and poppy taught me. So please, let me know those are tears of pride and joy."

His Mami began to shake, like many people in their 80's tend to do.

"Ÿo estoy orgullosa de ti hijo mio, yo nunca dudaría de ti. Yo crié un buen muchacho que se convertió en buén hombre," she replied. Translation: You are my pride and, my son. I would never question you. I raised a good boy. He became a good man.

With those words, Batman realized his Mami was fading, so he took her by the arm and led her to her bedroom, where she put her head on a petite pillow, covered by the most deli- cious white cotton, decorated at the hem with hand stitched blue half-moons. It was the same pillow she'd brought from Cuba when she and her family fled the Castro communists at age 45. At the time, Batman was only 6 years old. Forty-two years later, this grown woman still needed a tie to her home- land, and that small pillow, with the faded blue stitching, was that connection.

Batman kissed his sleeping Mami, walked into the front hall- way, picked up his suitcase, quietly opened the front door… and left.

CHAPTER #56

There was a "tom-tom" beating in Jez's head, and it wasn't the wine she'd consumed the night before. It was a pulsating drive of some kind that she'd never felt before... like someone had a rope around her neck and was dragging her into someplace she might not want to go. It was a hammering in her head, laced with tremulous fear and trepidation. There was a steady beat in her heart, but it was as if her heart was about to beat itself out of her chest.

Somehow she'd managed to show up for work Monday morning on time. But every person she passed in the halls either stared at her as if she was a leper, or hugged her as if she was the mother of the bride.

As she walked the halls of the station that had been her home for over a decade, her heart pounded louder! It was like an orchestra building up to some kind of crescendo by Rachmaninoff. Her body suddenly took on the hot flashes that she'd battled and won decades ago. Where were they coming from now?

Jez hadn't been at her desk more than a few minutes, when her phone rang. She could tell by the ring that it was an internal call. Her caller ID told her it was the general manager's secretary.

"Hi Cindy," she answered.

"Hi Jez." Cindy Delgado sounded almost pained. "Tab wants you in the conference room ASAP."

"I'm on my way." Jez hung up.

She took a deep breath and tried to gather her wits about her. What was going on she wondered, as she walked, supposedly with purpose, toward the station's fifth floor conference room?

Blood seemed to drain from her brain, leaving her lightheaded and a bit loopy. She had to steady herself against the wall in the hallway. She knew that by now, the higher ups would have seen the overnight ratings. If they were good or great, wouldn't Cindy have sounded a bit more upbeat, Jez wondered?

As she approached the closed door, she felt beads of sweat trickling down the small of her back. Her face was flushed, and oil began to seep from every one of her huge pores. She felt faint. "Get it together, she thought. You are "Underhanded!"

Taking the halting kind of steps a bride does down the aisle; Jez slowly approached the conference room. Standing before the door that held her future, she wondered, was she too young to become a Wal-Mart greeter?

She knocked... forcing herself to pound on the door not once, but three times.

"Come in," boomed Tab Tanner's voice.

Jez stared at the brass door handle. She then slowly put her hand on it, turned it, pushing the door open with such fear, she thought her knees would buckle.

As the door cracked open, Jez heard applause, then whistling and hollering. The people in the room were screaming her name. Everyone was standing and cheering! Jez was frozen. Her brain, so filled with fear, was having a hard time processing what was happening.

Tab Tanner walked toward her and wrapped her in a bear hug. Then he said to the entire room, "Last night I wanted to kill this reporter. Today I want to marry her!" Everyone erupted in laughter. Tab took Jez's hand and led her over to his laptop at the head of the conference table.

"Look at these 11 o'clock news numbers from last night, Jez!" Tab pointed to the screen. "Feast your eyes on the biggest numbers this news department has seen in 15 years!" Tab was positively giddy with excitement. The celebration continued to whirl all around Jez as she stared at the ratings chart.

"Wow!" was about all she could say. The fear she'd had a few moments earlier, had left her with cottonmouth.

"Jez, we're going to whip up big splashy promotions. We want it on the air by 2pm, so I'll need you in the studio in about an hour." Jez just looked at the promotions manager who was now talking.

"I can't hang around here because of a promo," she blurted out. The room suddenly went silent. "I assume you want to keep our ratings lead alive as long as possible, right?" She looked at Tanner. "Then let me out of here so I can go get another exclusive for tonight's news."

"But we need your presence in the spot," the promo guy insisted.

"You have plenty of videotape of me to create a presence, for God's sake. Let me go do my job!"

"She's right." It was Boris. He'd stood from somewhere behind a line of other employees. Jez looked stunned. She couldn't remember the last time he went to bat for her.

"She's got a job to do today. I expect nothing less than a kickass story tonight. Now go be a reporter." Boris almost sounded convincing.

Jez looked at Tanner. He nodded his head, giving her the signal to leave. In a flash, she was gone.

CHAPTER #57

In downtown Miami, the area surrounding the police head-quarters building had been transformed into a "Satellite City." Satellite broadcast trucks from every station in town, the major networks and even from other cities in Florida, had begun arriving around midnight and had sprouted like weeds in the dead of the night.

By 5a.m Monday morning, when most local stations were starting their morning newscasts, Satellite City was in full bloom! They were there for an interview, a picture... anything that would allow them to appear to have played catch up with 11 News and it's sensational exclusive the night before.

Lt. Dennis Black, the department's primary public information officer, finally came out at around 10:30, having spent the better part of the early morning hours in conference with the Chief of Police, the homicide detectives and the school system's Police Chief.

Other than issuing a "no comment" at around 3:30a.m.... Black had stayed away from the ever-growing media crowd. But he knew he had to say something for the noon news, or they'd riot.

"The Miami Police Department is committed to conducting a thorough investigation surrounding the death of Dep. School Supt. Dr. Hank Maine," Black began his press conference. "It would be irresponsible to discuss the details of our investigation, or comment on any news reports about our investigation. If any individual has tampered with evidence that is part of a criminal probe, I can assure you, that person or persons will be prosecuted."

"Does that mean one of your fellow cops, Lt.?" shouted one of the network folks.

"Are you referring to Jez Underwood?" shouted a local reporter.

"There is nothing more I can tell you," declared Lt. Black as he faced a room full of photographers and reporters. He hated the wolf pack. It was a nickname his staff had given to the media years ago. Boy, he thought, does that nickname fit, or what?

That didn't deter the herd of groveling reporters from trying to ask him questions he'd already said he wouldn't answer.

It was a typical moment in the annals of public discourse, reporters probed, targets refused to answer. Free speech is a great idea, if you can get people to speak freely!

Unfortunately, as Jez had long ago discovered, free speech didn't exist in the public school system, not if an employee wanted to keep their job, their pension, or not get killed.

Jez was watching the live press conference on the TV monitor in Emeril's news van. They'd driven into the private parking lot at the school board building, thanks to a wink and a nod from a friendly security guard. This allowed them to enter without being seen by their competitors, who were camped out in the lobby and on the sidewalks trying to get interviews with district employees about the child molestation video and Dr. Maine.

Jez and Emeril commented on how vacant the parking lot was, meaning that not too many of the top brass or school board members were at work... at least not yet.

There was no sign of board President Jewel Haynes' pale yellow Bentley Continental Flying Spur or Bitzy Champlain's Honda Accord.

Inside the system's headquarters, conversations were hushed and whispered. Although most employees had shown up for work, the top administrators were conspicuous by their absence. Some had had the courtesy to call with an excuse... "I have a dental appointment," "my child is sick," " I'm sick."

School board members were also invisible Monday morning. Staff was mum as to why each publicly elected official was missing in action the day after the district's most horrible public relations nightmare.

But in a twist of irony, Dr. Moses Moorehead, the most invisible of the school board members, was actually the only one in his office at 10:00a.m. Of course he was behind closed doors with his aide de camp, Franklin Elder.

"I'm told the media is camped out all around the building Mo," Elder informed his boss. "And that includes all the major networks and cable shows. Susie Q has already taken 20 messages from media outlets asking you for an interview."

"Give'm the standard response Franklin, ah don't do interviews." Moses took a puff on his cigarette.

Although smoking was prohibited in public buildings, Big Mo ignored rules he didn't like. Besides, he knew that no one in their right mind who wanted to keep their job in the school system would dare challenge him.

"Fine Mo, but how the hell are you going to get out of here without that Jez or some other reporter ambushing you? What the hell were you thinking coming in today? You never come in! Why today?" Elder stopped

"Beecuz you asshole... aah has thangs to take care of. Now leave me uhlone."

Jez had slipped into the halls of the school board member's offices when one of the cleaning people (who loved Jez) held the main door open for her. Jez winked at her friend as she slid past the secretarial gendarmes.

Emeril took a moment to say "gracias" to the woman as they passed.

"De nada señor," she said to Emeril.

Then the woman leaned into Emeril and whispered in his ear. "Jez is hero! Tell her."

"Si, Señora," said Emeril.

Just then Franklin Elder walked out of Big Mo's office... and that's when Jez saw Moorehead standing behind his desk. Big Mo's jaw dropped. Jez was equally stunned to see the "stealth" superintendent actually in his office since she hadn't seen his car in the parking lot. But what the hell was he doing in a public building with a lit cigarette, no less!

"Dr. Moorehead! I need a comment from you please about the child pornography found in Dr. Maine's home."

Jez was talking a mile a minute, fearful to lose this great opportunity. She headed straight past Franklin Elder toward Big Mo with her microphone in her hand. The camera was up on Emeril's shoulder. He'd been rolling from the minute they walked in the building.

Big Mo stepped around his desk and walked toward Jez. He was burning with rage. How had she gotten up here without an escort? Why was Franklin just standing there? What was he going to do to get rid of her?

"Ah understand you want a comment Ms. Underwood, but ah did not see your report last night and ah don't feel it's proper for me to tawk about something ah am not familiar with. Now you have uh nice day!" With that, Big Mo shut the door to his office, right in her face.

Without missing a beat, Jez banged on the door and hollered, "Then if you won't talk to me about Dr. Maine's pornography... maybe you'd care to comment on the $1 Billion dollars you ordered Superintendent Vascoe to remove from the Capital budget and put into a Cayman Bank?"

Jez hadn't realized that she'd been screaming at the top of her lungs, and now secretaries' heads were popping up all around the outer offices, and board aides were peering around corners.

Franklin Elder stood frozen in his tracks, listening to the whirl of the camera recording every second of this nightmare.

"One billion dollars Dr. Moorehead! Explain that to the tax-payers!" Jez waited for a response. None came. So she went for broke!

"We have video of you and Supt. Vascoe shuffling the mon-ey… illegally shuffling the money, Dr. Moorehead! Care to comment now?" Jez was breathless with the excitement of what she knew was her big story that night.

Suddenly, she turned toward Franklin Elder, who looked white, even though he was black. "Care to comment, Frank?"

She then turned toward the door and banged on it again with her knuckles. "I'm leaving now, Dr. Moorehead, but not be-fore I tell you what a pretty sanctuary the Church of the Great Believer has. I especially like those black lacquer offering plates your bagmen pass around." She paused for dramatic effect. Stared at Franklin Elder. Then she delivered her part-ing shot.

"I especially like the baby blue décor of Reverend "L's" sec-ond floor office, Dr. Moorehead. Know how I know what color it is? I bet you're dying to know how I know!" Again she paused, waiting for a response, she was almost certain wouldn't come.

"Would you care to comment on the money you disburse in the church's second floor conference room, Dr. Moorehead? I need to ask you about the video we have of you and others taking a cut of the kickback money and the parishioner's do-nations that you and your group take every Sunday. We have videotape. Care to comment?"

There was no response from behind Moorehead's door. At that moment, Jez turned to her left, then her right. She want-ed to see how many staff people were hanging on every word she was saying.

She then turned her back to the door, where Moorehead's name was centered at the top. She looked straight into Emeril's camera, and, with microphone in hand, Jez Under-wood recorded an unrehearsed "on camera" stand up.

"Although Dr. Moses Moorehead hides behind the closed doors of his school board office, refusing to answer our questions, the video of his presence in the conference room of the Church of the Great Believer this Sunday, speaks volumes about a criminal theft, corruption and kickback enterprise, our sources say he designed, ran and controlled. Jez Underwood Channel 11 News."

CHAPTER #58

Carlo walked to the door of Donna's hospital room and peered out into the hallway. He spotted one of the uniformed officers standing watch by the door.

"Officer," he began. "Could you please radio Capt. Cohen? Tell her she's needed in Mrs. Maine's room. Thank you." Carlo shut the door and sat down again. Silence hung in the air as he and Donna stared at one another.

After what seemed like hours, Capt. Cohen knocked and entered.

"What is it Mrs. Maine?" the Capt. asked.

Donna blurted out, "I want police witness protection!"

"Why would you think that, Ms. Maine?"

"I was drugged and left for dead! How many reasons do I need?" Donna huffed.

Capt. Cohen looked over at Carlo. He nodded at Donna, as if to say, "go ahead."

Donna shifted in her hospital bed. "Capt. Cohen, I know where all the school system's skeletons are buried! I can give you information that will have you making arrests from now until Christmas. But without serious police protection, I'll be killed before you can count to 100!"

Capt. Cohen replied, "Well, let's see what you've got and then I will take it from there."

Sheila Cohen pulled a chair around and sat down, as Donna began to talk about everything she knew.

Donna told her the story she had shared with Carlo about Hank, the unidentified male boyfriend, and the sex house called Royal Poinciana Ranch. She told Capt. Cohen about the offshore bank accounts, and the unauthorized movement of Federal funds into operating accounts. She withheld specific names... for now.

Capt. Sheila Cohen listened in a state of disbelief as the allegations flowed.

Lastly, Donna shared the story of the previous day... about the church, the club, and ultimately being left for dead. The sympathetic Capt. was beginning to understand the depth of Donna's fear and why she was insisting on police protection. Some powerful people could be feeling very threatened by what Donna Maine knew, thought Cohen, and one of them could be Hank Maine's killer.

Capt. Cohen's cell phone started to ring. She only saw the letters: Federal. Promptly, she excused herself and went out of the hospital room to answer the call.

It was FBI Special Agent in Charge Jose Ramirez. He introduced himself, saying that he was returning her phone call from Sunday morning. Capt. Cohen thanked him, and gave a brief overview of the homicide and its subsequent discoveries. She asked if they could meet to discuss any federal ramifications the case might contain. Agent Ramirez said he would meet her at County Line General, since the FBI office was close by.

Captain Cohen returned to Donna and Carlo, apologizing and explaining that she had to take that important call. She asked Donna if there was anything else that she remembered that could be of value to the investigation.

Donna shrugged, and replied, "I'm sure I'll think of 20 things after you leave."

"Write them down," responded Capt. Cohen. "You may not realize how small details can add up to big leads and have value to the investigation of your husband's murder. I wish you could remember the name of his young boyfriend. Who else might know?" Donna assured her that eventually she would think of his name; she was just too rattled now.

When Special Agent Ramirez arrived, Capt. Cohen showed him to a private waiting room, and began to lay out for him the past several days' events. He sat silently and listened. Then Agent Ramirez posed the question of accomplices.

"Did anyone else participate in the production of child pornography or any acts relating to crimes against children or pedophilia? If Dr. Maine was already dead, there was no prosecution for his crimes. Who installed the surveillance cameras? Who monitored the cameras? Was a copy made, and if so, who made it?"

He then gave Capt. Cohen a lesson in FBI strategies as it relates to child pornography and pedophilia. It was apparent that she personally did not have much expertise with this aspect, since most of her career had been spent in homicide. He explained the Federal violations involved with child pornography that included, receipt, transmission, distribution and possession. He advised her that the courts do differentiate between receipt and possession. He then enumerated, production, manufacturing, transmission, and distribution, and emphatically told her that the key to any of them is to prove that the violator knowingly intended to commit the crime. The burden of proof would be upon the federal government or state authorities, depending on how, or if, they split things up.

Capt. Cohen then thanked him for coming over to meet with her and also for his valuable time and advice. Cohen returned to the hospital room and apologized for the interruption, and told Donna and Carlo that she had to get back to the police station. "Remember Donna, jot down anything that comes to mind, things you may remember that you've not told me about today." Donna Maine nodded, and Capt. Sheila Cohen left.

******

While Carlo watched Donna sleep, the killer was sunning on the beach... again. The idea was to stay away from the school board building for as long as possible, while the authorities snooped around. A root canal that became infected should keep suspicions at bay, the "tanned one" thought. That was the excuse anyway for being absent from work on Monday.

Besides, what was another vacation or sick day after all? The school board's policy was "use it, or lose it."

"At least I'm claiming it as a sick day," the killer thought, unlike so many other district employees. The most egregious violators were always the ones with close ties to Dr. Moses Moorehead.

The killer remembered the time when a fellow teacher came back to school one day, bragging about a fishing trip he'd gone on with Big Mo, two deputy superintendents, and a Region Director.

"I don't have to use one sick or vacation day," the guy had bragged. "Mo is making sure the principal pays me for a day at work! How rich is that?" the guy chuckled. "I got paid for trolling for Marlin!"

He'd told the killer how the group had met at Black Point Marina, off Biscayne National Park, one morning. Big Mo, he said, had chartered a fishing boat. When the Captain asked for payment before shoving off, the killer remembered his colleague being shocked that one of the deputy superintendent's had handed the Captain a check for the day's offshore excursion. It was a Miami Public School System check!

"Taxpayers are so ignorant," the killer mumbled.

And so, with the morning newspaper in hand, and a beach bag on the shoulder, the murderous maniac headed off for a nice sunny day on the lush sands of Miami Beach.

CHAPTER #59

As Jez and Emeril were speeding back to the station to pre-
pare the two big stories of the day, Dr. Moses Moorehead
and his aide, Franklin Elder, huddled behind the closed door
of Big Mo's office, making plans.

"How the hell are we going to get out of here, Mo?" Elder inquired, as he nervously paced in front of Big Mo's desk.

"What if Underwood has our cars staked out, just waiting for
us to leave?"

"You mean your car, don't you?" Moorehead responded, re-
minding his trusted aide that he'd picked him up that morning, since his car was deep in a canal somewhere.

"Shit!" Franklin Elder cursed under his breath.

"We only have one way out," Moorehead informed his aide.
"The MetroMover. We'll hop that from the second floor plat-
form; take it East to the Omni. Then we'll use a pay phone
there to call Charlotte Mackey. She'll hide us at her house."

"Are you out of your fucking mind, Mo?" Franklin Elder had
stopped pacing and was now hunched over his boss' desk.

"She's the last person anyone would think to contact about
my whereabouts," Moorehead explained. "And, I'm confident
she'll take us in. God knows I've paid her and her family
handsomely over the years."

"You shot the woman in the hip, for God sake!" Elder reminded his boss. "What makes you think she's going to cover for
you or me?"

"Because, if she doesn't, I'll remind her that mommy and
daddy's six figure jobs with the school system will be gone
with the wind," he replied smugly. "I'm certain the little bitch
won't want that to happen."

Elder plopped down in one of the chairs opposite Big Mo's desk to think. Suddenly, memories of a night at the "Outpost Lounge" on Northwest 7th Avenue came flooding back to him.

It was the 70's, and Moses was on the fast track to greatness in the school system. He was climbing toward a deputy superintendent's position, faster than most of his other African-American counterparts. Franklin had become a close friend of his over the years, and the two enjoyed partying almost as much as they enjoyed fucking women. It didn't matter if the females were young, old, black or white; the two of them screwed anything in a skirt!

Franklin was married. Moorehead had been divorced for years. Franklin Elder knew that Moses used his sexual trysts with the ladies, to generate goodwill and loyalty among them. Hell, half the elementary school principals were in charge of schools for no other reason, than they'd had sex with Mo. He always took care of them. In return, they kept their mouths shut. But in the mid 70's, Moses Moorehead messed up big time.

He and Elder had gone to the Outpost Lounge one Friday night. The drinks flowed, and Mo's latest love was there getting hammered along with the rest of the group. Cocaine had infiltrated the bar scene in most Miami hotspots, so not only were Moses and Charlotte drunk, but they were high. Not a good combination, Elder remembered thinking at the time.

Around 1:00a.m. Mo got up to go to the bathroom. When he came back, he grabbed his wallet that he'd left on the table where he and Charlotte were sitting. Opening it up in order to pay the bill, Big Mo noticed that all his cash was missing. In his mind, Charlotte was the main suspect.

"You God damn cunt! You stole mah money!" he screamed at her... his Southern accent more evident because of the liquor.

"I did no such thing!" Franklin remembers Charlotte being almost believably indignant.

"Who else was sit'un at this here table, beetch?"

"Go fuck yourself," Charlotte yelled.

That's when Mo pulled his gun out of the back of his waist-band and started waving it, screaming at the top of his lungs how he was going to kill Charlotte if she didn't give him his money back. Charlotte bolted for the door with Moses right behind her.

Only the orange neon sign above the building provided any light in the parking lot. Charlotte was running like an escaped convict. But before Moses lost her to darkness, he took aim and fired. Her screams were loud and plaintive.

By now, other patrons, including Charlotte's sister were running past Moses, looking for the woman, they were almost sure was dead. Instead, they found her about 40 feet away, slumped on the ground, shot in her hip.

Franklin Elder shoved Moses Moorehead into his car and sped off. The bartender had already picked up the phone and called for an ambulance. Charlotte was taken to the hospital, where she was operated on. The doctors removed a .38 slug from her left hip. They told her that she might never walk correctly again.

As Charlotte lay in her hospital bed, Mo sent Franklin to broker a deal. Charlotte would not file a police complaint against him. In return, her mother, who was a guidance counselor in the school system, would be promoted to an assistant principal, and her father, who was an assistant principal, would be made a principal. And Charlotte, for her silence, would receive $10,000 a year for the rest of her life.

It worked like a magic potion. Nobody was the wiser, and everyone benefited, including Moses, who continued his rapid rise to the top, unimpeded by a gun slinging scandal.

Although the cops did their level best to find out who shot Charlotte Mackey, Moses had already paid off everyone in the bar that night in order to purchase their silence. The cops finally admitted defeat, and turned their attention to other matters, realizing they were up against a neighborhood code of silence.

Now, much to Franklin Elder's amazement, Big Mo was actually proposing contact with his hip impaired former flame!

"I think you're fucking crazy Mo," Elder informed his boss.

"I don't pay you to think, Franklin. Now let's get the fuck out of here." With those words, Moses and Franklin peeked out the office door, seeing no one, they headed for the elevator and punched the down button.

CHAPTER #60

As soon as Jez got back to the station, she ran to Boris Danken's office to inform him about the story she believed should lead the 6pm newscast that night.

"I have video from late Thursday night. It proves the top school system guys are in cahoots! It shows Moses Moorehead coming into R.V.'s office and ordering him to transfer $1 billion dollars from the capital construction account to a Cayman Bank." Jez paused for reaction.

"I don't recall authorizing overtime for Emeril for this shoot," he spouted.

"Oh, give me a fucking break boss!" Jez was beside herself. She had a major scoop, and all her boss could think about was overtime.

"Fine! If you don't want this story, then I'll just go back to my desk and cue up one of those mindless "evergreen" pieces you always insist we have in the can, and that can be the big scoop you promised Tanner this morning, when you urged the promo people not to tie me up on a promotions shoot. Capiche?"

"Show me the video," Boris shouted, realizing he'd been out foxed.

Emeril pushed the videotape into the boss' machine and hit play. Boris watched in silence. Only occasionally did Emeril or Jez offer any explanation of what he was seeing. At the end of the tape, Jez asked Emeril to insert the tape of her interview in front of Moorehead's office door from the morning encounter at the school board offices.

Again, Danken watched in silence.

When the interview ended, Emeril hit a button on the machine, as silence hung in the room like the humid air of a Miami summer.

"Do you have any comment from the cops?" Boris finally asked Jez.

"No. Why would I? They haven't seen the tape!"

"Well after you air this at 6:00, I'll want you to get a comment from them for the 11:00," he insisted.

"I think we need to talk about the 11pm news," Jez informed her boss.

"Why?" he leaned into his desk, suddenly curious.

"Because we have another separate exclusive for 11:00, that's why," she responded.

"You're trying my patience, Underhanded," he shot back.

"No, I'm trying to make you King of all Miami News Directors, Boris, so just sit back and listen to what I have to offer."

Jez then began to explain about the church surveillance and the video of the money and the offering plates and the people in on the deal... when Boris exploded.

"I know I didn't authorize any overtime for Emeril or Louise for Sunday! How dare you people just do your own thing!"

"Because," Jez began from a standing position now, leaning over Boris' desk, "if we didn't do our own thing, you wouldn't have another big exclusive for tonight's all-important 11pm news!"

"I don't care, you need my authorization," he insisted.

"You don't care about the 11pm news? Boris. I can't wait to tell Tanner that, and don't think I won't!" She was sounding almost threatening.

She then got up and popped the videotape out of the machine.

"Ferschte, Boris?" Jez was now speaking German, a language she knew he understood more than his phony Italian.

"Ich ferschte, Jez." I understand, he said.

******

At the hospital, Donna had finally opened her eyes, and was now sitting up in bed.

"I think I actually have an appetite," she told Carlo, who'd been by her side non-stop.

"Shall I ask them to bring your dinner, or do you want me to call Mario's for a delivery of Pasta Puttanesca?" She was considering his offer, when his cell phone rang. He saw that it was Jez on his caller ID.

"Hello."

"Carlo, it's Jez. Get the word out to all your sources and the gossips to watch Channel 11 at 6 & 11pm tonight. Two big... I mean huge exclusives. I'm breaking both of them. Get the rumor mill ginned up." She stopped.

"OK." It's all he had to say, or could say in the presence of Donna Maine.

"Is everything alright?" Donna asked him.

"Yes, of course," he said as he clicked his cell phone off. "I just need to step out and make a few phone calls, he added. "School business." He was out the door in two seconds furiously dialing numbers.

At about the same time, Dr. Moses Moorehead was dialing a very familiar phone number from a pay phone at the Omni MetroMover Station. After three rings, a female voice answered.

"Hello."

"Char, it's your hip doctor." That was the code phrase Moses used to let her know he was calling.

"My hip is fine!" Her response was terse and cynical.

"I don't think so," Mo responded. "That's why I'm going to have to make a house call and attend to it."

"What the fuck?" Charlotte Mackey was indignant, even after more than twenty years.

"Mommy and daddy are depending on you to take proper medical care," Moorehead responded.

There was silence for a few seconds. Charlotte was clearly trying to assess her options. Finally she said, "What time can I expect you Dr.?"

"As soon as you pick me up in front of the Plaza Venetia," he replied. "Move it!" He then slammed the pay phone down and ordered Franklin to start walking toward the condo building that was just two blocks away.

CHAPTER #61

At the Miami Police Department, detectives who'd been combing through Dr. Barbara Ross' office files had hit the mother lode. Buried in between files S-T, was a suicide note. "S" for suicide, they'd concluded.

The contents were shocking and all too common. It seems Barbara Ross had been catapulted to her death, by the most ordinary of motives... a love gone bad. In her case, the love was Dr. Moses Moorehead.

In the note they found, references to her passion for the "stealth superintendent," as well as her partnership with him, in what cops could only deduce, were criminal enterprises. But Barbara Ross had failed to outline any of those details. No, instead, she enumerated a long list of Moorehead's lovers... listing the names, promotions and perks each woman gained, as a result of sleeping with, or blowing, the powerful Moorehead.

There was Dina Moder, who went from a secretary to principal almost overnight because she agreed to have sex with Big Mo. After she died, Moorehead made sure a school was named after her.

When he decided to run for school board, he set up his campaign headquarters at the Overtown school, where the current principal, was helpless to object, since she too, had been giving Moses blow jobs for over two years, in order to get her coveted position.

Ross, named names, places and gave all the salacious details. The cops later told Jez, it was like reading a torrid romance novel with no end in sight!

Ross wrote about Madeleine Drysdale, head of the Title I Program. Although she was a mental midget, according to most people who worked for her, Drysdale's sexual escapades with Moses landed her in a very powerful position. Title I money, was the system's largest Federal grant program. It provided money for the underprivileged. In fact, 81% of Miami's school kids relied on Title I grant money for free breakfast and lunch programs.

Then there was the principal who also incorporated a "for profit" company that provided after school care for inner city kids. There was just one problem, as Ross so adroitly pointed out in her final statement, the principal, who'd had sex with Moorehead for years, was pressuring her teacher's to buy and to sell raffle tickets to a fundraiser for her childcare program. This type of arm-twisting was usually reserved for political fundraisers, but this woman had taken raffle tickets to a new height! All the money paid for raffle tickets was pocketed by her childcare center and amazingly; no one ever won the raffle. Who said it didn't pay to have friends in high places.

Ross also listed the names of paraprofessionals in schools across the vast district, whose sexual involvement with Dr. Moorehead allowed them to flaunt the job they were being paid to do. She wrote about one teacher's aide from Homestead Sr. High, who only worked when she wanted to. Another who taught at an alternative school, collected a $7,000 supplement as a band instructor, even though, the school had no marching band!

But Ross saved the best for last. After detailing a myriad of Moorehead's sexual exploits, Ross got down to brass tacks. She wrote about how Moorehead, in the months before and after Hurricane Andrew in 1992… advised his close friends and associates to buy land in the Southwest part of Dade county. Five of Moorehead's closest associates who were always in cahoots with the powerful Big Mo, purchased tracts of land, which appeared to be beyond the realm of development at that time.

A few years later, the population growth had begun to overwhelm Dade County. That land was sought after by the school district as needed for the development of two new, gigantic high schools. That's when Moses Moorehead and his land-buying friends, quietly and privately, sold to two major lobbyists, who then sold the land to the school board at a premium price. Taxpayers were again the victims of their own ignorance.

Even when the developers offered to lower the price, Dr. Moorehead insisted that the district pay top dollar, "to show we are good neighbors," he'd said at the time. The truth was, he didn't want to lose any money on his investment!

But before Barbara Ross signed off for good, cops learned that Moorehead, while principal of a high school, had asked students to buy cocaine for him. According to Ross' suicide note, when the kids came to Moorehead with the dope, he refused to pay them. If they objected, he threatened to have them expelled.

"Evil has many faces," Ross' note concluded. "Now you know their names."

CHAPTER #62

11 News had been teasing Jez's big exclusive about the movement of $1 billion dollars all afternoon. Now it was 5:58 pm... and Jez was about to tell the whole story.

Dean Sands began, "A taxpayer rip-off caught on tape! Tonight, an 11 News exclusive school system investigation reveals a one billion dollar scandal! Joining us here in the studio is 11 News Chief Investigative Reporter Jez Underwood."

The camera abruptly cut from a single shot of Dean Sands, to a two shot of Sands and Underwood, sitting side by side at the anchor desk.

It was an unlikely place for Jez to be. She hadn't spent much time at the anchor desk since her weekend anchor days ended eight years ago. But her close proximity to the main anchor, she knew, meant a signal to the viewers as to just how important her story was.

She began. "Dean, the report you are about to hear, will test our citizen's belief in truth. It will likely damage their trust in public officials, elected and otherwise. But what it won't do, is to continue to hide the corruption and malfeasance in which many in this school system participate every day."

The tape began to roll, the one that Emeril and Jez had shot from the parking garage rooftop.

Jez's narration began:

"On the night after his second in command was knifed to death in the halls of public education, we found Supt. Rod Vascoe in his office just before midnight. He was surrounded by a couple of his top executives, including Nestor Padron and Joe Nunez. Now look, as board member and former deputy superintendent of school operations, Dr. Moses Moorehead, enters the superintendent's office. Although there is no audio recording of what is happening. Channel 11 hired the nation's top lip reader to tell us what was being said.

At that moment, a male voice was heard.

"Vascoe: What are you doing here?"

"Moorehead: "We've got to move some major money before reporters start asking for public records requests."

"Vascoe: "Yeah, and if we do that, they'll ask even more questions. Are you nuts?"

Moorehead: "Are you nuts? Defy me and see who lives to tell the tale."

Vascoe: "What do you want me to do?"

Moorehead: "Transfer $1 billion out of capital reserves, into the Cayman account."

Vascoe: "No fucking way! Not with the cops breathing down my neck. Not now Mo!"

Moorehead: "What I know, is if you don't do what I say, the law will have a hard time finding your body in one piece."

Jez's narration continued. "Our lip reader ends his translation at this point, because, as you can see from the image our cameras captured, Superintendent Rod Vascoe did as he was told, without another word being spoken. Now what you will see, is a videotaped image of the superintendent trans-ferring $1 billion dollars from funds that are designated to build schools and classrooms for kids… to an offshore ac-count, that literally, can't be accounted for."

Jez's narration stopped, and the studio camera tally light flashed "red" letting her know she was back on camera.

"If you think what you've seen just now is an egregious viola-tion of taxpayer trust… stay tuned. Tonight at 11… we reveal hidden camera video of a criminal enterprise, allegedly orga-nized and operated by school board member Dr. Moses

Josiah Moorehead. Incredibly, we catch him using a church as his headquarters for corruption. Stay tuned. That story is coming your way tonight at 11... on 11 News. Dean, back to you."

******

Jez's report had prompted an emergency meeting at the Royal Poinciana Ranch, it had been called by the County Mayor.

"I told you we should have shut her up after that stupid story she did on our diplomas! But no! You "know it alls," said it would blow over, that the media never stayed on a story for more than a few days or weeks. Well it's been four long years, and that cunt hasn't gone away!" School Board member Dr. Jesse Joe Crandall pounded his fist on the bar, as if it were his pulpit.

"Yeah, but what really has come of all her efforts?" asked the Mayor.

"The public has turned on us, that's what," Crandall responded. .

"So what! The public has a short attention span and an indifferent attitude," the Mayor proclaimed. "As long as we keep the authorities at bay, what do we care about what the pathetic citizens of Miami think?"

"What about the district attorney?" The chief of personnel for the school system finally spoke.

"The D.A. will not be a problem," the Mayor said. "Not if she wants to keep her job. I've made that perfectly clear. The game plan is for her people to play dumb and act as if they can't really prove a crime. Meanwhile, she prosecutes the cafeteria worker who makes off with a school lunch. That way she looks like she's cracking down on corruption in the public school system."

"How long can she hold out with that strategy, as long as Jez Underwood is dogging us night and day?" The question came from the district's Deputy Superintendent of Facilities and Maintenance.

"As long as she wants to keep her job and stay alive, my friend." The Mayor put his hand on Padron's shoulder, as if to reassure him.

"You're all fools! Stupid, idiotic, alpha male, fools!"

Lily Molina walked into the living room and took center stage. As the only woman who'd ever been a member of the "sex house," she'd been listening to the men's conversation from the patio. It amused her that no one had noticed her absence, or the fact that the door to the patio was left open. These goofballs could fuck up a wet dream, she thought to herself.

The men were all staring at Lily. "Our dear D.A. will not possibly be able to tolerate the heat that is going to be generated by Mo's cameo as an embezzler. From now on, whatever that nosey bitch says will be taken as gospel by the very public you so generously described as pathetic, Mr. Mayor."

"Lily…" the Mayor tried to interrupt.

"Shut the fuck up you whimpering, pathetic excuse of man! I told you two years ago to clean up this mess! But NOOOOOO! You cavemen knew better. You chose to ignore the 800-pound gorilla in the room, and go about your merry way as if a microscope wasn't trained on your every waking movement. Now, you must realize that I was right all along."

Lily Molina was smug as she saddled up to the only open bar stool. "I'd like a double bourbon up," she instructed Nunez, who was standing behind the bar, trembling for fear of her temper.

"You're always full of Doomsday predictions!" her husband chided her.

"No, my pet. I'm just a realist." In one sweeping motion, Lily Molina swallowed her drink, put the empty glass on the bar, turned and walked out the front door. Had she looked over her shoulder, she would have seen a cluster of grown men staring with their mouths wide open. It would have pleased her!

CHAPTER #63

Carlo was sitting in his bedroom, swirling a martini, waiting for the late news on Channel 11. Samba sat beside him on the bed, looking longingly at her master, with her big brown eyes, wanting constant pets on her head. He hadn't been able to pay his four-legged companion much attention that night, because he'd spent the entire evening phoning all his good friends and family members, telling them to spread the word about Jez's exclusive report. Thankfully, his partner, Orlando had been there to give Samba her share of love and those much-needed walks.

Jez's 6pm report had triggered an avalanche of calls and speculation about what would be on at 11:00. Frankly, even Carlo didn't know. He liked it when Jez gave him plausible deniability, it beat having EDP... equal distribution of paranoia. That was his name for an affliction that was pervasive at the administration building.

EDP manifested at the most curious of times. Carlo remembered when Jez had requested payroll records for three system administrators. The school system didn't provide the information, but when Jez went on the air with the information anyway... all hell broke loose. Any person in the district who had access to that payroll information was cut off. Forget that principals, secretaries, and school treasurers had about 100 reasons for legitimately needing access to that information. The school system's leadership decided it was better to punish the many, for the sins of a few, in order to cut off the snake's head.

Carlo petted Samba, sipped his martini and vowed to one day do what he could, to expose the mania that threatened to destroy a community, the kids who needed an education, and the ignorant taxpayers, who so trustingly turned over their money to people who had no respect for their financial sacrifice.

When he saw the 11 News logo flash on the screen he disengaged the mute button on his remote, so he could hear what was being said. Dean Sands was full screen on his TV.

"Coming up tonight on 11 News, the church, the cash and the career educators all in cahoots allegedly abusing the public's trust. Investigative Reporter Jez Underwood has an exclusive report that will leave you wondering… "where is God, when education is so easily corrupted? Her report is just two minutes away!" Dean Sands stopped talking and looked seriously into the camera… as the station faded to a grocery store commercial.

Not unexpectedly, Carlo's home phone and cell phone began to ring.

The revelations about the kickback money, church contributions and the people involved in the whole sordid affair, didn't shock the few individuals who monitored the school system closely. For the rest of the ignorant public, it was an eye opener!

Even by Miami standards, this was corruption on a scale, rarely seen before. Legislators pocketed illegal campaign contributions, developers took millions to develop affordable housing and then built nothing, commissioner's and city managers accepted bribes and a major airline siphoned taxpayer dollars to build an airport terminal, as if it was money made by the citizens at a lemonade stand.

But using a church, broached the boundaries of even the most ethically challenged or inattentive citizens. Law enforcement and prosecutors could no longer look the other way. Or could they?

At the Miami D.A.'s office… high-level meetings were being held to discuss their response to these revelations.

Underwood's reporting is solid, said some… while others argued that the D.A.'s office couldn't indict on a TV report. It was the typical scenario of the tail wagging the dog.

"How can we get the same goods as the reporter?" asked the D.A.

Next to impossible, she was informed. Underwood's report would have shut down any further questionable activity.

"Well then, I guess there isn't much we can do," the D.A. announced to a shocked group of seasoned prosecutors.

"We aren't even going to try?" asked one.

"How can we?" the D.A. snapped back.

"My apologies. I forgot for a minute that we aren't really here to do the right thing!" the assistant D.A. replied sarcastically.

"Anyone who doesn't value their job security, is free to speak," the D.A. informed the group. There was nothing but silence.

It was understood, the school system would get away with whatever they were doing... at least as long as this D.A. was in charge of prosecuting crimes.

With their tails between their legs, each assistant D.A. left as soon as the meeting was adjourned. Silently, each wondered if there was enough hot water in the city of Miami to make them feel clean once they got home and showered.

CHAPTER #64
TUESDAY

The president of the school board, Jewel Haynes, popped another Xanax, hoping to tamp down her growing anxiety before her press conference. What was happening had her tied up in knots. How was she going to explain three dead administrators, videotape of a board member moving $1 billion from a construction fund for new schools, to a Cayman bank account... and tape of that same board member divvying up the cash spoils from kickbacks and a church collection plate! The press was going to chew her up and spit her out and there wasn't a damn thing she could do about it.

For years she'd been denying any problems in the district, explaining to that Jez Underwood, that the issues she'd been uncovering were isolated and not reflective of the district as a whole.

Jewel pulled out her compact to powder her nose. In the small mirror, she saw that her jet-black hair was perfectly coiffed, and her silk Shantung fuchsia suit was an ideal color for TV. On the surface, she looked cool and collected. But inside, the dread she had for the questions she would soon be asked had her stomach churning like a hurricane.

There was a knock on her office door. "Come in," Jewel shouted. It was her secretary Dinorah.

"Mrs. Haynes, the press is assembled and waiting on you." Dinorah saw the petrified look on her bosses face. Trying to reassure her, Dinorah said, "you'll do just fine Ma'am."

"Dinorah, make sure I have water nearby when I get in front of the microphones. I'm afraid I'll get a bad case of dry mouth trying to defend the insanity going on around here."

Jewel Haynes then stood and walked out of her office. Dinorah followed behind her, holding a silver tray with a small bottle of water on it.

By the time the President made her grand entrance into the media room, the other board members were standing and waiting on her like backup singers!

Jewel virtually ignored her colleagues as she walked up to the podium. First, she thanked the reporters for coming, and informed them she had some prepared remarks before she'd open it up for questions.

"The Miami Public School System is one of the largest in the country. It has always provided a quality education for the children of our great community and will continue to do so, despite the tragedies and difficulties all of us here have experienced in the last week. The board members and administrators are committed to cooperating with the authorities. We ask that the public and the press be patient, and let law enforcement officials do their job. I pledge to all parents and students that none of this will interfere with the daily operations of the school system, or the very important classroom instruction that must continue. Education is our only mission." She stopped, half expecting applause and a standing ovation.

Jewel, more than anyone else, believed her position as board president made her Miami royalty! Instead, she heard shouts from reporters peppering her with questions all at once.

"Please, please! I have one more announcement to make."

President Haynes was on the verge of losing her cool Dinorah thought, as she began to inch her way closer to her boss, just in case it was necessary to rush her out of the media room. Jewel Haynes tugged at her suit jacket, as if straightening out the wrinkles, would make her stand more erect.

"I have called for an emergency meeting of the school board at 9:00am tomorrow, Wednesday. The requirements of a public notice are officially waved by me, the school board president, due to the emergency nature of the situation we now find ourselves in. It is critical to the continuity of this school system to have leadership. Having lost our top two administrators, the board will convene tomorrow to select an interim superintendent." Jewel took in a whiff of breath before continuing.

"I will ask that whoever is named as interim Superintendent, not be eligible for the permanent position. I plan to ask the board to approve funding for a nationwide search for a new superintendent. It is important for the children of the school system to have the best leader that money can buy."

President Haynes continued, "I hope to show this community that education is our top priority, and that inspite of the tragic deaths our school system has suffered, we will unite to make sure that a seamless transition is achieved. It is the very least we can do for the children of Miami."

Jewel Haynes, bowed her head, then thrust it upwards to the sky and walked out of the room as if she were the Queen of England. She totally ignored the reporters shouting questions at her.

CHAPTER #65

Donna Maine sat on the sofa of her hotel suite, clutching a pillow to her chest; her legs were pulled up sideways. She was riveted to the TV press conference Jewel Haynes was holding. She was also finally feeling safe.

Capt. Cohen had arranged for Donna to be put into protective custody. Not only were two undercover officers stationed outside her door, but also she had two female officers inside the suite with her.

She grabbed her cell phone and started to call Carlo, when one of the officers took the phone out of her hands.

"Sorry Mrs. Maine. Capt.'s orders… no phone calls."

"What?" Donna was perplexed.

"We can't risk you talking with anyone. Your cell conversation might be picked up," the officer explained.

"Then I'll use the hotel phone," Donna said as if she'd solved her own problem.

"No Ma'am. Too much risk that the person you call might have a tap on their phone. I'm sorry." The officer walked off into the kitchenette area of the suite. "I'm going to make some lunch. Anybody want anything?" she hollered.

"I want my phone! I want to call Carlo Ferrini! You get Capt. Cohen on the horn and tell her what I require. That's what I want!" Donna Maine was her old bitchy self.

"Mrs. Maine, you can tell her yourself," the officer informed her. "She said she'd be stopping by later today."

Donna shrieked, "Fine!" as she threw the pillow in her arms, at the TV set.

Carlo Ferrini also wanted to call Donna, but he'd been told by Capt. Cohen that would be impossible for the time being.

They'd finally moved Donna out of the hospital late Monday. Carlo had been there when she left, but no one had told him where they were taking her. Frankly, he was relieved not to know details.

He'd returned to work Tuesday morning, only to find himself glued to the TV in his office listening to Jewel Haynes' press conference. She was so clueless, he thought. She must really believe this school system is all about educating children. How else could she say such things with a straight face? Either that, or she was one hell of an actress!

Suddenly, Carlo's phone was ringing. One solid ring versus two short ones meant it was his secretary.

"Marcello?" he asked.

"Sorry to bother you Mr. Ferrini, but Penelope is on the line."

"Thank you Marcello." Carlo punched line #1. "Hi," he said.

"You aren't going to believe what is happening downtown!" she whispered into the phone.

Penelope was his super-secret source for all things at the school system headquarters. He never asked how she got the information she passed on to him. He just knew she was always accurate and he was glad she kept him informed. It also allowed him to give Jez a "heads up" so she could beat her competitors with a big news scoop.

"I just saw Haynes' press conference," he replied.

"No! Not that! Something much better," she teased. "The cops are cleaning out Big Mo's office, and Nestor Padron and Joe Nunez have just been taken away in a squad car!"

Carlo was silent. He was trying desperately to absorb what Penelope was telling him. He wanted to sound surprised, but he really wasn't. After everything that Donna Maine had told the cops about Moorehead, Elder, Padron and Nunez, the Royal Poinciana Ranch and the kickbacks, his only surprise was that the cops allowed Jewel Haynes to assure the public that "all was right with the school system!"

He was sure someone would have to pick the board President up off the floor, when she heard this latest piece of news. Oh, speaking of news, he needed to call Jez.

"Thanks Penelope," he said as he hurriedly hung up and grabbed for his cell phone to punch in the special code he and Jez had pre-arranged years ago.

******

Lee and Lily Molina had called in sick on Tuesday morning. After watching the school board president's press conference, they'd headed to their six-person hot tub to figure out a way to capitalize on the leadership vacancies and turmoil in the school system.

They'd installed the spa in the backyard of their Pinecrest home, the year after Hurricane Andrew. The Jacuzzi tub was part of government grant that one of Lee's teachers had secured for the massage therapy class at his school. But when Hurricane Andrew hit, and the school was in chaos trying to find paper records of purchase orders and procurement authorizations, so Lee instructed his assistant principal to claim the hot tub as a loss on the FEMA paperwork. When it was finally delivered to the school, Lee had his chauffer redirect the delivery truck to his house, where it was installed.

To hide his nefarious deed, Lee Molina also had 10-foot high hedges planted around his property… hedges he also used school money to finance. The only way anyone was going to see his backyard and the taxpayer-funded hot tub, was by helicopter. A fact they learned when Jez got the station's chopper to videotape the stolen hot tub as part of her report on the school system's FEMA scams.

If the truth be told, Lee Molina was not the only school system administrator, principal or mid-level manager who had profited off the backs of the taxpayers following the devastation of Hurricane Andrew. Computers, TVs, musical instruments, even system-owned cars turned up missing... allegedly blown into Georgia by Hurricane Andrew! But Jez and Carlo knew that if anyone had just checked any driveway, backyard or family room of the "well connected," all that missing loot would have been located.

FEMA was treated like a bank ATM by top-level administrators. Money would arrive to replace school computers, for example. And new computers were purchased. It's just that they ended up in private homes. Meanwhile, teachers would be told the money was tied up in bureaucratic paperwork.

Although the district attorney's public corruption unit had been handed an outline of the thefts, malfeasance, and mismanagement, over the years, by insiders, they did nothing. It was as if these crime fighter's feet were stuck in quick drying cement.

In fact, when school board member, Amelia Salas met with prosecutors to inform them about the truckloads of "Free Meal" food, secretly being dumped in the county's landfill, they actually told her there was nothing they could do. They then, suggested she tell Jez Underwood! Salas had called Jez in shock! She couldn't believe that criminal prosecutors would have the nerve tell her to call a TV reporter, instead of tackling the corruption of wasted taxpayer dollars.

Jez, of course, ran with the story, learning that the district was dumping food that was, in some cases, 5-years old. Rusted cans of bad tomato sauce had been sent to a number of elementary schools. Concerned food service workers had finally contacted Salas, when they failed to stop the shipments of bad food commodities.

As Jez investigated further... a couple of food delivery truck drivers tipped her off to an even more alarming problem. Food was going bad, because the warehouse where it was stored had no air conditioning! The employees provided Jez with pictures of the food boxes that clearly stated on the outside that the food should be stored at 72-degrees. Other pictures they gave her showed the warehouse thermostat at 83-degrees. How could food storage not be air conditioned, Jez had wondered? Miami was hot nearly every day of the year!

That report had triggered outrage from parents and the federal government, which was paying for most of the food. As a result, the FBI and U.S. Attorney's office had launched an investigation.

Jez was curious why the feds were doing the district attorney's job. Then she discovered that the D.A.'s daughter was failing her senior year in high school. But because the D.A. played ball with the big boys in the system by turning her head away from obvious corruption and felonious misdeeds, the girl's principal was pressured to allow her to graduate.

So much for Governor James Barwick's "A +" Plan, Jez thought. The program was designed to make sure graduates were deserving of a high school diploma.

CHAPTER #66

Spotting the front-page headlines in the morning newspaper, a smug grin appeared on the killer's face. SCANDAL ROCKS SCHOOL SYSTEM! Poor Hank, thought the killer, he can't stay on the front page any longer than he could hold an erection without Viagra! The killer then crawled back into bed with a cup of coffee to soak up every written word!

In addition to the details of Channel 11's report on the money transfers to a Cayman Island Bank, and the kickback scheme at the church, was an article noting that funeral services would be held for Superintendent Rod Vascoe, that day at 3:00pm. The killer made a note of the time and place.

"I must be present. Such an event is critical to my career."

Draining the cup of coffee, Hank Maine's murderer, laid out appropriate funeral attire... and then got in a hot shower.

******

Capt. Shelia Cohen arrived at the hotel where Donna Maine was under guard. Her officers had warned her that Mrs. Maine was having a snit about not being able to use the phone.

"Hello, Donna," Cohen said as she entered the hotel suite. "I trust you're finding your accommodations comfortable."

"Capt. Cohen," Donna whined, "Your people will not allow me to use the phone! What the hell am I supposed to do all day? Watch re-runs of I Love Lucy?"

"If that's your favorite show, we aren't about to keep you from enjoying it," Cohen answered dryly. "The reason for the phone restriction is simple. We are trying to save your life. You asked for protection and we are providing it!" Cohen was starting to get pissed. Who do these people think they are, expecting the taxpayers to shield them from danger while they live like spoiled millionaires?

"It's a very simple arrangement that we have with you Mrs. Maine. You either play by our rules and provide us with the information we require, or we will escort you to the lobby and you are free to call whomever you wish, watch any TV show you want, and put yourself in the path of whoever you think is trying to kill you. After all, they've already put your husband six feet under. Do you really think they'll hesitate to do the same to you?"

Donna Maine was clearly sulking, but she knew Capt. Cohen was right. She'd traded a life of freedom so she could live... period.

"Can you at least make arrangements for Carlo Ferrini to visit me now and then?" Donna pleaded.

"I will see what I can do," Cohen replied. "But first, I need to know if you've remembered anything more since we talked the other night."

"Yeah," Donna said as she reached for the notepad she'd tossed on the couch. She was silent for a few seconds as she read her notations.

"Downtown parking!" she was almost giddy. "Last night while the officers and I were watching the news... by the way did you see that undercover videotape Jez Underwood had of Moses Moorehead? Whew! Whew!"

Sheila Cohen did not reply.

"Well," Donna continued. "There was this story about how there is no parking for the new Carnival Center for the Performing Arts. I mean what collection of county commissioners build a world class performing arts center and don't plan for parking?"

Donna had a point, Cohen thought.

"That made me remember that a few years ago, Hank came home one day in a total rage. He was shouting about some parking lot deal he was trying to broker with that scumball lobbyist... oh, what is his name?" She stopped to think.

"Sid! Sid Messing! You know, the guy who was part of the teacher's union healthcare scam that Jez exposed. Well, according to Hank, he and Messing had brought in a big time developer who wanted to buy the land and put a big parking garage on it, to service the new Performing Arts Center. But it was one of those deals that Amelia Salas managed to kibosh at a board meeting. She'd argued that the taxpayers would be better served by building an arts and entertainment magnet academy for kids, and that the district should lease the parking spaces in the evening and on weekends to the Carnival Center, instead of selling the land at the bargain basement price of $8 million! I mean, really, Capt., anyone with a 10th grade education knows that property across the street from the most modern performing arts center in the country, is worth more than a paltry $8 million. It does make you wonder who was going to be getting a piece of the action, doesn't it?" Donna stopped and looked back down at her notepad.

"Go on," Capt. Cohen encouraged her.

"Well Hank kept saying something about Royal Castle, you know, the hamburger joint. I guess that's what used to be on that property. He told me the land belonged to the father of a school system big shot. Hank was pissed that the person cultivated favor and promotions by getting his father to donate the land to the school system some years back."

"And..." Capt. Cohen said, trying to coax more information from her.

"And that's all I remember! Oh! Except, shortly after Hank came home ranting and raving, he got a call from Dr. Moses Moorehead... and he left to meet up with him. Hank never said another word about Royal Castle or parking lots after that. I really don't understand what all the fuss was about." Donna plopped on the couch and reached for the TV remote.

"Before we watch I Love Lucy, Donna, let's talk a bit more about this parking lot, shall we?" Capt. Cohen took the remote from her hand, put it on the coffee table, and got out her tape recorder.

"Let's get this on tape, Donna," she said as she pressed the record button.

CHAPTER #67

Big Mo and his aide Franklin Elder had holed up the night before at Charlotte Mackey's home. She was adamant that she wanted them gone first thing Tuesday morning, so Moorehead was furiously trying to get in touch with his charter boat captain at Black Point Marina.

"I want to go fishing in Bimini," Mo told the Captain.

"Wow! That's not like you Mo," the Captain chuckled.

"I don't recall asking you to assess mah destinations. As long as I'm paying you with good money, you don't ask questions and you take me where I want to go!"

"Sure, sure man." The captain knew something wasn't right, but he was smart enough not to cross Moses Moorehead.

"What time do you want to shove off in the morning, sir?" the captain asked.

"Forget morning, we're traveling at night. I'll meet you at the marina at 7pm." With that, Moses clicked his phone off and the boat's captain was left looking at his cell phone as if it had three heads.

CHAPTER #68

Joe Nunez and Nestor Padron managed to avoid the media "perp walk" as they were taken away by police since all the reporters and photographers were upstairs attending Jewel Haynes' press conference. They were driven to police head-quarters in separate patrol cars, and put in separate interro-gation rooms. Neither man was stupid, even if they weren't very smart. Both insisted on calling a lawyer before they'd answer even one question.

"So which one of you is waiting on Troy White?" Detective Hal Davis asked Joe Nunez. There was no response.

"What? You can't afford him?" Davis taunted. "Carlo Ferrini can. I don't think they're paying you enough, Joe!" Davis chuckled softly as he noticed a bead of sweat trickle from Nunez's forehead.

"Well, thank the heavens for small favors," Davis continued. "At least the TV cameras weren't rolling when we took you and Padron out of the building. They won't get a good picture of either one of you until we snap your mug shot! Right Joe?" Davis snickered. Nunez sat silently.

In the next room, Det. Gonzalez wasn't having any more success with Nestor Padron.

"We've got cops packing up all your files Mr. Padron. I heard them calling for a big U-Haul! It's just a matter of time before we figure out what you and the dead superintendent were up to." Gonzalez stared at Padron.

"Ever been in jail before Nestor?" Gonzalez let his question hang in the air.

"I didn't think so. Man, are you in for an education! Get it... education!" Det. Gonzalez was laughing at his own joke. Then he suddenly stopped.

"Let me tell you, Miami's downtown jail is one of the scummi-
est I've ever been in. Hell, the federal government nearly
shut it down a few years ago, it was so bad and I'm just talking about the physical facility. Never mind the nauseating dirt
bags who are in there with you, that is, when you get there.
But you'll be here for a while once your attorney arrives,
cause we've got lots of questions for you and Mr. Nunez."

"I'd like some coffee detective," Padron said.

"One coffee, coming up!" Detective Gonzalez repeated as he
stood. Then he glared at Padron. "But this will be the last
hospitality service you get before we lock you up. Or maybe
we'll just let the taxpayers you've ripped off have a whack at
you and your thieving friend."

Padron was staring at his clasped hands on the table. It
looked as if he was praying.

"Cream and sugar, American style, or do you want a shot of
Cuban coffee?" Gonzalez inquired.

"Cuban please," Padron responded without looking up.

CHAPTER #69

Jez had tried to sleep in on Tuesday morning. After her big exclusives at 6 & 11 the night before, she'd gotten Boris to agree to have another reporter cover Jewel Haynes' news conference. But once again, sleep did not come easy to Jez, so she got up, dressed and headed to the station around 10a.m.

At a stoplight, she dialed Emeril's cell phone.

"Good morning schlepping beauty," he said when he answered. He'd seen his caller ID indicate that it was Jez calling.

"If I'm the beauty, then you're the beast!" she replied. "Are you on your way in?"

"I've been cheer sentz 8:00 waiting on ju blondie!"

"Great! I thought we agreed to come in late, refugee?" Jez snapped.

"8:00 is late for me. Ju forget I'm scheduled 7-4," Emeril reminded Jez.

"Yeah, yeah! I'll meet you at your vehicle in 10 minutes," Jez insisted.

As soon as Jez and Emeril hooked up, they immediately headed for the school board building. Although they weren't there to cover the press conference, they'd considered dropping in, to at least listen. But no sooner had they parked, than they noticed a convoy of Miami Police cars lined up in front of the administration building.

"Shit!" Jez muttered. "What the hell is going on?"

"Maybe her Highness Queen Jewel requested police protection," Emeril responded giggling.

"I hope she's paying for it," Jez half whispered as she dug into her briefcase for her binoculars. "Are you just going to sit there, or are you going to get your camera?" she asked Emeril in a very bitchy tone.

"Chill, blondie," he huffed. "It's right here," he said, as he reached into the backseat and hauled the heavy camera up with one hand.

"Good thinking, refugee," Jez complimented him, knowing that usually, the photographers had to get out of their vehicles and open the heavy duty lockbox in the trunk, where the camera was stored.

Emeril hoisted the camera up onto his shoulder and began rolling videotape.

"That's Detective Gonzalez and Davis getting out of the first car," Jez announced as she peered through her binoculars.

"I'm getting it," Emeril replied.

"What the hell is going on?" Jez was clearly puzzled. At that moment, her cell phone began to ring. Immediately she recognized the code that she and Carlo had set up.

"Hey," she said. "What's up?"

"Nunez and Padron are being taken into custody and their offices are being raided, along with Moorehead's and Elder's," Carlo excitedly informed her.

"I wondered why the cavalry had arrived," Jez responded. "Thanks, we're here and we're rolling. Later." Then she flipped her phone closed.

After about 20 minutes, and nothing else had happened, Emeril was about to inform Jez that he needed to change tapes, when he heard her shout, "Look left! Look left!"

Emeril turned his camera left and saw Nestor Padron and Joe Nunez being walked to patrol cars and shoved inside.

Two seconds later, his camera began to beep, indicating he'd run out of videotape.

Jez grabbed Emeril's Nextel and clicked for Boris. "Boris this is Jez. Are you there?"

"Go ahead Jez." Danken was sitting in his office with his three chief minions all reading the overnight ratings.

"I've got tonight's exclusive lead!" she said teasingly. She began to laugh out loud, when she saw four of her competitors live truck operators all jumping out of their vans, pulling their hair out, as they realized a big story had just occurred and none of their crews were downstairs to roll on two administrators being taken away by police.

"What's so funny?" Boris asked, puzzled by Jez's laughter.

"There are four live truck operators who just realized they've been scooped on tonight's big story!" Jez was still chuckling as Boris began yelling at her to tell him what the story was.

CHAPTER #70

Carlo was one of hundreds who turned out for the funeral of Miami School Superintendent Rod Vascoe. The service was held at the Church of the Little Flower in Coral Gables. The Spanish style Catholic Church had an old-world feel and because of its size and beauty, was a coveted location for society weddings.

The first twenty rows in the church had been reserved for local dignitaries, including the school board members, an array of elected officials and leaders in Miami's business community. Most of the rest of those who attended were people who worked for the school system, many of whom owed R.V. for getting them their job.

As the plaintive organ music began to play, Bonnie Vascoe walked down the center aisle of the church, escorted by her son and daughter. The widow Vascoe was an attractive woman of about 55. She'd worked in the system as a teacher's aide, before marrying R.V. By the time he was named superintendent, she was suddenly an elementary school principal. More than a few tongues wagged about her getting the job because of her husband, and not because of her qualifications. Why people were so surprised, always tickled Carlo when he'd over hear the gossips talking about Bonnie. That kind of promotion was SOP... standard operating procedure in the Miami school system.

An hour later, as Bonnie Vascoe walked back up the aisle, her swollen red eyes, partially shielded by the large brim of her black floppy hat, she spotted Carlo at the end of one of the pews, and mouthed a "thank you for coming." Bonnie Vascoe then left the church, got into a black Limousine and left for a private family service at the gravesite.

Carlo was on his way home when he got a phone call from Capt. Cohen asking him to meet her in the parking lot of the Publix grocery store on Dade Blvd. on Miami Beach.

"I've agreed to let you visit our friend, but I don't want to discuss anything over the phone," Capt. Cohen had insisted.

Forty minutes later they rendezvoused in the parking lot. Capt. Cohen asked him to follow her.

They didn't drive far. The police had Donna Maine under guard at an offbeat boutique hotel, just two blocks from the beach. It was called the Abbey Hotel. An appropriate name, Carlo thought, since Donna was going to be living like a nun for the foreseeable future.

When they got to the lobby, Capt. Cohen gave him a stern lecture about the importance of secrecy. "If her presence here is discovered, trust me Mr. Ferrini, you will be the first suspect I lock up. Do you understand?"

"I have no desire to see the inside of your interrogation rooms ever again!" he replied. "I want Donna safe, and the system's secrets uncovered, more than you even know."

When the elevator opened, Capt. Cohen used a key to access the top floor. "You can come visit any time you want. All I ask is that you call and use this password so the officers will know it is you." Capt. Cohen then handed him her business card. On the back of it she'd written the code phrase he was to use and the number he was to call. Carlo studied it for a few seconds, then pulled out his wallet and put the card inside.

"I'm ready to take my vows," he declared.

"Very clever! Do I sense a theme emerging since we are at the Abbey?" Capt. Cohen replied sarcastically. "Save the commentary and just do as you're asked, Mr. Ferrini."

As they stepped off the elevator, three uniformed officers blocked their way. As soon as they saw that it was Capt. Cohen, they parted, and let their boss and Ferrini pass.

When Capt. Cohen unlocked the door, Donna Maine was sitting on the couch channel surfing with the remote. As soon as she saw Carlo, she was up on her feet screaming with joy as she ran to give him a big hug.

"God it's so good to see you, Carlo. I'm going stir crazy! They won't let me use the phone and you're the only visitor they're allowing." Donna Maine had grabbed his hand and was pulling him over to the couch. She took the remote and clicked the mute button, then looked over at Capt. Cohen.

"Thank you Capt. Thank you so very much!" Donna Maine was overwhelmed by the loneliness she'd been feeling, and she wanted Sheila Cohen to understand the depth of her appreciation at being allowed to have a visitor.

"I'm hoping Mr. Ferrini can help jog your memory, as much as I want to keep you happy, Mrs. Maine." Then Capt. Cohen turned and left.

Donna Maine, took Carlo's hand and pulled him close to her, whispering in his ear, "Carlo, what have I gotten myself into?"

"A safe place, that's what!" Carlo reached up with both hands and cupped her face. "Do I need to remind you that people want you dead?" He stared intently into her eyes waiting for a response.

"I guess maybe you do," Donna replied, her eyes shifting downward, away from his intense stare.

Carlo realized it was time to change the subject. "So, are you going to give me the nickel tour of your fine hideout?" he asked.

Immediately, she jumped up, took his hand and introduced him to the police officers both inside the hotel suite and outside in the hall, letting them know he was an approved visitor... as if they didn't already know that! She showed him the bedrooms; hers had a partial view of the beach, then the kitchen area.

"I guess I'll have to learn to cook, if I don't want to starve," Donna giggled nervously as they walked back into the main living room area of the suite.

"Your restaurant days are over my dear," Carlo stated emphatically, so as to remind her again, that her life had been unalterably changed.

"Oh, my God!" Donna screamed. Immediately her bodyguards jumped up, guns drawn... until they saw that she was pointing at the TV.

In the muted silence, all of them watched as Nestor Padron and Joe Nunez were shoved into Miami police cars. Donna reached for the TV remote and clicked the mute button off... just as Dean Sands was saying... "That story is coming your way at 6pm."

Donna turned to Carlo. "Do you know what's going on?" she asked.

"No," he lied. "I guess we'll find out in... 15 minutes," he said, as he looked down at his watch.

******

"I thought you assured my client that no media was around when you brought him in for questioning," shouted Nestor Padron's attorney as he burst into the interrogation room.

"That's right!" Det. Gonzalez snapped back. "The media was upstairs at Jewel Haynes' news conference. Why?"

"Clearly they weren't, Detective. On my way back from the men's room, the TV on one of the desks was showing videotape of Mr. Padron and Mr. Nunez being put in patrol cars!"

"Oh my lord," Padron mumbled as he lay his head down on the table.

"There wasn't a TV camera in sight!" Detective Gonzalez insisted.

"Is this your idea of a joke?" Padron was now pale and almost whimpering.

"What station? What video?" Det. Gonzalez said as he got up and went into the outer offices. He looked at the TV sitting on Det. Davis' desk just in time to see Jez Underwood sitting next to Dean Sands, followed by pictures of Nunez and Padron being walked out of the school administration building by uniformed officers.

"According to sources," he heard Jez say, "these top school system administrators are currently under interrogation by Miami Police detectives, in connection with the possible fraud and mismanagement of millions of taxpayer dollars. Sources tell 11 News, that at least four offices were raided by police today at the downtown administration building, following Channel 11's exclusive videotape of an alleged midnight, money moving, meeting in the late superintendent's office, the night before he died."

The sound from the TV abruptly went dead. Detective Gonzalez jerked around to see Capt. Cohen standing with the remote in her hand. "My office now!" she growled in a low, but serious tone of voice. "And bring Davis with you." She turned on her heels and was gone before Gonzalez could utter a response.

******

Meanwhile, at the Abbey Hotel, Carlo and Donna sat riveted by Jez's report.

"You know Hank always told me he thought those two were stooges," Donna said out loud. "But then, consider the source," she added. When Carlo didn't respond, she turned to him and asked, "Wasn't one of them your boss?"

"In a matter of speaking," Carlo mumbled, still glued to the TV.

They were stooges, he knew. On that, Hank Maine and he agreed. But R.V. often surrounded himself with stooges. Carlo always suspected that it made R.V. feel smart, something he clearly wasn't. That's the trouble with "yes men," Carlo thought to himself, they don't speak up to warn you when you're about to fall into an abyss, they just follow right behind you into the darkness.

Carlo realized Donna was still talking. "You know, Hank wasn't the most honest when it came to his educational credentials, but I remember him telling me that when Nestor Padron was Principal at Coral Gables High school, he used an ESE teacher to write his doctoral thesis, and put a substitute in her classroom for the whole year! Can you believe that? I mean, ESE kids, aren't they special education or something? Shouldn't that guy have used a gym teacher or someone a little less critical to the education of kids to do his personal work?" Donna stopped, waiting on Carlo to say something.

"But Padron isn't a PhD." Carlo said as he turned to face her.

"I know," said Donna. "I guess the woman's a slow typist or something!" She giggled. "I mean really, Carlo, how does the administration not catch on to the fact that they're paying a substitute for a whole year to teach a class in which the teacher is there every day! That's just nuts! Even stupid Hank caught on. He lorded it over Padron's head every chance he got. It was his typical blackmail scheme. That's how he made sure people were beholden to him. If Padron blew the whistle on Hank, then Hank would blow it right back at him!"

"I know," was all Carlo could say. It wore him out just thinking about all the devious fraud that went unchallenged in this school system.

"Didn't Jez Underwood catch Nunez using school maintenance workers to do construction and landscaping at his home during office hours?" Carlo asked Donna.

"She tried. But Hank told me Nunez got tipped off to her surveillance by one of his neighbors, and Joe immediately stopped the whole charade. At least for a while." Donna sat quiet for a moment, then jumped up and grabbed her notepad and pen. "Hey! I need to write all that down for Capt. Cohen," she exclaimed.

"Add this little nugget to that list," Carlo instructed Donna.

"What?"

"Make a note for Cohen to check out the system's deal with the company that got a $17 million dollar contract to retrofit all the school buses with air conditioning." Carlo paused as Donna wrote. "The good Capt. might just discover that, R.V.'s wife has a cousin, who is part owner of that company."

"No!" Donna gasped.

"It gets better! The cousin is also head of the district's transportation department... you know... the department that operates and maintains all the school buses!"

"Holy, Mary, mother of God!" Donna was writing as fast as she could.

"There's one other thing we want to give Capt. Cohen the heads up on." Carlo stopped.

"What?" Donna looked at him, her pen poised in her hand, as if she might actually know how to take dictation.

"Just jot down FEMA payments for portable classrooms after Hurricane Andrew." Carlo smiled. He'd waited years to find the right moment to drop that dime on the top educators who were always in cahoots. Now was that time.

CHAPTER #71

It was 6:45pm Tuesday night, and Captain J.R. was at Black Point Marina, gassing up his 48-foot Hatteras for the trip to Bimini. The Captain was no fool. He knew there was something amiss about this whole trip, but as long as he got paid, he didn't care.

J.R. was not your typical charter boat captain. Instead of looking like he rarely bathed, with a scraggly beard and bandana tied around his head, Captain J.R. was movie star good looking. His 6-foot frame was chiseled like a Greek God and he sported a thick, dark mustache that made him look like Clark Gable's twin.

He'd come to Florida as a college student. But after graduating and working for a national moving company as a salesman for several years, he'd traded his business suits for a pair of shorts and a muscle shirt. He bought his first boat with the money he'd earned doing catalogue modeling, and eventually was able to upgrade to his beloved Hattaras, which allowed him to run charters to the Bahamas and overnight sport fishing ventures in the Florida straits. As long as the money was green, he kept his mouth shut and did what his customers wanted.

In a shaded section of the marina's parking lot, Moses Moorehead and Franklin Elder skulked behind the front visors of Elder's car, observing the surroundings. They wanted to make sure they hadn't been followed, and that Captain J.R. hadn't tipped off authorities to their plan to flee the country.

"Wouldn't a "go fast" boat be a better idea, Mo?" Franklin quizzed his boss. "I mean that's what all the human smugglers are using these days to get Cubans to Florida's shores."

"That's brilliant, you brick head!" Big Mo responded. "Let's give thuh Coast Guard a ruhlly good reason to check us out, whuy don't we!" He then hit Franklin upside the head with his hand, causing him to whine an, "I'm sorry Mo."

By 7:00pm, Big Mo was satisfied that they were in the clear, so he and Franklin headed off toward the fishing boat that would put them on course toward a new life, or so they thought.

As the two men, with suitcases in hand began running for Captain J.R.'s boat, they heard the distinctive whine of a Coast Guard helicopter. It stopped them dead in their tracks. Both looked up at the sky, just as the familiar orange whirly-bird banked right toward the marina. A voice, almost God like, projected from a megaphone... "This is the United States Coast Guard. Stop right where you are!"

Both Moorehead and Elder froze. How could they have found out about us, each wondered silently? Then another order came from up above.

"Stay on your boat. Do not get off the boat." "¡Quédense en el barco! ¡No se desembarquen!

"Boat?" Moorehead said to his sidekick. "We aren't on no boat."

That's when Franklin Elder, standing poised as a statue, spotted the boat the helicopter was hovering over.

"They aren't talking about us, Big Mo!" Elder informed his boss... as he pointed to the "go fast" boat heading toward the marina.

"Move it," Big Mo ordered and both men hightailed it for Captain J.R.'s big rig charter fishing boat.

"Welcome aboard mates," Captain J.R. greeted them as they jumped onto the stern. It seems the action follows you guys wherever you go." The Captain was pointing at the boat 50-feet away, where dozens of Cubans were scampering into the water in an attempt to reach shore.

"Yeah, well get us away from all this action," Big Mo commanded.

"Money first, Dr. Moorehead." Captain J.R. extended his arm with his palm up.

"Just get us the hell out of here," Big Mo repeated as he pulled a wad of cash out of his pant pocket. "You don't have to file a flight plan, or boat plan or whatever do you?" he inquired as Captain J.R. counted his $10,000.

"No sir!" he mumbled. "No flight plan is required for Captain J.R.'s charter boat. We just go where you tell us. Now get your ass below deck and stay there till I tell you the coast is clear."

As Captain J.R. maneuvered his Hattaras out of the dock space... Big Mo and Franklin could hear the sirens of police cars arriving at Black Point Marina. Immigration agents would be right behind them, they knew; ready to decide if the boatload of Cuban refugees had technically reached dry American soil. The "wet foot/dry foot" policy meant the difference between a boat trip back to their Communist homeland, courtesy of the U.S. government, or a new life in America.

Unlike the passengers in the "go fast" boat... Moses Moorehead and Franklin Elder were in search of dry land that was not American soil. Their plans were to vanish for a while.

CHAPTER #72
WEDNESDAY

Nothing in Miami ever started on time. That's because Miami was on Cuban time, as it was gingerly referred to. So when the clock ticked 9:25am on Wednesday morning and school board president Jewel Haynes finally approached her chair on the dais, it was no surprise to anyone.

God forbid these people might ever work in TV, Jez thought from her seat in the back press booth. Not only did she work in an industry where seconds mattered, but she was part German. Her genetic timepiece was wound as tight as a finely tuned Bavarian cuckoo clock.

"It's a god damn emergency meeting," she squawked to Emeril, who'd joined her in her private booth, once he saw there was no hurry to begin the meeting. "You'd think, just this once, they could start on time."

"Blondie, ju are just going to have to take one of jur chill pills," he told her.

"I hate it when people are late!" she snapped.

Jez watched as Jewel took her seat, followed by Bitzy Champlain, the Reverend Jesse Joe Crandall, Amelia Salas, Patty Sable, Hammond Garfield, Dr. Cecil Raymond... and last, but not least, the unintelligible Mario Castro.

"Hey Paul," Jez shouted to the audio booth guy in the adjacent room. "You got your subtitles software qued up?" Paul knew she was referring to Mario Castro.

"Mumbles might have something to say!" Jez then burst into laughter at the nickname the media had bestowed on the English challenged board member. As Emeril got up to go stand by his camera, he shot Jez "the look." It said, I can take your shit, but be careful who else hears you say these things.

"Oh I'm sorry Emeril. Did you think I was talking about you?" Jez then doubled over as she and Paul snickered over her Spanglish joke.

"God will get ju blondie!" Emeril muttered as he left the pressroom. "See if I bring you any cookies today."

Since Jez had stopped working in the official pressroom, she often asked Emeril to bring her some of the district's most delicious chocolate chip or oatmeal raisin cookies. It was about the only thing she missed from that beehive of brainless wonders that called themselves journalists.

"My hips don't need the calories," was her retort.

"No they don't!" Emeril shouted back.

"Touché!" she heard Paul say, just as President Haynes pounded the gavel and called the meeting to order.

"Asshole!" She muttered, just loud enough for Emeril to hear her as he left the pressroom.

"Please stand for the Pledge of Allegiance," she heard Jewel Haynes announce. So Jez stood. It was one of her pet peeves, people who didn't stand, put their hand over their heart, say the pledge out loud or sing the National Anthem. She'd seen so many big name athletes and celebrities, chew gum and stand mute, that she vowed anyone watching her, would never question her patriotism.

Being an American was a privilege, not a right. She lived in a community where as many people appreciated their citizenship, as those who simply felt entitled to it, but held none of the morals and ethics, for which most Americans stood. Being called an American was not the same as "being" an American. But distinguishing between the two was getting harder and harder in Miami.

Jez sat down when Jewel Haynes called for a moment of silence. It was only then that she realized it was exactly one week, at this very moment in the board meeting, when she'd heard Hank Maine's wail of death. So much had happened, she thought.

President Haynes called the meeting to order and told her fellow board members that there was much from the previous week's meeting to accomplish since the meeting was aborted because of Dr. Maine's murder. So much more was about to happen, starting with the selection of an Interim Superintendent.

True to her word, President Jewel Haynes first proposed an emergency item calling for the appointment of an Interim Superintendent who would not be eligible for the permanent position. She also asked the board to approve funding for a national search for a superintendent.

There was little debate from her colleagues, who voted for both items without any discussion. Conspicuously absent from the dais was Dr. Moses Moorehead. Not one word was said about his empty chair, which caused Jez to chuckle to herself. Was it true? Was the Stealth Superintendent suddenly irrelevant? Or was he like the Wizard of Oz? Able to pull the board members strings from behind some hidden curtain?

Jez didn't have to wait long for the answer. As soon as nominations commenced, Moorehead's fingerprints blazed as brightly as a full moon over the Atlantic Ocean.

"I jominash, Lily Molina." It was Mario "Mumbles" Castro. Score one for the Cuban mafia, Jez thought. Molina would make a real working superintendent. Working on her knees, no doubt.

Amelia Salas opened her microphone next. "I nominate Dr. Noelle Baptiste." A Cuban nominating a Haitian, interesting. Jez pondered the ramifications for Salas.

Hammond Garfield stayed alert long enough to put up the name of R.V.'s Deputy Superintendent of Transportation... Jeremy Harris.

"Dr. Raymond?" Jewel Haynes flashed her adoring eyes at the silver fox.

"Yes, madam President. I'd like to nominate Lourdes Rubenstein, Assistant Principal at Miami Beach High."

"He's nominating his own niece!" Jez was talking to herself. Astonished, she grabbed for something to get Emeril's attention. Her Tic Tacs were nearby, so she got one and aimed at his head. When he felt the pelt of the tiny breath mint, he looked around to see Jez asking him if he was rolling on Raymond's audacious nomination.

"Jes Jez, I'm rolling," he informed her as he rolled his eyes.

Jez watched Jewel Haynes look at both Rev. Crandall and Patty Sable, neither of whom had indicated they had a nomination. Just as Jewel was about to open her mouth, Jesse Joe Crandall beat her to the punch, nominating a former football coach to be superintendent.

"I buhlieve that Dr. Frederick Noonan has the command of leadership and the temperament of a disciple to steer this school system in its time of great need," Crandall pontificated.

Jewel then looked at Patty, who waved her off, indicating she didn't want to be a part of any of this nonsense. Jez knew Patty was still distraught over R.V.'s death. She'd always been one of his biggest defenders, inspite of his reputation as a simpleton.

"Well, if all the other board members have spoken, who wish to make a nomination, then I will conclude this process," President Haynes announced. "I believe it is my duty and my privilege to nominate Dr. Cecil Raymond to be the Interim Superintendent."

There was a gasp from the audience. No one had figured that a board member would nominate another board member. But Jez was privately smiling. What a power play! She had to hand it to Jewel, it was a brilliant stroke of politics.

By nominating Raymond, she was trying to remove him from the board, just two months before the board would be required to elect a new president. Everyone knew Dr. Raymond was campaigning to become the next board president. Hell, he'd already managed to get a school named after himself... becoming board president would be a walk in the park for this guy! But Jez knew that if Jewel could get Raymond named the interim superintendent, he wouldn't be eligible for board president... and with Moses Moorehead apparently on the lamb, Jewel was calculating that she only needed to garner four votes, to be re-elected. That was easier than the five she would need if all board members were present and accounted for.

"You go girl!" Jez said to no one in particular.

By noon, when President Haynes called for a one-hour recess the board was on its 30th ballot, and not one person had changed their vote or withdrawn their nominee.

As Jez and Emeril walked outside to head to a nearby café, she informed him, "I think this may take more than the 100 ballots they went through two years ago, to elect a board president."

"I'd better get more tapes," Emeril informed her.

"Yeah, and I'd better get a thicker cushion for my ass!" Jez knew she was looking at a political stalemate that would test everyone's patience and fortitude... especially hers.

CHAPTER #73

It had been a full week, and the homicide detectives who were investigating Hank Maine's murder, had zero suspects, and very little forensic evidence.

They'd identified the weapon as a Semper Fi Collectible Marine Corp knife, 10½ inches long. There were no witnesses, no fingerprints, but plenty of motive. The tox screen came back clean, and the Medical Examiner's report stated that Maine died of internal injuries caused by a single knife wound in the gut. About the only new piece of information they'd uncovered, was where Maine had purchased his sexy ladies lingerie at the Victoria's Secret store in the Aventura Mall.

They'd at least managed to close out the death of Superintendent Rod Vascoe as natural... a heart attack. And the M.E. had ruled Dr. Barbara Ross' plunge to the cement sidewalk, as a valid suicide.

Now they were hunkered down, pouring over the mounds of documents collected from the offices of Dr. Moses Moorehead, Franklin Elder, Nestor Padron and Joe Nunez.

"Has the geek squad finished the forensics on the four computers?" Capt. Sheila Cohen had just arrived, carrying a McDonald's bag in her hand. Breakfast would be fast food today.

"Not yet Captain," Davis replied.

"Get me a time frame," she shouted just before slamming her door shut. She wanted to eat her breakfast burrito in peace and quiet. She should have known better. Thirty seconds later her phone rang. It was the detail at the Abbey Hotel calling to tell her that Donna Maine had a new list of things to discuss with her.

"I'll try to be there by 11," Capt. Cohen said in between bites, and a sip of coffee. Indigestion was already sending her stomach an alert, when the phone rang again.

"Cohen here."

"Are you watching the school board meeting?" She recognized the voice as that of the police chief.

"No sir. You said detectives didn't need to be watching TV's in their offices when I put in for them in last year's budget request."

"So I did," he responded, half back peddling in his tone. "Well get down to Public Information and check out one of their sets. Dr. Moses Moorehead is a no show for today's big emergency meeting. Do we have a handle on his whereabouts?"

"No sir. We put his house under surveillance around noon yesterday, but he hasn't shown up. Neither has Franklin Elder. The units at the airports and bus depots report no activity. It's the same at the train stations."

"What the hell are we doing to find them?" the chief was getting huffy.

"We issued a BOLO to every agency yesterday, but there is no way we can cover all the ports and marinas. We just don't have the staff, sir."

"If I find out they paddled their way to the Bahamas in a row boat, somebody's going to lose her stripes, Capt. Cohen."

"Yes sir." Cohen needn't have tried to respond. The chief had already hung up.

As Sheila Cohen attempted to finish her late breakfast, a light bulb went off in her head. "The Bahamas!" She jumped up from her desk and swung her office door open.

"Davis! Where did Jez Underwood say that church money was being sent by Moses Moorehead and his band of thieves in her report the other night?"

"The Cayman Islands, Captain."

"Well what are you waiting on? You and Gonzalez book a flight to the Caymans and find Moorehead. And don't come back until you have him in handcuffs!" Cohen slammed her door shut.

Gonzalez and Davis looked at one another in shock. Traveling to exotic locales was not something the Miami Police department did very often. Before either Detective could call travel services, the bureau's secretaries and other detectives had formed a Conga line and were singing the familiar commercial jingle... "The Cayman Islands!"

"Bite me, you jealous assholes!" Gonzalez shouted, as he dialed the travel agents number.

******

50 miles off the Florida coast, Dr. Moses Moorehead was just waking up. They'd docked in Bimini around midnight, and had decided to sleep on Captain J.R.'s boat instead of checking into a hotel. Neither Moorehead nor Elder had phony documents, so they'd have to use their real names and real I.Ds to travel to the Cayman Islands. It was a risk. But they had no options.

"I smell coffee," Big Mo grumbled as he climbed the stairs topside from the cabin area.

"Well, good morning to you too," Captain J.R. replied. "Where's your friend? Still sleeping?"

"I reckon." Moorehead was in no mood for chitchat. "Can I get some coffee, or was $10,000 not enough for a little cabin service?"

"Help yourself Mo. It's down below in the galley."

As big Mo turned to head back down the stairs, the Captain stopped him. "Hey! I need to know how soon I can clear out of here. I don't like lying to the Customs people about how many are in my party, if you know what I mean."

"Give me an hour to make arrangements. You should be able to head home by this afternoon." Mo took his grumpy self down to the galley in search of hot coffee and food.

CHAPTER #74

Carlo had been on the phone all morning with Penelope, as they both watched the emergency board meeting.

"This place is going nuts!" she exclaimed. "The idea that any of those people besides Dr. Baptiste, would become the superintendent has staff retching in the bathrooms! Have you talked to Jez yet?" she asked Carlo.

"No. I'm trying to keep my calls to the bare minimum in case either of us is being monitored."

"Good thinking." With that, Penelope hung up, leaving Carlo staring at his handset. His mind was swirling. Lily Molina? Frederick Noonan? What madness was this? Who in their right mind, he thought, would put a skank or a dumbshit in the superintendent's seat? He answered his own question. The school board, that's who. They were all in cahoots.

"Marcello," he hollered at his assistant. "I'm going out for lunch. I'll be back in about an hour." Carlo was a blur to Marcello as he raced to his car.

He began fishing through his wallet to find Capt. Cohen's card. He dialed the number she'd given him, and spoke the code phrase. Then he put his sporty Mercedes roadster in gear and headed for 20th and Collins Avenue.

When he arrived at Donna's suite, she was sitting with Capt. Cohen going over the notes they'd drafted the night before.

"Hello Mr. Ferrini," Cohen said as she got up to shake his hand.

"It's good to see you again, Capt." he replied.

"It seems the two of you jogged each other's memories pretty good last night." Cohen was still standing and smiling.

"I'm glad you're here," Carlo said as he walked toward the two women. "I'd come over to give Donna more details on the FEMA money and the portables, but I see I can give it to you in person. That's great."

"Have a seat Carlo," Donna implored.

"I believe I will. Are you going to take dictation Donna?" he asked.

"Sure! Whatever that is!" Donna giggled as she sat back down.

"How about I use my tape recorder, Mr. Ferrini? Wouldn't that be better?" Capt. Cohen began digging through her purse to find it.

"That would be perfect," Carlo responded. "Just perfect!"

After an hour, Carlo was still explaining to Capt. Cohen how the district had scammed the Federal Emergency Management Agency after Hurricane Andrew. It had begun when the feds offered to pay the district for nearly 400 new portable classrooms to replace entire schools that had been blown away by the fury of Andrew's wrath.

Carlo explained how the district had double billed its insurance company and FEMA for the portables lost during the storm, as well as many that weren't lost. He'd been privy to some meetings, he said, in which R.V., Joe Nunez, Nestor Padron, Hank Maine and Moses Moorehead, had cooked up the entire double billing scam.

"How did they get away with it?" asked Capt. Cohen.

"They almost didn't!" Carlo detailed how things began to unravel, when an inspector for the State of Florida began trying to track the money and the physical trailers that FEMA had sent.

"The way FEMA works, is to get the state government to guarantee that the state, i.e. the Governor, takes responsibility for making sure all the money the Feds send is legitimately spent. But when a group of state inspectors and auditors showed up three years later, and couldn't document the spending or even prove that the portables they were looking at were the ones the government sent in... R.V. went nuts. He thought the scheme was a home run."

"What was missing?" Cohen jumped in.

"It's my understanding that these auditors found serial plate numbers shaved off a number of portables, or missing altogether. The rumor mill said that the auditors even began to suspect, that the school system had not used the FEMA money to purchase new portables, but instead, had moved older portables from the Northern part of the county, to the Southern part, where Andrew hit the hardest. That meant, the district was pocketing both the insurance money and the FEMA funds... and doing lord knows what with the trailers FEMA had shipped in."

"How much money are we talking about?" Cohen checked her recorder to make sure the tape was still rolling.

"I remember seeing a letter about $3 million dollars for 52 portables. FEMA apparently had paid for an estimate only, not the actual trailers. That's what got the auditors revved up. They felt they could prove that the school system was defrauding the Federal government. But when R.V. got wind of their suspicions, he pulled the rug out from under them."

"How'd he do that Mr. Ferrini?" Cohen asked.

"Don't quote me, because I can't say for sure. But what I do know is that R.V. was very tight with Congressman Billie Weeks. They'd worked together at the same school when Weeks was an art teacher and then when he was elected to the state legislature, they renewed their friendship, because R.V. was a lobbyist for the school system. The story I heard was that R.V. called Weeks and asked him to call off the taxpayer watchdogs."

Carlo got up and went to the kitchen to get a glass of water, but kept talking.

"It must have worked, because the questions stopped, and the auditors vanished." Carlo walked back into the room and asked if he could get Donna or Capt. Cohen anything to drink.

"No thanks," they replied.

"But, how could the auditors have proven their suspicions?" Capt. Cohen asked. "I mean, beyond paperwork? How could they physically prove their assertions?"

Carlo, sipping his water, cocked his head. Good question he thought. "Well, if I were an investigator, I'd talk to the people who had classrooms in those portables. Teachers and students would certainly know if their portables were new, old, or the same ones messed up by the storm."

There was a pregnant pause. Then Carlo put his glass of water down on the coffee table. "I think I'd also make use of the county's Tax Assessor "fly over" photographs."

Carlo was referring to the aerial photos that were taken every year for tax assessment purposes. Much like Internet sites today, that show aerial satellite photos of properties, this was a similar, but a more rudimentary version of the same thing.

"Exactly!" Capt. Cohen cried out.

Suddenly, Donna had questions. "I just don't understand how the government and the insurance company wouldn't eventually find out that they'd each paid for the same thing?"

"Oh, but they did!" Carlo responded. "That's when I began to hear that things were getting tricky. FEMA apparently sent a letter to R.V. insisting that the school system repay the Feds, $6 Million dollars. That's what they'd confirmed had been collected in double billing."

"Did the district pay the money back?" Donna asked.

"No way!" Carlo stood and started pacing the floor. "Donna, you of all people should know that the school system is in the business of collecting money, not repaying it. That was part

of the reason R.V. called Weeks. He sat on the House committee that had oversight of FEMA. Convenient huh?" Carlo
continued to pace. He'd waited so long to tell someone about
this.

"Capt. there's something else you need to know, in order to
connect all the dots, if that's what you really intend to do. And
I hope that it is, otherwise, I'm not sure why Mrs. Maine
should spill her guts or remain a captive at the Abbey Hotel."

"Let me assure you both, I want to know everything. I'm a
law enforcement officer, and I intend to enforce the laws of
this city, state and country." Capt. Sheila Cohen paused. "I
have never, nor will I ever capitulate or compromise my oath
to uphold the law. They will have to fire me or kill me first. So
please know, that you both can talk freely and with my as-
surance, your information will not be given in vain."

Donna and Carlo looked at one another, but said nothing.
Carlo kept pacing, all the while rubbing his temples as if trying to ward off a growing headache. Finally he sat back down
on the couch.

"I've never told anyone about this before, in my life! But the
money the Feds wanted returned was the exact amount of
money, the district was going to have to spend to bring almost 400 portables up to code."

Capt. Cohen wasn't sure she was following Carlo. "I'd expect
that new portables would have stricter building code guide-
lines than older one," she said.

"No, you don't understand." Carlo stopped and took a gulp of
water. "The $6 million dollars is what the district was going to
have to spend even before Hurricane Andrew hit."

"I'm still not sure I'm following you, Mr. Ferrini."

"Capt., the district had paid $6 million dollars, the year before
Andrew, for nearly 400 portables that were nothing more
than homemade tree houses. When building officials refused
to certify them for occupancy, the district began scrambling
trying to find the money to bring them up to code. Andrew

was the slush fund they didn't have before August 24th of 1992."

"Why didn't the district just sue the manufacturers for violating the contract?" Capt. Cohen inquired.

"They couldn't. The contract had purposely been written in violation of the code. It's how the company could then come back to the board for a second contract to fix the portables, and, of course, collect more money. Besides, some of the portables had been built by district staff, the others were supplied by a company that was owned by Moses Moorehead's brother."

There was silence for several minutes.

"Carlo, you do realize the implications of what you are telling me, don't you." Capt. Cohen looked down at the recorder, and realized it was about to run out of tape. She held up her hand as if stopping traffic, flipped the tape over, and then nodded, letting Carlo know he could respond.

"Yes. It means Donna and I might become roommates."

"Do you know the names of these inspectors who were shut down, Carlo?" Cohen knew she needed some more concrete leads than just Carlo's memory.

"A name? No. His residence? Yes."

"What do you mean?" Cohen asked, completely puzzled.

"You'll find one of the inspectors at the Eastside Psychiatric Hospital in Tallahassee; the state's loony bin. That's where they sent him when he refused to cooperate and threatened to go to the media."

CHAPTER #75

The emergency board meeting reconvened around 1:30pm. Penelope was trying to reach Carlo, but he wasn't answering, and his assistant kept telling her that he wasn't back from lunch yet.

In her private pressroom, Jez Underwood was scribbling a draft of a script that had the board electing an Interim Superintendent... and on another page, was a script that had them still deadlocked. Which one would make air, she wondered? By 4:00, she'd have to put one of them into play, as she'd have to record a story for the 5:00, whether it was outdated or not.

Rules were rules at Channel 11... and the rules demanded you have a taped report, especially if you'd been on a story since 9:00a.m. It pissed Jez off. She was more than capable of ad-libbing a live shot with the latest breaking information, meaning, she could and should wait until the last minute to deliver her report. But NO! Not at 11 News. Common sense had no place in the mind of the News Director, Boris Danken.

******

Meanwhile, Captain J.R. ferried his passengers from Bimini to Nassau where he dropped them off at a marina and then headed back towards South Florida.

At the Nassau, Bahamas International Airport, Dr. Moses Moorehead was in a pay phone booth, listening to the board's meeting, through a link with one of his "plants" on the dais.

He heard President Jewel Haynes call for another ballot.

"The board will now begin voting on the 85th ballot for the Interim Superintendent."

Moorehead spoke into the phone. "Doc, you better figure out a way to get Baptiste off the ballot now, or plan your retirement."

"I'm a god damn nominee, Mo, how do you propose I do that without looking like I'm up to something?"

"It wouldn't be the first time people said that about you, so get over it!" Moorehead was furious. "Ask for a recess. Then get your people to strong arm Jesse Joe to drop Noonan, tell Jewel you are withdrawing your name and Lourdes', and promise Jeremy Harris a raise if he'll withdraw his name from contention. Then make sure those votes are cast for Lily Molina. We need someone we can control, and we need you on the board to run against Jewel. Don't you see what she's up to?"

"But Mo…"

"Just do it!" Big Mo hung up on his "plant," Dr. Cecil Raymond.

The two had always been unlikely allies, except for their drive to control everything in the district. Mo had the staffing to the do the job, while Raymond had the richest community of any school board member and enjoyed the financial backing of the Republican Party through his close friendship with Governor James Barwick. It was money vs. manpower… a combination that forced the two men to play ball together.

At 3:50pm, President Jewel Haynes, patting her increasingly sweaty nose pores, called for a vote on the 94th ballot.

"Madam President." It was Dr. Jesse Joe Crandall. "In order to help this board come to some agreement, I am withdrawing the name of my nominee, Dr. Frederick Noonan.

"Madam President." It was board member Hammond Garfield. "I respectfully ask that my nominee's name be removed from this ballot. Mr. Harris has informed me that he is unwilling to put this board through the angst of more ballots, in hopes that a consensus can be reached."

"Thank you Mr. Garfield and Dr. Crandall... we will officially remove the names of your nominees. So now I will call for the 94th..." she was suddenly interrupted by Dr. Cecil Raymond.

"Madam President, I too, want to help bring this important decision to a conclusion, sooner, rather than later. Therefore, I am removing my name as a nominee and that of Lourdes Rubenstein."

"Very well sir," Jewel was seething with anger. She'd been so sure Raymond's ego would prevent him from withdrawing. What had happened between ballot 1 and ballot 93? Jewel smelled a rat, and his name was Big Mo.

"Shit! They always do this to me!" Jez was 10 minutes from having to record her report, and now the board had just played 52 card pick up with her scripts.

She threw a few more Tic Tacs at Emeril's head. "Yo! I think we're going to have to wing it "E.""

"Ju know the boss doesn't like that Jez."

"Yeah, well, I can't control the momentum of a story. I just report it. Call the station and tell them we've had an 11th hour upset of biblical proportions, and I will have to tap dance over video."

Jez then put out her hand, signaling to Emeril that he should give her all his tapes. She gathered them into her arms and ran to the live truck. As she dumped them on the floor of the technologically advanced vehicle, capable of communicating with satellites in outer space, Jez instructed the operator to feedback anything to the station, that he fancied.

"It's all the same," she assured her live truck operator. "One ballot looks and sounds just like the next."

"But there are 12 tapes, Jez," Andy screamed.

"I know! Good thing there aren't 15," Jez hollered back, as she ran for the auditorium door.

CHAPTER #76

In the school board auditorium, President Jewel Haynes had just called for the 94th ballot to begin. There were now only two candidates left to vote on, Dr. Noelle Baptiste and Lily Molina. Either one would make history, because there hadn't been a female superintendent, even an interim one, in all of Miami's history.

"Mr. Garfield?" Jewel was again calling on the board members according to the seating from left to right.

"I cast my ballot for Lily Molina," Garfield said before closing his eyes for a catnap.

"Mrs. Sable?"

"I'm again voting for Lily Molina," Patty Sable insisted for the 94th time.

"Dr. Raymond?"

"Madam President, I am proud to cast my vote for Lily Molina," he said.

"Ms. Salas?"

"I again cast my vote for Dr. Noelle Baptiste, Madam President."

"Mrs. Champlain?"

"Oh, this is so difficult, because I think both women would be simply superb... but... I don't know... I... um... Oh dear!" Bitzy was being ditzy. It was a known phenomenon that occurred with her, whenever it was a black vs. white issue. Being a good Democrat, she always liked looking progressive and pro African/American, or in this case, Haitian/American. But she knew politically, insiders in the district wanted her to vote for Molina. Inevitably, her Democratic inclinations won over.

"I believe I am going to vote for Dr. Baptiste.

That's three to two, Jez thought, as she tallied the results on her homemade notepad ballot.

"Reverend Crandall?"

"It is with great joy in my heart that I vote for Noelle Baptiste as our Interim superintendent," Jesse Joe thundered as if he were at his pulpit.

Emeril whipped his head around to look at Jez, whose mouth was somewhat agape.

"I didn't see that coming," Emeril whispered to her. "Did ju?"

"No way! He's defying Big Mo's plan," Jez said. "But why? What's he going to gain?"

"He does have lots of Haitians in his district," Emeril pointed out.

"True," Jez replied still trying to calculate the politics of the situation. "I think it's his black power thing going on," Jez added. "Even Big Mo can't control Crandall's reverse racist thinking."

"But Big Mo isn't here!" Emeril reminded her.

"Sure he is "E" we just can't see him!"

"Mr. Castro?" President Haynes looked at "Mumbles" to her right.

"Magnum Prejudinsh, I jominasheted Mrs. Molina, ank I am agin voshing for jer."

Jez looked up at the TV monitor as it flashed the subtitles that read… "Madame President, I nominated Mrs. Molina, and I am again voting for her."

"This is pathetic!" Jez said to herself, hoping Emeril wouldn't hear her.

"Well, I guess it all comes down to my vote," President Haynes half whispered into the microphone. She sounded as if she was contemplating sending someone to the electric chair! Jez realized Jewel could tie the vote, or tip it for Lily Molina, who had 4 of the 5 votes needed.

"I am saddened that my nominee has chosen to take his name off the ballot. Dr. Raymond is, in my opinion, the best candidate for this job. But since he has left me no choice," Jewel paused to sip from her miniature bottle of water. "I believe it is my duty to vote for Dr. Noelle Baptiste."

"A fucking tie!" Jez threw her head back, as her hands clawed through her thick blonde mane. "Shit! Just get me out of here!" She was not a patient person, and today's meeting had tapped her out. She looked at her watch. It was 4:10pm.

"I am calling for a 15 minute recess," announced Jewel Haynes as she got up and all but ran to the door that led behind the dais.

Just then, Jez heard Emeril's Nextel beep. He handed it to her. "This is Jez," she answered.

It was Sophie, the producer. "Jez, the feed room says you haven't sent back a taped report yet. Can you give me some idea how long it will run?"

"Just shoot me!" Jez mouthed to Emeril, who was listening and smirking.

"No! I can't Sophie, because there won't be a taped report. It's 4:10; they just had a tie vote and are taking a 15-minute recess. By the time they return, it'll be nearly 5:00. So I'm going to ad lib over video, which the feed room should be receiving any minute now."

"But Jez!" Sophie sounded panicked. "You know the rules. We have to have a taped report."

"Of course I know the rules, Sophie." Jez was talking in a very soft, but condescending way, which she knew would go right over Sophie's head.

"But those are the newsrooms rules. Out in the field, where the real reporting is done, the reporter rules. And this reporter is telling you that there will not be a taped report… so just deal with it!" Jez was now yelling at poor Sophie. "QSL?"

There was no response from Sophie. Not good, Jez thought to herself. She suspected Boris had been standing next to Sophie's desk listening to the conversation, and had snatched the Nextel from her. She was right.

"Jez? This is Boris. When you are finished with your assignment, I want to see you in my office immediately. Capiche?"

Jez clicked the Nextel with dread. "No problem!" She tried to sound cheery and unphased, but in truth she was nervous as a tit on a boar hog.

CHAPTER #77

The selection of Lily Molina as Interim Superintendent came as no surprise to anyone who followed the incestuous, inner workings of school system politics.

On the 95th ballot, President Jewel Haynes had switched and voted for Molina. She'd used her vote for Baptiste to extract promises during the 15 minute recess that she'd be re-elected President. The wheeling and dealing behind the scenes, was never about what was best for the children in the public school system... but about what was best for the powerful insiders and board members. Haynes had played her hand like a pro!

As she walked to the superintendent's seat to assume her throne, Lily Molina suddenly froze. Her goal had been achieved; her wishes granted. Yet she was immobilized by fear. She hadn't gotten here by smarts. The platinum blonde, Anna Nicole look-a-like, had always put power above personal happiness. She'd married for it, sucked cocks for it, slept with pencil-dicks for it, and had generally debased herself in any way, shape or form... for power. But now, how could she give an entire school system a blowjob, she wondered? And what about the media?

Until now, she'd hidden behind the district's apron of silence, meaning, if you didn't want to talk, the district's spokesman spoke for you. Now she was in the hot seat, and silence was no longer an option.

"Be careful what you wish for." Those words her mother spoke on her deathbed, suddenly haunted her and echoed in her head like a troublesome ghost.

"Stop it!" she shouted out loud.

"Mrs. Molina, are you o.k.?" asked President Haynes.

Lily suddenly realized she'd spoken, not to herself, but on the public record.

"I can't stop it… the feeling that I'm so unworthy of your endorsement," she explained, trying to recover from her misstep. "But I promise to make this community proud in the short or long term. Know that I am here to serve the children of Miami."

"I'm going to vomit!" Jez said, listening to the live feed of the school board meeting in the satellite truck.

Emeril wasted no time responding. "Just make sure ju open the door in time to vomit on the sidewalk, blondie."

"Funny ha, ha!" she retorted. "Can you believe this garbage she's doling out?

"You and I have covered dis school board for how many jears, Jez? Of course I can believe it. Dis is the crazies at deir finest!"

Jez sat silently, pondering the absolutely accurate point that Emeril had made.

"Five minutes, blondie. Powder jour shiny nose and get jour ass in fronf of my camera."

Jez reached for her makeup bag and dug for her compact. As she flipped the mirror open and saw herself in it… she suddenly clamped it shut.

"Emeril, go find Ms. Salas now! Tell her I need her for my live shot. Andy can man the camera for you in case you miss the top of my live shot."

"What the hell?" Emeril looked totally baffled.

"Go! Now! Bring me Ms. Salas!" Jez was yelling as she clipped her microphone on her jacket lapel, and put her earpiece into her ear, grabbing for the black box that she'd plug into, allowing her to hear "on air" audio.

"Go!" she yelled again, realizing Emeril was not moving. She then tilted her head down and spoke into the microphone on her jacket. "Andy, please come out here and handle the camera for Emeril."

"Jez, you know that's against Union rules," the live truck operator informed her.

"So is eating in the live truck! So put your Big Mac down and operate this camera."

At that moment, Jez heard Sophie give her the 2-minute warning in her ear. "Showtime!" Jez thought, wondering if she'd be able to pull off her little scheme.

******

"Oh my God!" Penelope was screaming in Carlo's ear. They'd been on the phone, simultaneously watching the board meeting from their respective offices. "Lily Molina? Did Moses Moorehead die, go to heaven and gain supernatural powers?"

"Must have," was all Carlo could say.

"How could they elect "Cocksucker Lily?""

"By a 6 to 4 vote, apparently." Carlo wanted to be as upset and surprised as Penelope. But it just wasn't in him. He was way too familiar with the treachery that lurked behind the scenes of every decision the school system made.

"Are you on Channel 11?" he asked Penelope.

"Of course," she replied. Her deep throated intonation indicating she thought he was high on drugs for assuming she'd be watching any other channel. He knew she was devoted to Jez Underwood's revealing investigations.

"She must be the lead story, don't you think?" Carlo stammered. He was almost dizzy by the obvious corruption of the process.

"Are you o.k.?" Penelope inquired.

"Yeah. Just tired. I haven't been sleeping well these last few nights. It must be catching up with me."

Penelope seemed satisfied with his response, so she didn't pursue it further.

"How could Lily get that job without Big Mo being present?" Penelope pushed her friend to respond.

"Maybe he was, and we just didn't see him."

"You mean, he was like, pulling strings behind the curtain?"

"Perhaps." Carlo paused. "It's been done before. Remember when Supt. Johnson was indicted for installing gold plated bathroom fixtures in his home?"

"Yes."

"Well, Mo wasn't on the board then, but he made sure that the board didn't take the appropriate disciplinary action the prosecutors required in order to nail him for fraud." Carlo stopped, waiting for Penelope to respond.

"Oye Vey!" Penelope exclaimed.

"Mo was absent today. Do you know why?" Carlo was pressing Penelope.

"His office said he was on vacation."

"Yeah right!" Carlo couldn't understand how anyone would believe such a story.

"Penelope, Mo is calling the shots. It's the only way to explain the sudden turn of events, with four names being removed from nomination on the same ballot. He's giving orders from somewhere. The question is where."

At that moment, both of them saw Channel 11 put Jez Underwood full screen. "Call me after her report," said Penelope and they both hung up.

"Dean," Jez began, "the new leader of the Miami School System is Lily Molina... a veteran of the district, having risen from the ranks of teacher, to Associate Superintendent. You may recognize her name, from past reports here on Channel 11. Three years ago, we detailed how she and her husband Lee Molina, used district funds and school employees to pay for and work at their sumptuous wedding. Much of the money used to pay for the celebration was part of her husband's slush fund, collected from phony attendance records, purchase orders and bogus enrollment fees. Yet this is the person the school board chose to put in charge of a $5.9 billion budget."

Jez paused waiting for Dean Sands to respond. But he was already stunned by her words. He had no response.

"So to wrap up today's events, let me just inform the public that when Lily Molina was principal at Homestead Middle school, she killed a plan to add a science wing for students. Instead, she expanded the administration offices, at a cost of $2.7 million dollars. To date, science scores in the Homestead area, remain grossly lagging behind the national science scores. One has to wonder, what that science wing could have meant to those kids, and our school system in general."

Jez's pause was only because she saw Emeril running his poor Cuban refugee ass off... tugging Amelia Salas behind him.

"Dean, in order to put things in perspective, I've asked Dr. Amelia Salas to join me for a live interview."

Emeril thrust Salas toward Jez, who quickly blocked her fall and held her up, while at the same time, thrusting a microphone in her face.

"Thank you so much for joining us, Ms. Salas. I know you've had a long day, and a lot of ballots. But can you give us your assessment of what occurred today? I mean, you guys did go to 95 ballots before naming Lily Molina as Interim Superintendent."

"Jezebel, it was a very long day."

Jez winced at the sound of her full name. For some reason, Amelia always did that. Perhaps because she was such a proper person, that she couldn't bring herself to use nicknames.

"And at the end of the day, I am pained to understand how the board could ignore such a qualified individual as Dr. Noelle Baptiste. The entire process smacks of being corrupted."

"Bingo Bango," Jez thought to herself. "I couldn't have written this script any better if I'd tried."

"Oh my word, Ms. Salas," Jez exclaimed, sounding baffled, "whatever do you mean?"

"Jezebel, Dr. Moses Moorehead orchestrated this entire charade!"

"But Ms. Salas, how could he? He wasn't even present." Jez was setting the stage.

"He doesn't need to be! That man can turn green turnips into red tomatoes if he wants. His powers are demonic I tell you! I've been on this board for over seven years, and I've seen what he does with the members of this board when he wants to exert his power. I don't give a damn if they say he's on vacation, he is pulling strings like a puppet master makes Elmo move."

"Ms. Salas, we are out of time, but I'd like to thank you for joining us and sharing your outlook on today's events here at the Emergency Meeting of the Miami School System."

"You are very welcome, Jezebel." With that. Amelia Salas turned and left the sidewalk where she'd been interviewed by Jez.

As Jez was signing off, shots rang out. Jez ducked, covering her head as part of some automatic reflex. As she slowly stood upright again, Jez turned, just in time to see Amelia Salas fall in the middle of the street, gunned down by a mystery shooter.

"NOOOOOOO!!!!!!!" Jez was screaming so loud, Emeril thought his eardrums would shatter.

Andy, the live truck operator, wasn't a skilled cameraman, but he knew when to focus on a subject, and the subject he was focusing on now, was the twisted body of Ms. Amelia Salas, lying in the middle of the street. As he slowly zoomed out, Jez Underwood could be seen running to her, dropping to her knees and screaming for someone to call 9-1-1. All of this was being fed live, back to the Channel 11 newsroom... and into the living rooms of their viewers.

"Stay on the dead gal!" screamed Boris Danken. "Tell the photographer to stop shaking! What is Emeril doing?"

"It's not Emeril," the feed room operator informed her boss. "It's Andy. And he doesn't have a clue what he's supposed to do."

"Where's Emeril?" Danken demanded.

"Pulling Jez off the dead body, according to the video I'm looking at," the feed room operator informed the boss.

Danken whipped his head around to look at the bank of monitors he'd had his back to. That's when he heard Dean Sand's soothing voice.

"Ladies and Gentlemen, there appears to be another tragedy at the Miami School Board Headquarters. We are efforting to find out just what happened, but as you, no doubt can tell from the video you are seeing, the situation is total chaos. Our reporter Jez Underwood is clearly on the scene, but her involvement may prevent her from sharing with us what happened. We can now see police cars arriving, and that is a signal that there will be, yet another, law enforcement investigation into the situation at the Miami School System."

As soon as Dean Sands stopped talking, the piercing sounds of sirens shattered the quiet of anyone who was tuned to Channel 11.

As the camera stayed trained on the crumpled body of Ms. Amelia Salas, video showed Jez Underwood pumping her chest in an effort to revive her... pounding the pumping motions of CPR... screaming like a banshee for help.

Amelia wasn't just another board member; she was also Jez's friend. What had started as a source relationship had grown into a true friendship. They often socialized, having dinners together, or Amelia and her husband had Jez over to their home for a weekend barbeque. Jez had given Amelia some guidance on her public speaking abilities, which were often disjointed, so Jez had encouraged her to write out important speeches, so she wouldn't trip over herself searching for words in her head.

As soon as the paramedics arrived, Jez informed them that she'd felt a slight pulse. They immediately shoved Jez out of the way as they went to work trying to save Ms. Salas.

"Come on Jez. Jou've done all ju can do. Let the pros take over." Emeril was doing his best to get Jez up on her feet. As she stood, he saw that her pink suit was bloodied, as were her hands. There were also flecks of blood on her face. As they began walking toward the sidewalk, he saw that the red tally light on his camera was lit up. Jesus! He thought. We're live! At that moment he saw Andy waving the microphone at him, indicating that the station wanted Jez for a report.

"Are you crazy?" he mouthed. But Andy just kept waving the microphone.

"Jez? Jez, honey? I think the station wants ju to do a report."

Jez stopped walking and looked over at Emeril, with a look of shock, horror and puzzlement. Then she nodded her head, yes.

"Are ju sure ju can handle it?" Emeril didn't think it was such a good idea for Jez to talk just now. After all, she barely kept her mouth in check when she wasn't in shock!

"Jez, please… let me just tell dem ju aren't up to it. Really, I don't sink ju are." Emeril's pleadings fell on deaf ears. Jez pulled away from him, walked over and took the microphone from Andy, and stood in front of the camera.

"She's gonna talk Dean. Throw it to her now!" Boris was giving Dean Sands orders through his earpiece.

Dean obeyed his orders, even though he thought it was a terrible idea.

"I believe we have Jez Underwood back with us, so perhaps she can tell us what she knows. Jez? Can you hear me?"

Andy gave her a handle signal to begin, since she'd ripped her earpiece out on her way to revive Ms. Salas.

Jez seemed catatonic.

"Jez? Can you hear me? This is Dean."

Innately, Jez new what an anchor would be saying to a talent that didn't have IFB. So automatically she began with, "Dean, I can't hear you. But I'm going to assume that you can hear me." There was another long pause, as Jez appeared to try and collect herself.

"Just moments after finishing our live interview, Ms. Amelia Salas was shot. She was shot right here!" Jez pointed to the middle of her chest, indicating the location of the wound.

"I tried… I tried… I tried to give her CPR, and I believe I felt a faint pulse when the paramedics arrived." Tears began to roll down her cheeks, smearing some of the droplets of blood that covered her face.

"If Amelia doesn't live, then this community will have lost its only true guardian of our taxpayer dollars." Jez sniffed as her nose began to drip. Suddenly, she seemed much more in control.

"If assassination is what awaits the good people of Miami, who try to fight for what is right, then we are all doomed."

Emeril had a growing unease about Jez's demeanor and her words. So he slowly reached up and put his hand on the video output cable to the camera, knowing Andy couldn't see what he was doing while he was looking through the viewfinder. Emeril would unplug her, before he'd let her go unhinged on the air.

"Earlier today, Ms. Salas did what many in the community cannot do. She put aside ethnic divisions, and nominated a Haitian as Interim Superintendent. She should have been praised for her independence and congratulated for finding this district a superb human being to do the job. Instead, she was gunned down and left bleeding in the middle of the street!" Jez had gone from weepy to warrior in the blink of Emeril's eye. His hand tightened around the cable connection.

"There is a sickness in this school system, that will infect all of us, if we do not demand accountability and honesty. Where is your outrage, Miami? How much of the diseased corruption does the media have to throw in your face, before you march in the streets?"

Oh shit! Emeril thought as he began to slowly twist the cable.

"How many bad Principals will you allow to lead your schools because they slept with a powerful person? How many sick children are too many because of mold that seeps into school walls, the result of shoddy construction, kickbacks and payoffs? How much of your hard earned money will you let them steal from you without demanding that someone go to jail? Huh? I can't hear you Miami! Where is your voice?"

No mas, Emeril thought to himself, as he twisted the cable from the back of the camera, letting it drop to the sidewalk, as he ran to grab Jez and rushed her to his news VAN.

"What the hell just happened?" demanded Boris. "What happened to our feed? Tap dance," he shouted into Dean's ear.

"It seems we've lost our connection with Jez Underwood. While we try to sort out the technical snafus, let's take a commercial break. We'll be right back in two minutes." Dean stared into the camera, daring the director, not to go to black and run some commercials. As soon as he heard the theme song for United Airlines, he grabbed the anchor desk phone and screamed for Boris Danken.

CHAPTER #78

At about the same time as Dr. Moorehead and Franklin Elder
were boarding a Bahamas Air flight to the Cayman Islands,
the Miami police were receiving a fax from the Bahamian authorities, that the two men they were looking for, were heading to the Cayman Islands. Luckily, and Capt. Cohen had her
detective's one step ahead of the scoundrels. She immediately called Davis and gave him the flight information for Elder and Moorehead. It was 4:00pm. Davis and Gonzalez
were just arriving at their hotel.

Moses Moorehead pushed his seat back and let his tray table down, so the flight attendant could serve him his "double
brandy." His left hand went up, and gently touched his banana flipped hairdo.
"Thank yew," he said as the radiant young black woman with
shoulder length braids, delivered his cocktail. "Yew make a
mahan want to visit the Cayman Islands more often," he
drawled in his most Southern way.

"May I steal that as a compliment for the Bahamas, sir. You
see, I am Bahamian," the flight attendant corrected him.

"Yew may accept it as uh compliment intended only furh
yew," he said trying not to let her admonishment irritate him.

As she walked away, Franklin turned to Big Mo and said,
"ooopps!"

"Shut up, shit for brains!" Mo threw back his double brandy
and let the warm liquid sear his insides as it made its way
down into his body, and back up into his head. He closed his
eyes. He needed to think. As he did, he wondered if his orders had been followed. If so, his adopted hometown must
surely be in chaos, he thought, as he drifted into the fog of
sleep.

At about the same time as Big Mo was nodding off, detectives Gonzalez and Davis were talking with the Bahamas Air
ticket agent at the Grand Cayman International Airport.
They'd flashed their badges and asked to speak to the Supervisor.

"May I help you?" A kindly gentleman in his early 60's approached the two cops from Miami.

"We have two suspects arriving in 30 minutes on flight #54 from Nassau. We need access to the gate and the ground area. Can you help us?" Detective Gonzalez tried pleasantries before he'd let Davis use threats and intimidation. They had the "good cop, bad cop" thing down pat.

"Please understand that I will require your badge numbers in order to confirm that you are who you say you are. After that, we should be able to assist you." The supervisor wrote down their information and disappeared into a back room, where they assumed he would call the Miami Police Department.

"I'll handle the gate," said Davis.

"Fine. I'll do the ground area in case one of them has decided to imitate a suitcase in the baggage compartment," Gonzalez replied.

"There'll be no umbrella drinks until we get these bozos, you know," Davis informed his partner.

"Yeah! I know how bad you want an umbrella drink, Pussy!" Gonzalez teased his colleague.

Just then the supervisor reappeared and informed them to follow him. Each man was in place as the plane taxied up to the gate and stopped.

As the passengers began to deplane, Mo informed Franklin that he wasn't feeling well and bolted for the front toilet. "Go on," he instructed his aide. "I'll catch up with you at baggage claim."

Mo didn't like anyone to know that he hated to fly. He'd contained his queasiness as long as he could. That double brandy hadn't helped he had to admit. If anything it made him sicker. Just as Mo was wiping his hands with a towel, he heard voices right outside the cockpit.

"What police? Where? Oh, my god! That was the guy sitting in row 4."

Mo had a bad feeling. He and Franklin had been sitting in row 4. He was positive they're travels had been tracked, since they'd been forced to use their real I.Ds. Mo quietly unhooked the lock. He knew it would show up in the cockpit that the door was locked, and the last thing he wanted to do was give the crew a reason to check the lavatory. Then he put the toilet seat down and sat on top of it, to ponder his next move. Clearly, it sounded as though Franklin had been apprehended. How could he avoid the same fate?

He didn't have to wait long. The next sound he heard was the cleaning crew entering the cabin. Slowly, he pushed the door open just a sliver. He saw a male janitor working on the first row, with at least three other janitors all working the plane's tail end and middle section. In a split second, Mo exited the lavatory, hooked his hand around the janitor's mouth, and dragged him back into the lavatory. It was a tight squeeze, but Big Mo had no options.

"Take off your clothes!" Moses Moorehead was wrapping his tie around the man's mouth so he couldn't speak. "I said take off your clothes!"

The man made some sounds like he was trying to say "ok." Then he began to unbutton his shirt and unzip his pants. Mo was doing the same thing. The man looked horrified. Was he about to be raped, he wondered?

He needn't have worried. Moses Josiah Moorehead was a dyed in the wool skirt chaser. His only interest in this man was the disguise his janitor's uniform could give Big Mo, as he attempted to escape the clutches of law enforcement. As difficult as it was for two grown men to exchange clothes in an airplane bathroom, Mo managed to do so… leaving his hostage tied up in his skivvies, curled in a ball in the cramped lavatory.

Mo even sacrificed his banana flip, Condoleezza Rice, hairdo… shoving his manicured wig up into the ball cap the janitor wore. As he exited the bathroom, he looked around and then headed for the jet way. Unsure whether it was wiser to exit into the airport, or use the jet way stairs to the ground level... he paused. There weren't enough people on the ground level to evade notice, he thought. So, he chose the airport terminal for his escape. As he walked off the jet way, he stopped to empty a few trashcans. It gave him time to surveil the area for cops. He then moseyed over toward the bathrooms. In front of the women's room was a tripod sign that read "temporarily closed for cleaning." He grabbed it and moved it in front of the men's room. Then he headed for a stall and locked it. He needed to think.

CHAPTER #79

Detective Bobby West was going crazy. I need to work, he thought, as he sunned himself by the pool in his backyard. Bobby Jr. was blissfully playing on his Shamu the Whale inflatable. West had taken some time off, mostly to cool down emotionally, but also to spend time with his son.

West Sr. was trying real hard not to let his emotions get the better of him. But every time he looked at Bobby Jr., he had the urge to pound his fist through a wall. He decided he'd call Capt. Cohen and tell her he was coming back to work tomorrow. There were certainly plenty of other school board investigations he could help with, besides Hank Maine's homicide and pornography case.

As he walked inside to get the phone, the TV caught his eye. It was something about a shooting at the school headquarters. Furiously, he began looking for the remote so he could turn up the volume. He'd all but dismantled the sofa, when he found it jammed between two cushions. He began pumping the volume "up" button.

"Amelia Salas, a Miami School Board Member, was shot in the chest in front of the school system's administration building. She's been taken to Jackson Memorial Hospital's Ryder Trauma Center, where we're told that she is currently in surgery. As soon as we get any information on her condition, we'll of course, bring it to you." West watched as Dean Sands recapped what had happened. He now realized how badly he must be needed back at the department. He quickly dialed Cohen's number. She answered on the second ring.

"Captain, its West. Where do you want me to go?"

"Oh, thank God. Are you free now?"

"Sure," West replied.

"Get over to Jackson and wait for word on Salas. If she makes it, see if you can get a statement from her," Capt. Cohen ordered.

"I'll be there in 20 minutes," he said, half running to the pool to get Bobby out, and make sure his mother knew he needed to leave, so she would look after the boy.

******

In the emergency room, a team of doctors was furiously trying to assess the extent of Ms. Salas' injuries. The entrance wound in the front of her chest was indicative that the bullet entered her heart. They immediately ordered a chest X-ray... and rushed her into the operating room. The trauma surgeons on duty cut open her chest to determine the severity of damage. After cracking her sternum, to reach the penetration site, they realized that the left ventricle held the bullet. Doctors at South Florida's premier trauma unit didn't have any trouble extracting the bullet from Amelia Salas' chest, but they were having a devil of a time, stopping her internal bleeding. There was severe tissue damage. A Cardiac Pulmonary Bypass Machine kept the blood circulating in her body, since her heart wasn't pumping. Hours went by before surgeons finally believed they'd sutured and repaired the damaged tissue.

Thinking they'd halted her internal bleeding, they removed the bypass machine and her heart started pumping again. But something wasn't right. They realized that there was a small leak coming from the wound location. So they put Ms. Salas back on the bypass machine. The surgeons went in and tediously reinforced the original sutures to capture any small punctures. To their dismay, a small amount of tissue damage was noted in the posterior ventricle. They sutured the additional site and reassessed once more.

She held her own after being taken off the bypass machine for a second time. Not seeing any additional evidence of blood coming from the wound site... they closed up her chest... and prayed that she was a fighter.

By the time Det. West got to the hospital and checked in with the trauma center supervisor, he was pleased to know that he, at least, had some ballistics evidence they could process. The doctor handed him the bullet they'd removed from Salas. It was already bagged and tagged for him.

"Any idea when she'll be out surgery?" he inquired.

"It could be awhile. She's on her third transfusion, and last I heard, they were calling for a fourth," he was informed.

"Not good," West said.

"But she is in good hands. Take your bullet to forensics," the doctor instructed him. "By the time you get back, I may have better news."

"I hope so." West extended his hand, shook the doctor's hand and then ran for his car.

CHAPTER #80

Lily Molina was sitting in the superintendent's chair at the superintendent's desk, inside the superintendent's office. She hoisted her champagne flute and saluted all her friends, family and close colleagues, who'd gathered in the office to celebrate her naming as Interim Superintendent.

"I love you all!" she declared.

"To the first female superintendent of Miami Schools!" It was her husband Lee, who was smiling so wide, he looked like a hockey puck was stuck in his mouth.

"To Lily," the gathering cheered. And they all immediately began swilling their bubbly.

Before most could finish their first gulp, a phalanx of Miami police officers burst in with guns drawn. The bubbly group went flat.

"Is everyone here ok?" quizzed the first cop in the door.

"Excuse me officer!" Lily was incensed that her party had been crashed by the cops.

"Ma'am, we have a school board member who's been shot, and we need to secure the building."

"Shot! Who?" screamed Lily as she lowered her flute. Instantly, the board members in the room began calculating the members who were present. Mario Castro. Check. Hammond Garfield. Check. Patty Sable. Check. Dr. Cecil Raymond. Check. Jewel Haynes. Check.

"Oh, my God," Jewel Haynes exclaimed as she wilted into a nearby chair. "This can't be happening."

"Well who got shot?" It was Hammond Garfield, the resident curmudgeon, gruffly demanding information from the cops.

"Ms. Amelia Salas," the officer replied. There was silence, except for the sound of champagne glasses being set down.

Nine floors below the gathering in the superintendent's office, police were wrapping the street in crime scene tape... effectively shutting off a major shortcut for truck drivers trying to get from the Port of Miami, to I-95. And for the third time in a week, the administration building was on lock down.

"This can't be happening," sobbed board President Jewel Haynes.

"Lily, you must hold a press conference immediately. Show that you are in control." Lee Molina appeared to be trying to show that he was in control, and Lily Molina knew it.

"I'd like to suggest that Jewel and I hold a joint press conference, if that's O.K. with Jewel."

Jewel, who was fanning herself with a magazine she'd picked up off a nearby table, stiffened. "I'm not sure I can face those heathens again. Yesterday's "meet the press" nearly undid me!"

"Jewel, you're the God damn President of the board." Dr. Cecil Raymond was now speaking. "If you're too delicate a flower to handle the pressure, then I'm gonna suggest you step down and let Mario, here, handle things. He is, after all, the Vice President."

"Mumbles? Are you insane," Patty Sable whispered into Raymond's ear. "He'll only remind our entire community that they already think we're a collection of nitwits!"

"I jould be cheery jonored to spill in for ju Yewel." Mario Castro bent at the waist, bowing before the board President.

"I'm sure you would be very honored to fill in for me, Mario, but that will not be necessary," Jewel instantly replied. "I think a joint news conference is a fabulous idea. Lily set it up as soon as we are released from our imprisonment here." With that, Jewel lifted her glass of champagne, tilted her head back and sucked down every drop. "Who's got the bottle?' she asked, when she came up for air.

******

At Jackson Memorial Hospital, Amelia Salas had finally been stabilized and moved to the Intensive Care Unit. Doctors listed her condition as critical, but stable. There was hope.

"There's no way she's going to be able to answer your questions," the chief surgeon was telling Detective West. "She's heavily sedated, and I plan to keep her that way until she shows signs of improvement. I promise to call you as soon as she is able to have visitors." With that, the doctor walked back into Ms. Salas' room.

West then got on his phone and called Capt. Cohen with the information. "I'll be back here first thing in the morning," he told her.

"West," Cohen began. "Thanks. Glad to have you back on the job." Then she hung up.

West was also glad to be back on the job. Not only did he need the work to keep his mind and worries off Bobby Jr., but by being back in the loop, so to speak, he could quietly keep an eye on what his colleagues were learning about the porn they'd found in Maine's condo. West strongly suspected Maine hadn't done this just for his own personal gratification. He was pretty sure there was a ring of other sickos that Maine was involved with. If even one of them lived in Miami, West wanted to know who it was. He'd set aside any moral dilemmas for later.

******

In the Cayman Islands that night, Franklin Elder was keeping his lips sealed. The Miami cops had apprehended him as soon as he stepped off the plane and taken him to the local police headquarters for questioning. But he'd stood firm, insisting on a lawyer first.

"Fine!" barked Gonzalez. "If you don't want to talk, then you can spend the night in this local hell hole, thinking about the wisdom of your decision."

With that he and Davis had the Cayman authorities allow him to call his lawyer, then lock Elder up on suspicion of fraud, theft and misappropriation of federal money.

"Nighty, night," Davis teased as they left. "Don't let the bed bugs bite!"

Several miles away, Moses Moorehead sat in a large bath-tub, filled to the rim with bubbles. He'd lined up an array of alcoholic beverages from his hotel room's minibar, and was systematically downing each of them, one at a time. He reached up to massage his banana flip wig, out of habit, when he realized for about the 12th time, that he no longer had his hairpiece on his head.

In an effort to escape detection, as he fled the airport, he'd heaved it into a vat of cooking grease, sitting outside the back door of an airport restaurant. Moorehead had slipped out of the airport by using an exterior exit, marked for em-ployees only.

Thankfully, the Cayman Airport wasn't as secure as most American airports, and since he was dressed as a janitor, he figured he wouldn't draw much attention, unless someone spotted his signature hairstyle. That's why he'd dumped the wig and fled into the night, bald as a newborn baby.

He'd stolen a silver Vespa motor scooter from the airport parking lot, and driven several miles until he found the Hyatt Grand Cayman Hotel. About six blocks from the hotel was an arcade where a bunch of local kids were hanging out. He left the motor scooter in the arcade parking lot, hoping the au-thorities would assume some mischievous youths had used it to get to their favorite hangout. He then walked the six blocks back to the hotel, where he'd used his dwindling stash of cash to pay for a room, using an assumed name. He was now safe. At least for the time being.

Any video of his arrival at the hotel lobby would show a bald, black man, not one with a mane of "That Girl" hair. It would hopefully keep authorities at bay until he could get to the bank the next morning and put his hands on more money.

After pushing a chair under the door handle of his room, and pushing a chest of drawers up against the chair, Big Mo, finally felt safe enough to undress and crawl into a bubble bath.

He'd already put his plan together in his head. He'd stop at the hotel gift shop in the morning and buy a pair of Cayman Island shorts, a tee shirt and a hat. Looking like a goofy tourist should help with his disguise. Then he'd head to the bank where he and his band of thieves had their offshore account, and he'd withdraw a hundred thousand dollars in cash. Then he'd transfer the rest to an account he'd set up several months ago with Banque Suisse in Geneva, Switzerland.

He hated to turn on the boys like that, but shit happens, he thought. Besides, it had been his plan all along to make off with the loot. He just used the other fellas to help give him cover and to accumulate more money. They'd fallen for it, and had made out quite nicely. At least that's how he justified what he was doing now. He wasn't so sure they'd see the reason in his logic.

Big Mo was half hammered from his cocktail concoction of little minibar bottles of alternating beverages; Brandy, rum, scotch, tequila and vodka... then repeat. Moorehead slid down into the bubbles up to his chin, forcing his feet to the surface. Big Mo was suddenly fascinated by his big toe. Ever so slowly, he began to wiggle it into the tub's faucet. At the same time he began to sing a song from his childhood memory.

"The itsy bitsy spider, climbed up the bathroom wall," he crooned, as he slid his toe further into the faucet's opening.

"Down came the rain and..." Mo's body suddenly jerked. "What the fuck?" He was yanking with all his might on his right leg. It was then that he realized his big toe was stuck in the faucet. He yanked and he pulled and he tugged and he yelled. But nothing helped release the grip the faucet had on his overheated, and swollen toe.

"NOOOOO!" he howled, realizing that he was about out of liquor, and couldn't get to the minibar for more. This was just before he passed out, toe fucking a faucet.

CHAPTER #81
THURSDAY MORNING

Jez, uncharacteristically, awoke around 6am Thursday morning. That's when she remembered that Boris had given her the day off. She then tried to go back to sleep.

Lily Molina woke up, remembered she was the new superintendent and jumped in the shower singing.

Moses Moorehead woke up shivering in a bathtub of cold water with his big toe stuck in the faucet, and every inch of his skin, shriveled and wrinkled, even more than normal. "Gawd damn it!" he mumbled... just as his toe fell from the faucet's orifice.

"Hallelujah! There is a Gawd!" Shivering, Moses Moorehead immediately stood up, grabbed a bath towel and rolled himself into the bed he was supposed to sleep in the night before.

At Jackson Memorial Hospital, Ms. Amelia Salas had remained stable throughout the night. Doctors upgraded her condition to serious with noted improvement. One of them called Detective West.

And in his parent's plush mansion, Daniel Estrada, got out of bed, took a leak and then stopped in front of the bathroom mirror to admire his body with its growing pot belly. He put his hands on his breasts, then slowly stroke himself down over his rib cage, down and around his hips, turned and admired his tight butt, then moved his hands over his muscular thighs and caressed his ever hardening cock. It's a shame to waste this, he thought. So he slid back into his bed and shared his hardness with the kid who shared his bed.

Marcos Alfaro blinked his eyes and moaned. "What if your parents find out I'm here?" he whispered.

"Say good morning," Daniel responded coyly

******

"Good morning," Capt. Cohen shouted boldly as she strutted through the homicide offices. "Anybody got anything for me?" Grown men jumped up to answer her inquiry.

"West called in. Said Ms. Salas has been upgraded to serious and he might get a chance to talk to her today." Det. Ingersoll was determined to make an impression on the boss.

"And Gonzalez and Davis are on their way back from the Cayman's with Franklin Elder, who isn't talking."

"Has he lawyered up?" Cohen asked as she threw her purse on the floor and dumped her Burger King bag on her desk.

"Seems so, Captain."

"What about Moorehead?"

"No sign of him. The boys said the Cayman guys were more laid back than they'd hoped. Seems they don't know the basics of a lockdown and search."

"Great! What else?" Sheila Cohen asked as she pulled a square shaped cardboard box from the BK sack.

"French toast sticks?" Ingersoll inquired, half drooling, in hopes she'd offer him one.

Instead, Capt. Cohen slapped his hand away. "Suspects?" she asked.

"None. Nada. Zip!" Ingersoll replied.

"Find one!" Capt. Cohen said as she dipped one of the French toast sticks into a cup of syrup and took a bite.

Ingersoll left her office with his shoulders hunched. He was suddenly obsessed with getting his hands on some BK French Toast Stiks. "I'm out of here," he said, gathering his car keys and heading for the parking garage.

As soon as he left, Cohen picked up the phone and called the Abbey Hotel. "Is Mrs. Maine awake yet?" she inquired. "Good, put her on." Capt. Cohen licked her fingers as she finished her first stick and waited for Donna Maine to get on the line.

"Hi, Capt.," Donna said as she picked up the extension in her hotel room. She was still in bed, but awake, reading the morning paper.

"I guess you know about Salas?" she asked Donna.

"This is getting out of control," Donna said, sounding ever so grateful to be trapped in a safe environment. "Who would want to shoot such a nice lady?"

"I'm hoping you might have some ideas, Mrs. Maine." Capt. Cohen reached for French toast stick number two. As she dipped it in the thick, rich maple-flavored syrup, she said, "I'll be by around 10:30. We'll talk."

"O.K. Capt." Donna Maine then hung up the phone and grabbed a pillow, which she held to her chest. She then began rocking back and forth... trying to think, but feeling afraid all over again.

Before Capt. Cohen left headquarters, she checked in with the rest of her detectives in the special crimes division. One group had been combing through all the papers and computers they'd removed from Moorehead, Elder, Nunez and Padron's offices, with the assistance of detectives from the public corruption unit. Another group was focusing exclusively on Maine's murder and the child pornography. And a third unit was now dealing with the attempted murder of Amelia Salas.

"Does anyone have any good news for me," she asked the group buried in documents.

"Not if you're looking to bust Moorehead or Elder," sighed one of the female detectives from public corruption.

"Yeah, we don't have bubkiss on those two," her male partner chimed in. "Nunez and Padron, on the other hand, are looking promising."

"Do tell?" the Captain inquired.

"Well, we still have mounds of shit to go through, but we've found a few internal memos, referencing a huge pot of money, that doesn't seem to have any purse strings attached to it," the detective began to elaborate. "As best I can tell, without getting my hands on additional documents, one of the adult education principals was hoarding all the GED fee money that students paid to each school. Since Nestor Padron was in charge of that division, he'd then authorize the fee money to be transferred to this school. There's a memo in here asking Padron what kind of investments he wanted to set up, since the cash pile had grown to over $300,000."

Cohen leaned over to read the memo the detective was fishing out from a stack of papers. "Hmmm. What principal has $300,000 just sitting around, unmarked for any type of use?" she pondered out loud.

"Not my kid's Principal," the female detective replied. "Hell, we even had to have a fundraiser just so the school could buy toilet paper for the last three months of the school year!"

"And my kid's school has a mud pit instead of a playground, because there's no money to pay to sod the field," the male detective added.

"Subpoena the school's records and all of the documents from any audits of that school for the last five years. And bring the principal in for a little Q & A, why don't you." Captain Cohen then crossed the hall over to the group working on Maine's sleazy life before death.

"Can anyone here spell progress?" Cohen asked the group, all of whom were hunched over videotape players, DVD machines and viewing monitors.

"P-O-R-N! Progress!" It was Cohen's problem child, Detective Christine Rodriguez.

"You're a damn spelling bee champ, aren't you Rodriguez," Cohen shot back.

"Shit Captain! This crap is beyond disgusting! I mean look at the vegetable lady here. I've spent my morning watching her do things with squash, zucchini and cucumbers… to the point that I don't think I can ever shop in the produce section again!"

"Then buy frozen veggies, Rodriguez," Cohen responded dismissively. "Are we having any luck with the surveillance tapes from the 9th floor hallways?"

"Not yet. Sgt. Leventhal just got them this morning. He's scanning as fast as he can," Rodriguez informed her boss. "But we may have a lead off Maine's home computer though. The IT guys are seeing if they can identify the servers used to send a couple of the kiddie porn pics we found on his computer," Rodriguez paused, hoping for an "atta girl" from the Captain.

But all she got was a, "keep me posted," as Captain Cohen left the room.

Her last stop was to check in with the forensics lab. "Is our bullet talking yet?"

The crime scene analyst looked up from his microscope. "Yes. He says his name is a .284 Jarrett. A 30-caliber bullet, most likely fired from a Jarrett Signature rifle. They're high-powered with good velocity… so I'm guessing our shooter did his damage from a distance. There's no way she'd have survived that bullet if it had been fired at close range."

Captain Cohen started to say something, but the lab guy interjected. "Yes, we calculated the distance, and the techs are back out re-examining all the areas we mapped out. The best bet right now is the Annex Building."

"The building across the street from the main parking garage?"

"That's the one. I'm guessing the shooter was on the roof, or one of the top floors. He'd have had a clear shot at her and the distance would most likely account for her momentary survival. I hear she's serious, but stable."

"You hear right," Cohen said as she turned to leave. "Good work. Call me as soon as you know anything more."

As she was driving to the Abbey Hotel, Capt.. Cohen called her husband, who was a firearms instructor at the police academy.

"Honey, what do you know about the Jarrett Signature Rifle? Why does that name sound so familiar?"

"How could you forget, Sheila? A cache of Jarrett's were re-covered when the feds raided that camp in the Everglades, a few years ago, where the F-4 Commandos were training the Venezuelans who were hoping to overthrow President Chavez. I guess it was their weapon of choice that year."

Eliott Hernandez adored his wife, even if she hadn't taken his last name when they married. But he couldn't believe how little she knew about firearms, especially being a police offi-cer. It just wasn't her area of interest, but it was most certain-ly his. He figured they were just like most married couples, with some interests and hobbies rarely crossing paths.

"Why are you asking," he inquired, realizing she hadn't replied.

"The F-4 Commandos? Do you mean that whacked out-group of Anti-Castro terrorists? Aren't they all in nursing homes by now?" Cohen suddenly slammed her brakes, as the traffic on the MacArthur Causeway came to a halt.

"Wishful thinking my dearest," Hernandez teased.

"Aren't they the ones that your darling parents refer to as the mafia? The group that appointed itself to decide who is Cuban enough?"

"Bingo, Babe! They seem to believe that they have a litmus test for deciding who is and who isn't a "true Cuban exile.""

"Shit! Got to go honey. See you tonight!" With that, Cohen abruptly terminated her phone call with her husband and dialed Detective West's cell phone.

"West here," he answered.

"West, it's Cohen. Start researching the F-4 Commandos. Salas was shot with a .284 Jarrett, most likely from a Jarrett rifle... the same kind the feds confiscated from those anti-Castro nuts a few years ago. Maybe they didn't like Salas' politics. She did nominate a Haitian woman to be the Interim Superintendent."

"Holy shit! You don't think...." Before West could finish his sentence, Cohen said... "Yes, I do think. Call me later." And she hung up.

CHAPTER #82

Lily Molina's first day as Superintendent was shaping up to be a glorious one, or so she thought. The famous Miami sun was shining, blue skies sparkled as if bejeweled by chunks of Aquamarines, set among pearly clouds.

The platinum blonde arrived at district headquarters wearing her signature color... red! In fact, if it weren't for her blonde hair, she'd have looked like a red balloon. Her jacket was red; her skirt was red, as were her shirt, pantyhose, shoes and jewelry. She even sported a large red flower on her lapel, which drew the eye to her bulging cleavage.

As she pulled her car into the private garage, nearest the entrance to the elevator she'd take to the 9th floor, security guards, janitors, and any other school system personnel, who encountered her, bowed their heads. It was their way of disguising their nauseous reaction to her redness! But of course, Lily Molina was vain enough to believe that they considered her royalty.

Just as the elevator door was about to shut, to ferry her up to her lavish office, a hand reached in between the doors, causing them to open wide again. There stood Jez Underwood.

"Lily!" she crowed. "Or should I say Superintendent Molina. Good morning."

"What are you doing here?" Lily growled.

"I wanted to be the first to interview the first female superintendent of the Miami school system." Jez glared at Molina. "I never took you for one of those shy retiring types. Don't tell me you have issues with publicity, Mrs. Molina?" Jez smiled coyly.

"I have issues with you!" Lily Molina all but spat at Jez, just as Emeril started lugging his massive amount of equipment onto the elevator. As soon as the doors shut, Lily turned and got right into Jez's face.

"Don't think you'll get the first interview with me, or any interview with me... ever! I'd rather eat fire than talk to you... you... bitch!"

Jez flinched a little from the spittle that was flying out of Lily's mouth. Then she turned and looked at Emeril. "Did you get that on tape?" she asked.

"Ju bet I did Jez" Emeril had his camera on his shoulder and Jez could see the red tally light lit up.

Just then, the elevator stopped and opened up to the 9th floor offices.

"Security! Security!" Lily Molina fled the elevator cab. She looked like a streak of red painting the hallways, as her huge breasts bobbed up and down like lobster trap buoys in the Atlantic. She was the brunt of many school system jokes for wearing her clothes one size smaller than her actual measurements.

"What's her problem?" Jez asked Emeril.

"I don't know Jez. After all, we do have 9th floor passes." Both of them looked down at the orange laminated tag that was clipped onto their clothing that displayed a big number 9.

"And here we are on 9! Let's go Emeril," Jez said... grinning from ear to ear. And so off they went in search of the new superintendent, for a little more harassment.

Although Jez had been given the day off, her mind wouldn't let her just stay in bed. She'd called Emeril around 7a.m. and told him of her plan to ambush Lily Molina on her first day on the job. Emeril had loved the idea. So here was the workaholic, chasing after the woman in red, when she could have been lying in bed watching old movies. Jez wondered if she didn't have some kind of sickness that prevented her from unwinding

At the Abbey Hotel, another woman was frazzled, but for a very different reason.

No sooner had Captain Cohen arrived, than she'd gotten a phone call from one of her detectives. They'd captured the image of man entering Dr. Maine's office, the morning of his death, from a hallway surveillance camera. It was only the back of his head, but it was something. They were sending a copy over to the hotel for Donna Maine to look at.

"I'm trying to remember, but I can't. As far as I know, I never met this person that Hank was so obsessed with. All I know is he was around 20, and that was a few years ago. Hank described him to me, but I refused to listen. I mean, what wife wants to know about her husband's gay lover!" Donna plopped down on the bed and grabbed a pillow. It was swiftly becoming her version of a security blanket.

"Please Donna," pleaded Capt. Cohen... "I'm begging you to try... try and remember what Hank said about what this guy looked like."

"I can't! I won't!" screamed Donna. "This whole thing is re-volting!" She then began to sob into her pillow.

Captain Cohen walked over to one of the bodyguards and ordered her to call Carlo Ferrini. If anyone could calm the hysterical Mrs. Maine, Captain Cohen was willing to gamble on Ferrini.

Thirty minutes later, Carlo arrived, having called in his code phrase and all the other silliness that was required to see a state witness under protection. As he entered the hotel suite, he saw Captain Cohen pacing the living room floor.

"Ah, Mr. Ferrini. Thank you so much for coming over. I'm afraid we have a hysterical witness on our hands, and I didn't know who else to call. Perhaps you can calm Mrs. Maine. We are expecting a snapshot of a surveillance camera to ar-rive, and before I show it to her, I need to know what she re-members about this young guy she told us that Maine was seeing." Cohen paused. "Remember the person she told us about?" she queried.

"Yes," Carlo responded, "but I don't recall her giving much of a description."

"True. But back then I didn't care. Right now I care a lot!" Captain Cohen then escorted him towards Donna's bedroom where she was curled up in the covers staring at reruns of I Love Lucy.

"Donna," Carlo called out quietly.

Donna was up in two seconds with her arms around Carlo's neck. "Oh thank God you're here. Did Sheila tell you what's happening?" Donna looked into his eyes with a pitiful, weepy, helpless expression.

"Shit can the 'Damsel in Distress' attitude, Donna." Carlo all but barked at her, and she recoiled.

"These officers have saved your life, provided you a safe place, and all they ask in return is your cooperation trying to find the person who killed your husband. The least you could do is give it your best shot, without the dramatics!"

"So much for his calming effect on the widow Maine," Captain Cohen whispered to one of the bodyguards.

"How can you be so mean to me, Carlo!"? Donna was screaming and crying as she threw herself onto the bed.

"It's called tough love, my dear!" Carlo reached for her arm and pulled her up.

Just then, there was a knock at the hotel room door. One of the cops, pulled her gun, and walked over to the door. She then spoke a code word, while peeking through the eyehole.

"Detective Ingersoll walked inside waving an enlarged photo, of what he firmly believed, was Hank Maine's killer.

CHAPTER #83

Dr. Moses Moorehead was deep into REM sleep, when a banging on his hotel room door brought him quickly out of his deep sleep cycle.

"Housekeeping! Housekeeping!" a shrill Caribbean accented voice hollered.

"Not now," he huffed, as phlegm stuck in his throat.

"OK sir. But checkout at noon, sir," the female voice informed him.

Moses looked at his watch. It was 11:45a.m. Damn, he thought. "Yeah! Yeah! Noon."

Moorehead then ran to the bathroom, turned on the shower, and was walking out of his room 10 minutes later.

After a quick purchase at the hotel gift shop, he headed to the lobby area men's room, where he changed into a pair of Cayman Island logoed shorts, tee shirt and a straw hat. Without his wig, he felt naked and needed the hat to make him feel a sense of security. A true tourist, he thought, as he glanced in the mirror, before exiting and hailing a cab in front of the Hyatt Grand Cayman.

"The Cayman Island National Bank at 25 Main Street," Moorehead instructed the cab driver.

A few minutes later, Big Mo was standing in the lobby of the massive bank, waiting on the group's banker, Harry Kimble.

"Dr. Moorehead!" a deep voice boomed behind him.

Startled, Moses jerked around, suddenly feeling really silly in his Minnesotan tourist getup.

"Mr. Kimble. How good to see you. It's been so many years." Mo waited for a reaction. There was none.

"Is there someplace private we can talk?" he asked Kimble.

"Of course," Kimble said as he led Moorehead off toward a private office.

"What can I do for you sir?" Kimble inquired as he closed the door to the office.

"The situation in Miami has changed, and my group finds it necessary to transfer our deposits elsewhere... at least for the time being." Big Mo waited for a reaction from the very proper Mr. Kimble, but there was none.

"All I need are your instructions, Dr. Moorehead. If memory serves me correctly... only your name is required for a transfer of funds."

"Your memory is very good," Moorehead replied, clearly impressed by the services of the Cayman Islands National Bank.

"I have an account number at the Banque Suisse. Transfer all but $100,000. The remainder, I wish to be paid to me in cash," Mo instructed the banker.

"Dr. Moorehead. The transfer is no problem, although I do regret that we are losing your business." Mr. Kimble paused. "But there is a procedural problem with the structure of your account and your request for a $100,000 cash withdrawal."

"What's the problem?" Moorehead was suddenly starting to perspire.

"A cash withdrawal of that amount will require a second signatory. Bank protocol. I'm sure you understand."

Moorehead started to cough. God he needed coffee! "I can't honestly say I'm familiar with those terms of our agreement," he lied.

"It's right here, Dr. Moorehead. Your signature is on the left side of this document." Kimble then thrust a piece of paper under Moorehead's nose.

"So it is!" Big Mo was trying his best not to be flustered. If only he had a gun, he thought. I'd just shoot the motherfucker and be done with him!

"Well, as you say, a second signature is required, Mr. Kimble." Moses Moorehead then reached into his short's pocket and pulled out his wallet. He opened it and began going through it as if his ass was on fire.

"Here!" he finally yelled. "This is Thaddeus Brown's signature. Now you have two signators."

Dr. Moses Josiah Moorehead, was actually, and unbelievably, presenting an IOU from Thaddeus Brown, signed four months earlier, as a second signature to Mr. Harry Kimble.

"Dr. Moorehead, I'm afraid I can't…"

Before Harry Kimble could finish his sentence, Big Mo stood, leaned in toward the proper banker, and closed the deal.

"If you don't accept this as a second signature, Mr. Kimble, I can assure you that you won't live to dispute my account of this meeting." Kimble was trembling.

"Uh huh!" he muttered.

"Now, Mr. Kimble, start playing banker!" Moses Moorehead sat back down and lit a cigarette. "And thank you, Harry. I'd love a cup of coffee," he said.

"No problem," was Kimble's only response.

CHAPTER #84

As soon as Detective Ingersoll stopped waving the mystery man's picture around he dropped it on the coffee table in front of the couch, along with nine other photos of men entering Hank Maine's office... all had been copied from surveillance videos. But to protect the integrity of this rudimentary line up, Mrs. Maine wouldn't be told which photo was taken the morning of the murder.

Donna, hugging her pillow, slowly walked over and sat down. Carlo peered over her shoulder, and glanced at each photo, one at a time. Trying to remain expressionless, he stopped on one of the photos and thought to himself... it's him!

"Mrs. Maine," Captain Cohen began. "Please take a good look at these photos. Tell me if you can identify any of the people entering your husband's office."

"How can I?" Donna whined. "I can't see their faces."

"Just do your best, Donna. You know so many of the people your husband worked with. There's no rush. Just do your best." Cohen looked up at Carlo, who refused to meet her glance.

One by one, Donna lifted each picture off the table to get a better look at each one. As she studied the third picture, she said, "This looks like Dr. Cecil Raymond, the school board member."

"OK," Cohen said softly.

"Oh! This is definitely Dr. Moorehead." Donna was holding picture number four. "I mean who else do you know has such a ridiculous hairdo?" Donna tossed the picture back down. She then proceeded to scan the fifth picture, then the sixth picture, the seventh and eighth.

"Number nine looks like Nestor Padron," she announced. "And this is R.V.... number ten!"

At that point, Captain Cohen removed numbers 3, 4, 9 and 10 from the table.

"Now take a look at these remaining photos," she instructed Donna. "Do any of them match anything that your husband might have said in describing this young man he was so infatuated with?"

Donna began studying the pictures again. "I remember he talked about running his hands through his hair." She lifted picture #1. "I guess that would eliminate this guy. He's bald." Donna handed the photo to Captain Cohen.

"And I don't think Hank would have been talking about greasy hair. So that eliminates number 8."

Donna was starting to get into this little game. She handed her security pillow to Carlo, who walked into her bedroom and threw it on the bed. He was glad for the few seconds it gave him time to think about what he should do.

As he returned to the living room, Donna was handing the Captain the 7th photo, saying the hair looked gray and would mean he wasn't young enough. That left pictures #2, 5, and 6.

As Donna studied the last three remaining photos, Cohen again tried to lock eyes with Carlo. But he was non-responsive, appearing to be studying the pictures just as intently as Donna.

"Hank said something about him being an impeccable dresser. So this guy, number 2 is probably not the guy. He looks like a fat slob, with his shirt half tucked in his pants, and no suit jacket."

"Alright." Capt. Cohen realized she'd been holding her breath, and exhaled as she took picture #2 off the table.

"Young, lots of hair, an impeccable dresser..." she paused, her eyebrows wrinkled as she looked at both pictures. "And tall!" Donna squeaked as she grabbed for the fifth picture.

"This guy looks tall, and he matches all the other descriptions I remember Hank talking about."

She proudly handed the fifth photo to Captain Cohen. "So who is he?" Donna asked Cohen.

"You don't know?" Sheila Cohen was hoping to trip her up.

"No!" Donna stood. She was getting angry. "I told you, Hank never mentioned him by name, and I frankly never asked!" She then stepped past Cohen and walked over to Carlo for a hug.

A few minutes lapsed, as Carlo comforted Donna. Ingersoll got up and helped himself to a Coca-Cola from the refrigerator, and Donna's bodyguards began patrolling the windows, checking out the scene down on the street below their hotel suite.

Finally, Carlo unglued himself from Donna and escorted her back to the couch, urging her to sit down.

"I think Donna is telling the truth," he finally said. "It's highly unlikely that Hank would have given her a full name. He was too protective, especially about his secret life."

Cohen was listening intently. "Captain, I'm a gay man, and even I didn't know about Maine's lingerie fetish!" He paused. "But I do believe I know the name of the man in photo #5."

Donna jerked around, staring at Carlo. Captain Cohen stood. "Do tell, Mr. Ferrini," the Captain urged.

And Carlo did.

CHAPTER #85

"His name is Daniel Estrada," Carlo began. "He's the son of a very prominent and wealthy Hispanic businessman. He lives with his parents in their Golden Beach ocean-front mansion."

Carlo sat down on the couch, realizing that everyone in the hotel suite was hanging on his every word.

"I first met Daniel when he was a part-time clerk at his former high school, Miami Beach High. Often times, his principal would ask him to hand-deliver something of importance to the downtown administrative office. On one of those occasions he met Hank. The reason I know this is because Daniel is also gay, and he confided in me."

Carlo stopped. "Could I get a glass of water?" he asked.

When Det. Ingersoll returned with the water, Carlo continued.

"He told me that he introduced himself to Hank one day when he'd been sent by his principal to deliver something to the administration headquarters building. He was patting himself on the back about how he'd told Hank that he saw him on TV all the time. Daniel admitted that he shamelessly flirted with Hank. I guess it worked, because according to Daniel, Hank asked him to stop by his office before he returned to his school. Daniel told me that he remembered the exact minute that Hank Maine hit on him. It was 12:44pm... a Monday. He said he was staring at a wall clock over Maine's desk, when Hank got up, walked around to the visitors chair Daniel was sitting in, grabbed Daniel's thick head of hair in his hands, and planted a passionate kiss on his lips."

Carlo realized he was sweating. He was extremely uncomfortable talking about this, especially in front of Donna.

"Go on," Captain Cohen urged him as she grabbed her tape recorder and pressed the record button.

"Daniel must have thought that because I was gay, I'd be comfortable hearing all the salacious details... but I was not! I stopped him and told him I wasn't interested. But a few days later, he cornered me again and asked me if I'd like to know more about the Great and Powerful Dr. Hank Maine? I insisted I didn't, but he began talking anyway."

Carlo took a sip of water. Donna ran into her bedroom and slammed the door shut.

"Frankly, I'm glad she's gone," Capt. Cohen said to those in the room.

Carlo continued. "Daniel told me all about how he and Maine groped each other's crotches, kissed in silence, but never once removed any clothing. According to Daniel, Hank seduced him with tales of his unbridled power. He gave Daniel his card with his private number and told Daniel to call him to get together for lunch."

"And?" Cohen pressed.

"Daniel confessed he played hard to get, waiting a few days to make that call. But he clearly was fantasizing about what Hank could do for him if they did hook up. After two days, he told me he called Maine, who suggested they meet at an intimate bistro on Lincoln Road. It was a place that Maine was confident they wouldn't run into any school board employees. I guess after that lunch the two of them couldn't keep their hands off one another. Daniel was very candid that he didn't like to frequent bars or gay clubs, so the fact that he'd met Maine in such a private way really had him boiling over with testosterone and ambition. He told me that he figured Maine could satisfy both his needs... and he was right!"

"Why do you say that?" Det. Ingersoll asked.

"Because, Hank maneuvered school board policies and procedures to get close to his new flame! Maine made sure his new lover rose rapidly through the ranks. One minute this kid was a part-time school clerk... the next thing I know, he's moving downtown to take an important position in the personnel department."

"Why Personnel, Carlo?" Cohen asked.

"It's just my guess but probably because another closeted bi-sexual male was in charge of that department and he was easily manipulated by the Nazi! Hank controlled the entire process... so it was all too easy for him to stack the deck, so to speak."

There was silence in the room as his audience processed everything Carlo Ferrini had told them.

"You sound very close to this person, Mr. Ferrini?" It was Det. Ingersoll.

"I found myself in that position by accident. Not only had Daniel confided in me, but his parents came to me about his sexual orientation. It bothered them greatly!"

"Explain," Cohen insisted.

"The father found out that he was wining and dining a 17-year old student at Beach High, after he got a $15,000 credit card bill. They knew I was gay and a school administrator, so they approached me. They were ready to toss Daniel out of their eight bedroom, nine bathroom home. The father hated the fact that his son was gay, and worried about how his son's sexuality would reflect on him. The mother worried about never having grandchildren. They'd nearly tossed him out of the house twice, once when he'd dropped out of college after only one year, and again when he rang up that huge credit card debt."

"So why didn't they?" Ingersoll asked.

Carlo quickly explained. "He landed that big job in personnel and so his parents allowed him to stay, but under one condition."

"What was that?" Capt. Cohen checked to make sure the tape recorder was still rolling.

"His father brought in a psychiatrist from South America, who he thought would turn Daniel into a heterosexual. He told me he didn't trust American psychiatrists. But when the "shrink for hire" informed the father and mother that Daniel would never be heterosexual, and to accept their son's sexual orientation… they threw in the towel and decided to learn to live with their son. They loved him. They just didn't love who he was."

"OK," Captain Cohen began. "This Daniel guy is young, hot, gay, a college dropout, power hungry and rich. But is he a killer?"

Her words hung in the air like humidity in Miami.

"Are you asking me?" Carlo inquired.

"Yes!"

"He's a sociopath Captain. That much I know. Does that make him a killer? I'm not an expert." Carlo stood, sipped his water and looked out the hotel window.

"That's a pretty strong indictment of the man, Carlo." Cohen didn't push any further.

"It's a pretty accurate indictment too," Carlo responded. "Maybe you'll find that out for yourselves, once you begin to investigate Daniel."

"Maybe we will, " Sheila Cohen conceded. "Is there anything else you can tell us about this guy, Daniel?"

Carlo paused, considering his words carefully. "Daniel often talked about bringing Hank to his parent's house. He was detailed, in his description of their sexual liaisons. In my mind, Maine was a willing player… not an innocent."

With that, Carlo asked if he was free to go. He was led out, and put on the elevator by Donna's bodyguards. Although he was physically independent of the cops, he wondered if his safety would be better served staying near them rather than driving away from them.

CHAPTER #86

Jez Underwood's Noon News report, showing the new interim superintendent cursing her in the elevator, sent Lily hiding behind closed and locked doors. She'd called the school police chief and demanded round the clock security. The chief, who couldn't stand Lily Molina, informed her it was an inappropriate use of tax dollars, and he'd report it to authorities if she pressed him.

"God damn him!" she screamed at her secretary. "Get me his employment contract. I need to find a way to fire him and put a putz in that position who will do what I say."

"Yes, ma'am," her secretary responded, before hurrying out of the superintendent's office. As soon as she reached her desk, she picked up the phone and called the police chief, informing him what the "woman in red" was up to.

Lily Molina was so full of herself that she was completely clueless as to how many enemies she had. It would be her undoing. But for now, those enemies were playing their cards very close to their vests… just like any good spy.

This was typical of the treachery that infected the nation's fourth largest school system. Lily was just doing what she'd observed so many others do over the years. Manipulating the system and getting away with it was a hobby for most school administrators. Lily simply didn't know any better, having been born without a moral compass.

Jez and Carlo had had lengthy discussions about the decrepit morality that ran through the blood of so many high profile Miamians. Were they born without an ethics gene, or was it a learned behavior? Not being scientists, they never reached a conclusion, but their debates invigorated them!

Jez was back at the station after her noon live shot from in front of the school administration building, when her cell phone rang.

"Hello," she said.

"You might want to be at Miami International Airport to greet the 4:40pm Cayman Airways flight #33," said a strange voice.

"Why?" Jez asked.

"So you can be the first to welcome Moses Moorehead home from vacation!" All Jez heard after that was a click and then a dial tone.

Jez immediately did two things. First, she called Emeril and told him to bring the news car around. Then she dialed a special number and informed the person who answered what the caller had just told her. She grabbed her purse and brief-case, headed downstairs to the news desk, where she in-formed Allison that she'd have a lead story for the 5:00 maybe, the 5:30 probably... but the 6:00 definitely.

"What is it?" she heard Allison screaming as she bolted for the door and jumped in Emeril's vehicle. "M I A," she told him.

"Ju got it!" Emeril then hit the accelerator and they were off.

"We can't have a rogue operator in the newsroom!" Allison Wheeler was in Boris Danken's office pitching another fit over the fact that Jez had left without telling her what story she was working on.

"I agree," said Boris. "I'll fire her, and we'll simply do without those rating numbers she pulls in. The bosses upstairs won't mind, will they Allison?"

"I know she's good, but so does she! I thought it was your philosophy never to let the talent know they were talented, Boris." Allison was dripping with sarcasm. "It seems you're breaking your number one rule."

"It's not like I tell her, Allison. But shit! She can read a ratings sheet same as anyone in this building. She isn't stupid. She knows what quarter hours spike, and what stories she had in that time frame. You make it sound like I send her flowers and chocolates, with a note that says 'you're a ratings star!'"

Boris slammed his mini refrigerator door shut, having removed two small, green plastic bottles of water. He tossed one to Allison, who tried to catch it, but missed.

"All I'm asking is that you set down some rules. How am I supposed to keep the rest of the staff under control when they see Jez doing her own thing without any repercussions?" Allison was fuming as she crawled under Boris' desk to retrieve the bottle of water she'd dropped.

Just then, the executive director, Warren Fletcher walked in. At first, all he saw was Allison's ass playing peek-a-boo from underneath Boris' desk. He then saw Boris sitting in his chair, grinning.

"Am I interrupting Allison's oral arguments about Jez's behavior?" Warren inquired sarcastically.

"Hardly!" Boris stood up to show Warren that his pants were firmly zipped. At the same time, Allison squiggled back out from under the desk and showed off the small, green bottle of water, she'd found.

"Boris throws like a girl," Allison declared, as she held up the bottled water, looking like an Olympian with a gold medal.

Warren just shook his head. As hard as he tried to understand his boss, sometimes Warren felt like he was working in an insane asylum.

"Jez just called. She's at MIA waiting on Dr. Moses Moorehead to arrive from the Cayman Islands," Warren informed them.

"I thought he went AWOL!" Allison jumped in. "The cops have searched his office and have his house under surveillance. Has he really been on vacation?"

"I don't know, Allison," Warren responded. "But I'm sure we can count on Jez to get us the real facts." With those words, he let the boss' door close, leaving Allison and Boris alone to drink their bottled water.

CHAPTER #87

As Mo departed the immigration and customs area wearing his straw hat, he was greeted by Detective Ingersoll and two uniformed officers.

"To what do I owe the pluhsure?" he asked… showing no sign of surprise.

"Save it for your lawyer," Ingersoll sneered. "We're just going to escort you downtown for a little chat."

"I had no idea the po-leece would be so interested in my vacation." Moses Moorehead remained cool as a cucumber. Then just as they passed the security checkpoint and entered the main terminal area, Jez and Emeril stepped out from behind a thick pillar. Moorehead squinted at the brightness of the light on top of the big video camera. By the time his eyes adjusted, Jez had the microphone in his face.

"Were you running from the police?" she demanded.

"Just a vacation. That's all," he replied, gritting his teeth.

"Oh really? Where'd you go Dr. Moorehead?"

"My business, not yours." Moses was growing angrier by the second.

"How was the weather in the Cayman Islands?" she pressed. "I mean, you look like a walking billboard for the place," she half laughed.

Shit! He thought to himself. The last thing I need is for the boys to figure out where I've been. He kept walking, refusing to look at Jez or answer anymore of her questions. As the exit doors to the airport swung open, Jez got in one last question before Moorehead was unceremoniously pushed inside a squad car.

"You do know it's illegal to transfer money for school construction into an offshore bank account, don't you, Dr. Moorehead. I mean you are a smart man. Or are you?"

She knew she'd pushed one of his buttons, from the glare he gave her as the cops slammed the car door shut. There was a lot about Moses Josiah Moorehead you could say, but no one ever questioned his intellect.

As the cop started the car, Jez suddenly realized that Moses Moorehead looked different. Damn! She suddenly realized, Moorehead wasn't sporting his trademark "That Girl" flipped hairdo.

"Hey, Dr. Moorehead," she shouted at the closed window of the patrol car. "What happened to your hair?" Just then the police car pulled out and Jez turned to Emeril with a big grin on her face. "He's missing his hair, for Christ's sake! Moorehead has lost his flipped locks!" Jez then began to laugh so hard she was crying.

Emeril just shook his head. This crazy reporter loves to play with fire, he thought… just before he began to chuckle too.

CHAPTER #88

"You want to run that by me one more time." Det. Christine Rodriguez was on the phone with the cops' computer geeks.

As they started into their computer bibble babble, Rodriguez interrupted them. "Boil it down to me in English. Save your techno language for the witness stand," she instructed the person on the other end of the line. She was scribbling notes on a legal pad as fast as she could.

"So the bottom line is that some of that child porn came to Maine's home computer from the school system?" She said it out loud on purpose, so her fellow detectives would perk up and pay attention. They did.

"But you're saying he didn't mail it to himself from his office computer. Well do you know where in the district it came from?" She was writing notes again.

"OIT? What's that?" There was a pause, after which Det. Rodriguez repeated what she'd been told… "The Office of Information Technology. O.K. I got it. Now have you linked it to a particular computer in that office?" There was silence as she wrote down what the computer geek was telling her.

"A supervisor? Well of course we'll get a subpoena for his computer. Good job guys." Christine Rodriguez hung up the phone and glanced at the other detectives who were staring at her. "I think we may have unearthed a child porn ring operating out of the school system, fellas."

"Man alive!" shouted one of her colleagues. "I'm pulling my kid out of that public education horror show first thing tomorrow," he informed the group.

"Good idea," Rodriguez responded. "But first I need you to get a search warrant and meet me at the OIT office in West Dade. Now who's coming with me?" she inquired. Four other detectives stood up, grabbed their coats and headed for the door.

Just as they got to the elevators, Rodriguez's cell phone rang. It was Captain Cohen.

"Hey! I was just about to call you," Rodriguez began, but Cohen cut her off.

"I need you to get over to Golden Beach. We may have identified Maine's killer," the Captain informed her.

"I… well… you see…" Rodriguez was stammering.

"That's an order Rodriguez!" Cohen was in no mood to deal with her problem child.

"I can't Captain. We're on our way to the school system's office of information technology. The computer geeks in forensics have identified some of Maine's child porn as coming from that office… a supervisor to be specific. They say it may be part of a child porn ring, Captain. I'm efforting a search warrant, as we speak."

Cohen was nearly speechless. "Then go! Do whatever you have to," she insisted. "And keep me posted."

"You got it," she said as she flipped her cell phone closed. Rodriguez then informed the other detectives what Cohen had said about a possible suspect living in Golden Beach.

"I guess even the richest among us, don't get a pass on murderous desires," said one of the men. "But if I lived over there, I think I'd be more concerned about my stock options than homicide."

"Maybe that's how they get so rich," Rodriguez chimed in. "They just kill the competition. Literally!"

"Maine was a cross-dressing, Adolf Hitler, look-a-like," insisted one of the other detectives. "Who was his competition? Eva Braun?" The group starting laughing as they got into their cars and drove off.

CHAPTER #89

Moses Moorehead seethed with anger during the entire drive from the airport to the police station. He wasn't as angry about being met by cops, as he was, knowing that Jez had ambushed him without his famous hairstyle and his cronies would soon know that he'd been in the Cayman Islands. That was a secret he'd wanted to keep as long as possible. He'd figured they been on the lookout for him, and since he was forced to use his real name to fly back to Miami... the greeting committee was all but expected.

As the cops drove him back to the station, Moorehead prepared to be met by more reporters. To his surprise and joy, there wasn't one camera crew. "I want to call my lawyer," he insisted.

"Now why would you want to do that Dr. Moorehead? Being as, you've been asserting your innocence since we picked you up," Detective Gonzalez asked.

"Innocent men get lynched by the system all the time, boy! But then maybuh you Cuban fellas don't know anything about Jim Crow." Moorehead was fuming. Damn Hispanics, he thought, they come here, work for next to nothing, and make my people look like lazy slobs, when all we want is a level playing field.

"Sorry, Moorehead. I never met your friend Jim Crow," responded a jarhead looking, muscle-bound, Cuban-American uniformed cop, who looked to be about 25-years old.

You idiot! Moorehead thought to himself.

The next thing he knew, he was being hustled into an interrogation room, where he was allowed to call his lawyer. He reached K.T. Jones on his cell phone.

"Moses! How are you?" Jones asked when he heard Mo's voice.

"Not ree-uhl good, Jones. I'm at the Miami Police station for a chit chat they tell me. I ain't talk'in until you get here, K.T., so take your time, or hurry over... either way, I don't care."

"Is this about that video of you in Vascoe's office last week?" his attorney asked.

"I'm figur'in it is, although they haven't said so."

"I was wondering why I hadn't heard from you when that video was broadcast all over town," Jones replied.

"Yeah, yeah. We'll talk about that later, but I also need you to move fast to get Franklin Elder released. They picked him up yesterday and held him overnight. I guess they wanted to put the heat on me, by using him."

"Mo, do they have all your papers?"

"They raided my office, yes. Beyond that, nothing." Mo's left hand automatically went up to his head, as if on autopilot, searching for his flip curl, when he remembered he didn't have a flip anymore. He again, cursed Jez Underwood.

As soon as he got home, he'd put on his second wig. But how could he explain having hair, only hours after she'd videotaped him without his signature flip hairdo? That fucking bitch! Now the whole damn town would know he wore a wig! What would his lady friends think?

"Mo, listen," his attorney was instructing him on what to do. "Say nothing. Don't let them goad you into a conversation. Let me first take care of Franklin. So just sit tight until I get over to you."

"Yeah, that's fine. Do it." With that, Moses Moorehead hung up the phone. Two seconds later, the cops, who'd been watching from the adjacent room, walked in and sat down.

"So, can we talk?" asked Gonzalez.

"No we cun not! But you cun get me some coffee and an ashtray," Mo instructed the detective.

"Coffee, si. Ashtray, no. This is a government building Dr. Moorehead. You can't smoke in here. I'm surprised you'd even ask, considering that the school board building is public too."

Moses Josiah Moorehead was suddenly regretting letting his attorney take care of Franklin first. He wasn't sure how he'd manage not to smoke for 5 minutes or five hours! This was hell on earth, he thought. As soon as I get out of here, he vowed, I'm getting curtains or shutters or something to cover the windows in my office and the superintendents, god damn it! With that, he began to chew on his yellowed, warped, and misshapen fingernails.

CHAPTER #90

Two Golden Beach police officers stationed their patrol cars along the center medium of the tony, enclave of monster mansions. Their orders were to wait for Miami police, and detain anyone from leaving the burnt yellow Mediterranean home that was barely visible behind the wall of hedges and a gigantic wrought iron gate.

The cop's presence on the street would hardly alarm anyone. This was a department famous in Dade County for actually enforcing the 35 MPH speed limit. Those who drove this section of A1A, actually expected to see patrol cars. Running radar was about all the dozen members of the Golden Beach police department had to do with their time. The uber-wealthy who lived there had elaborate security systems. Some even had their own security personnel. Speeding was about the only offense, for which a Golden Beach police officer, ever got the chance to write tickets or reports.

They'd been sitting there for about an hour, when three Miami police cars arrived, two of which were unmarked. Captain Sheila Cohen got out and walked over to introduce herself, as the two officers exited their vehicles.

"Any sign of activity?" she inquired.

"Nothing," they responded simultaneously.

"Good," said Cohen. "I'd like it if one of you would stay here, and the other would accompany us to the house. Do either of you know anything about the people who live there?" she asked, pointing to the house on the east side of the road.

The tallest officer informed her that the owners were Mr. and Mrs. Jorge Estrada. They'd lived there 15 years, and the cops had only been called to the house once, when a burglar alarm went off. The report said it was probably triggered by a lightning storm that was in the area at the same time the alarm was triggered. The report noted that a number of other homes in the area had also sounded false alarms.

"What about a Daniel Estrada? The son?" Cohen asked.

The two cops shrugged their shoulders. "It's a pretty quiet neighborhood, Captain."

"That could change," Cohen informed them. "We're here to question a possible murder suspect."

The two Golden Beach officers shared a wide-eyed glance at one another, just as Cohen pointed to the tall one and asked him to go with her team.

Cohen and the Golden Beach cop walked over to the home, and punched the security box next to the gigantic locked gate.

"Hola!" They heard a female, Hispanic voice answer.

"Hola, Señora," Captain Cohen responded, as she waved to one of her Spanish speaking detectives to come over, just in case there was a language barrier... real or imagined.

"My name is Captain Sheila Cohen. I'm a detective with the Miami Police Department. I need to speak to Daniel Estrada. Could you please let us in?"

"Jes! Jes! Please do come," answered the Hispanic woman, sounding a bit flustered. Just then the big wrought iron gates began to part, and Cohen began her walk up the driveway to one of the most spectacular homes she'd ever seen. Her team followed behind her in their cars.

Inside, the housekeeper, a 64-year old Cuban named Maida, hit the intercom button to Daniel's room. "Meester, Estrada, sir... there are police here to talk with ju." There was no response. "Meester Daniel! Meester Daniel!" Again, no response. Maida was all but certain Daniel was home. She'd seen him come in from the beach nearly an hour earlier. Just as she was about to head towards his bedroom, she heard the doorbell ring. "Dios Mio!" she said, crossing herself and heading for the front door.

When she opened the door, she saw a woman in a pants suit who was showing her a police badge. Behind her were two other men in regular suits and two uniformed police officers.

"We need to speak with Daniel Estrada, please." Captain Cohen could see that the housekeeper was frightened. "Is he home?" she asked.

"I thought so miss. I saw him come in from the beach about an hour jago. But he didn't janswer the intercom when I called."

Just then, Daniel Estrada entered the foyer, pulling a tee shirt over his head, looking like he'd just gotten out of the shower.

"Maida, did you say I had guests?" When he saw the cops, he didn't even blink. "May I help you?" He was calm, almost smug.

Captain Cohen introduced herself and her team, and Daniel then took them all into the living room. Cohen asked the Golden Beach officer to remain at the front door.

As they walked into the "living room," or the "great room," as the Estrada family called it, Daniel took the chair of importance in the room.

As Captain Cohen took a seat on a charmeuse-upholstered sofa, she noticed that her two detectives were gawking at the opulence that was on display. The room screamed the kind of wealth, most city cops could never imagine. The two-story room had windows that appeared to reach from the ground to heaven with views to the pool deck, beach and Atlantic Ocean. Each was draped with silk charmeuse swagged draperies with fringe. There was a Travertine marble-encased fireplace that stood 7 feet tall. And above it hung a painting that Cohen suspected was an honest to gosh Van Gogh. Hanging from the cathedral ceiling was a gigantic crystal chandelier. Cohen quickly motioned for the plain-clothes detectives to close their open mouths and be seated.

Captain Cohen began. "Mr. Estrada, we are here to ask you some questions about the murder of Dr. Hank Maine. Did you know Dr. Maine?"

"Well, yes, everyone knew Dr. Maine," Daniel began. "He was the face of the school system on TV. He commanded enormous attention and respect as the second in command to the superintendent. Everyone is really upset about his murder, and the death of the superintendent."

"Did you get along with Dr. Maine?" Capt. Cohen asked.

"Of course!" Daniel was acting indignant at the Captain's line of questioning. "He was an educational leader. We all aspired to be like him, to be one of his army." Daniel pretended to get chocked up about the loss of the flaming, cross-dressing, degenerate.

Cohen was studying everything about Daniel... the way he sat, how often he ran his hands through his hair, how often he blinked... even where he chose to sit.

He'd chosen a chair that put him in a position of power. His legs were comfortably crossed, and his hands hung casually over the edge of the armrests. There was no indication that he was nervous, scared or remotely phased by the presence of so many police officers.

What Capt. Cohen didn't know was that Daniel had been taking Lexapro for some years to combat his Generalized Anxiety Disorder from which he had long suffered. In fact, anxiety was the primary reason he'd dropped out of college. The medication allowed Daniel to remain cool, calm, and collected, while really nervous inside. He knew that he couldn't show it or the cat would be out of the bag.

After a pregnant pause, Cohen shot another question at Daniel Estrada. "Why did you enter Dr. Maine's office on the morning of his murder?"

Daniel crossed his arms over his crossed legs, leaned in to Captain Cohen and informed her, "I had to deliver something to him from my boss in personnel," he responded.

"And you couldn't leave it with his secretary?"

Daniel quickly fired back, "I have a relationship with most administrators who want things to go directly into their hands. I went to Dr. Maine's office as I normally did. His secretary wasn't at her desk, so I had no idea he wasn't in his office." He leaned back in his chair, uncrossed his arms and let them casually resume hanging limply over the armrest of the maroon, winged back, leather chair. Daniel slowly uncrossed his legs, then, with manicured precision, re-crossed them in the opposite direction.

Capt. Cohen didn't respond. Instead, she studied him. Daniel felt as if she was boring a hole through his body.

"You mentioned relationships. So just what exactly was your relationship with Dr. Maine?"

"We were professional colleagues as most administrators in the downtown office are," responded Daniel.

"Are you sure you were just professional colleagues?" Cohen let the question and the implication, hang in the air.

Daniel said nothing.

"We have learned that your relationship was much more than that of casual colleagues." She had dropped the bomb and waited to see what, if anything, exploded.

Daniel confidently replied, "Well, of course we were. When you work with someone night and day, you become friends, close associates. I'm sure Captain Cohen, you must know what I'm talking about."

The captain's response lacked any degree of bullshit.

"We have reason to believe that you had a romantic or sexual relationship with the deceased for some time. Our sources have identified you as someone whom Dr. Maine was seeing... personally, not professionally. We also know how and why he orchestrated your rapid rise through the ranks of the district."

"Would you like a drink Captain?" Daniel Estrada got up and walked over to the massive mahogany bar next to the two story Mahogany French doors that led out to the pool.

"No thank you, Mr. Estrada," Cohen responded... watching closely to see what he poured for himself. A glass of red wine was all.

As he walked back to his chair in center stage, Daniel decided there was no point in trying to bullshit his way out of the conundrum, he now found himself in. So, he began to recount his relationship with Hank Maine.

"Yes, Captain... Dr. Maine was interested in me. But it was strictly sexual," Daniel said with an emphatic and self-assured voice.

"Elaborate, please." Cohen suddenly wished she had that drink he'd offered.

Daniel swigged his Merlot as if it were Kool-Aid. As he sat the glass down on the end table next to the winged back chair, he stared up at the ceiling holding the huge crystal chandelier. It was a Pike's Peak pyramid of glass that let in the sun and the clouds... mimicking the atmosphere at the beach or maybe the pyramid in front of the Louvre in Paris

"I fucked him. He fucked me. End of story, Captain. There was no romance... no fondness, no tenderness. Just screwing!" Daniel went silent. "In the beginning, I fantasized about what Hank could do for me... professionally speaking. But I soon realized that Hank had a fantasy too. He was curious about what I could do for him sexually!"

"Did Dr. Maine ever socialize with you after office hours or away from the office building?"

"On occasion, we would meet for drinks." Daniel paused.

"Captain, do I need to get an attorney before answering any more questions?"

"Mr. Estrada, we haven't charged you with anything and this is just an informal inquiry or you would have been read your 'Miranda rights'. If there is anything at all that you can contribute to this case, it is important that you inform us now, not later."

"Yes, he helped me get several promotions, and for a while, I was crazy about him. The day we had lunch after I first met him, he was rather frank about his inner desires. So we set up a meeting for the following day. But he, like many others in the district, was a bisexual or gay married man, and I knew from the beginning that it was just a fling. I figured I'd enjoy it while it lasted, and I certainly didn't mind the perks and promotions. Know what I mean?" He winked at Cohen. It almost made her sick.

"Was his wife aware of your relationship?" Cohen shot back.

"I don't have the vaguest idea! I fucked Hank, Captain. I didn't try to get inside his mind, and I frankly never thought about his wife."

Daniel licked his lips before he continued. "Generally speaking, Hank didn't like us to be public. As a result, I often brought him here, to my parents' house. This is where we usually made love!" Daniel paused, hoping to elicit a reaction. But none was forth coming, at least not from the cops.

"The first time I brought him here, it was because I wanted to impress him with my family's wealth. It also gave us privacy. The maid and cook had Fridays off, because usually the entire family got together and dined out that night. But on this particular Friday night, I was dining on Dr. Hank Maine!" Daniel smiled devilishly; his interrogators wanted to throw up.

Daniel was suddenly deep in thought, remembering the first time he and Hank had had sex. While showing Hank his room, he lead him towards the large French doors to a wrought iron balcony facing the Atlantic Ocean. Daniel had assured Hank that he needn't be anxious about someone walking in on them. That couldn't happen, since he'd activated the alarm system.

At that very moment, Daniel grabbed Hank and kissed him, even more passionately than Hank had kissed him in his office that first time. This wet and passionate kiss entwined tongues to the deepest chasm in their mouths. From there, Daniel began to unbutton Hank's shirt and lick his hairless chest and touch his hard nipples. He then licked them and took tantalizing bites at them.

Hank began to respond… but Daniel wanted to make Hank his love slave, and show Hank his many skills. So he'd pushed Hank onto the bed and began running his tongue down Hanks chest, along his belly, then he moved his tongue into Hank's navel. Oh yes! Daniel was experienced and bragged about his oral skills, especially when someone needed excitement.

He then deftly removed Hank's belt and unzipped his pants. He fondled his average-sized cock, dropped to his knees and gulped it into his wide-open mouth. Hank moaned, and that made Daniel become even more excited. Then Daniel took Maine's hot nuts into his hungry, wet mouth and rolled them around. They were a mouthful, but Daniel was up to deep throating a cock and loved the thrill.

Hank pumped his hard cock in and out, gyrating his hips as Daniel sucked on his hard penis. Hank was gazing out at the ocean, in pure rapture. When he could no longer contain himself… he let out a final thrusting moan and shot his load into Daniel's mouth. Maine knew this would not be a "Lewinsky" with DNA evidence, as Daniel swallowed every drop.

Daniel then sat on top of Maine… and masturbated over Maine's torso. As Daniel neared climax, he screamed and ejaculated all over Hank's bare chest.

Captain Cohen then jerked Daniel out of his trip down memory lane. "How many others knew about your relationship with him?"

Daniel was starting to get huffy. "In a perfect world, not a soul knew about us. But we lived and worked in the school system, so I suppose it's not beyond the realm of reality to think that the system's fabled rumor mill was working overtime, speculating about my easy access to the number two man. Some people knew what we were up to. Hank wanted me downtown, so that I was nearby. It suited his needs. So, he helped me get promoted. This is typical in the school system of many men with their concubines or male lovers. There's a saying in the system, 'it's not what you know, it's who you blow!'" Daniel threw his head back and began to laugh. "I suppose it's the same at the police department, huh, Captain?"

Captain Sheila Cohen sat stiff as a statue. She was not going to let this little shit, get to her.

Daniel realized his joke had been a dud, with the very proper Captain Cohen.

"I don't know if his wife knew about us, but he told me that their relationship had deteriorated into one of convenience. He said he figured it was better to stay married than to divorce. Frankly, he needed the cover of a wife because of the generation he came from. Hank used to say that it would have shocked the taxpaying public, to find out just how many of their elected officials and top business leaders were leading this same kind of double life."

"How frequently did you get together for sex and where?" Captain Cohen was going to places she really didn't want to go.

"We got together at least a couple of times a week. Sometimes we'd do it in his office. Other times we got together at the sex house." Daniel decided it was his turn to stare a hole through the Captain.

"The what?" Cohen was trying not to sound surprised.

"The sex house! At least that's what I called it." Daniel again paused.

"Why?" Cohen wasn't sure she wanted to hear the answer.

"Because that's all that went on there... sex!" Daniel grinned. "Am I embarrassing you, Captain?"

"Did Maine own this house?" Cohen quizzed... refusing to respond to his silly question.

"I really don't know who owned the house, but I doubt it was Maine," Daniel responded, smugly.

There was silence. Cohen wasn't sure what she'd bumped into, and Daniel wasn't sure how much he should say. He realized he was treading on thin ice.

Cohen continued to probe. "Do you want to tell me about this place?"

"Not really!" Daniel got up and poured himself another glass of Merlot.

"So why did you bring it up, Daniel?"

"Because I'm curious." Daniel turned as he sipped his wine, and looked into Sheila Cohen's dark brown eyes.

"Curious about what?" she replied.

"I'm curious about what the authorities find more reprehensible? Murder, or depravity?"

"Why don't we talk about depravity, Mr. Estrada." Capt. Cohen was determined to pop a few surprises of her own. "Was Dr. Maine into pornography?"

"Absolutely. He loved it, and he had lots of it." Daniel didn't flinch at the Captain's question.

"Sometimes he brought it to show me... and frankly, we got off watching it." Daniel grinned an almost demonic smirk, as if daring Captain Cohen to press on.

"What part of it did you like?" Cohen probed.

"The part that you wouldn't like," Daniel responded. "Care for a drink yet, Captain? Or does duty prevent you from dousing your discomfort with a tonic?"

Cohen just stared at Daniel. She was not about to let him see her sweat at his foul suggestion and intonations. She stood, looked at her detectives, who followed her lead, and walked right up to Daniel.

"I'm not finished here Mr. Estrada," she hissed quietly into his face. "If you dare to leave this county, consider yourself a hunted fugitive. Do you get my drift?"

The stare off between the two, passed in seconds that felt like minutes. Finally. Cohen broke the silence. "The tragedy for you, Mr. Estrada, is that I am the law, and I am on to you."

With that, she turned and exited the "great room," leaving her detectives to follow behind her like chicks following a mother duck. The uniformed Golden Beach officer, turned swiftly to open the door for her, as soon as he saw Cohen coming. Not a word was spoken. Cohen got into her car, as did her detectives and drove off. Only a single wave of appreciation was spoken between Cohen and her Golden Beach counterparts as she left the 2-mile community of the "Ultra" rich.

CHAPTER #91

K.T. Jones had wasted no time getting Franklin Elder out of jail, and getting Moses Moorehead released as well... without having to answer any questions from the cops. His ability to pull off the impossible was one of the reason he was the top lawyer in Miami's black community.

"I want you both to go home, take care of whatever you need to take care of, and then disappear. Check into a hotel, or stay with a friend or relative. Call me as soon as your ass is parked somewhere and let me know how to get in touch with you. We're going to have to face the music eventually, but for now, you have some breathing room," K.T. told them as they got into his car. "Now, where are your cars, gentlemen?"

Moses and Franklin looked at each other. They weren't about to tell K.T. that their vehicle was an hour away in Cutler Bay at the Black Point Marina. Moses winked. It was his way of telling Franklin to chill.

"At board headquarters. Take us to the school board building, K.T.," Moses instructed his attorney.

"Sure thing." With that, attorney K.T. Jones put his black 4-door Mercedes 500SL in gear and drove off.

******

Meanwhile, Christine Rodriguez had pulled up in front of the school system's Office of Information Technology. She sat and waited for the marked units to arrive.

Against protocol, she had not notified the school system's police department, fearing they'd tip off the suspects. She wanted to catch the sickos unaware.

Nobody in law enforcement trusted the school police department, no matter how hard they tried to gain respect. The leadership, had, with only one notable deviation, been pawns of the corrupt administrative leaders, who pulled strings as if the cops were puppets, not police. The bottom-line, they weren't the trusted, fellow officers, people like Detective Rodriguez would confide in.

Rodriguez had stationed her fellow detectives at different locations around the OIT facility. It was part mobile office trailers at the back, fronted by an unattractive 1970's designed, flat, windowless, uninspired, office building, with a trail of glass blocks on each side of the front door. It looked like an attempt had been made to stamp the communistic looking façade, as art deco.

"Rodriguez to unit 23," she clicked.

"Unit 23 here. I'm on the North side over by the elementary school and I have the search warrant."

"QSL." Rodriguez then called all three of the other units that had arrived with her... all unmarked. "Any departures of note?" she asked over a general channel.

"Negative," was the response that bounced back to her from each unit. Just then, Rodriguez saw the first of six marked units arrive. She contacted them and informed them to guard all exits... and then she instructed each of the undercover units to move in.

Based on the information they'd gotten from the geek squad in forensics, the location of the computer that had sent Maine the pornography, was located in a back office in the main building. So Rodriguez had her plainclothes officers cover every exit of the main building, while several of the uniformed officers kept a close watch on the mobile trailers... just in case.

Rodriguez pushed the intercom button at the front door of the anonymous looking building, which also had no sign indicating what the place was.

Fifteen seconds later, there was no response. Rodriguez buzzed again. This time, a woman answered, "OIT. How can I help you?"

"Miami Police Detective Christine Rodriguez... open up, please, we need to talk to the person in charge." Rodriguez didn't know what to expect.

Then came the female voice again. "Have you contacted the system's public information office? They handle all questions."

Rodriguez rolled her eyes as she turned toward her partner, who was starting to laugh. Rodriguez then took her index finger and pushed the intercom button for what seemed like two minutes. When she finally released the button, there was silence for a brief moment before the female voice came back on... only to say "Hello."

Rodriguez was chaffed. "Listen baby doll! I'm not the press, I'm the police! I don't go to the public information office, I come with a badge, and if you don't open this God damn door in three seconds, I'll have a battering ram knock it down, just before I shove it up your ass! Got it!" Rodriguez looked over at her partner and grinned. At that moment, the door buzzed, indicating it was open and they could enter... which they did.

As Rodriguez threw open the door, in no mood to be nice or pleasant, she ran face first into a woman. She assumed it was the female voice from the intercom. The woman's first words confirmed her suspicions.

"This is really very unorthodox," the woman insisted.

"So is child pornography being sent from school system computers!" Rodriguez retorted. "Now, here's my badge," Rodriguez displayed her gold shield. "I want an escort to the back warehouse area, where a Mister Goldman... excuse me... Supervisor Goldman hangs out. Do you know it miss? I'm sorry, but I don't believe we've been introduced." Rodriguez waited for the woman to speak, but she was clearly petrified to say anything.

Finally, Rodriguez spoke. "Your boss. Is he or she here?"

"Yes ma'am," the woman responded as she fled into the bowels of the office building. Rodriguez looked at her partner, raised her eyebrows and signaled him to follow the frightened winch.

Rodriguez wasn't going to wait on any office boss... so she drew her gun and slowly began to walk in the direction of the back office, according to the building's blueprints she'd ordered one of the marked units to bring to her. Slowly, she made her way through a maze of winding hallways, until she reached two large, double doors, like you see in a TV studio, but these doors were shut.

Rodriguez got on her radio. "I need back up at the rear of the main building inside."

"QSL," came a response. Rodriguez would wait. She decided, maintaining her ready and response posture, with her gun just above her shoulders was the best idea.

The silence was deafening. Rodriguez greeted every creak and sound in the building with suspicion. Her hearing seemed heightened in a way she could only imagine the blind could appreciate. She heard sounds of laughter, speech and more laughter. But it was garbled. The doors were thick metal.

Rodriguez's curiosity got the better of her as she waited for her backup. Slowly, she let her left hand drop from her pistol, and reach for the mammoth door handle. Gently, she began to pull on it towards her.

Yet instead of opening, the door gave only half an inch before it clanked... mimicking the sound of a locked door. Instantly, the garbled laughing and chatter she'd heard seconds earlier, stopped. Shit! She thought, wishing that she'd waited for back up before doing something so stupid.

"Reckless thoughts, and thoughts of bravery will get you killed." Those were the words her police academy instructors had tried to drill in her head. She thought they'd done their job. But apparently now, she realized their words must not have fully penetrated her psyche.

Just then she heard the clip clop of footsteps... her back up, she believed. Thank the lord! As she turned to greet them with a silent hand signal... she suddenly felt a heavy object crashing into her skull... her eyes flashed like a fountain of fireworks, launched on the 4th of July and she dropped like a meteor to the ground.

When she awoke, Detective Christine Rodriguez was in an ambulance, on her way to the hospital... an oxygen mask covered her mouth and nose. She tried to talk, but her partner, who was sitting next to her, pushed his hand against her breathing mask, refusing to allow her to take it off.

"Stop trying to be a Saint, or a heroine, would you please?" he implored her.

Her eyes were wide with curiosity and bafflement. She didn't remember a thing that had happened to her, but clearly it hadn't been good. She blinked, trying helplessly to ask her partner to please explain why she was in an ambulance on oxygen. He must have understood the desperate pleading in her look. He began to talk.

"Chris, someone tried to kill you. We found you unconscious outside the backroom door. By the time we arrived, Goldman and his cronies were gone. All the computer hard drives are missing. I'm so sorry. You were right on target, but now you have to focus on your recovery. They hit you with a two-by-four. We found it lying next to you. The sons of bitches didn't even try to get rid of the damn weapon!" He held her hand and squeezed it as he continued.

"That fact alone indicates cold blooded bastards, if not killers." Christine Rodriguez blinked, to let him know that she understood what he was saying.

"Chris, the entire department has been mobilized, twelve on and twelve off. Nobody is taking the attempted murder of a fellow officer lightly. We'll find the assholes who did this to you." He paused. "But most importantly, we are going to solve this pornography case."

Detective Rodriguez blinked again, acknowledging his declaration, and sending him her own personal signal that said… "You're damn straight, we will." Just then, the ambulance pulled into Baptist Hospital's Emergency Room doorway… and a crowd of hospital personnel rushed Detective Rodriguez into an examining room.

******

Meanwhile, behind the wheel of the ambulance, sat a man, who, an hour earlier, had made sure that Det. Rodriguez was knocked out of her mind. Keep your friends close and your enemy's closer, thought the ambulance driver, as he flipped through a book of swinger pornography he'd brought with him.

Just as he was about to leave, he heard a nearby cop's radio, declare that the police were looking for an Adam Goldman. A BOLO, or "be on the lookout" would follow. A BOLO was not something Goldman wanted to play with. So he turned on the ignition to the ambulance, and drove out of sight and out of the county.

CHAPTER #92

Jez was the first reporter to get the tip that a Miami cop had nearly been killed at the school system's OIT headquarters. After making two additional phone calls to other sources, she had enough information to do a "Breaking News Desk" report.

As soon as she finished, Boris came up to her as she was unhooking the microphone from her jacket lapel and unplugging her IFB from the receiver box.

"I need you on this story tonight, Jez." Boris tried to sound firm, but he was really pleading.

"Not a problem. I figured as much," Jez replied, sounding almost agreeable.

Boris Danken was immediately on alert. It wasn't like Jez to be agreeable, so easily. He usually had to drag agreeability out of her. So he decided to make sure his hearing hadn't failed him.

"You realize I'm asking you to work a double shift, don't you?"

"Sure, Boris!" Jez grinned as she pulled her earpiece out, and wound it up in a tight ball. "It's my exclusive. Who else would work the story?" Jez paused waiting for Danken's reaction.

"My exact thought!" he quickly replied. But his scrunched up face, made him look like he was waiting for her to throw a knife in his eye, or that he was terribly constipated.

"See you on TV," Jez said cheerfully, as she ran off in search of Emeril.

Boris scratched his head. One second his best reporter tormented him beyond belief with her willfulness, the next minute she was a cheery, obedient, employee. What the hell was with her, he wondered, as he left the station, headed home, while Jez worked a double shift.

He'd find out soon enough. Jez had a plan for her boss, and it required her to be passive and pleasant. She all but patted herself on her back as she hoisted herself into Emeril's huge SUV, and they drove to Baptist Hospital where Det. Rodriguez was being hooked up to an IV.

Doctors wanted to stabilize Rodriguez's fluids, first. Second, they planned to have her undergo a CT Scan. They needed to know if the whack by a 2 x 4 had caused a concussion, or worse. But right now, they were doing battle with Captain Sheila Cohen, who'd arrived and wanted to have some time with her problem child detective. So she ordered the doctors and nurses out... telling them to come back in 10 minutes. "Her CT scan can wait ten minutes!" she all but shouted.

"Rodriguez?"

"Yes, Captain?"

"Who else is in cahoots with Goldman in this child porn ring?"

"His mid-level, manager chums," Rodriguez informed her boss, clearly pained by the throbbing in her head.

"Names?" Cohen asked.

"Oscar Bernal, Anthony Palotta, and Conrad Carson."

"We're on it, Rodriguez. Get well." As Captain Cohen got up, she noticed Rodriguez appeared to fall asleep. She quickly called for the doctors, knowing it wasn't a good idea for Rodriguez to nod off, until they'd figured out the extent of her injuries.

But now, armed with names, Cohen could launch a full assault on the individuals, Rodriguez had named. And that's what she was on her way to do, when Jez Underwood suddenly appeared out of nowhere, as Capt. Cohen exited the Emergency Room door.

"Captain Cohen," that's as far as Jez got before Cohen waved her off.

"Not now Ms. Underwood."

Jez let her walk a few more steps and then she pulled out her trump card.

"Sheila!" Captain Cohen stopped dead in her tracks. "Don't play coy now," Jez insisted.

"I'm not," Cohen responded as she turned to face the reporter. "But if you think I want anyone to see us talking like this right now, you are crazy!"

"Then get in your car, but don't start the engine until after you've called my cell phone," Jez ordered.

"Done!" Cohen then walked off into the night and the darkness of the hospital parking lot, where she climbed into her undercover SUV and dialed Jez's cell phone.

"Isn't this better, and more private?" she asked Jez, as soon as Jez answered her phone.

"Whatever trips your trigger, Sheila! Now what the hell is going on? I need information? And you need me to get the information out, so play ball, will you?" Jez stopped talking and waited for a reply.

Cohen was aware how tricky it could be for a cop who had a source relationship with a member of the media. She was also aware how beneficial it could be to make sure a reputable reporter leaked certain information. She and Jez had collaborated on this kind of thing before, but the series of deaths and threats on cops, made Cohen suddenly worry about heading down an old and trusted path. Then it dawned on her that if Jez revealed the names of the suspects, it would most likely mean they'd be ratted out by their "not-so-friendly friends," or enemies. It could possibly hasten the capture of these crooks and derelicts.

"I'm going to give you four names, so get your pen and paper ready. I won't sell them or repeat the information," Cohen cautioned Jez.

"Go!" said Jez.

"Adam Goldman, Oscar Bernal, Anthony Pallotta, and Conrad Carson." Cohen went silent.

"Got it," said Jez... and she repeated each name. Then suddenly, Jez gasped.

"Whoa! Wait a minute Captain! Isn't Conrad Carson, Donna Maine's brother?"

Captain Cohen's eyes popped out as if shot by a blowgun. Jez was right! Carson was the brother of Donna Maine. Shit! Cohen wondered if she'd live to regret giving Donna Maine police protection. Cohen was suddenly sweating in her air-conditioned cop car, as if it had no air conditioning.

"Sheila?" Jez was saying her name again. "Sheila!"

At that moment, Captain Sheila Cohen cranked the ignition, shoved her drive shaft into reverse, backed up, put the car in drive, and peeled out of the hospital parking lot, headed for the Abbey Hotel.

"Oh shit!" Jez said out loud. "She just realized what I know!" Jez turned and looked at Emeril, who was starting up his SUV.

"Do ju want me to follow a polish car?" Emeril asked as he accelerated.

"Yes, I do," Jez answered him. "And don't lose the polish car! I have a feeling the polish car will take us to a very important place."

So, as Emeril plowed through one red light after another, he kept a close watch in his rear view mirror, hoping against hope, not to see the flashing lights of a cop car in pursuit.

It all worked beautifully, until they drove off the MacArthur Causeway onto 5th street, headed for South Beach. Suddenly, his vehicle was blocked by a fence of Miami Beach Police cars and officers, some of whom had their guns drawn up above their heads.

"Shit!" he heard Jez scream.

"Dis isn't goot, Jez."

"Stay where you are. Don't leave the car," Jez ordered. "Let me handle this."

With that, Jez exited Emeril's vehicle, waving like she was Miss America, to the cops blocking her roadway.

"Hey, guys! How are those radios working for you?" As soon as the beach cops saw that it was Jez Underwood who'd they'd stopped, they immediately dropped their weapons.

"We didn't know it was you Jez," one of them claimed. "We were just told to stop the red Jeep Cherokee."

"No problem, man," Jez reassured her uniformed friend. "I guess if I hadn't gotten you those upgraded radios, you wouldn't have been able to receive the call from Captain Cohen, since you guys never shared frequencies, until I convinced your City Manager to bring you into the 21st Century!" Jez smiled.

"You got that right, Jez," one officer agreeably admitted.

"So, who can escort me to where Captain Cohen was headed before she had you stop an honest journalist working on a major story?"

"I can!" shouted a female patrol officer. "Just make sure you forget my face."

"Done!" said Jez, as she jumped back into the Channel 11 SUV. "Follow that cop car," she instructed Emeril.

"Ju want to tell me how ju did that, or where we're joing?" Emeril inquired quietly... not expecting a response.

"Nope!" Jez was adamant, and then went very quiet.

So, Emeril did the only thing he could do... he drove.

CHAPTER #93

Just as Jez and Emeril were pulling up in front of the Abbey Hotel, having given the Beach cop a wave of thanks, they heard the assignment desk calling them on the Nextel.

"We have the information on those four names you called in," the desk informed her.

As Emeril had been blasting through red lights following Capt. Cohen, Jez had asked the assignment desk at the station, to run the names Cohen had given her. She wanted addresses and phone numbers.

"OK, thanks. But right now, I can't do anything with the information. I'm following another angle of the story. Can you get another crew to go check out that information?" she asked.

"Boris said this is your story, Jez!" It was Allison being a bitch. Jez mockingly hit her head against the window of the SUV. It was her way of telling Emeril that Allison was driving her crazy. Finally, Jez responded.

"Hey, Allison! I'm so glad when Boris has such confidence in my decision making to say 'this is my story!' To that end, I guess I'm calling the shots on My Story! So get another crew to check those addresses, while I work, what I'm working on. Capiche?" Jez was mocking her boss, and she knew Allison would rat her out, but she didn't care.

"We have other stories we're working on for the 11:00 news, Jez," Allison announced.

"Fine! If that's what you want to tell Boris when he asks why we didn't follow up on the names we were given, exclusively! It's your butt, not mine, Allison!" Jez was smirking when she caught Emeril's eye. He just shook his head and got out to collect his equipment.

"I'll see what I can do!" Allison shot back.

"Good!" said Jez. "I'll make sure that I tell Boris that our success on this story was due to your yeoman's effort. I'll call you later, once I know what I have here on the beach."

"What are you doing on the beach?" Allison inquired, sounding almost panicked.

True to her rebellious form, Jez didn't reply. Let her sweat that tid bit of information, Jez thought.

Having loaded all his equipment into his photographer's cart, Jez and Emeril were all but walking through the hotel's front door, when they ran into Carlo Ferrini, who was on his way out.

"Small world!" Jez exclaimed.

"Oh my God! You scared me half to death," Carlo whispered breathlessly, turning his head in every direction, trying to make sure he wasn't seen talking to Jez Underwood.

"Come here often?" Jez replied, half laughing.

"Not now Jez," Carlo informed her.

"Wait a second!" A light had suddenly gone off in Jez's head. Carlo wasn't here because this was a popular beach hangout of his… he must be here for the same reason Capt. Cohen was here. Donna Maine! Suddenly, all the pieces of the puzzle were coming together.

"Carlo, talk to me." Jez had grabbed him by his arm and was pulling him into an unlit area to the left of the hotel's front door.

"I can't! Later," he told her.

"Not later! Now!" Jez stared at him. "Why are you at the same hotel as Capt. Cohen?" There was no response. "Is this where they're hiding Donna Maine?" Jez was pushing. But there was still no response. Finally, she let go of Carlo's arm. "Go home. I've got the big picture and you didn't say a word." With that Carlo took off.

As Jez walked inside the hotel lobby, she could hear Emeril speaking in Spanish with the front desk clerk. Of course, she had no idea what was being said, but from the flailing of arms she was witnessing, she assumed the two men were arguing. Body gestures were the international symbols that broached all language barriers, she thought to herself.

"What's the problemo?" she asked Emeril.

"He says he can't let us up to any of the rooms unless we are guests."

Jez looked around. It was one of those darling and intimate hotels on Miami Beach that had been refurbished... wiping away all evidence of its former life as a heroine/crack hotel, to a chic place, where a famous chef had put his name on the restaurant. And along with the restaurant was a bar.

"Tell him fine... we'll just park our assess at his bar and drink until we get what we came for!"

With that, Jez headed for the 6-stool bar area that shimmered in the light of gigantic candelabra. As she sat down, she used her index finger to indicate to Emeril that he should follow her. He did... and there wasn't a damn thing the hotel clerk could do about it.

******

Meanwhile, on southbound Card Sound Road, Adam Goldman was dumping an ambulance in the scrub brush and mangroves of the upper Keys, not far from the tony Ocean Reef Club. Not that the prickly, little plants would hide the blazing red boxed vehicle, it's just that he'd finally caught up with his ride, who would take him away.

"Where to?" his chauffer asked.

"Key West," Goldman ordered.

"Then what?"

"I don't know, you fool! Just drive, Carson," Goldman demanded.

CHAPTER #94

Carlo was home mulling over the events of the last hour, when Penelope called.

"Did you see Jez's report on the OIT thing?" she asked.

"Sort of," was all that he could say at the moment. He'd been with Donna in her suite at the Abbey Hotel, when they'd seen Jez's breaking news report. But running into Jez had rattled him a bit. He didn't need the system's brass knowing about his confidential relationship with the one reporter in town they all wanted to kill.

"I'm not surprised," he managed to say.

"I always knew those sick computer fucks were up to something! I just didn't realize they'd have the balls to use district computers," Penelope responded.

"How can you be so naïve?" Carlo asked his friend. "These sickos operated with absolute immunity! Anyone who dared question them was demonized, anyone who hinted at their sickness, was reassigned, and anyone who lifted an eyebrow at their behavior was banished to the system's version of Siberia! God, Penelope, you of all people should know that. They did it to you!" Carlo went silent.

Moments passed before either Carlo or Penelope spoke. Carlo broke the ice first.

"Do you remember Daniel Estrada?"

"You mean "Little Lord Fauntleroy, from Beach High? Sure. Why?" Penelope asked Carlo.

"Not over the phone," Carlo declared. "But work your sources. I think you'll be pleasantly surprised!"

Carlo then clicked the off button on his phone and headed for his bar. It was time for a Martini, and some quiet "quality" time with Samba and Orlando.

Penelope hung up. Of course she remembered Daniel. How could she forget him? He was the cause of one her most painful memories… having to fire a single mother of three children.

As she flashed back, she remembered how, one day she was forced to contact the parents of one of her students who had more than 30 absences. When the parents came in the next day for a conference, Penelope opened the school's attendance records in the computer. She was shocked when the student's computer records showed only three absences… not 30! But fortunately for Penelope, she had the hard copy of his records that she'd printed the day before.

As soon as she discovered the record inconsistency, she notified the principal, who summoned the attendance clerk… the single mother. She was accused of altering the state's official attendance records. It was a criminal offense, since attendance determined the amount of state money schools received. The clerk was offered the option of resigning or facing criminal fraud charges.

Penelope felt terrible to be the cause of this woman's dismissal. She was the only breadwinner, and Penelope hated that she'd been the one to take food out of the mouths of this family.

Two years later, a former student informed Penelope that he was one of a select group of male students, who had their attendance records altered by Daniel Estrada. At the time, Daniel was a student aide in the high school working in the attendance office. He'd managed to acquire the attendance clerk's password. According to her former student, Daniel had used his ability to eliminate absences and tardies, as a way to gain popularity with the high school boys he was trying to make a move on.

That's when a light bulb went off in Penelope's brain. It was Daniel, not the attendance clerk, who'd altered the records she'd discovered. She was nauseous when she realized that Daniel was the reason the poor attendance clerk lost her job. The woman had been completely innocent! But as Penelope knew, in the school system, "the end justifies the means."

CHAPTER #95

These days, Daniel Estrada didn't need to alter attendance records. His big promotion to an administrative position, now allowed him to sign out the object of his desire. And so he did... often.

Daniel sauntered up to the clerk in the office at Miami Beach High and asked for the student sign out sheet.

"Oye chica! You are looking fine today." He always tried to use his charm on the poor, frumpy, office woman... in hopes it would eliminate any questions she might have about why he was frequently signing the same boy out of school.

"Oh Mr. Estrada, you are a tease!" she replied, blushing as she reached for a hall pass to hand to one of the student "gophers."

"Is that a new dress Nina? It really shows off your assets. If you know what I mean!" Daniel winked at the pathetic clerk and then blew her a kiss. "Tell Mr. Alfaro, I'm out front waiting on him will you doll?"

"Of course Mr. Estrada." Nina giggled as she looked away.

A few minutes later, Marcos Alfaro threw open the main door to his school and ran to the dark green Corvette convertible. He hopped in, closed the door, and planted a big, open-mouthed kiss on Daniel for the entire world to see.

"I thought you'd never get here," he exclaimed breathlessly. "Five more minutes and I'd have had to take a fucking alge-bra exam."

"Saved by a sexual addict!" Daniel then hit the accelerator and drove them off campus as fast as he could. As he drove North on Collins Avenue, he couldn't help but smile. Marcos had unzipped his fly, and was sucking his cock like the pro Daniel suspected he was.

"Easy does it," Daniel cautioned his young friend. "You don't want me to get a speeding ticket if I climax driving through Bal Harbour. You know they have cops everywhere."

By the time they reached Daniel's secluded Tiki hut on his parent's private beach, the two had stripped off all their clothes and were devouring one another, as only two animals can. Marcos stood over Daniel as he lay on his back. The kid wasn't tall, maybe only 5'8" but he had a cock that hung like a curtain pull. Daniel had teasingly called him "tripod" the first time he'd seen the size of Marcos' penis.

"Are you intimidated?" Marcos had asked him.

"I'll tell you after you fuck me!" No, Daniel thought latter. I'm not intimidated' I'm delirious!

That first encounter with the kid had been the beginning of the end of his sexual trysts with Dr. Maine. Now that he had his big shot job at the headquarters, and all the perks that went with it, like getting to sign Marcos out of school on a whim, Daniel didn't need Hank. He dodged his invitations more frequently and ignored his phone messages for days on end. Maine was livid. He'd called Daniel to his office one day and railed on him about his aloofness.

"What would daddy say if I sent him a copy of that videotape we made at the ranch?" Maine was in his face whispering venom.

"What would Donna say?" Daniel shot back.

"Don't think for one minute that you can fuck with me," Hank spit on Daniel.

"No, I just fuck you and you love it, Hank," Daniel retorted. He stood to leave, but Maine grabbed him around the throat. All he could see was Maine's wall of military memorabilia. All he could hear were Hanks vindictive words and threats. Is this the last thing I see before I die, he wondered, just as Maine let him go, pushing him toward the door.

"Get the fuck out of my sight!" Maine screamed, as Daniel made a hasty exit out the door.

A week later, Maine was dead, and Daniel was free to romp with Marcos, without guilt.

CHAPTER #96

Daniel Estrada was sipping his 10th glass of wine, since the visit by the police. He thought it would help him figure out a plan. Instead, the alcohol had muddled his brain to the point that he'd seen nothing wrong with calling his father's pilot, and putting the Estrada's private jet on stand-by at the Ft. Lauderdale Executive Airport.

"Destination?" the pilot had asked.

"I don't know right now Howard," Daniel declared as he hung up on the pilot.

Shit! Thought Howard Marks. A rich puppy with access to daddy's play toys is a recipe for disaster. So, he did the only thing he thought was responsible, he called the senior, Mr. Estrada.

"Don't you move that plane one inch!" Daniel's father was beside himself with anger when he learned that his son had tried to activate the family's private jet.

As soon as he hung up with the pilot, he stormed out of his bedroom, and marched downstairs to his son's room. He grabbed the door handle, turned it and pushed. Nothing. He turned and pushed again. He now realized it was locked. Then he began beating on the door. "Daniel! Daniel! Open this door."

Suddenly, the door swung open, and there on Daniel's bed lay a nubile looking, blonde male, about 18 years old, who was bare naked, accessorized only by the smile he wore when Papa Estrada came bursting into Daniel's room. Señor Estrada froze.

"Good evening father," Daniel said. "Join us, why don't you! I always thought your homophobia was the result of your own sexual conflict." His words slurred as he tried to maintain his composure.

"I will do nothing of the sort!" barked Jorge Estrada. "I only want to know why you've contacted Howard Marks and asked him to get the plane ready?" The father was glaring at his son.

"I thought I'd take my lover Marcos here, on a flight of fancy. Got any problem with that pops?" Daniel, who was standing naked in front of his father, grabbed his cock and flicked it at his dad. It was the equivalent of a "fuck you" finger movement, except his dick was the finger.

"Out of my house!" the elder Estrada screamed. "Out of my house now, you sick mother fucker! And take your prostitute with you!" Just as Jorge Estrada turned to leave, Daniel dropped his bomb.

"If I go, what will you tell the police, who were here today questioning me about the murder of Dr. Hank Maine? You'll look like an accomplice, father dear. They'll think you orchestrated my vanishing act, and they'll have the call from this house, to the pilot, ordering him to fuel the plane!"

Daniel gazed at his father, with a look that did not betray the hate he felt for his old man. All the while, Daniel played with his cock, knowing it would drive his father insane!

"Howard knows it was you who called!" Jorge Estrada declared.

"Don't be so certain Papi! You know how often we are mistaken for one another on the phone. Howard won't be able to tell the difference, any more than Mami can."

"But I spoke to him and ordered him to halt any takeoff plans." Señor Estrada was sounding desperate.

"For all he knows, that voice could have been mine!" Daniel grinned. "Do you see the trap you're in Papi?"

"I'll kill you myself!"

Just as the father lunged for the son, Marcos arose from the bed, grabbed a large conch shell that decorated the bedside table, and hit the father with it, in the back of his skull. The father fell to floor without uttering even a whimper. Daniel then yanked the jagged edged shell from his lover's hand, and began pummeling his father with it... bashing his face and brains in. When he was finished, Daniel instructed Marcos to get dressed, as he started packing a number of suitcases. He was ready to leave the country and escape the cloud of suspicion that hung over his head.

As the two murderous lovers left Daniel's room, Daniel muttered "Nighty, night Papi. Sweet dreams!" He then pulled the door quietly shut and disappeared into the night.

CHAPTER #97

"This is the Golden Beach Police Department. Captain Sheila Cohen gave me this number to call if there was any movement on the part of her subject. Well, we have movement. What does she want me to do?"

Cohen had left the tall Golden Beach cop on surveillance at the Estrada home, just in case. He'd be paid out of the Miami Police Department's overtime budget.

Not having received a message, the Golden Beach cop clicked his radio again and inquired, "Can anyone put me in touch with Capt. Sheila Cohen?"

"This is Cohen here. Go ahead."

The puzzled Golden Beach cop regained his composure in time to respond, telling the Captain, "The subject is on the move. I'm following. QSL?"

"QSL," was the response he got back from Cohen. "Keep me posted. Use this channel for all communications."

"QSL," the officer replied as he floored his patrol car, in order to keep up with the speeding dark green Corvette that had just pulled out of the Estrada's driveway.

"I've got other problems, you can't begin to comprehend," Capt. Cohen informed Donna Maine. "So I need you to be real up front and candid with me, now!"

Sheila Cohen had arrived at the Abbey Hotel, in a flourish of anger and resentment. She felt she'd been conned by Donna Maine. She'd gone to the Abbey to confront her and find out if her protected witness was really in need of protection.

"Did you know your brother was involved in a porno ring with your husband?" Cohen was pacing up and down the carpet of the hotel suite, never taking her eyes off Donna.

"No!" cried the widow Maine. "I didn't know what my husband was up to, or my brother. You have to believe me!" The fits of sobbing and whining were starting to irritate Capt. Cohen.

"I don't have to believe one word of what you say, Donna. Don't you get that?" Cohen was playing rough.

"But I swear to you Captain, Hank and my brother lived in a world they didn't share with me. Do you think I find any solace in knowing what those two degenerates were up to?" Donna Maine got up from the couch and headed toward the kitchenette.

"I used to hide in my kitchen, chopping onions, carrots, you name it, just so I wouldn't hear the bleating of male pleasure coming from my husband's office. Hank used to try to entice me into his little sanctum, but I'd never go. Then he tormented me with the sounds of his sexual satisfaction… knowing full well, I was in the other room and could hear his moans and groans."

"Am I supposed to feel sorry for you, Donna?" asked Cohen.

"I don't know!" Donna was flying into a rage. "I don't know what my husband did or didn't do! I don't know what is normal and what isn't! I met the man when I was a student. I'd never had another lover, and still haven't to this day! Am I a woman without experience? Yes! Should that condemn me to a life with a bastard like Hank? No!" Donna then threw herself onto the bed in the hotel suite and cried into her pillows, knowing that few women, like Capt. Cohen were able to understand her situation.

What Donna didn't know, is how well Cohen related to her plight. It was, after all, the reason Cohen had become a cop.

CHAPTER #98

As Sheila Cohen drove back to police headquarters, she couldn't help but think about what Donna had said to her earlier.

It reminded her of the time in her life, when she'd been horribly, betrayed by a man, the love of her life or so she'd thought at the time. She too, had been a meek and milder version of her current self when she'd met Frank. He couldn't have been nicer and more caring. It was what attracted her to him. Yet inspite of his niceness, Frank was a card carrying sociopath, who was hell bent on destroying her life.

It wasn't like she had much of a life. She'd been a 5th grade school teacher in Atlanta for the ten years before she met "psycho man." He convinced her that she was the Queen of Sheba, and she'd, of course, believed it. So she'd quit her teaching job and moved in with Frank. Almost instantly, her nice and caring love became an abusive and controlling monster. He prevented her from seeing her friends. He wouldn't allow her to visit family members unless he was present. He told her what to wear, how to act, what to eat or not eat and he took her car keys away from her. He made sure she was totally dependent on him for everything. At the time, Sheila didn't know that she was in an abusive relationship. She'd grown up in a loving home. Abusive behavior was not part of her psychological vocabulary. But the day Frank threatened to kill her was the day she fled.

Although she'd lived with Frank, they hadn't yet married. So when he demanded she falsely sign his tax return as his wife… she'd refused. She knew it was illegal, and she wasn't about to go to jail for the bastard. Wanting to intimidate her, he'd gotten his gun and threatened to kill her if she didn't sign.

"Please Frank! Don't do that honey," she pleaded. "I'll sign. Just please let me go to the bathroom, first, I'm having terrible menstrual cramps and I need to take some Midol."

Sheila then headed for their bedroom, closed the door, locked it, and escaped out the French doors that led to the back patio. Without her purse or wallet she fled through the backyard gate, into the street running until her legs turned to jelly. Finally, she saw a taxi, hailed it, and had the driver take her to the home of the one girlfriend Frank had never met.

Four weeks later, she moved to Miami and signed up for the police academy, determined, that if psycho man ever entered her life again, she'd know how to put a bullet square between his eyes.

She had risen through the ranks and was now Capt. Sheila Cohen, who had an unsolved murder of a deputy superintendent on her hands, and the attempted murder of a school board member. She had a bunch of porno hungry tech guys, who may have splayed her ferocious Detective Rodriguez in the head, and on top of everything, she'd committed to protect a woman who was related by marriage and birth to two men who were A-1 degenerates!

Cohen's trance was broken by a phone call from Det. West who was stationed at Jackson Memorial Hospital with Amelia Salas.

"She's gonna make it," declared Det. West. "The doctors say two weeks recovery in the hospital. Her liver and heart suffered the worst of it. So, what do you want me to do now? Salas has no memory of the events... hell she doesn't even remember talking to Jez. I say you'd need a knock out pill for an elephant, not to remember a conversation with that pitbull!"

"Can your commentary," Cohen instructed West.

"Listen, I need you to hook up with a Golden Beach cop. He's tailing our chief suspect in the Maine murder. Are you up to it?" Sheila Cohen knew she'd pulled West off of the Maine investigation because it had gotten so personal for him. But she needed his expertise, more than she needed him babysitting a comatose board member.

"Is the Pope Catholic?" Det. West replied.

"Keep it strictly professional and by the book, will you? I mean it West. Don't make me regret giving you this assignment."

"No worries," he assured her. "Give me the information."

******

As Detective West headed North on I-95, Goldman and Carson were headed south toward Key West. They weren't really sure why they were going to the "Southernmost Point" in the United States, but they needed to get somewhere and think.

"We need to dump these hard drives," Carson informed his passenger.

"We'll toss em off the Seven Mile Bridge when we get there. It's tall enough," Goldman answered back.

"Sure, but is the water there deep enough? Or is some fisherman gonna snag one the next day?" Goldman realized that Carson has a point. The waters in and around the Keyes were shallow by most standards. They'd need to be out at sea to dump those hard drives deep enough. That's when Goldman had his idea. A cruise ship!

"Ever been on a cruise?" he asked Carson.

"I get sea sick! Are you kidding?" Carson was starting to turn green at the very thought. He'd always wondered how he'd managed to make South Florida his home. He hated water, except the kind that came out of the shower head. He didn't speak a foreign language, and barely had command of the English language. Hell, he was just a Southern Cracker, who liked his feet to be on dry land, and his fish to come from a creek.

The blonde hair of Carson's youth was now dirty brown and thinning. He usually skulked around in overalls and a John Deere ball cap. He was a hick, who had a brain for computers. And, as luck would have it, he'd fallen into a job with the school system, about the time that people with computer skills were in great demand.

Originally, he'd been the brain behind the idea of using district computers to alter records... for a fee, of course. He hadn't had a difficult time convincing his boss, Goldman, to go along with the idea.

For example, teachers who didn't want to exhaust themselves attending "continuing education" courses paid the two men $600 in cash, to manipulate their records, indicating they'd attended the required courses. Students who didn't want to study in order to graduate, paid them $500 to massage their grades from an "F" to an "A" in the computer. It was a very lucrative side business!

Eventually, Carson and Goldman recruited Pallotta and Bernal. They called themselves the "four geeks." Eventually, they branched out into the Satellite card business... using the system's OIT offices to provide illegal satellite TV cards... for a price.

But it was Adam Goldman, who brought the seedy world of child pornography into their computer geek world. Apparently, Goldman had been using the school system's computers to trade pictures with unknown friends throughout the world ever since he'd been promoted to supervisor and became the authorizing administrator for all the system's mainframe applications. Translated, that meant he had control of everything and everyone who used the schools' computer system... including the superintendent and the board members. If only they'd known what had been done in cyberspace using their names!

"If you want to get on a floating hotel, be my guest," Carson informed Goldman. "I'll take you to Key West, but I'm driving back to Miami. I don't have no urge to spend even a day trying to walk with rubbery legs, and hugging the porcelain bus, inside some broom closet called a bathroom!"

"Fine! Just drive! But we've got to talk about what the four of us are going to do next, now that we know the cops are hunt-

ing for us. Where'd Pallotta and Bernal say they were headed?"

"They didn't say. That's what's got me nervous," Carson was
staring at his fuel gauge, which was getting close to empty.

"So, while I was off whacking the blonde cop and hijacking
an ambulance… those two losers just left?"

"No! They helped me load the hard drives into the truck and
then they left." Carson nervously reached up and turned his
John Deere ball cap around backwards.

"Those fuckers!" Adam Goldman was a big, burly guy, with
salt and pepper hair, and a gruff voice, which sounded all the
worse, when he was mad. He'd gained about 100 pounds
since his promotion to Supervisor at OIT. Sitting on one's ass
all day in front of a computer will do that to a person. He was
married to a woman who worked at the local animal shelter
as a volunteer. She preferred to be around any animal but
Goldman, while he preferred to have sex with anyone, except his wife. It was a match made in hell, for sure.

"Give em a break Goldman," Carson pleaded. "You know as
well as I do, that things happened real fast tonight. None of
us had planned on this, and we're all damn lucky we got
away. Wherever they are, they'll find us, or we'll find them.
But right now, we've got a shitload of evidence in our possession. Evidence, I want to get rid of as soon as possible.
So let's focus on our plan for hard drive disposal. Are you
with me?" Carson asked Goldman.

"Yeah! Just drive. I need some shut eye for a few minutes."

With those words, Adam Goldman, slipped into a foggy world
of half sleep… where his real world, dumping an ambulance
in the marshes off the Keys… collided with his fantasy world
where 5-year old girls, made up in eyeliner and rouge, sat
hairless and innocent, and spread their legs for him… and
only him.

For some reason, known only to the psyche, this little girl
was posing on a gurney inside an ambulance. Who said our

sub-conscience didn't have a sense of humor and irony... Goldman thought to himself, as he fell deeper into sleep.

As Carson drove, he flashed back to the events that had led him here... on the road to Key West with a pickup truck full of stolen school system computer hard drives.

The "four geeks" had been in the back room at OIT, where they made the illegal Satellite Cards and shared pornography with one another. It was around 7:30pm, and they knew most OIT employees had already left. Besides that, all OIT employees knew better than to disturb them if those big metal doors were closed. They'd been uploading some new child porn, delivered from one of their contacts in Germany, when they'd heard the doors rattle. Goldman quickly glanced at the security camera monitor in the office... and saw a blonde woman with a gun crouched on the outside of the doors. He immediately knew it was a cop. Silently, he gave the signal to his partners that told them to grab all the hard drives and head for the secret tunnel. Immediately, their emergency preparedness plans went into action.

When the group was first formed, they'd always anticipated a raid by police. So they'd decided they needed a secret exit. They obtained the blueprints for the OIT headquarters, as well as the adjacent elementary school. Next they got their hands on the utility plans from the county. They discovered an abandoned 60-inch sewer line underneath the building. Conveniently, it connected to the adjacent elementary school parking lot. Their exit was a water and sewer manhole cover, that Carson, or one of the others, always parked their car right next to. In case they had to evacuate the hard drives, the tunnel would give them an escape hatch beyond the fences of the OIT parking lot, which would no doubt, be under surveillance by cops.

As his three cohorts grabbed hard drives and disappeared into the secret tunnel, Adam Goldman snuck out a side door, grabbed the two-by-four he kept nearby, put on the yard gloves that sat on the thick wooden weapon, snuck up behind the blonde cop, and whacked her in the head as hard as he could. Considering his girth, his swing had to have been dangerously strong. Goldman waited just long enough to watch the cop collapse. He then dropped the weapon... and ran back into the back office and entered the tunnel. Suddenly, Goldman realized how much tighter the tunnel was than he remembered it being, when they'd dug it two years earlier. Of course, that was about 100 lbs. ago. Huffing and puffing, he managed to get himself to the exit manhole, where he had to rely on his three accomplices to help him up and out. That's when he heard the screams of an ambulance siren coming his way.

"Get outta here," Goldman ordered his cohorts. "I'm going to see to it, that our brain damaged cop doesn't ever say another word."

Immediately, Carson, with a pickup truck filled with school system hard drives, peeled out, turning right toward the winding side streets. Pallotta and Bernal followed for about two miles before they turned off and headed in a different direction. Carson realized he couldn't bother with them at the moment. He then searched for a place to park his truck and wait for Goldman to get in touch with him.

After he watched his partners exit the elementary school parking lot, Goldman huffed and puffed his way to the middle of the street... laid down and waited.

In a matter of minutes, an ambulance came racing around the corner barreling toward the OIT offices. All Goldman heard was the sound of tires screeching as the ambulance tried to stop when the driver saw Goldman's considerable body in the middle of the road. The ambulance stopped just short of Goldman. In a flash, the driver and the ambulance attendant jumped out and ran over to the body they'd nearly runover. As soon as the two men got in his face, Goldman cold-cocked one guy with a right hook, then grabbed the other guy by his hair and bashed his forehead into the pavement. Just to make sure they stayed out of it long enough for him to do his thing... he lifted the one guy's head up and smashed it into the pavement a second time. He then did the same to the attendant he'd slugged. Leaving the two county employees bleeding and lifeless, Goldman stripped off one of their jackets, put it on, got inside the ambulance and drove it up to the back of the OIT offices... where cops were flagging him down. He then helped the police load their fellow officer onto the gurney and into the ambulance. He grabbed the vehicle's walkie-talkie and informed Baptist Hospital that he was on his way with a police officer near death! No one was the wiser. It was just as he had hoped.

******

From Key Largo, where Carson picked up Goldman, it was about a three-hour trip to Key West. During the day, the drive down US 1, just a two-lane road, was tolerable, since you had the Atlantic Ocean on the left side, and Florida Bay on the right. At least there were sights to see and beautiful shades of shimmering blue and green water to look at. But at night, it was a boring and dangerous drive and Conrad Carson was not amused that he had to negotiate the road without anyone to talk to him, and keep him awake. The stress of the evening was starting to catch up with him... as his eyes begged him for permission to shut.

Just when he thought he was fading, a flash of light, pin-pricked one of his brain cells, and he was instantly awake, alert... and alarmed.

"Hey Adam," he said to Goldman, as he pushed at him to make him wake up. "Yo! Sleeping Beauty!"

"Huh? What?" Goldman was groggy and grumpy.

"We got company, behind us. Lights are flashing but no siren. How do you want me to play it?"

Adam Goldman jerked his head around so fast Carson wondered if it was attached to his shoulders.

"Cops! How the hell did the cops find us? Were you speeding?" Goldman was starting to sweat like a stuck pig.

"I don't know! I mean, I don't think so. But I was kind of fall'n asleep."

"You fuck'n retard, cracker!" Goldman was blind with anger at their predicament. Their escape should have been so easy, he thought.

"Pull over!" Goldman instructed. "No sense making the guy angry. Let's just assume he hasn't gotten that BOLO, and all we'll get is a speeding ticket. Otherwise, you're gonna have to pummel him with that "ceement birdbath" you've got in the back end of this pickup truck."

"I will not! I bought that for my wife. It's our anniversary to-morrow."

"Even if you make it home to give it to her, you're not likely going to be able to stay long enough to see any birdies splish-splashing around in that thing. We're wanted men."

Goldman was just being truthful. "We got cops looking for us you fool. Let's just pray he isn't one of them." He then point-ed to the rear view window and both men watched as a Mon-roe County Sheriff's Deputy slowly approached their vehicle.

CHAPTER #99

Daniel Estrada had never felt as free, as he did when he fled his parent's home. His father was dead, and in a perverse way, that liberated him… even if getting caught might mean a lifetime of imprisonment.

Daniel was also drunk and behind the wheel of a muscle car. It was a recipe for disaster.

"Where are we going," his lover wanted to know. He too, was shit faced and it wasn't just the alcohol that had him slobbering in the Corvette. The two had done a few lines of cocaine before being interrupted by daddy Estrada, and that was combined with Daniel's daily dosage of Lexapro

"Are we flying somewhere?" Marcos managed to slur.

"Yes. But not where I wanted to take you. Daddy put the brakes on that idea before he died," Daniel explained very slowly and precisely, like a man who was uttering words for the very first time.

"I got to get some stuff from the office," Daniel explained, "Then we're getting the hell out of Dodge!"

As Daniel crossed over the William Lehman Causeway, headed west, he thought he saw a police car behind him. He shook his head, closed his eyes, opened them again and looked in his rear view mirror again. It was gone.

I must be imagining things, he thought to himself, slurring his words as if he was the drunk that he was. As Daniel turned left onto Biscayne Blvd. he became more concerned about keeping his car from swerving in and out of lanes. But it was hard to see the lane markers. Daniel was so hammered he was seeing double sets of lane stripes. Shit! He thought.

So with his right hand on the steering wheel, Daniel put his left hand over his left eye… and magically the extra set of lane markers disappeared. This "patch over the eye" approach to driving may have straightened out his vision, but it didn't give him much leeway to scan the road for cops.

By the time Daniel and lover boy Marcos pulled through the intersection of 79th and Biscayne, Det. Bob West had joined the surveillance detail in his undercover car. As he pulled in behind Daniel, the Golden Beach patrol car, fell back a few blocks. They didn't want his marked unit to spook their suspect. Little did they know their suspect was navigating the streets of Miami, with one eye closed, and likely couldn't have spotted the cop or Mount Everest even if he had tried.

As soon as Det. West was in place behind Daniel he phoned Capt. Cohen.

"It looks like he's headed to his school headquarters' office, Capt.," West informed her. "He's also weaving horribly. I think he's sloshed. What do you want to do?"

"Stay with him until he lands someplace. Then haul him in for questioning. At least arrest him for DUI. I'm going to send back up for you, so I need to know as soon as he stops, but I'll get some crews headed to the school board building."

"QSL," West responded.

West pulled down the visor in his Crown Victoria, and looked at the small picture of his young son that he'd clipped to the corner. He put his index finger to his lips then planted it on the picture. "I swear Bobby, daddy will make sure you get justice," he said out loud to no one but to himself. He then flipped the visor back up and continued following Daniel Estrada south on Biscayne Boulevard.

In a matter of minutes, Daniel had pulled up in front of the school system's administrative building. Det. West noticed he stumbled getting out of his macho corvette. As he crossed the street headed for the auditorium entrance, Det. West held up his badge, and announced himself to a very surprised Daniel Estrada.

"You seem to have some difficulty staying in lanes, sir. I need to see your driver's license please," West then reached out his hand for the license.

Daniel Estrada's balance wasn't good, so as he was trying to find his wallet in his back pocket, he nearly fell over in the middle of the street.

"Offisher," he slurred, "I'm jush going to my officshe. I shwill be staying here tonight, sho you don't havsh to worry about my driving. I'm an admisher... adminshidator... I'm a shul board administrator, offisher."

"I'm sure you are, sir. But you're going to sleep this one off in a holding cell," insisted Det. West.

At that moment, he turned around to give the signal to the Golden Beach cop to radio Capt. Cohen about their location, when, out of the corner of his eye, he saw Daniel bolt for the doors of the school board building. Before West could pull his weapon, Daniel was inside and running down the hall-way, past the "Wall of Shame," as district employees called the hallway, where every one of the last 11 school superin-tendent's pictures were hung.

West radioed dispatch as he ran inside after Estrada. "I need back up! Suspect Daniel Estrada is fleeing inside the school board building.

As West rounded the corner running down the "Hall of Shame," he heard a door slam shut. As he ran out of the hallway, he had to decide whether to go right, into the garage, or left toward the east side exit doors. He chose east, just in time to see Daniel Estrada running southbound toward an empty parking lot the board owned.

Daniel's drunken stupor was quickly wearing off. His fear and adrenaline were now in control of both his brain and body. As he sprinted down NE 2nd Ave. toward the entrance to I-395... he suddenly had an idea.

Looming like an elephant in a china shop was the Carnival Center for the Performing Arts. Although the facility was still under construction... it presented an ideal spot to elude his pursuers. It was lit up like a Christmas tree on the outside, but because it wasn't open, it had minimal security... just the

$10.00 an hour rent-a-cops, who didn't carry weapons, and would probably shit themselves before pursuing an intruder.

Daniel bolted across the street, to the Ziff Ballet Opera House... slamming through an unlocked fence gate. He then high tailed it through the mammoth back stage, loading dock entrance, where spectacular scenery would one day be delivered, to adorn the nearly half a billion dollar facility.

Pumping his out of shape body down the sidewalk, Det. West lifted his radio and informed dispatch, "The subject has just broken into the Opera Ballet house... the Performing Arts Center... the Ziff place! Copy?"

"Copy," dispatch responded. "Units and SWAT are on the way."

As Det. West slammed through the same unlocked fence gate... a startled security guard, who must have been about 75 years old, looked up, pointed inside, and then ran away from the cavernous arts center, as quickly as his arthritic knees would let him.

CHAPTER #100

There wasn't anything Capt. Cohen could do about the potential sighting of the porno tech guys down in the Keys, but she was only blocks from the chase underway at the Carnival Center for the Performing Arts. Jeez, she thought, as she ran toward her unmarked SUV... this place isn't even open yet, and already it's going to be Miami's next monument to crime!

She'd just grabbed her seatbelt, when her radio crackled. It was dispatch.

"Captain, we just got a call from the address in Golden Beach where you were earlier today. Someone in the house is reporting the death of a Mr. Jorge Estrada."

"What the fuck?" Sheila Cohen stammered after hearing the news.

"Call Golden Beach Police and inform them that this death may be related to another murder and a chase we're in the middle of. So tell them to secure the scene and wait for our investigators to get there. QSL?"

"QSL, Captain," dispatch responded. "But FYI, Golden Beach has already called for county investigators to handle the death. They don't have homicide detectives in their small department, so it's protocol."

"QSL. Just get our CSI people moving in that direction now!" Cohen clicked her seatbelt, started her vehicle and peeled out, headed to the new Performing Arts Center, where the Miami Police Department was about to take center stage.

******

Conrad Carson and Adam Goldman had pulled their truck over to the side of the road in front of the Dolphin Research Center in Marathon, in the middle Keys. They watched as the

Monroe County Sheriff's deputy sauntered toward their pick-up truck.

Carson rolled down the window. As hard as he tried to act cool, he just couldn't hide the beads of sweat dripping down from his forehead, rolling along the side of his pointed nose, and landing on his shirt, as soon as it trickled off his chin.

"License and registration," the deputy demanded.

"Sure officer!' Carson was trying to sound innocent and help-ful. But he was squinting in the glare of the deputy's large flashlight that was beaming in his face, almost blinding him as he tried to wrestle his wallet out of his back pocket. He was shaking as he opened the black leather wallet. It took him three tries to remove his Florida Driver's License from the clear, plastic holder it was in. He handed it to the deputy, who stared at it with a deep intensity.

"Registration," the deputy barked.

"Right!" Carson repeated. Then he reached across Gold-man's lap and opened the glove compartment. It was filled with papers. In the dark, Carson was having a hard time see-ing what any of them were, so he just grabbed the entire contents, and pulled them out.

"Officer, it may take me a minute. I have a lot of junk in the glove compartment... but I know the registration is in here somewhere," Carson informed him, as he sifted through gro-cery receipts, two gun licenses, four maps, direction to his parents' house in Ocala, something that looked like home-work his son should have turned in months ago, and all of his truck insurance renewal slips.

The deputy said nothing. He just held the flashlight, in hopes that it would help the driver find the registration more quickly.

"Mr. Carson?" The deputy was peering inside at papers that were flying in every direction. It gave him a good chance to look at Carson's passenger.

"You guys been partying?" he asked.

"Oh hell no!" Carson almost started to laugh. "I mean, no officer."

"I followed you for several miles and you were weaving a good bit," the deputy informed the men.

"Well, my friend here fell asleep and wasn't keeping me company, so I think I sort of started to nod off," Carson quickly explained. It was the truth!

"I should have pulled over and taken a cat nap, but I thought I could fight off the urge to sleep. My apologies deputy." Carson looked right at the deputy and grinned sheepishly.

"Out of the car, Mr. Carson. I need you to take a sobriety test." With those words, the deputy put his hand on the driver's side door and opened it up... indicating with his hand that Conrad Carson should exit the vehicle.

Just as Carson was stepping down onto the gravel of the road shoulder, he heard the deputy's radio come on.

"Attention all units! Attention all units! Miami Police have issued a BOLO for a Conrad Carson and Adam Goldman. Both men are white, middle aged, possibly fleeing in a red ambulance."

Carson locked eyes with the deputy for what seemed like 30-minutes, but was really only 3 seconds; basically the time it took the deputy to reach for his gun.

"Hands up!" he commanded.

"No!" came the sound of Goldman's voice. "Your hands up deputy." Goldman stood on the passenger side of the pickup truck pointing a rifle at the deputy.

"Down on the ground, nice and slow officer," he instructed.

Slowly, the deputy dropped his gun, and began to bend at the waist, as if he was about to drop, as instructed. Then in the blink of an eye, he dropped hard to ground and rolled his body under the pickup truck, grabbed his shoulder radio and screamed, "I have Carson and Conrad... Marathon!"

The second he disappeared under the truck, Goldman fired a shot, missing the deputy by a mile. "Shots fired!" screamed the deputy into his radio.

Goldman and Carson stared for half a second at one another, and then took off on foot, headed for the Dolphin Research Center. If they had to hijack Flipper to get away from the cops... Goldman had already decided that's what they'd do! Unfortunately, a locked chain link fence around the dolphin's holding area stood in their way. So Goldman used his rifle to shoot up the lock. In an instant, both men disappeared into the blackness of night, and the sanctuary of the world's smartest water mammal.

CHAPTER #101

Carlo had hung up with Penelope and then decided to call Donna. She was crying when she answered.

"Donna? What's wrong?"

"Oh, Carlo! My life is such a mess! Hank and my brother… they were… the porn… oh God I'm going to be sick!"

Carlo could barely understand what she was saying, but he knew she was in distress. "I'm coming over! Tell your guards. I'll call in the password as soon as I'm in my car." Carlo hung up quick, grabbed his car keys and ran out of his condo.

As Donna looked up, she realized her bodyguards were huddled around their police radios listening to a bunch of chatter. Suddenly, her tears stopped, and as she grabbed for a tissue and blew her nose, she began to hear some of what was being said.

"We've got an officer down in Marathon," she heard a voice announce over the radio. "His last transmission, said he had Carson and Goldman. Backup units are on the way. Capt. Cohen is also mobilizing the SWAT Team to the Carnival Center for the Performing Arts, and CSI is on its way to a home in Golden Beach, where they've got a dead guy at the home of the chief suspect in the Maine murder. But from everything I've heard, it sounds like that suspect is the one they're chasing in the arts center complex. I'll get back to you guys when I know more, but keep a sharp eye out. Mrs. Maine could be in danger."

Just then, the bodyguards realized that Donna Maine was standing in the doorway and had heard everything! That was about two seconds before Donna fainted, dropping like a brick to the floor of her bedroom.

******

In the newsroom at Channel 11, the scanners had started going crazy as soon as the BOLO on Carson and Goldman went out. The freelance scanner junkie in the Keys, had called the desk about the deputy down, and immediately, the desk had dispatched one of the night crews to meet up with Chopper 11 and head to Marathon.

Next came the call out of Golden Beach about a possible homicide. Two minutes later, Jez called in and said she had a tip about a manhunt at the Performing Arts Center. "I'm on my way in," she informed the desk. "So is Emeril."

"Did you get overtime authorization from Boris, for him?" Allison asked in her very snippy way.

"NO!" Jez snapped back. "I got approval for an overnight in Marathon! Did you get similar approval for the crew you just dispatched?" Jez waited for Allison's reply. Instead, all she heard was the intern on the desk, say "QSL."

"Good!" Jez snorted into the phone. "QSL!"

Within about 20 minutes, Jez was parking her car on the NE 2nd Ave. side of the school board building... just shy of the perimeter the cops had set up around the Ziff Ballet Opera House... one of two gigantic performing arts centers, that the citizens of Miami had waited on, for 20+ years, and paid nearly $300 million in additional change orders and over budget dollars, in hopes of seeing that the project was completed before the end of the world!

Although it was nighttime, she could see the dark shadows of the black-clad SWAT guys, manning the rooftops of nearby buildings, with their high-powered rifles trained on the façade of the "reportedly fabulous" Cesar Pelli-designed Ballet Opera House.

How fitting, Jez thought to herself... opera and ballet often centered around themes of tragedy, murder, and sexual liaisons. It seemed frighteningly appropriate to her, that the man the cops were chasing, had had sexual liaisons with his first murder victim, and tragically, may have murdered his father. Opera at its best!

Jez had gotten a call earlier, from one of her cop sources who'd filled her in. There wasn't much about Daniel Estrada she didn't know at this point, except what he looked like... and of course, his fate.

CHAPTER #102

It didn't take Carlo long to get to the Abbey Hotel. As he brought his roadster to a screeching halt in front of the hotel, he barely turned the engine off before jumping out and running inside. The uniformed cops, recognizing him, bypassed the silly code words and phrases, and quickly escorted him onto the elevator.

"Thank you!" he shouted as the doors closed.

This time, he was prepared for the sight of cops with their guns drawn when the elevator doors opened onto Donna's floor. "Chill guys! It's just me."

"Sorry, Mr. Ferrini," they apologized, as they quickly holstered their firearms. The one closest to the entrance to Donna's suite grabbed a key from his belt and unlocked the door for Carlo.

The first thing Carlo saw was Donna laying on the couch with a couple of cops fanning her as if she was a Southern Belle, who'd passed out from the heat and tightness of her corset.

Her long, flaming, red hair cascaded down the side of the couch. She was wearing a pair of jeans and a white tee shirt that had the school system's insignia on it in the upper left hand corner. Although her eyes were shut, the cops kept talking to her as if she were wide-awake.

"Donna! There you go! Good girl!" What the hell, thought Carlo, she's out of it!

Carlo ran to her, pushing cops out of his way, like a swimmer doing the breast-stroke.

"Donna! Donna!" he pleaded. "Wake up, Donna. Wake up," he said shaking her and then clutching her to his chest. "Somebody get some water," he shouted at the clueless cops.

If they'd thought he planned to give her a drink, they were wrong. Two cops arrived with large glasses of water, which he grabbed from them and thrust in Donna's face. Immediately, she came around.

"Donna, we need to talk," was all Carlo could say.

Donna Maine shook her head yes, put her arms around Carlo's neck as he lifted her up, and together they walked slowly into her bedroom and closed the door.

CHAPTER #103

Every on duty cop in Golden Beach immediately responded to the call about a dead man. In one day, the Estrada home had gone from being just another spectacular mansion on the beach, to the center of the department's attention.

The first cop at the scene, found a hysterical woman, who identified herself as Mrs. Estrada. In between screams and sobs, she managed to point the cop towards one of the two floating circular marble staircases leading to the second floor and Daniel's ocean view bedroom. The door was wide open, and the body of a man lay on the carpet. As the cop got closer, he realized that the man's face was missing, having been pulverized by whatever was used to kill him.

"Jesus Christ!" The cop thought he might be sick, and quickly turned to leave the room, just as two other officers were running down the long hallway.

"Bad?" one of them asked.

"Horrific! Sorry, but I can't handle this," he said as he put his hand up to his mouth.

"Go secure the front door," one of them ordered. "And stay with the Mrs., until the county guys get here. We'll secure the scene."

Within minutes, Miami-Dade homicide detectives had arrived, along with CSI technicians from the Miami Police Department. It was left up to Golden Beach's Police Chief to explain all the cross-jurisdictional issues, involving the Estrada family. Finally, it was decided to let Miami process the scene for forensics, and the county folks would handle the investigation.

At about the same time as cops were wrapping crime scene tape around the exterior entrance to the Estrada home, Jez and Emeril were contemplating various ways to circumvent the police tape around the Opera House in order to get their story. Suddenly, Jez's cell phone began ringing. Before she answered, she checked the caller ID. It was Carlo. He'd used their secret code.

"What's going on?" she asked, instead of answering with a "hello."

"I'm with Donna. She's passed out. It seems her brother is involved in the Maine thing and pornography stuff and is running from the cops in the Keys and she's wilting!" Carlo was breathless.

"I know!" Jez said pointedly. "Listen, Carlo, I need your help."

"Anything Jez," Carlo responded.

"I need a description of this psycho Daniel Estrada. He works for the school system in its headquarters. And the cops are hunting for him inside the Ziff Ballet Opera House. Do you know him? Or anyone who does? Please! It's critical mass here! They think he killed the Nazi and maybe his father too."

After a pregnant pause, Carlo gave Jez all the information she needed. "He's about 5'9", short sandy blonde hair, thin build, a slight pot-belly and demonic. He'll kill you before he thinks twice," Carlo cautioned. "Be careful Jez. He's loco."

"I hear you," she assured her friend. "Now take care of Donna. It's her testimony that's going to take down the school system's corrupt leaders, and maybe put some of these sickos in the electric chair! Got to go. I'll call you later after I give Emeril a tour of the new performing arts center... if you know what I mean? Bye now." She then turned her cell phone off. She didn't want any ringing to interrupt her mission.

Carlo laughed. But it was a half-hearted laugh. Her cryptic language told Carlo that she planned to go inside the performing arts center. It worried him, knowing Daniel, but he knew that she could survive in that place if anybody could. Why? Because he'd been with her the day he'd arranged their private tour of the facility… just Carlo, Jez and three others.

It was the most private, of private tours ever given. They'd been told about the inner workings of the firewalls that could segregate smoke to one small area, without panic, or the knowledge of anyone sitting in the audience seats.

They'd watched as the stage hands, practiced handling the 108 scenery rigging cables, and huffed and puffed up the stairs to the catwalks, and then back down again to the basement, where the spiral lifts underneath the stage and orchestra pit, could move scenery and actors, up, down and around. The lifts operated like gigantic screwdrivers. It was the most modern of engineering designs, replacing the traditional hydraulic lifts that were still used in most theaters and performing arts centers.

Carlo knew that Jez knew more about the performing arts center than the cops, who were poised to storm the place. And he wouldn't be surprised if Jez ended up hiding in an air duct. The damn things were 9 feet tall! The tour group was dwarfed by them on their way through the back areas of the two performing arts center halls.

Their guide, the project manager for the Knight Concert Hall, had explained how a computer programmed the temperature and used a system of continuous and constant flow, eliminating the off/on sounds that most air handlers make. Underneath many of the seats in both halls were mushroom-looking buttons, about the size of a salad plate that rose about 5 inches off the floor. The air handler pushed the cold air out from above, and the mushrooms trapped the return air without creating a direct draft, sending it back into the system to be cooled and recycled.

Carlo hung up, knowing that his chief job was to care for Donna. With that knowledge, he pulled Donna's bedspread back, made sure she was tucked into the comfortable sheets and snuggled by the comforter. Then he sat in a chair near her bed and fell asleep. Sometimes, bodyguards weren't as effective as angels. And at this moment, Carlo was Donna's angel.

CHAPTER #104

"I have an idea!" Jez announced to Emeril. "Follow me."

Penetrating the police guards at the Opera Ballet House wasn't going to happen, Jez realized. But there was no police perimeter around the Knight Concert Hall across the street.

"Do ju know where we're goink?" Emeril asked Jez, almost pleadingly.

"Jes! I... I... I mean, Yes!" Jez stammered in a whisper that she knew Emeril, who was hard of hearing, might not hear or understand.

"How do ju know where ju are goink?" he pushed.

"Because, god dammit, I've been here before!"

They both stopped and stared at each other.

"Dis place is still under construction! Hard hats required! See, dat's what da sign says. How could ju have been here before?" Emeril was grinning as he huffed and puffed lugging the camera equipment.

"Ju were here making luff to one of your boyfriends, weren't you?" Emeril taunted her with a teasing, off the cuff comment.

"I will just let you think that!" Jez sassed back.

They'd managed to get past the Hispanic "rent-a-cop" at the Concert Hall, by greasing his palm with about $60 dollars. Emeril told him in Spanish that Jez was an American TV reporter. The guy had nodded and grinned so big, that Jez even threw in an autograph for him. They left him beaming and thanking them profusely in Spanish.

As they stepped into the lobby, Emeril stopped to look around. "Wow!" Jez heard him say.

"Pretty isn't it?" Jez turned around to see Emeril staring up at the etched glass balcony railings by local artist, José Bedia. Each glass panel depicted fish, the sun, people and different musical instruments, such as a violin, and saxophone. The wavy lines throughout represented sound and ocean waves. He then looked down at the ochre and black terrazzo floor in the lobby. It was a vision of fish and suns surrounding the centerpiece... that was an open palm of a hand... outstretched, ready to "greet or clap," as the artist described it.

"So this is what jey've been doink with our tax dollars?" Emeril observed.

"Yeah!" Jez was already half way up the lobby staircase that led to the orchestra level seating area. "Wait till you see the Cinnabon!"

"The what?" Emeril asked.

"The acoustical canopy. Come on, you'll see why they call it the Cinnabon." Jez motioned for Emeril to join her.

Emeril was truly in awe of everything he was seeing. He was also thinking that maybe he should bite the bullet and buy season tickets. He knew his wife would love the idea. He'd seen the announcements about a number of performers that were to play there, by noted local Cuban musicians.

As he reached the top of the staircase, Jez was holding the door open for him.
"Come on!" she insisted.

As Emeril walked through the doorway and entered the main concert hall, his jaw dropped.

In the middle of the cavernous hall, was a gigantic wooden looking swirl that indeed, looked like a mammoth Cinnamon Bun... without icing! The massive circular centerpiece was suspended, about even with the third box tier... high enough above the stage, but low enough not to interfere with the workers who were still painting the ceiling and installing the lighting equipment.

"This big thing is what, I was reliably told, will make this concert hall have the best acoustics of any similar hall in the world," Jez informed him. "Depending on what kind of sound they want, they can raise or lower the various layers of the Cinnabon. Each circular fin is not connected to the others. Isn't that cool?" Jez was suddenly reliving the giddiness she felt when she first saw the gorgeous hall.

"Ju really do know dis place!" Emeril said, sounding impressed, as he surveyed the plastic covered orange seat cushions and blonde wooden floor, railings, and balcony shields.

"Then follow me, because I'm afraid your private tour will have to wait." Jez then indicated that the two of them should leave the hall... and Emeril followed her up to the next level.

Jez was making her way up to the next level, or box tier, towards the "walk bridge" that connected the Concert Hall to the Ballet Opera House across Biscayne Boulevard.

"Jez? Are ju sure dis is a good idea? We've never broached polish lines before."

"Just follow me, will you refugee? We aren't breeching the police lines... we're just getting ahead of them. Oh! And by the way, take pictures please!"

"Why do I luff her?" Emeril thought to himself, as he ran after Jez, the pain in the ass reporter, trying to catch up with her.

CHAPTER #105

Interim Superintendent Lily Molina had been working late, when she heard all the sirens. When she looked out her 9th floor window, she saw a sea of cop cars. Some were stopping in front of the administration building others kept on going, southbound on NE 2nd Ave.

God! What now, she wondered. One day on the job, and still, the flashing lights of law enforcement surrounded her world.

Lily had been pouring over real estate documents of all the property the school system owned. It wasn't as if she needed the information. She already knew the properties, known and unknown to the public, which were owned by the system. But she used the ruse, so no one would suspect what she was really up to. If she did nothing else as interim superintendent, she was going to get rid of the "ranch!"

Lily knew the guys would never agree to sell their little piece of sexual paradise. But she also knew, that with Maine's murder, Vascoe's death, Ross' suicide, Moorehead's troubles, and Nunez and Padron under suspicion, it was just a matter of time before the cops, or Jez Underwood, found out about the "sex ranch." She was finally in a position to save all of them from themselves. She planned to put the ranch on the market first thing the next morning.

As she was dictating a memo to the head of the school board's real estate department, she was suddenly startled by the sound of her outer office door slamming. Then she heard the voice.

"Lilluh Belle? Oh, Lilluh Belle?" It was Moses Moorehead. She promptly dismissed her stenographer secretary who scurried through a concealed side door, closing it behind her.

Before Lily Molina could make a move... Moorehead was waltzing into her office.

"Aah!" Lily screamed, sounding more like a crow, than a superintendent. "Why are you bald?"

"Shut up, you cunt!" Dr. Moorehead was in no mood for Lily's disparaging remarks.

"But Mo, I, I, I've never seen you... without... I mean like... you know... with... with... with... without your hair!"

"We need to have a little talk, Lilluh." Moses Moorehead then sat in one of the black leather visitor chairs facing Lily's desk.

"What do you want?" Lily had regained her composure, and now sounded more like the bitch that she was known to be.

"Well whatever I want, you're going to do it for me." Moses was looking down and twirling his diamond pinky ring around his finger.

"Don't think you can just saunter in here and start giving orders," she barked. "I'm not Rod Vascoe!"

"No, you are not. You are so right about that. Rod Vascoe was an appointed superintendent with a contract. You my dear, are just the interim superintendent. And you have me to thank for throwing that little nugget your way. Hell, Lilluh Belle, you wouldn't even be stand'n here if it weren't for me. We both know you worked on your padded knees, many a night, in order to get yourself a job title that would allow you to even be considuhd for this poe-zi-shun. And what Big Mo gives, he can also take away," he paused for effect, and stared right at her.

Lily knew he was right. She'd have to play his game, or lose everything, because Moses Moorehead wouldn't just stop at taking away her current job. She knew he'd destroy her and Lee. Their careers would be over.

"What do want," she asked again, dialing back her attitude a bit.

"Two things. First, you're gonna call the motor pool and have them bring me a car."

"Where's your car?" she asked.

"It's... it's flooded you might say."

"Alright! I'll get you a God damn car. What else? Cause I'm sure there's another reason you're here threatening me."

"You always were a smart cookie," he said grinning. "You're gonna call the head of OIT and request that a little doctor'n be done in the system's mainframe. I want that transaction that R.V. and I did, the night Jez Underwood was spying on us, to disappear. I want that transaction reversed, no record that it ever occurred."

"I can't do that! It's illegal! Besides, that's what you're under investigation for. The cops have already cleaned out your office."

"Lilluh, they found nothing in my office, and I know for a fact, that the cops haven't seized the mainframe records yet. But it's just a matter of time. So make the call and get this done! Promise the computer guru a raise if you have to, but get it taken care of, ya hear?"

"But Mo, Jez has you on tape doing the switch." Lily was desperate to find her way out of this mess.

"Lip read'n ain't proof. Besides, this way it'll make that bitch reporter look like a liar! If there's no proof of the transaction, we can accuse her of shitty reporting. Those journalism heathens hate to have their accuracy impugned. Maybe by discrediting one of her reports, we can poke holes in the public's opinion of her. Now wouldn't you like that, Lilluh?"

Lily loved the idea! Taking that Underwood woman down had been a dream of hers for years. Her reports had trashed both Lee and Lily, and it had caused both their blood pressures to spike.

They were so vengeful that they had sought a "Santera" to do something about her. But so far, the "spell rendering old Cuban woman" hadn't done much. So much for Santeria, a religion that developed long ago on the island of Cuba. It was basically a combination of African tribal rituals, Catholicism and a bit of Voodoo.

"You are good Moses, I'll give you that. But if I get busted for this, I'm taking you down with me. So make sure I don't go to jail, cause you'll be joining me." Her threat wasn't even subtle, and Moses knew she meant it. She was a shrewd devil, he thought. But he wasn't about to push his luck. He'd gotten what he'd come for. He'd let her feel she won something, too.

"I believe ya Lilluh. Now make that call."

CHAPTER #106

Nine stories below Mo and Lily, sat Marcos Alfaro in the passenger seat of Daniel's Corvette. He'd hunkered down, the second he'd seen Daniel talking to a guy who'd gotten out of a car, that looked suspiciously like an undercover cop car. When he finally got the nerve to lift his head and peek out of the window again, he saw Daniel running, followed closely by the guy in a suit.

"Not good!" Marcos was quickly sobering up. It was time to distance himself from his rich lover and that meant leaving the incriminating conch shell in the bag they'd stashed it in. He then loaded it into the vet's trunk, along with the other suitcases filled with clothes.

Marcos wasn't worried about leaving his prints on the shell. He'd wiped it down with Clorox, which he found under the sink in Daniel's bathroom. Even if cops found his fingerprints in Daniel's room, it wouldn't connect him to Jorge Estrada's murder, since he was a frequent visitor to the house.

"You're on your own Daniel," he thought to himself as he opened the passenger side door, and fled Northbound up NE 2nd Avenue. His plan was to cut east over to Biscayne Boulevard and blend in with the gay hookers who worked that area, before disappearing into the night, and then head over to SoBe when the time was right. He would never be spotted there with the other buff bodies of the young boys.

******

Moses Moorehead was also on the move. After Lily had called the head of OIT and instructed him on what she needed him to do, Mo had headed down to the garage and gotten the keys to one of the school system-owned cars. Pulling out of the gated parking lot, he was suddenly terrified to see so many cop cars, speeding down 15th street, with lights flashing and sirens blaring. For about two seconds, he didn't breathe, fearing they were after him. But he quickly realized they were all heading south on NE 2nd, and he convinced himself that he was just panicking for no good reason.

He turned left out of the parking lot, accelerated and departed the area, taking the back roads through Overtown to NW 7th Avenue and north to home.

When he arrived, he saw the undercover cop car assigned to watch his house. It was parked in his neighbor's driveway. As he got out of his car, he turned and waved to the cop. It was his way of letting them know, he was on to them. He then unlocked the front door and walked inside.

During the drive home, he'd been thinking about his predicament. He knew the gang would get suspicious when they learned he'd been in the Cayman Islands. His first priority, now that he'd gotten Lily to remedy his computer transaction with R.V, was to pacify the boys, so they didn't tip off the authorities. A big reward might just buy their silence.

That's when he'd hatched his plan. He'd buy them off before anyone else could. He threw the satchel with the $100,000 on the sofa. He unzipped it and looked at the mounds of bundled $100 dollar bills.

Although he'd planned to use the money for his own needs, like paying K.T. Jones, Moses was a smart man, who knew when not to get greedy.

In college, he'd boxed welterweight. He'd learned the art of moving left when your opponent went right; backing up and going forward. You never stood still in boxing. Now was just another moment in his life when he'd have to bob and weave and most probably give up the $100,000 that sat on his couch.

Although Moses Moorehead hated using his telephone, he was going to have to, if he was to implement his plan. Grudgingly, he lifted the handset, running the code phrases through his head. He and the boys had planned for this day, hoping it would never come, but now it had. He was calling an emergency meeting at the church.

"Rev. "L!" Moses had called the righteous Rev. Daschle Hamill.

"Hey! Mo! Glad to hear you're back from vacation." Hamill knew better, but figured he play along.

"Reverend? What is your favorite biblical passage?" Mo asked.

The silence told Mo that "L" was probably freaking out at hearing the beginning of the code phrase.

"I... I uh... well... I'd have to say that I like Psalms 24. The Lord is "my shepherd; I shall not want..."

"That's nice." Mo said. "But I like II Kings. "And the king sent, and they gathered unto him all the elders of Judah and of Jerusalem."

With that, both men hung up. Protocol required the person who was called to make the next phone call, and so on, until all six of the members who were in cahoots had been noti-fied. The phrase told the others, that the King, Moorehead, was asking for all of them, meaning the elders, to gather at the church immediately.

Moses then went to the satchel and began separating the bundled money into five individual batches of $20,000 each. He'd give each bundle to his pals, in hopes that whatever concerns they might have in the coming days, would be van-quished by his generous payoff.

CHAPTER #107

In the Keys, money wasn't what Carson and Goldman needed as badly as an exit strategy. After blowing the fence lock
open at the Dolphin Research Center, the two men found
themselves wandering around in the dark. But thanks to a full
moon, they at least had a distant spotlight.

After running for several yards, they found themselves in the
middle of large pools of water, separated only by narrow
wooden walkways. They were trying to be quiet, but the
minute their feet hit the first planks of wood, the water in
each of the huge pools began to make noise. They heard
splashing sounds, some squeaks, and something that
sounded like teenage girls chattering on the telephone.

"I guess they really do have dolphins here," Carson whispered to Goldman.

"Duh! That's why it's called the Dolphin Research Center you
moron!" Goldman knew his sarcasm wouldn't get him out of
there, but it made him feel better.

"So what do we do now, Mr. "know-it-all?" Carson asked.
"We've got a cop who will be in here with back up any second now, and the only way out of here is a free ride on a dolphin!"

"What keeps the dolphins in here?" Carson asked Goldman.

"How should I know? This is my first time here."

Under the light of the full moon, Adam Goldman began running up and down the wooden walkways. "There's fencing on
the outer boundaries of each dolphin pool. If we can figure
out a way to open those fences, we can get out of here,"
Goldman exclaimed.

"I'm not a good swimmer, Adam," Carson informed his en-
thusiastic co-worker.

"You won't have to swim, Conrad! The dolphins will be your
ticket out of here, that's why they call the attraction, 'Swim-

ming with the Dolphins', because they'll pull us along for a free ride to freedom."

"Are you insane?" Carson was starting to sweat. He didn't like the ocean during daylight, never mind at night!

"Shut up and help me find a way to open these fucking fences," Goldman ordered.

"I'm not getting in the water, Adam."

"You will if you don't want to go to jail! Now help me." As soon as Adam Goldman said that, he jumped into the water and began feeling around with his hands, in hopes of finding some kind of latch or lock.

Conrad Carson stood frozen. The idea of getting into the water with dolphins gave him the same "creep out" factor, as if he'd been asked to jump into a pool of sharks. Carson hated water and anything that lived in it.

Just then, Goldman found the hook latch on the fence.

"I found it!" he hollered at his friend. "Now jump in, hop a dolphin and grab hold of a fin. This is our ticket outta here!"

But before Carson could respond, dolphins from every one of the pools, lept over the walkways, squeaking and squawking. It was clear, their mission was to keep Goldman inside the confines of the gated pool. They nosed him with their version of a jab. Then they nipped at his hands as he attempted to push the gate open.

"What the fuck? I'm trying to set you kids free!" Goldman shouted, as one of the Atlantic Bottle-nosed Dolphins goosed him. "Shit!" he screamed.

That's when he heard the same dolphin laughing... or what sounded like a human's laugh. "Ach! Ach! Ach!"

"You fucking flippers! I'll have you fried and frittered for dinner!" Goldman barely had those words out of his mouth, when a pack of four dolphins, barreled into him, lifting him high into the air, and tossing him over the fence.

"Carson!" he shouted. "Carson! Help me!"

Under the water, the lead dolphin named "Queenie," made sure that the latch on the fence lock was clicked. She'd known for the better part of her 12 years, how to get in and out of the pools. But escaping one of the most prestigious aquatic preserves was not in her nature. Knowing a bad ass when she swam with one was the reason she was called "Queenie!"

As Carson stood staring into the darkness, that was only infrequently illuminated by the moon as clouds passed by… he wilted when he heard the word "FREEZE!" He knew the jig was up! So, hands over his head, he turned toward the sound of the cop's voice and surrendered.

CHAPTER #108

Adam Goldman was treading water with great difficulty because of his considerable size. He was trying to figure out how he was going to survive in the night waters of Florida Bay, when he heard the cop order Carson to freeze. Goldman then realized his only option was to swim.

As he began stroking, not knowing where he was headed, a bright light suddenly illuminated the water around him... and he heard a loud noise overhead. He immediately stopped and looked up. There in the sky over his head was the Monroe County Sheriff's helicopter with its searchlight scanning the dark waters. Adam immediately ducked under the water's surface, but realized this was not a long-term solution to his predicament.

Goldman's lungs began to burn from holding his breath, so he was forced to surface. That's when he heard another noise. It was the sound of a motorboat. Just then, the spotlight from the chopper zeroed in on him. That's when he saw the boat turn slightly to the right, and head straight in his direction. Goldman stopped swimming, having finally realized there was no place to go, except into the police boat that was on its way to pick him up.

As Monroe County deputies handcuffed both Goldman and Carson, other units arrived on the scene and were preparing to search the suspect's vehicle. They'd been asked by Miami police to secure the scene until officers could get down there. Meanwhile, the two suspects, one wet and one dry, were taken off to the Marathon Detention Center.

******

At Jackson Memorial Hospital, Amelia Salas was starting to wake up. She was surrounded by her family. Immediately, her son ran to tell the doctors and the cops, who were standing guard outside her private room.

When they contacted Captain Cohen about this development, she immediately dispatched a detective to the hospital.
Sheila Cohen doubted Ms. Salas would be able to remember
anything of significance, but she had to try.

Meanwhile, the team that had gone back out to the scene of
the Salas shooting, had determined that whoever had shot
Amelia Salas, had done so from the roof of the Annex Building. It was a secondary administration building, used by the
school system, which had long ago outgrown its nine-story,
main headquarters.

The thinking was, that the shooter likely had no idea that Ms.
Salas would be doing an interview with Jez Underwood, but
did know that the school board member would have to exit
the secured parking lot behind the main building… and drive
directly toward the Annex Building. The police theory was
that the shooter probably planned to fire on Salas in her car,
as she was driving away. The fact that she was an easy target as she crossed the street following her interview, was
most likely just "dumb luck."

As soon as Capt. Cohen finished ordering detectives to the
hospital… her phone rang again. This time the news was
about the arrests of Goldman and Carson.

"Send Horton and Herrera to Marathon," she ordered. "I want
those porn-addicted, sons of bitches back in Miami by morning. If Monroe County gives our guys any grief about that,
have the Sheriff call the Chief. I'll fill him in as soon as I hang
up."

Sheila Cohen reached up and began massaging her temples. A headache was creeping up on her, as she thought
about all the jurisdictional issues she'd have to deal with; first
Golden Beach and Miami-Dade County… now Monroe
County! Her next call was to the Chief, to bring him up to
speed on all the late breaking developments.

******

Channel 11 was handling the developments by breaking into
programming with a special report.

"Good evening, I'm Dean Sands. We have breaking news in the effort to find the person who murdered Miami's Deputy School Superintendent, Dr. Hank Maine. According to sources, police are hunting a man by the name of Daniel Estrada. He is identified as a school system employee, who works at the main administration building. Right now, Miami Police believe he is hiding in the Ziff Ballet Opera House, located adjacent to the school headquarters. We can report that the SWAT team has been activated, and is heading to the unfinished performing arts center. In a tragic irony, the man believed to be Daniel Estrada's father has been found beaten to death in his Golden Beach home. We can also report, that the Monroe County Sheriff's office has arrested two men, both of whom are identified only as school system employees. We are uncertain, what, if anything, their arrests have to do with the hunt for Daniel Estrada, but we have a crew headed to Marathon to find out more. We have the best reporters in all of South Florida covering each aspect of this story, and we'll have the very latest for you, right here on 11 News, at 11:00pm. We now return you to regular programming."

Carlo was sitting in Donna's hotel living room watching TV with the cops, when Dean Sands' breaking news announcement came on.

"Oh My God! I knew Daniel's father," he informed the bodyguards. "That poor man. He tried so hard to understand his son and do right by him."

"What do you mean understand his son?" asked one of the cops.

"Daniel is gay. Not that being gay is any big deal, but many Hispanic families, are homophobic and shun gay relatives. It tore his father apart, especially when he discovered that not only was Daniel gay, but he was a gay predator. He liked teenage boys."

"Does Captain Cohen know any of this?"

"Yes. I told her about him when she brought those pictures for Donna to look at. I recognized him." Carlo just sat there, starring at the TV.

Just then the bedroom door opened and Donna came out. "I just heard the news clip," she said. "Is it true? Did Daniel kill Hank?" Her eyes were puffy from crying, mascara was smeared down her cheeks, and her red hair was matted and wild.

Carlo immediately rose and put his arm around her. "Come on honey and sit down with us. Hopefully, we'll find out more at 11:00, that is, unless Capt. Cohen calls here with the in-side scoop." Carlo gently lowered Donna onto the couch. "You need to eat something, Donna."

"I'm not hungry."

"Maybe not, but you still need to eat something." Carlo was insistent. "I'm going in the kitchen and find you a snack."

As Carlo left the room, Donna sat in a stupor wondering if the arrest of Daniel Estrada would mean she wouldn't have to hide out any more. Then she remembered that the real reason she was locked inside a hotel, was because of Moses Moorehead. Even if they arrested him tomorrow, there was no way she was safe to return to her old life. She knew too much, and there would be a lot more school system employees who would want to shut her up. The very thought was too depressing to handle, so Donna put her head down on the end of the couch and closed her eyes.

CHAPTER #109

It was 10:25pm, and no one at Channel 11 could get in touch with Jez or Emeril. Boris was beyond angry! They'd teased her report all night, and now, with only 35 minutes till show time... his lead reporter was AWOL! He couldn't help but think that the stress this bitch caused him would give him a heart attack one day.

"I'm going to reshuffle the entire rundown," he shouted as he exited his office.

The announcement made the producers and video editors shrink. Chaos reigned whenever Danken "reshuffled the rundown." He could have cared less how this affected his staff. After all, he was the boss. But the morale of the people who had to work in this volatile environment, disintegrated with every order that came out of the boss' mouth.

"Lead the news with the death in Golden Beach... then go into the son at the performing arts center," he ordered. "But before we go to the PAC for a report, play up the late breaking facts out of Monroe County. Take live reports from each location. But do a constant tease about the situation at the Opera House. Maybe by then, Jez will have graced us with her presence!"

"Did it ever occur to you she and Emeril might be in trouble at their location?"

The voice that was challenging Boris was that of the general manager, Tab Tanner.

Boris whipped around to face Tanner. Neither spoke. After about five seconds, Tanner turned and left the newsroom. Danken immediately hustled himself over to the assignment desk and told Allison, "Assume the dynamic duo is in peril. Act accordingly."

He then shouted to the producer pod, "Take Jez out of all rundowns until further notice. Don't tease any of her stuff. Take live pictures from the performing arts center, but don't mention Jez being there. Got it?"

The hushed sounds of producers saying "got it," was all he wanted to hear. Frankly, they were in shock. The producers were used to a lot of shit, but hearing Boris take Jez out of a rundown was not one of those things. They all looked up and stared.

"What are you looking at? Get back to work and assume Jez is a no show!"

With that, he stomped back into the safety of his enclosed office.

CHAPTER #110

For once in his pathetic life, Boris had done the right thing. Jez and Emeril were indeed in a situation that didn't allow them to do any reporting. Hell! They were beginning to wonder if they'd ever see their loved ones again!

After crossing the "walk bridge," from the Knight Concert Hall and into the Ziff Ballet Opera House, Jez and Emeril found themselves in total darkness. At first they were surprised, considering how much light was glistening in the concert hall they'd just left, even though, not one patron was there to see or listen to a violin or trombone.

"Now what blondie?" Emeril whispered to Jez.

"I don't know refugee!" Jez snapped. She hated it when she wasn't in control, and right now, she was not in control. The lack of light spooked her, and she was desperately trying to remember everything she learned on that tour, in order to get the two of them to safety.

Her biggest fear wasn't the psycho, but being mistaken for the psycho by the SWAT team that had surrounded the Opera house almost an hour ago. Since they didn't know she and Emeril were inside, she realized they were ripe for the picking!

"Emeril," she whispered.

"What?"

"We have to put some distance between us and the possible action."

"Really Jez! Do you sink?" Emeril's sarcastic reply didn't go unnoticed.

"OK, you can say I told you so later," Jez responded, almost sounding humble. "Let's make our way to the top... the fourth row tier. That's where the follow spot booth is. We can turn on the spotlights and then you'll be able to videotape anything that happens, and we'll have a bird's eye view of anyone who might be trying to come after us. Capiche?" She suddenly hated the fact that she was mimicking her news director, but damn that phrase fit all bills!

"OK Boris!," Emeril snidely responded as the two ran out of the mezzanine level and headed quickly up four more flights of stairs, entered the fourth tier and headed for the follow spot booth.

They were stealth enough that Daniel Estrada didn't hear them moving up to the very back top row. That's because Daniel was hiding under the stage among the huge spiral lifts. He was suddenly wishing, that as a gay man, he'd taken drama in high school. Then he might know about all this stuff, including pulleys and counter weight riggings that would one day hoist large scenery changes and/or performers, depending on the need, for productions such as Aida, Rigoletto, Sleeping Beauty, Giselle or Madame Butterfly.

For their part, the cops were just standing by on the perimeter of the Opera House. They were waiting on the final set of blueprints of the facility. Unfortunately, as they were about to find out... there were no final blueprints. As with most public construction projects in Miami-Dade County... construction was started long before a final architectural rendering was sanctioned by local building officials. In other words, the architect provided schematics for 2/3rds of the building's design... and the contractors began digging holes, pouring concrete and basically building a facility based on those designs.

Then, when the local building officials came along and wanted to see how the work compared to the renderings... the honchos, who didn't have the final renderings would: A.) claim ignorance... or B.) claim that a fired employee had double crossed them.

Then the contractor would promise to take care of all issues, and the building inspector would issue a TCO... a Temporary Certificate of Occupancy.

It would most likely be to everyone's advantage that Daniel had no idea where he was too. But who could be certain of that. Even Emeril didn't believe that Jez knew her way around this place. The cops were now confronted with a reality that they had a suspect holed up in a facility they knew nothing about. Although the county's fire department had regularly toured the facility as part of the fire inspections... police didn't learn about a new building until there was a crisis. It was the reason the SWAT leader put his team on standby.

"We don't go anywhere we don't know everything about." He was speaking to Capt. Cohen.

"I couldn't agree more," she said.

"Then get us some Intel," he insisted.

"I'm doing my damn level best!" Sheila Cohen was in no mood to be messed with, by some out of control macho man!

Cohen had already placed a call to county officials and requested they get the project manager on the scene. When she checked on him, she was told he was three blocks away. In a matter of minutes he arrived, nearly out of breath from running.

As soon as Captain Cohen spotted him, she hurried him over to a nearby patrol car, where he rolled open his working schematic papers on the hood of the cop car. Cohen immediately summoned the head of the SWAT team. The three of them were now ready to formulate a plan.

"I think your best option is for me to activate the fire suppression system. That will activate the various fire zones in the building. All the fire zones are self-closing and self-latching. It's the best way to detect his movements through the building," the project manager, Lance Toomey explained, "Especially since you have no idea where he is."

"Explain," the head of SWAT demanded.

"There are monitors in each of the fire zones. If a fire zone is activated, the building management system, or BMS, can detect if one of those fire doors is opened. The closed circuit cameras and security door system monitors would then allow us to track his movements.

"Give us a for instance," the SWAT leader commanded.

"Well, for example, if a fire alarm went off on the right side of the stage, the entire area that separates the stage from the audience, called the back of house, including all the mechanical rooms, can be secured from the public spaces. Using the monitoring system, if he was on stage right, and tried to get out, we could track him the minute he breaches the monitored doorways in that zone. From the BMS we can see every place he is moving, because he'll be opening monitored doors in fire zones. It will light up on the fire panel display like a Christmas tree!"

"I like it," said Cohen. "So how do we get to the BMS office?"

"I'll have to take you there," Toomey informed them. "There's something else you should know," he informed the cops.

"What?" Cohen demanded.

"Once you get your people into position in each sector, go to radio silence."

"What good will that do?" asked the SWAT leader.

"Because of the acute acoustics that have been installed in each hall of the performing arts center... you'll be able to hear his footsteps. Hell, if he dropped a dime on stage, you'd hear it like it was a tympani drum."

"Damn!" Captain Cohen muttered.

"I'll also give you keys to access all the exterior doors... and you can surround and move in, or whatever you people do, as soon as you get me safely into the building management system office." The project manager also said he'd make the fire door remotes available to the cops, so they could search each monitored area, once he activated the BMS.

"I'll call and warn the fire department that this is just a drill," Capt. Cohen offered. "We don't need any firefighters showing up for a fire that isn't a fire!"

"Good idea," Toomey said, "Because they know this place like the back of their hands, and your sharpshooters don't!"

"Done!" the SWAT Leader exclaimed as he headed off to brief his men on the plan.

CHAPTER #111

As Daniel Estrada cowered underneath the Opera stage amid the imposing spiral lifts, he began to worry about being crushed by them if the cops decided to lower the stage or orchestra pit. His claustrophobia was also kicking in. He needed somewhere else to hide.

Grabbing a construction flashlight that was left sitting on the floor, he surveyed his options. A singular stage light that had been left on, gave him a hint as to how to get back to stage level. From there he began to climb the stage stairs up toward the attic, where his plan was to get onto the light bridge.

But in a flash of eye burning light, Daniel suddenly realized the entire stage had been illuminated. He froze, trying to figure out what to do next. While up on the fourth tier, Jez and Emeril were high fiving themselves for figuring out how to turn on the follow spot lights.

As Emeril focused his camera on the stage and orchestra seating, Jez whirled the spotlights up and down and around, trying to locate the murder suspect.

Daniel's ascent to the attic stopped at the box tier level. He immediately leaped off the staircase and into the hallway. He had no idea where he was or where he was going... so he just ran.

In the follow spot booth, Jez and Emeril had heard his footsteps as if they were right in front of them.

"Da acoustics in dis place are stupendous!" Emeril remarked.

"Yeah, but where is our psycho buddy?" Jez asked.

"Not in the house anymore," Emeril responded.

"Shit! He got off on the box tier level!" Jez screeched. "He can use the "walk bridge" from that level. We have to move now!"

As Jez and Emeril raced down three flights of stairs, the cops were cautiously moving toward the Opera House... carefully protecting the project manager who would take them to the all-important BMS office.

When they entered the Opera House, Lance Toomey knew something was wrong. "There's too many lights on," he said.

"What do you mean?" asked the SWAT leader.

"All the follow spots are on! We never leave the building with the follow spots on."

"So what does that mean?"

"It means someone else has been here and turned the spot-lights on!" Toomey was now very worried.

"Does this mean our plan is busted?" Captain Cohen pressed.

"I'd say so." Toomey then noticed an open door to the box tier level. "Someone has used that door," he said pointing to the open door leading out to the fourth tier lobby.

"What's on the fourth tier?" Cohen asked.

"The follow spot booth, but it's empty." Lance Toomey scratched his head. He looked all around. Then he saw it. The door to the fourth tier lobby was open.

"Whoever was in the spot light booth left out the lobby doors."

Instantly, they all began running in that direction. As they reached the fourth tier lobby... Toomey looked out the mas-sive wall of glass that faced southeast.

"The walk bridge!" he shouted.

"The what?" Cohen queried.

"The pedestrian walk bridge that connects the Ziff to the Knight Concert Hall! Jesus! He could be in either center!"

"How do we get to the walk bridge?" the SWAT commander asked.

"Follow me." Toomey then took off like a rocket.

Unfortunately, he was about 10 minutes too late. Daniel Estrada had already found his way from the box tier level of the Opera House, into the main kitchen, which he then discovered led to the exterior terrace and the walk bridge. He was inside the Knight Concert Hall in seconds.

But unbeknownst to the murderous sociopath, a Channel 11 camera crew was on his tail.

"Hurry!" Jez whispered to Emeril, who regrettably had to run with a 40-pound camera on his shoulder. The 60-year old photographer wasn't in the best of shape, and this kind of task, taxed him to the max!

Jez had led them off the fourth tier and onto the box tier level that she knew led to the walk bridge. Just as they'd entered the terrace, they'd seen Daniel Estrada open the door to the Knight Concert Hall.

"We have to call the cops," Emeril insisted.

"We will, as soon as we know where he is," Jez whispered back.

"This is so against every journalistic rule!" Emeril managed to say in between gulps for air.

"So is dumping your ass and mine because we aren't 23 and cheap, but that doesn't stop management from canning our colleagues!" Jez was defiant. "Remember, Emeril, we're only as good as our last story! Now follow me!"

They were running like crazy people. As they entered the concert hall, Jez took an immediate left down a hallway, then a right into the first box tier level. They hunkered down, as Jez instructed Emeril to go silent.

"From here we should be able to hear his movements," she told her photographer.

"Ju've got to be kidding me!" Emeril was not convinced. But as the two of them went silent, except for their breathing and beating of their hearts… they heard it! Footsteps.

"He's going up," Jez whispered to Emeril.

The exhausted cameraman tilted the tool of his trade upward, and zoomed in to the next level, then the one higher, and ultimately, all the way to the top.

"Nothing!" he informed Jez.

"Stop and listen, Emeril. The acoustics will tell us where he is."

Before Emeril could roll his eyes in doubt, he heard it! My god, blondie is right, he thought. He immediately trained his camera on the area where he'd heard the footsteps. They were on the third tier. As he zoomed and focused, he saw him! There was Daniel the monster, walking right onto the acoustical canopy, or Cinnabon as Jez has called it earlier. It had been positioned flush with the third tier seats. The guy didn't even have to jump!

Then in a split second, Daniel disappeared.

"He's on the bun thing, the canopy," Emeril whispered. "I can't see him. He must be hunkered down."

"He doesn't have to," she informed her photographer. "Those acoustical fins are eight feet tall!"

"So what do we do now?" Emeril asked Jez.

Before she could answer… she saw a light go on in the concert hall's control room.

"Focus on the center of the Cinnabon!" she instructed Emeril. "See those doors in the center? They're called Bombay doors, and they can be opened from the control booth. Don't stop rolling! Got it?"

"Got it," he replied as he zoomed into the center of the Cinnabon.

"What am I looking for?" he asked.

"What you'll see," Jez responded.

Jez suspected that the light in the concert hall's control booth meant that the cops had figured out that Daniel was in the Concert Hall… not the Ziff Ballet Opera house. She thought she saw a silhouette of Sheila Cohen.

As she squinted, she saw a SWAT person and Lance Toomey, the project manager who'd given her the private tour of the two performing arts centers… standing in the control booth. Suddenly, the acoustical canopy began to rise. Up, up, up it went, until it was as high as it could go.

"What the hell is going on?" Emeril whispered.

"I'm not sure. Either they know Daniel is in the canopy and this is their way of trapping him… or they wanted to get it up to clear their vision of the stage area. Either way, his goose is cooked!" Jez was watching the control booth, while Emeril kept his focus on the Bombay doors that were now about 60 feet above the stage.

"Did you hear that?" she quickly asked Emeril.

"What?"

Jez noticed Lance exit the control booth and stand. He was listening to the same thing Jez was. Then she saw Lance go back inside the booth.

"Get ready!" she whispered in a half yell to Emeril.

"I'm fucking ready!"

Five seconds later, the Bombay doors that were in the center of the acoustical canopy opened... and Daniel Estrada fell through them... to his death.

He landed center stage, where any good actor worth his salt would hope to end up. But instead of standing and delivering a monologue, he lay crumpled... his body parts twisted like a pretzel and his neck snapped like a twig. A fall from 60 feet will do that to a person, Jez thought.

"Let's go file an exclusive!" she announced to Emeril.

"But what about the cops up there," he asked pointing to the control booth.

"We'll run behind the acoustical curtains that line every wall, until we can exit safely," Jez informed her photographer.

"Have I told ju lately that I luff ju?" he asked.

"No! But save that mushy stuff for your Cuban wife!"

Jez and Emeril then took cover behind the acoustical curtains that surrounded the entire concert hall's tiers. By the time they got out of the Knight Center, it was 11:25pm. Jez clicked on her Nextel, informed the desk they had an exclusive, and the two of them ran like bats out of hell for the live truck three blocks away.

CHAPTER #112
SATURDAY

The next morning, Moses Moorehead woke up completely unaware of what had happened at the Carnival Center for the Performing Arts the night before. That's because he'd spent his evening, handing out wads of cash to his church buddies, hoping to buy their silence, at least for a while.

They'd all shown up at the Church of the Great Believer around 10:00pm, except one. Nobody had been able to locate Vince Calvo. The podiatrist's mother said he was on vacation. But Big Mo had an uneasy feeling. Calvo hadn't been seen or heard from since Sunday. Since then, video of the church guys passing the cash had turned up on Channel 11. Mo didn't want to believe that one of his handpicked men was a turncoat, but Calvo's absence was leaving him little choice.

As he began making coffee, he turned on the TV. The news was all about some SWAT action involving a Miami school system employee and the Performing Arts Center. They were even suggesting the murder of Dr. Maine might have been solved.

Just then Moorehead's phone rang. "Hello."

"Moses!" It was Lily and she was sort of whispering.

"Speak up Lilluh Belle, I can hardly hear you."

"I can't! I don't want anyone to hear me making this call," she insisted. "We've got big problems!"

Moorehead wondered why she always had to be dramatic. "What is it Lilluh? He was only half listening to her as he dumped some coffee grinds into the filter of his coffee maker.

"This place is crawling with Federal agents, Mo! That's what."

Moses Josiah Moorehead was now paying very close attention to everything Lily was saying.

"Why? What department are they in?"

"Not one department Moses! Every department... finance, OIT, Title One, Adult Education, Alternative Education, K-12, Attendance... oh yeah, and your favorite departments, Facilities, Maintenance, Construction and Land Acquisitions. Am I forgetting anything? Oh, did I mention Procurement?"

Moses Moorehead was barely breathing as he sat down at his kitchen table. "Are you sure they're feds and not the D.A.'s people?" was about all he could muster the energy to say.

"Yes I'm sure! Their cards and badges say FBI, not MDPD, God damn it! At first I thought it was just a few suits helping the District Attorney. Then the FBI Special Agent in Charge, a Jose Ramirez, informed me that the D.A.'s office isn't involved at all. They said this was strictly a Federal investigation."

"What are they investigating?" Mo wasn't sure he wanted to hear her answer.

"Anything in this district that involves federal money! Jesus, Mo! I've been the superintendent for two days and the feds move in! How will this look on my resume?"

"I don't know, Lilluh. But jail ain't gonna look too good on your resume either!" Mo sensed that Lily was starting to come unhinged.

"Jail!" Lily screeched.

"Just calm down and keep me informed," Moses told her. "You have to remain calm and collected. Don't let them see you sweat, Lilluh Belle."

"Keep you informed? You mean you're not coming down here?" Lily was in full panic.

"Are you out of your mind? The cops have already cleared out my office and have me under watch here at home. I've got my own problems. Now hang up and go back to work,

Lilluh. You are the superintendent. Or should the board ap-
point someone else?" With that he slammed down the
phone. He needed to clear his head and get a handle on
what was happening and what he should do. But first he'd
call his attorney.

******

Jewel Haynes was driving into work, when her secretary
called her.

"Dinorah, what is it? I can hardly understand you. Are you
crying?"

Through the sobbing and whispering, Dinorah managed to
inform her boss, the President of the School Board, that the
FBI was executing a Federal Search Warrant on the administrative headquarters, seizing computers, paper files, and just
about anything else that they were granted by the Federal
magistrate who signed off on the warrant that was carefully
crafted by the FBI and U.S. Attorney's Office.

Jewel Haynes heard the words Dinorah was saying, but she
couldn't comprehend the reality of those words. The school
system, her school system was perfect! They didn't have
problems. There was no corruption. That's what she believed, and that's what she always told the public. There
must be some mistake, she thought. I am President of the
nation's fourth largest school system, and it has so much to
be proud of.

Jewel then began to list, in her head, the many important
measures she'd spearheaded, designed to improve the
school system.

She'd sponsored an item that banned a children's book that
depicted Cuban kids as living a happy and fulfilled life on the
island. Although the student government board representative had spoken out against the ban, the board's attorney
had warned them this could lead to a costly lawsuit, the
board had voted to exorcise it from school libraries. The action mirroring the very press censorship, they claimed to ab-

hor under the Castro regime. The student government had then sued the school board along with the ACLU.

Then there was the resolution to denounce the conditions of cocoa bean workers in the Ivory Coast. She pushed the board to turn "chocolate" into the category of a four-letter word, but managed to keep them from banning all chocolate products, outright.

She sponsored a resolution proclaiming March as Hispanic Heritage Month.

She'd pushed to get Supt. Rod Vascoe a contract extension and she'd proposed an amendment to allow school district employees to run for elected office without having to give up their school jobs. The press had portrayed the measure as "double dipping." Jewel was convinced that having elected officials as employees gave the board greater influence over legislation.

Missing from all her resolutions, proposals and amendments, was anything that resembled a cause for kids, and the betterment of their education. But that fact eluded Jewel Haynes, just as it eluded most of her fellow board members.

As Jewel drove her pale yellow Bentley into the secured parking lot where board members parked, she was shocked back into reality, when she saw all the undercover Fed cars. They'd even parked in her specially designated parking space, forcing her to parallel park her fancy car up against the chain link fence, far from the cushy and prestigious spot she normally had near the garage elevator.

Jewel got out of her car, beeped the remote lock and began walking towards the building, when she suddenly broke out in a massive sweat! God damn it! She was having a hot flash, and it was a bad one. By the time she got to the building, her shoe polish black hair was sticking against her face like strands of black straw, and her navy blue suit was soaked in perspiration, giving it a two-toned navy effect... especially under her arms.

As she entered the building and felt the air conditioning en-velope her in a cocoon of chilled air, she suddenly stopped dead in her tracks. There stood a dark suited federal agent, who escorted her to the lobby, where she was forced to stand among an overcrowded assembly of employees.

When she tried to go to the bathroom, she was forced to stand in a long line, only to discover that there was no toilet paper or paper towels. It was a scene that any teacher would have recognized as resembling one of their poorly supplied school bathrooms, but when had Jewel ever concerned her-self with such trivial matters as toilet paper.

Finally, the bosses were getting a taste of the reality they sanctioned, facing every kid who labored to learn and most teachers who labored to teach, in the Miami School System.

CHAPTER #113

For years, FBI agents sat on their collective backsides, as the Miami School System degenerated into a quagmire of corruption, mismanagement, and an assortment of criminal enterprises. Various whistle blowers had given them a glimpse into the treacherous world of the school system. But they'd paid little attention. And that fact was about to bite them in the ass.

In the last week, the events that had stacked on top of one another had brought the catatonic government agents out of their stupor. They'd decided not to wait on the local District Attorney to act.

Because her office routinely passed on other public corruption probes, the Feds had little confidence that she'd do anything about these latest revelations. So they'd taken the initiative. The fact that they'd been pushed by leaders in Washington also had something to do with their sudden interest in the Miami School System.

Capt. Sheila Cohen was frankly grateful for the Feds involvement. She had a lot on her plate, and wasn't about to get territorial. The cool-headed Miami cop had already begun to deal with, and process all the points of her various investigations.

She'd finally connected the dots between Hank Maine's vast pornographic collection and it's connection to the OIT department. She'd learned that Maine's brother-in-law had been handling the international peddling of child porn… most of it going overseas. The stuff Maine had captured on camera in the school bathrooms and in the classroom, was apparently just for Maine's personal enjoyment. None of it had shown up in a search of Carson's home or office, or any of his computers. She knew how relieved Det. West would be to learn that his son, Bobby, had not been exploited internationally.

But it was still an uncomfortable feeling, knowing that the system's top computer geeks were sick pedophiles. Even more stunning, was when she learned that several of those working in the Office of Information Technology were convicted felons.

It seemed the system ignored criminal background checks whenever it was necessary to hire cronies. She wondered how many other crooks would show up on the school board's payroll, once the FBI got finished scouring the records of nearly 40,000 employees.

The fact that Goldman and Carson were also running an illegal TV satellite card side business was just another nugget revealing how lax the system was when it came to controls on top officials. The school cops always managed to arrest a cafeteria worker who took home some leftover food, to feed a family that lived in poverty, thought Cohen. But it was clear that any focus on administrators was discouraged.

Why, she wondered? What were they protecting? Who were they protecting? Captain Cohen assumed she wouldn't have to wait long to find out, now that everything about the school system was under investigation by the Federal Government.

CHAPTER #114

"Dean, sources are telling me that the school system is under major scrutiny by the FBI."

Jez was on the air at noon, reporting as much as she knew. She'd been given a heads up by her sources at the administration building. But she still couldn't process what was happening.

"Behind me you can see a line of unmarked FBI cars, and that's just on one block. The school system's headquarters is literally surrounded on all four sides by government vehicles. It is an unprecedented show of force, and apparently this isn't the only facility being searched. I'm told the OIT offices in West Dade are also being raided by the FBI."

Jez was doing a live shot, standing on the sidewalk across the street from the administrative office building, so her camera could get a wide shot. In addition to the line of unmarked FBI cars, there was a line of Miami Police patrol cars. The feds had called them in to provide additional security outside. The FBI wasn't about to involve the school police since, for all they knew, the department was dirty.

"This all began around 10:00 this morning, Dean. We haven't been able to reach anyone with either the FBI or the school system for a comment. We've also not seen anything being brought out of the building, at least not yet. Obviously, no one is being allowed inside and no one is being allowed to leave. My sources tell me everyone is being clustered in groups in the hallways, bathrooms, conference rooms... just about any place that is far away from computers and file cabinets."

"Jez, do we have any idea what prompted today's raid by the FBI?" the anchorman asked.

"No, not really, Dean," Jez responded. "And there's something else that is puzzling. When we contacted the District Attorney's office for comment, the spokesman told us that the

D.A.'s office was not involved in this operation. He said he didn't even know about it. So, clearly, this is strictly a Federal operation, and for whatever reason, local police and prosecutors have been left standing on the sidelines."

Just as Jez was about to throw it back to Dean Sands, she saw Emeril furiously pointing at something behind her. When she turned and looked, she saw a convoy of Ryder box trucks pulling up in front of the administration's headquarters.

"Dean, stay with us for a second," she instructed the anchorman. "It looks like the FBI may be preparing to load up whatever they are in there seizing. You can see this parade of storage trucks pulling up right now. I've never seen anything like this. It looks like they're preparing to empty every office in the building!"

"Jez, if that's the case, wouldn't it amount to a Federal takeover of the school system?" Dean Sands waited for a reply.

"I, I, don't really want to speculate, since I don't know for sure, but I don't know what other conclusion could be reached, given what we're seeing." Jez was almost speechless.

"Are you aware of the Feds taking over any other public school system, Jez?"

"Dean, I only know of one other similar raid. It happened in 2001 in San Francisco. As I recall, millions of dollars in bond money, intended for school construction were missing, and city leaders asked the Feds to determine if criminal activity had occurred. That's it."

"But Jez, isn't that the very thing that one of your recent stories focused on... the movement of construction money into an offshore bank account?"

"Yes. You're right, Dean. But even if that is what they are here to investigate, I can't imagine that they would need this massive display of manpower."

Dean Sands, sensing a lull in the story, at least for the moment, instructed Jez to get back to him as soon as anything else developed at the scene.

The minute they were off the air, Jez and Emeril began plotting their next move. They needed to try and get video of what was happening inside the building, and the best place they could think of, was up on top of the same parking garage where they'd videotaped one of the money shufflings.

"Things are coming full circle," Jez commented as Emeril unlocked his camera from the tripod.

"Ju got dat right, blondie!" The two of them then headed toward the parking garage.

CHAPTER #115

Inside the administration building 110 Federal agents were searching every office. The FBI Miami Division had even called in agents from the Tampa and Jacksonville Field offices to assist them. City of Miami Police officers were being used to monitor the groups of employees that had been segregated away from office areas, to provide crowd control, and outside perimeter security.

Interim Superintendent Lily Molina stood in a cluster of 9th floor employees in the hallway nearest the North bank of elevators. She was humiliated, but she was also terrified. What would happen if they discovered how her husband was using his school money to pay for "things" unrelated to school business? What if they discovered how Moorehead and Barbara Ross had used secret companies to funnel kickbacks from vendors? What if they discovered how she'd rigged the appointment of hundreds of principals and assistant principals, by stacking the selection committees with her cronies, whom she then paid off for turning a blind eye to the most competent candidates?

Then she remembered the real estate documents she'd left on her desk the night before. Her knees nearly gave out on her when she realized the feds would discover that the district owned the Royal Poinciana Ranch.

Superintendent Lily Molina wanted to die at that moment. A search of that house would bring down some of Miami's most powerful people... and they'd blame her. She was as good as dead when that happened, she knew. That's when she began to cry.

Thankfully, the feds hadn't pulled the curtain shut in the superintendent's office, and Emeril was able to get some good video of their search. Mostly, they were packing boxes with papers. Every drawer was open and being emptied, a technician was unhooking computer parts, and her desktop was already empty of everything except pens, a stapler and a picture of Lily's family.

"It looks like a clean sweep," Emeril told Jez as he panned to other offices, where the scene was the same.

Just then, Jez saw several agents exit the building with boxes stacked five high on a dolly. The back door of one of the Ryder trucks was opened, as agents began loading the boxes inside.

As Emeril panned down to the street level to videotape the boxes, he noticed a few employees leaving the building. They trickled out slowly, as Jez and Emeril raced down the parking garage ramp to try and get interviews.

With her microphone in hand, Jez ran up to employee after employee, all of whom refused to comment. No one said they were told not to talk to the media, so she figured it was just their normal paranoid reaction to a news crew.

Finally, a secretary to one of the board members walked out. She'd always been friendly with Jez. Jez was hoping now wouldn't be any different.

"Norma! Norma! Can you tell me what's going on inside?" Jez pleaded as she thrust her microphone in the woman's face.

"I, uh… I don't know much. The agents just asked us all to leave our offices. We stood in the hallway until they'd carted away the stuff they wanted, and that's when they told us to go home. It looks like they're releasing employees as they finish with each office."

"Did they question any of you?"

"No… at least not anyone I was with," Norma answered.

"Do you have any idea what they're looking for, Norma?"

"No clue. Frankly, I don't want to know. I know that I haven't done anything wrong and now all I want to do is go home." With that Norma walked off.

Jez and Emeril ran to their live truck still parked around the corner.

"Heads up!" Jez hollered at the engineer. "Call the station and tell them we have video and interviews to feedback, if they want to do a special report."

******

After spending the night at the Abbey Hotel with Donna, Carlo had left early the next morning, gone home, gotten dressed and then headed into work. He'd turned on his office TV, but muted the sound... that is until Penelope called him and asked if he was watching Channel 11. He later learned that almost every school in the district was tuned to Jez's report with many employees glued to the screens.

He sat at his desk, listening to Jez report on an FBI raid of the school system's administrative offices. He was in total shock. Never did he think he'd live to see the day that this cesspool of corruption, called a public school system, would be so vulnerable to being exposed. Finally! He thought.

As he and Penelope talked on the phone, Carlo tried to fend off the rush of employees and students wanting to get in and talk to him about what was happening. Were classes being cancelled? Was the FBI coming to their school?

"I don't know anything beyond what I heard on TV. We still have a job to do... it's called education. So until further notice, carry on." He then ordered everyone back to class or back to their offices.

Meanwhile, at FBI headquarters in North Miami Beach, Special Agent in Charge Jose Ramirez and his staff were notifying all news outlets that he'd be holding a news conference at 2:30pm. They'd had to wait for the Governor to fly down from Tallahassee and for one of the Deputy Secretaries from the U.S. Department of Education to arrive from Washington D.C.

As Ramirez was going over his speech, he got a call informing him that the first three Ryder trucks had arrived at the warehouse.

Two days earlier, the FBI had rented a gigantic warehouse in Doral... knowing the massive amounts of paperwork and computer equipment that agents would be seizing, would not fit into any space at the Miami Division headquarters. Ramirez had assigned a 40-person task force to set up temporary offices in the warehouse to catalog and organize all the potential evidence. A call was placed to the FBI Headquarters in Washington, DC to request that the FBI send agents to South Florida to provide 24/7 security on the newly rented warehouse facility.

It was a call from the President of the United States, the Secretary of Education, the Director of the FBI, and the Commander at South Com, that set in motion today's raid. Ramirez was curious about South Com's involvement, but he knew better than to ask questions. He simply followed orders. He was instructed to orchestrate a Federal takeover of the Miami School System, and that's what he was doing.

Just as Sheila Cohen was hanging up the phone, having been called by Ramirez to attend the 2:30 press conference, Det. West knocked on her door.

"We may have a suspect in the Salas shooting," he informed her.

"What have you got?"

"Well, ballistics traced the bullet to a rifle, which we know was purchased by a Diego Diaz at the Ft. Lauderdale Gun and Knife Show last year. Then, four months ago, Diaz reports the rifle stolen. But the Ft. Lauderdale police weren't buying his story. The incident report noted that nothing else was missing from his home, and that there was no sign of a break-in."

"Go on," Cohen said.

"I talked to the burglary detective who wrote the report. He said he suspected insurance fraud, but it wasn't of enough value for them to bother with, given the backload of work they had. End of story."

"What do we know about Mr. Diaz?" Cohen asked as she stood to put on her jacket and grabbed her purse.

"Walk and talk," she instructed West. "I'm due at FBI Head-quarters in 45 minutes."

"Diaz works for the school district. He's some administrator in Federal Grants. He's also a member of that loco Cuban exile group, the F-4 Commandos!"

"Get over to the school board building. They've got every-body on lock down while they raid the place. See if he's still a captive there, and pick him up for questioning. If not, find him." Cohen then got in her car and drove off.

CHAPTER #116

At 2:30, Special Agent in Charge Jose Ramirez walked to the press podium at FBI headquarters in Miami, accompanied by Governor James Barwick and the U.S. Deputy Secretary of Education, Perry Mitchell. The trio looked out at the sea of video cameras, still cameras and reporters, all poised with pens and notepads.

"Thank you for coming," Ramirez began.

Click, click, click, click, click. The sound of the still cameras threatened to drown him out. So Ramirez spoke louder.

"Today, the Miami Field Office of the Federal Bureau of Investigation raided the administrative headquarters of the Miami School System, as well as the Office of Information Technology in West Dade. We initiated this action at the request of the President of the United States, the U.S. Secretary of Education, and the Director of the FBI. We were assisted in our efforts by agents from the Tampa Bay and Jacksonville field offices. It is a highly unusual move for the Federal government to take control of a local school system, but it is not unprecedented. It is not an action the Federal government takes lightly." Ramirez paused to breathe.

"At approximately 9:30 this morning, agents entered the school board building and began seizing any potential evidence further described in the Federal Search Warrant prepared by the U.S. Attorney's office, and signed late last night by a Federal Magistrate. Employees were segregated away from all offices, and put on lock down until our agents were finished in each office. Employees are being sent home as soon as their offices are cleared by agents. There have been no arrests. I can't comment on the specifics of the investigation... except to say, that for the President of the United States to order a Federal takeover, indicates the seriousness of the situation."

Reporter's hands were in the air... each one shouting a question simultaneously.

"Please, hold your questions for a moment," Ramirez pleaded. "I want to give my other guests a chance to comment further on today's action. Allow me to introduce, Governor
James Barwick."

The Governor changed places with Agent Ramirez and ad-
dressed the media.

"It pains me greatly to see my hometown embroiled in such a
controversial action on the part of the Federal government.
But based on all the briefings, to which I've been privy, I have
reluctantly agreed to take the following steps, to insure that
this investigation is fair and untainted. Moments ago, I signed
an executive order suspending all elected members of the
Miami School Board. I am also appointing a special prose-
cutor to handle any criminal cases that do not fall under the
jurisdiction of the U.S. Department of Justice. I am doing this
to avoid any hint of a conflict of interest involving the Miami
District Attorney and her staff."

A collective gasp went out from the reporters and photographers in the room.

"Additionally, I have activated a number of National Guard
units. Each of them was assigned to a school or to district
offices outside the scope of the downtown headquarters.
Their mission is to secure all offices until the FBI can get
agents inside to conduct an investigation. I'm told that the
guardsmen and women have all reported to their assigned
location."

Governor Barwick let out a small sigh.

"Let me assure the citizens of Miami, that this takeover by
the Federal government will only last as long as is absolutely
necessary, and that I have pledged to cooperate fully. The
school children and the taxpayers of Miami deserve to know
the truth about the operations of their public school system.
In the coming weeks and months, you may not like what you
hear. I may hate what this investigation uncovers, but this is
the only way to get at the truth. Now I'd like to introduce Perry Mitchell, the Deputy Secretary at the U.S. Department of

Education. He's going to elaborate on how the schools will function, in light of this takeover. Mr. Mitchell."

As Perry Mitchell approached the podium, a few reporters ran out of the room with their cell phones in hand to call in the earth shattering news to their bosses.

"It is with great regret that I come to Miami under these circumstances. However, I want to assure the citizens of Miami, that the job of educating children will not be interrupted. Let me outline the Department's plans."

Reporters were furiously writing down notes on who would be doing what as far as running the school system. Perry Mitchell would take over as superintendent and handle all the day to day operations. Tomorrow, other officials from the U.S. Department of Education would arrive to handle areas such as transportation, finance, accounting, construction, food service, maintenance, and computer operations. The feds were temporarily suspending all business dealings in areas such as Land Acquisition, Federal Grants, ESE, After School programs and Adult Education. All hiring would be frozen.

"This is going to be a painful and time consuming task. But it must be done. The nation's fourth largest school system has apparently operated unchecked and without the necessary controls to insure that tax dollars, meaning federal, state and local, weren't squandered, misappropriated or used for fraudulent purposes. All that stops today!"

As soon as Perry Mitchell opened it up for questions, the room was in chaos.

Off to the side of the press room stood a man in a military uniform. He'd chosen to stay out of sight, in the shadows. As the reporters began pummeling the dignitaries with questions, the Commander of South Com, hit the redial button on his cell phone.

"Department of Defense," a woman answered.

CHAPTER #117

As TV and radio stations broke into programming to broadcast reports on the FBI's news conference, and websites
dinged alerts to members... phone calls went out to members of Miami's business community.

The Beacon Council, the standard bearer for all things business in Miami-Dade County, was dialing its board members
calling for an emergency meeting at 5:00.

A Federal takeover of the school system was the doomsday
scenario for the business community in the Magic City. Re-
cruiting businesses to Miami was hard enough, given the
state of the public schools. Dilapidated buildings, poor test
scores, a teacher shortage, overcrowded classrooms and a
constant drip, drip, drip of news reports on alleged corruption
and mismanagement, had hampered the Beacon Council's
efforts, for years, to recruit new businesses and industries to
Miami. They desperately needed the public to approve a new
bond issue for school construction, but their polling indicated
that the taxpayers didn't have faith in the school system's
administrators to properly use the money. Now a bond issue
would be impossible and recruitment would be cut off at the
knees.

Meanwhile, Miami Mayor Javier Castillo was fuming! He'd
been left out of the loop and had to find out about the Federal takeover, just like everyone else... on TV. The Democratic
Mayor blamed the Republican administration for dissing him.
It never occurred to him that he was under suspicion too. Of
course, that was the main reason the Feds had left him in the
dark.

A year earlier, the Mayor had been part owner of a huge par-
cel of waterfront land in Coconut Grove, which was sold to
the school board for nearly $70 million dollars. When Jez re-
vealed that the appraised value was $50 million... the Mayor
had brushed off her questions, and called her a "troublemak-
er." He went on to say that he'd have gotten twice that if he'd
sold to a private developer, but because he knew how badly

the school board needed land for new schools, he and his partners had sacrificed their potential earnings. The public exploded, and a petition was circulated, demanding he be recalled. The courts were now trying to decide the validity of the petition signatures.

Mayor Castillo hurriedly called his own press conference for 4:00.

"This is a grotesque violation of the separation of state and Federal powers," the Mayor railed.

The snickers from reporters were now chortles of laughter. A female reporter from the NBC station raised her hand. "Are you a product of the Miami School System, Mr. Mayor?" she inquired.

"I am proud to say that I am!"

A soundbite was born. It would be the quote heard round the world. As if Miami didn't have enough problems, their Mayor had proven himself to be a total ignoramus.

By the time the Beacon Council board gathered an hour later they all looked as if they'd been embalmed.

For years the community's business leaders had worked overtime to protect the image of the Miami School System. They'd convinced the publisher of The Miami Herald to water down any damning reports, and to keep his investigative team away from the school board. Only basic information from board meetings ever made its way into print.

In return, the Beacon Council and Chamber of Commerce made sure their business members spent millions in advertising dollars with the local daily. Then one day, Jez Underwood began unearthing nasty details about the school board, and the newspaper could no longer fade the competitive heat. Business leaders could do nothing but watch the public school system unravel. Now, as they gathered, the Beacon's board members had to deal with a moronic Mayor.

"How can the Mayor be such a blithering idiot?" asked the board's chairman.

"He's a product of our school system," responded the vice-chair. No one laughed.

"Who was in charge of dealing with Rod Vascoe?" the chairman asked.

"I was." It was the head of the Latin Builder's Association. "He couldn't be handled, because he was already being controlled."

"By whom?" the chair inquired.

"Dr. Moses Moorehead is the person who really runs things. I brought this to your attention a year ago, but the board didn't want to do anything for fear of appearing racist. Now look at our predicament."

"We can't be seen trying to oust a prominent member of the black community," declared another board member.

"Fine! But now what do we do?" asked the chairman.

There was silence. Then from the back of the room came a faint response. "Black Ops."

Everyone turned to look at the man who had stealthy entered the meeting room undetected. He looked like a vision out of some Iraq War movie. He wore a close-cropped haircut, green pressed uniform, with enough ribbons and medals to decorate a large shadow box.

"Black Ops," he repeated. "A secret mission handled by secret military forces. That's what you need."

"Sir! Identify yourself," the chairman demanded.

"I'm General Gage McAfee, Commander of South Com. And I'm here to restore the fairy tale that Miami is a good place to do business. Any questions?"

"Yeah," said the vice-chair. "What's in it for South Com?"

"Allow me to explain." With that General Gage McAfee began to outline the problems facing the City of Miami and its business leaders.

"The Federal government is convinced that Miami and its leaders are operating this important county like a third world country. The graft and corruption in South Florida is out of control. We can't protect the Florida Peninsula, if the leaders are acting like banana republic dictators, mired in financial and sexual scandals that would rival any Hollywood movie plot!"

"What sexual scandals?" the Beacon Council chair asked.

"Stay tuned to your favorite TV station, sir. It's just a matter of time before you find out."

"I don't know who this guy is, or if he's even the real deal," shouted another board member. "I say we adjourn until our leaders can verify McAfee's identity."

A chorus of yeah and yeses filled the conference room. "This meeting is adjourned," the chair declared. He then walked over to the General, grabbed his arm and said, "Come with me."

"Not until you take your hand off my arm!" The chairman let go immediately. "Don't ever touch me again!" The General then followed the chairman to his office.

CHAPTER #118

The General hadn't shared everything with the Beacon Council. That would come later. As he sat in the chairman's office watching him make phone call after phone call, General McAfee got up and turned on the TV in the corner of the chairman's office. It was straight up 6:00, and leading the newscast on Channel 11, was Jez Underwood.

"Tonight, the Miami School System is controlled by the Federal government. A raid on the board's administrative headquarters was the opening salvo in a takeover that shocked everyone, including the city's Mayor.

Next was the soundbite of the Mayor raging about the erroneous separation of powers and his pride in being a product of the Miami School System.

"A takeover of the public school system is Miami's cross to bear tonight," Jez declared. "Here's a minute by minute breakdown of what happened today, and why."

Jez then began to recap the days FBI raids, her interviews with employees, the FBI's press conference with the Governor and Dept. of Education, the Mayor's news conference... finally ending with a prepared and pat statement from the Chamber of Commerce and the Beacon Council.

As Jez stood in front of the locked school board building, she had Emeril turn his cameras on the spontaneous, but massive group of parents who'd gathered to protest the Feds actions. On the other side of the street, was a smaller, but equally vocal group, who held handmade signs cheering the demise of the current school board administration.

Jez and Emeril agreed that the groups were small now, but as night fell, they'd likely grow. So each of them put on their bulletproof vests. Riots were never out of the question in Miami.

CHAPTER #119

Captain Cohen had returned to the police station after the FBI's press conference. Detective West rose when he saw her enter.

"Good news, Captain," he announced. "Diaz confessed! He's even proud of trying to kill Amelia Salas. Can you believe that? Said she wasn't a true Cuban because she nominated that Haitian woman to be the interim superintendent."

"Has he lawyered up?" Cohen asked.

"Nope! Says he'll represent himself."

"The sign of a true psycho! Have you notified Salas' family?"

"About an hour ago. They were ecstatic."

"Good work, West!" Cohen then headed toward her office... grateful that another case was wrapped up. She then phoned the Chief to give him the good news.

Earlier, she and the Chief had encouraged the FBI to put a priority on finding information about the Royal Poinciana Ranch. They'd outlined what they'd learned about the type of community movers and shakers who frequented the ranch. The FBI had promised to make it a priority, but Cohen knew, that given the volume of evidence that had been seized, it could be weeks or months before anything was learned.

Cohen was rattled out of her deep thought by the ringing of her phone.

"Cohen here."

"Captain, it's Jose Ramirez. I think I have something you want."

"Special Agent Ramirez, it's good to hear from you. Is this about the ranch property?"

"We've just finished going through the documents taken from the superintendent's office," Ramirez informed her. "She had a stack of real estate documents on her desk. One is a property in West Kendall that appears to mirror the description you gave us of this Royal Poinciana Ranch. We've verified that no school board office or school sits on that site. I've got our helicopter heading to the address, in order to get video. Are you able to get back here to take a look at what we get?"

"I'm on my way!"

For once in her life, Captain Sheila Cohen didn't mind navigating the hellacious rush hour traffic on I-95. In fact, she decided she'd use lights and sirens to get to FBI headquarters faster.

As soon as she arrived, she was ushered into Ramirez's office, where he was staring at a big screen TV monitor. On it was the live feed being transmitted from the FBI's chopper as it hovered over a large home in the Kendall area.

"Does this look like the place?" Ramirez asked.

"It does. But to be sure, we need to get someone here who's been there. And right now I don't have one single person who can identify this house. Daniel Estrada is dead, so is Hank Maine. Beyond that, I've got nobody!" Cohen was thoroughly dejected.

Ramirez had an idea. "Why don't we bring in the interim superintendent, Lily Molina? After all, these documents were found on her desk."

"Do you honestly expect her to volunteer that this was the infamous sex house?" Cohen asked.

"No! But I do expect she'd have an explanation as to why the district owned the property." Ramirez waited for Cohen to reply.

"Go ahead," Cohen replied. "What do we have to lose?"

As Ramirez began making calls to his various agents, Capt. Cohen dialed the Abbey Hotel. "I need to speak to Donna," she announced.

"This is Donna."

"Donna? It's Sheila Cohen. I need to know if you'd recognize the sex house if I showed you a picture."

"Captain, I already told you I'd never been there."

"Is there anyone you can think of who might have been? This is a very important question, Donna." Cohen paused, waiting for a response.

"Sheila," Donna began, using the Captain's first name as a way of letting her know her sincerity. "Hank partied with a number of top district officials. Which ones might know about the house, will be your job to find out. But I'll tell you who he played with, at least as best as I knew."

"Tell me," Cohen urged the widow Maine.

"Nestor Padron, R.V., Joe Nunez, Lee and Lily Molina, Alexander Martinez, Hammond Garfield and of course, the dead Daniel Estrada."

Cohen was almost speechless. "Alexander Martinez, the County Mayor?" she asked.

"Yes."

"Hammond Garfield, the school board member?"

"The very one," Donna replied.

"Well I'll be go to hell!" Cohen was stunned. "I'll be in touch," she told Donna Maine and quickly hung up.

"We've got a tiger by the tail," she informed Ramirez.

"Meaning?"

"Our jobs could be in jeopardy if we reveal what we are about to uncover." Cohen paused.

"I didn't sign up for job security in order to cover for criminals," Ramirez explained.

"Neither did I." Cohen was stoic. "But I think you should know what we're up against."

"Consider myself informed. Now tell me what you know." Ramirez and Cohen then huddled at his desk.

CHAPTER #120

Outside the school board building, the crowds were growing, just as Jez and Emeril had predicted. Despite an enormous police presence, the crowd was developing a mob mentality.

"Allison, this is Jez. Can you get another crew down here?" Jez knew that she and Emeril wouldn't be able to handle this story, if the crowds got out of control."

"What is Emeril still doing on the clock?" Allison Wheeler demanded. "You know we are not approving overtime."

"Screw you!" Jez screamed. "We're wearing our bulletproof vests. This isn't a tea party I'm asking you to cover. The crowds are swelling and they are angry!"

"Tell Emeril he has to go home," Allison ordered Jez.

"And what? Leave me here alone?"

"I'll get another photog to you as soon as they finish their dinner break," Allison informed Jez.

Emeril had been listening to the conversation and watching Jez's veins pulse. So it didn't surprise him in the least, when Jez held the Nextel at arm's length, clicked the announce button, and screamed!

"FUCK YOU!" With that declaration, Jez threw the Nextel on the ground and began stomping on it.

"We're on our own," she informed Emeril, who'd already figured that out. Just then, a fight broke out in the crowd that had gathered in front of the school board building.

"Are ju sure ju want to stay here?" Emeril asked Jez.

"Positively!"

With those words, the two of them waded into the angry crowd, tape rolling and microphone in hand.

******

Back at the Channel 11 news desk, assignment editor Allison Wheeler kept talking into her Nextel.

"Emeril? Jez? Do you copy? Jez respond. Emeril respond." After there'd been no reply for more than 10 minutes, Allison dispatched another news team to the school board building. Their instructions: deliver a working Nextel to Jez and Emeril.

But when the second news crew arrived, they found the crowds in front of the school administration building in a full-scale riot. Cars had been lit on fire, newspaper dispensers were upended, and the mob was running toward the line of live trucks that surrounded a two-block area of the school building.

"Unit 10 to the desk!" an 11 News photographer screamed.

"Go ahead, Unit 10."

"We've got a riot here! Send back up, now!"

"What kind of riot?" asked the clueless bimbo desk assistant.

"A fucking car burning, gun firing riot! Copy?"

"You're pulling my leg, because you know I'm a rookie," declared the desk assistant. "This is hazing isn't it?"

"No!" screamed the photographer. "But if you don't do something now, I'll see to it you never work in this business ever!"

"I was warned by Allison that one of you guys would pull a stunt like this!" The desk assistant sat back in her chair and put her feet up on the assignment desk.

"Now, are you ready to give up your nonsense?"

"As soon as I call the News Director, bitch, you are toast!" With those words, the Channel 11 photographer hung up and dialed Boris Danken's private number.

But before the first ring was completed, a Molotov cocktail exploded three feet from where the photog was standing... and he collapsed on the ground as his reporter screamed hysterically.

CHAPTER #121

No sooner had Captain Cohen hung up the phone with Donna, than her police radio began chattering like crazy. There were reports of shots fired and rioting in front of the school board building.

"Damn!" she said. "This ranch thing will have to wait, Ramirez. I've got to get back downtown."

"Go," he said, as she bolted for the door.

As Cohen drove south on I-95, she heard dispatch sending a number of units to the scene. She heard fire trucks and ambulances also being sent. By the time she got to her exit, Miami Police had already blocked it off, in an attempt to limit access to the administrative offices. She flashed her blue light and drove around the blockade... only to encounter two others that had been established along Biscayne Boulevard and at 15th street.

From his top floor condo, Carlo and his partner Orlando were watching the rioting from their terrace. They alternated using the binoculars they kept on the patio table.

"Oh my God!" Carlo exclaimed as he honed in on the street in front of the school board building. "What do these people think they're going to accomplish?" he wondered as he watched the mob trying to rock over one of the TV station's live trucks.

Up and down the Boulevard he could see the flashing lights of police cars, fire trucks and ambulances. Some were headed into the melee... others appeared to be keeping their distance, as if on standby. "Turn on Channel 11," he ordered Orlando. "See if Jez is reporting from this carnage."

Just as Orlando turned to go inside, they heard a huge explosion followed by flames leaping in the air. It seems the mob had managed to overturn the live truck and it had exploded.

Suddenly, Carlo began to worry about what might happen if the rioting spilled over to the nearly completed performing arts centers. The Concert Hall and Ballet/Opera House were only blocks away from the mayhem, and the construction materials that still littered the properties would make ideal weapons and firewood. He could only hope that it was true what he'd learned on his private tour of the facilities... that they were the best fortresses in town, in the event of a hurricane. He hoped the same was true of riots.

"The anchorman says it's too dangerous for their crews to go live!" Orlando shouted from the bedroom. "He says Jez is down at the scene, but they've lost communications with her and another news crew. They've got their chopper up and they're showing aerials of the rioting."

Just then, Carlo spotted the Miami Police department's large, anti-riot, armored truck pull up to the intersection of 15th and Biscayne. Behind it was a massive line of cops, all in riot gear, walking straight into the danger zone.

"Carlo! It's Jez! She's on the phone with the anchor guy," Orlando shouted.

Carlo immediately dropped the binoculars on the patio table and ran inside. On the TV screen he saw a still photograph of Jez and heard her breathless voice.

"Dean, my photographer, Emeril and I were standing in front of the school board building, when a group of people protesting the Federal Government's takeover of the district, began to clash with those who supported the takeover. At first it was just a lot of shouting, then we heard gunshots. We managed to get out of the middle of the crowd, and we've made our way to a safe area. I don't really want to divulge our location, in case any of those crazies on the ground are listening to this report. But for now, I can tell you that we are safe, we're wearing our bulletproof vests, but we are still in the center of this riot. We are videotaping what we can, but without access to our gear, our camera will soon lose battery power or we'll run out of videotape. I'm not sure which will happen first."

"Jez," Dean Sands began, "do you have any idea where Darcy and Lionel are... our other news crew?"

"I wasn't aware the station had sent a second crew over here, so no, I have no idea. But I can tell you that the mob overturned one of Channel 23's live trucks moments ago. That was the big explosion you might have heard earlier."

"For our viewers who don't know, Channel 23 is our Spanish language sister station, and my producers are telling me that the Univision engineer has been taken away in an ambulance," Dean Sands informed his audience. "We'll try to get more information on the engineer's condition and bring it to you just as soon as we can."

"Dean!" Jez shouted into the phone. "I can see the riot police now. They've just arrived and are walking straight towards the mob. They're in full riot gear, meaning helmets and shields. Oh shit!"

"Jez? Are you o.k.?" Dean asked tentatively.

"Yeah. Sorry for the language, but someone just shot out one of the street lights." There was another popping noise. "They just nailed another street light. I don't know if it's the mob, or the cops trying to darken the streets," Jez informed viewers.

"Jez, the producers are telling me that the police have ordered all news helicopters out of the air space over the school board building. They've put their own choppers in the air to assist the forces on the ground. Can you see them?" Dean asked.

"Yes. Yes, I see them. They're using their spotlights to help the cops on the ground see what's going on. I would also assume that if the crowds begin to scatter, the choppers will keep tabs on them."

"Where do you think she's hiding?" Orlando asked Carlo.

"I don't know, but I'm glad she's safe." As Orlando headed back out to the terrace, Carlo decided to call Donna.

"I can't believe what is happening," Donna Maine said as soon as she answered the phone. Of course, she knew it was Carlo, since no one else knew where she was. "I can't help but feel that I am somehow to blame," she whimpered.

"Donna, that's just ridiculous. The authorities have known for years about the corruption in the school system. They just chose to ignore the many warnings. Then when Jez ramped up the focus and her competitors had to stay current, that's when all of this began to explode. You just helped focus the attention on certain areas." Carlo was trying to keep her calm. "It's not like you had a lot of firsthand knowledge," he explained.

As Carlo talked, he kept a close eye on the TV. It had been nearly 20 years since Miami had seen a riot of any sizeable proportions.

The removal of Elian Gonzalez, from his uncle's home in Little Havana, in April of 2000 had triggered some sporadic tire fires, and a lot of shouting, but nothing major. Now Carlo was watching his nearby neighborhood burn, all because the Federal Government had finally acknowledged the sickness of corruption in Miami's public school system. Who would be against that, he wondered.

Suddenly he saw Jez's picture back on the TV screen. "Donna, I'll talk to you later," he said as he hung up. He wanted to find out if Jez was still safe.

"Dean, the riot police have moved in and appear to be taking control of the situation," he heard Jez inform her anchorman.

"What exactly are you seeing, Jez?" Dean Sands asked his reporter.

Jez then began to describe the way the police pushed their way into the angry crowd, using batons to whack any unruly and uncooperative protestors. As soon as the crowds started to disperse, they were confronted by a blockade of more riot police, who'd stationed themselves on all side streets. No one was going to get away if the police had their way.

"Right now we're seeing a lot of arrests, a lot of people handcuffed, and lots of people still trying to escape police. So for now, the rioting appears to have stopped as members of this mob try to get away," Jez reported.

Just then, Emeril indicated that his battery was dead.

"Dean, I think we're going to try and make our way back to our vehicle. We've lost battery power on the camera, and since it looks like police are getting control of the situation, I think we are safe enough at this point."

Dean Sands was concerned, but knew that Jez was trying to signal to him that he needed to talk to the other crews on the story, so she could get to their equipment van. "Jez, we'll let you go, but be careful, and get back to us when you can."

As Jez and Emeril made their way down from the top of the parking garage, they were immediately stopped by police and ordered to leave the area. Their news car, if it was still in one piece, couldn't be moved anyway, until police wrapped up their investigation. So the two of them walked toward the Boulevard in search of another crew from Channel 11.

"I'm tired, hungry, dirty and my feet hurt," Jez groused.

"Try lugging dis camera on jur shoulder," Emeril mumbled.

"Is this the glamorous part of being on TV?" she asked.

"Yeah! Ju look real glamorous right now!" he teased. They both began to laugh, as if punch drunk, as they hobbled toward a live truck.

CHAPTER #122
SUNDAY

As the sun peaked out from behind the horizon of the Atlantic Ocean the next morning, the carnage from the rioting the night before, still littered the area around the school board building. Police officers were still on the scene, and the early morning news shows were finally broadcasting from in front of the administrative headquarters. They reported 112 arrests, 19 injured, two serious, and hundreds of thousands of dollars in property damage, mostly to vehicles.

At around midnight, Mayor Castillo had gone on TV and urged calm. He also assured the citizens that the education of children would continue, uninterrupted. It was wishful thinking on his part. The next morning would find that most parents had decided to keep their children home from school.

But like most principals, Carlo showed up at his school, not knowing what to expect. He'd only been there an hour, when Captain Cohen called, asking him to meet her at FBI headquarters.

"Am I going to be arrested," he half joked in response to her request.

"Not unless you want to be," she teased. "We need your help. Nothing more. I promise!"

Forty minutes later he was being escorted into the office of Special Agent in Charge Jose Ramirez.

"Thank you for coming Mr. Ferrini," Ramirez began. "Captain Cohen has told me about your assistance in the many cases that have been dropped on her plate these last few weeks."

Carlo turned and looked at Sheila Cohen who was sitting in the seat next to his. She'd not said a word since he arrived.

Ramirez continued. "I'm hoping that because of the trust Captain Cohen has placed in you, I can do the same."

Ramirez walked around from behind his desk and sat on the front corner of the large glass tabletop. He looked right at Carlo.

"I need a guide. I need someone who has institutional knowledge, who can school my agents in the budget and accounting procedures of the school system, so they don't have to waste a lot of time deciphering all these financial records we've seized. I need someone I can trust... and Captain Cohen here assures me that you're the guy! Time wise, we must ensure that the inconvenience to the actual classroom and school site educational process be kept to a minimum. Parents and students should not have to suffer for the offenses of a few renegades. First and foremost, we need to keep the payroll and procurement systems operational while we investigate."

Carlo was speechless at first. "Agent Ramirez, I'm a principal, not an accountant."

"Understood. My guys are accountants, but they don't know, for example, a 101 account from a 02 account. That's the help I need from you. Give them a primer and they'll do the detail work." Ramirez paused. "Can I count on you?"

"What about my job as principal?" Carlo tentatively inquired.

"You'll still be paid, but you'll have to be away from the school for a while. Do you trust your staff to handle things in your absence?" It was Captain Cohen's first comment.

"Absolutely! They are the best. I have complete faith in their abilities," Ferrini opined.

"Then you'll do this?" Ramirez asked.

"I suppose so. But first, I need to talk to my administrative staff. Everyone is on pins and needles right now. I'm sure you can understand."

"Of course, Mr. Ferrini. How about you take today to handle what you need to, and meet me back here tomorrow at let's say 10a.m."

Carlo glanced over at Capt. Cohen, who nodded approvingly. "There's a lot of people I could have recommended," she said, "but your name is the only one I can endorse."

"I guess I'll see you tomorrow Agent Ramirez," Carlo said as he stood. The two men shook hands then Carlo gave Capt. Cohen a bear hug. "Thank you," he whispered in her ear as he clasped his arms around her. "I'm truly honored."

CHAPTER #123

After Carlo Ferrini left, Ramirez and Cohen picked up where they left off the day before... looking at aerials of what they believed was the Royal Poinciana Ranch.

"My agents ran property checks. This place has been called the Royal Poinciana Ranch since 1918," Ramirez informed Cohen. "Property records indicate the school board purchased the land in 1992... right after Hurricane Andrew."

"Who was the seller?" Cohen asked.

"A consortium as best we can tell right now. It appears they used a fictitious name, which in and of itself is not illegal. But one of the directors is a lobbyist. Does the name Sid Messing ring a bell?"

"It rings bells and whistles!" Cohen responded. "The guy is a scumball extraordinaire! He was busted a few months ago for possession of heroin. Drug court didn't make much of an impression on the low life. He kept failing his quarterly drug tests. Finally, the judge threatened to send him to jail, and he suddenly got clean. Who knows if he bought the bench, or actually got clean. Now he's a proselytizing do gooder, who's throwing money at every bad apple on the school board."

"What do you have on him besides a drug charge?" Ramirez asked. "Hell, half of Miami could be indicted on the same charges!"

"He's ugly, and has a pitiful comb over!" Cohen responded.

"Oh! Those are charges that will stick!" Ramirez laughed. "Why don't we indict him for stupidity and bad taste!"

"That would be my first choice," Cohen chuckled in response.

Suddenly, there was silence, as the two thought about how to uncover the ranch house.

"I assume you've asked Mr. Ferrini about this sex house," Ramirez asked Cohen.

"Clueless," she replied. "This was a big ass secret only a select few were privy to. That's why we have to figure out how to proceed. The names of the people who were, "in the know," will kill us before they'll let this secret out."

"They'll be staring at "Old Sparky" if they try to take down a federal agent or law enforcement officer!" Ramirez exclaimed.

"They don't care! Don't you get it?" Cohen pleaded, "they don't fucking care! Everyone in Miami is expendable! Badge or no badge."

Cohen couldn't believe she was having to educate the head of the FBI Miami Field Office on the politics of the community… but apparently she had to.

"Power is their drug of choice. They don't see their sexual predilections as an issue… unless exposed. Publicity is their enemy if it doesn't enhance their power. They use sex to gain power. Therefore, any publicity about their sexual prowess or inclinations, that is unacceptable in the public domain, becomes a liability. They can't allow for liabilities, so they shut them down before they become public." Cohen stopped. "Am I making any sense?" she asked.

"Not to my way of thinking," Ramirez answered. "I think you just drew a circle on top of a circle."

"That's the problem with you Feds! You have no imagination!" Cohen screamed. "It's not like I'm a figure skater tracing figure eights! When one of your agents warned you guys that Middle Eastern men were learning to fly planes, but not how to land them… you fucking blew it off as loco! Now look who is loco?"

"Captain Cohen." Ramirez was stern and to the point. "We can either work together and crack some heads, or square off against one another and get nowhere. What is your choice?"

There was a long and pregnant pause before Capt. Cohen responded.

"I want us to nail the men or women and/or both who've stripped money from our kid's schools, who've cheated the taxpayers of this county, and who've aided and abetted the corruption of a governmental entity. That's what I want, Agent Ramirez. Now! Can you make that happen?"

"I can, Capt. Cohen. But I'll need your help." Ramirez went quiet.

"You have it, Special Agent. Now let's get to work busting some bad guys or girls!" Cohen and Ramirez shook hands.

"Let's organize a raid of the house," Cohen suggested. "You guys have control of all the school board property. Let's get in there and see what's behind the closed doors, at the very least. Who knows, maybe we'll get lucky!"

"I'll get the chopper over there to secure the scene," Ramirez responded. "Mind if I drive?"

"I love being chauffeured!" Cohen grabbed her purse and the two of them headed to the parking lot as Ramirez talked into his phone dispatching other agents to the ranch.

CHAPTER #124

As Ramirez and Cohen turned west onto the Dolphin Expressway off of I-95... the chopper called in.

"We have eyes on the ground here," one of the agents reported.

"Whose eyes?" Ramirez asked.

"School police... just sitting outside of the perimeter wall."

Cohen and Ramirez looked at one another. "Any vehicles inside the wall?" Ramirez inquired.

"No sign of any."

"OK. Stay in the air till we get there. Make sure nobody comes or goes," ordered Ramirez.

"Copy that."

"Well it is school board owned property," Cohen commented.

"Yeah, but we ordered the department to stand down. They were put on desk duty only." Ramirez then turned on his siren and flashing blue light in order to get through traffic more quickly.

"Maybe these guys didn't get the message," Cohen offered.

"Maybe on purpose!" Ramirez was getting angrier by the minute. "They could also be renegades... sort of a private police squad for that location only. That's what concerns me."

"Why Special Agent Ramirez, I do believe you're catching onto the game we've found ourselves in the middle of." Cohen was being catty... a fact that Ramirez didn't appreciate one bit. They drove the rest of the way in silence.

Twenty minutes later, Ramirez and Cohen rendezvoused with the other four FBI units at a gas station about 5 blocks from the ranch. The plan was for the four units to block each of the cop cars from the front and back simultaneously. The chopper would provide air cover, and Ramirez and Cohen would enter the property.

Thankfully, the two cops in each car were taken by surprise. One had been sleeping the other was reading a magazine. They didn't put up a fight at all. Both were detained for questioning. But that would have to wait until the FBI had searched the entire ranch.

To their great relief, no one was inside. After each agent had given the all clear, they were ordered to turn the place inside out.

The house itself was homey looking, nicely furnished, but nothing that hinted at extravagance. At the back was a pool, sheltered under mosquito fencing. Inside, the house had five bedrooms and six and a half bathrooms… a huge kitchen that looked unused, a large living room, dining room and gigantic family room with a large wet bar.

As Cohen searched the kitchen, she heard one of the agents shout for Ramirez.

"In the family room," he hollered. The agent was standing in front of the big screen TV. The video looked like a home movie of some sort, but it was far from being a video of a trip to Disney World. No, it was more like a homemade porno flick. At first it was video of the backside of a woman riding a man like a cowgirl. Then the naked body of a second man appeared. He was fully erect, walked up to the bed and put his dick in the mouth of the man the woman was fucking. Suddenly, there was a gasp from the three people in the family room, watching the video.

"It's the county Mayor!" Captain Cohen plopped down on the nearby couch. She was referring to the second man, who was now in the throes of a passionate kiss with the man on his back. Then suddenly, the woman stopped humping her partner, and rolled over, lying next to him. That's when the

viewers recognized her as Lily Molina, the interim superintendent.

"Jesus!" mumbled Ramirez.

"And that's my murder victim on his back, sucking dick! Exclaimed Cohen. "It's Dr. Hank Maine."

"Find every videotape, DVD, CD, audio tape, and 33 LP!"
Ramirez ordered the agent in the family room, as he ran off
to order the agents searching the bedroom to locate cameras
and all recording equipment. "Tear the ceilings apart! I want
this stuff found, now," he shouted, as he ran out the front
door to get some air.

Cohen waited a few minutes before she went outside. She
spotted Ramirez standing under an avocado tree, smoking a
cigarette.

"I didn't know you smoked," she said softly as she approached him.

"Only when I can't handle the stress." Ramirez then went
silent again, so Cohen just stood there. Finally, he took his
last puff, threw the cigarette butt on the ground and twisted
his shoe over it.

"I've dealt with bank robbers, kidnappers, drug dealers and
crooked judges... but this! This is... " he stopped.

"Sick?" Cohen said trying to finish his sentence.

"Sick and tragic and disgusting and... I don't even have the
vocabulary to describe what I'm thinking right now!" Ramirez
grabbed his thick mass of black hair and acted as though he
might pull it out.

"Get it together Ramirez! Your agents don't need to see you
like this. We've turned over a rock that has exposed the underbelly of society. Deal with it! I have a feeling there is more
to come, and you need to cope now... not tomorrow or next
week... now! Put your macho Latin sensibilities in check and
cope! If you need to see a counselor, see one. But right now,

you are the guy in charge here. We all need you to be in control." Cohen had grabbed him by the shoulders and was shaking him.

He let go of his hair, dropped his hands and looked up at Captain Sheila Cohen. "You are right. I'm sorry. Thank you." With those words, the two of them headed back inside in silence, to supervise the gathering of evidence.

As they entered the main foyer, Ramirez's radio clicked. "Special Agent, we have company in the air," the chopper pilot informed him. "Channel 11 is up here with us. Copy?"

"Shit!" Ramirez cursed, as he looked over at Cohen, who was shrugging her shoulders, as if to say, I don't know how they found out.

"Turn the TV to Channel 11," he ordered the agent who was in the family room.

There were aerials of the ranch being broadcast as Jez Underwood narrated.

"This ranch style house in far West Kendall, is the focus of an FBI search, according to our sources," Jez was saying. "We've seen agents hauling bags of, what we can only presume is evidence, from this house... which according to our property records search, is owned by the Miami School Board. In fact, we can see two Miami School Police cars sitting on the outside of the wall that surrounds the property, which my producers now tell me is known as the Royal Poinciana Ranch. But why the FBI is here and what they are taking from the house is still unknown. Live from Sky 11, I'm Jez Underwood."

Across town, a Mayor, a county commissioner, an interim school superintendent, her husband, and several of their administrative friends were standing on knees that were turning to jelly, as they realized that their secret lives were about to be exposed.

CHAPTER #125
THREE MONTHS LATER

When Carlo arrived at his school, his office was decorated with balloons and banners saying "WELCOME BACK!" He was applauded and hugged by his staff who'd managed to keep the school running in his absence.

"You are the best!" was all he could say, overwhelmed with emotion. He was a principal again... an educator. It was all he'd ever wanted to be. He was home again!

Since he'd last been at the school, so much had happened.

Jez had broken the story about South Com's involvement in the Federal takeover of the school system. The community had been stunned when she reported that military authorities at Southern Command had deemed Miami-Dade County a threat to national security!

It seems the military and intelligence community believed that the County's Mayor and the school system's superintendent, Rod Vascoe, had been acting against the laws of the State of Florida and the U.S. government.

For months, a secret unit of South Com had been working with an equally secret FBI Task Force, investigating the two leaders... who'd been acting more like dictators in a third world country. At last, they'd finally come up with enough information to have the Defense Department go to the President of the United States, and ask him to initiate the unprecedented takeover action.

They targeted the school system first, fearing that a Federal takeover of county government services would destabilize the community. By making an example of the school system, it was hoped that the other local governments would clean up their act out of fear that the Feds would do the same to them.

But the county Mayor and his chief aide hadn't waited around to find out that bit of information. The day the FBI had raided the Royal Poinciana Ranch, the lovers fled to Uruguay that evening... before the FBI could file pornography and public corruption charges against the two men. They'd finally been nabbed two days before Carlo returned to his school, by a Special Operations unit of the Department of Defense. A fact that was unknown to the citizens of South Florida, at least to date.

Lily and Lee Molina were arrested outside Nashville, Tennessee as they checked into the Opryland Hotel three days after the raid on the ranch. They'd planned to escape to Canada... but never made it. Both had been indicted in Federal Court on charges of public corruption, fraud, theft and a litany of other offenses, including the transmission of child pornography across interstate lines. It seems the Molinas had been selling their sex videos to adult porn sites around the world... some of which also displayed child porn... so the Molina's found themselves guilty by association.

Joe Nunez, Nestor Padron, Sid Messing and Hammond Garfield were also picked up and charged with embezzlement, public corruption and fraud. Once the FBI got into the finances of the school system, they discovered how Padron, Nunez and Rod Vascoe acting in cahoots had cooked the school board's books with phony change orders and illegal money transfers.

Garfield and Messing were in cahoots on the Royal Poinciana Ranch land deal, and Messing, along with the entire school board was being accused of racketeering, when the Feds discovered the health insurance scam that Messing had rammed down the school system's throat. He'd collected nearly $2 million dollars in lobbying fees for his efforts.

It was determined that Daniel Estrada had killed his father and Hank Maine. His lover, Marcos Alfaro was also arrested as an accomplice in the murder of the Senior Mr. Estrada. And the scene of Daniel's death, the Knight Concert Hall, had eventually opened to a full audience for the premiere performance that featured Miami's symphony in residence, the Cleveland Orchestra.

As the Feds combed through the attendance records of every school, they discovered that 104 Kindergarten through senior high schools had altered attendance records to illegally collect money provided by the state of Florida for every student. Seven high school principals and athletic directors were charged with changing grades for high profile athletes... and every single alternative school was found to be cooking the attendance and grade books, essentially committing fraud. All were shut down, including one that was run by a prominent city commissioner.

A hand full of adult education centers were found to be enrolling foreigners without the requisite official documents. In essence, these schools were allowing foreigners, even illegal aliens, to be educated at taxpayer's expense.

And when the Feds pulled Hurricane Andrew documents out of cold storage in Atlanta... they uncovered massive fraud on a scale that astonished even seasoned FBI agents. The school board had made claims for losses that never existed, charged FEMA for items such as computers and TVs that ended up in the living rooms of administrators, and stripped FEMA trailers of ID numbers in order to relocate them to the Everglades, where they were subsequently shipped out to other states. The money for these trailers was all being collected by school board member Dr. Moses Josiah Moorehead.

"He and Barbara Ross ran a trucking company that handled all the shipments," the U.S. Attorney informed the courts during a hearing. "She detailed all the leads in her suicide note. And we confirmed her information by comparing school records to FEMA documents."

"What is the dollar amount of the fraud?" the Federal Judge asked.

"Your honor, we stopped counting at $50 million."

"Why?" asked the Judge.

"Because, frankly, there isn't a punishment that is worse at $51 million than at $50 million. In addition, so much money was laundered in a scheme using the Church of the Great Believer, that it's impossible to know how much more there was that we could go after and find."

"Are you filing charges in district court?" the judge asked.

"Not at the moment, your honor." The U.S. Attorney then informed the judge of the evidence they'd uncovered, showing that the local District Attorney had ignored leads and covered up information that could have led to white collar criminal investigations of the system's construction program.

"She appears to have turned a blind eye to every tip or hint that came her way when it involved the school board or any of the school administrators. The Federal government is recommending that Florida's Governor remove the D.A. from office and consider charging her with neglect of duty. So we are not cooperating with her office at this point in time, your honor."

"Incredible!" the federal judge mumbled. "What is happening with the bench warrant I issued for Dr. Moses Moorehead?"

"Your honor, he fled the country and has so far eluded us. We have tracked him to a Cayman Island account that he emptied, shortly before our takeover of the school system. But current laws prohibit us from finding out where that money went. We suspect, but can't prove that he has a Swiss bank account."

"Are you on his trail?" the judge asked.

"That's not a question I care to answer in open court, your honor," the U.S. Attorney responded.

"Understood. Court is adjourned," the judge declared.

Special Agent Ramirez and Capt. Sheila Cohen had been in the courtroom listening to the proceedings. As the two of them walked out of the federal courthouse, their gaze locked on the gathering storm coming in from over the Ocean. The skies were black, the clouds ominous, the thunder and lightning threatening.

"Looks like we're in for a drenching," Cohen said.

"Did you bring an umbrella Captain?

"No. I always like to take my chances, Special Agent."

"I thought so! In that case, allow me!" With that, Ramirez grabbed Cohen's arm and began running… pushing her along the sidewalk in downtown Miami.

"What is this?" Cohen asked as her legs raced to keep up. "I've already passed the physical training course!"

"Good!" shouted Ramirez… "then you won't mind beating me to the car before we get soaked!"

With that, both Ramirez and Cohen began running as if their lives depended on it… headed for the Federal Courthouse parking lot. They were about two steps ahead of a dark cloud that would bring a rejuvenating rain to a community in desperate need of cleansing.

THE END